THE STENCH OF FRESH AIR

C.J. HENDERSON

The Stench of Fresh Air is published by Dimensions Books, an imprint of Elder Signs Press, Inc.

This book is © 2008 Elder Signs Press, Inc.
All material © 2008 by Elder Signs Press and C.J. Henderson

Cover art © 2008 by Ben Fogletto.
Design by Deborah Jones.

Publication History
Published by the Berkley Publishing Group under the title "Some Things Never Die," 1993.
Published by Marietta Publishing, 2004.

The name "Kill By Inches" © 1992 by Kevin Oriol and is used with Mr. Oriol's expressed permission.

FIRST EDITION
10 9 8 7 6 5 4 3 2 1
Published in June 2008
ISBN: 1-934501-12-3
Printed in the U.S.A.

Published by Dimensions Books
P.O. Box 389
Lake Orion, MI 48361-0389
www.dimensionsbooks.com

THE STENCH OF FRESH AIR

C.J. HENDERSON

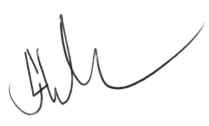

2008

I have learned a great deal over the years from a number of different people. Some of them taught Socratically, some have lectured, some have merely offered their own lives up—the good and the bad—as a set of examples, each to be studied for their individual value.

One of the men I have known, however, did all three, skipping from one to the other as easily as other men walk an uncrowded sidewalk on a sunny day. He was kind and loving and ruthlessly intelligent. He was an artist of many stripes, but first and foremost he was a thinker,

perhaps the finest I will ever meet.

He was a good friend—one of the best I have ever known or am ever likely to know. He taught me more than any other single person in this world, and for no more gain than the joy he derived from the passing on of knowledge.

Thus, this book is dedicated to the memory of:

Kevin Peter Norton

who, if he had lived another ten thousand years, would have still died too soon

"Here I stand—I cannot do otherwise. God help me. Amen."
—Martin Luther

"How old would you be if you didn't know how old you are?"
—Satchell Paige

"Dust thou art, and unto dust shall thou return."
—Genesis

PROLOGUE

JIMMY LU REALLY SHOULD have known better. After all, considering who his mother was, considering all that had happened, considering everything he had been taught since childhood, one would think that someone with as much going for him as Jimmy would have had the simple common sense to avoid Hester Street that night. He did not, however, and that simple failing was what started the nightmare.

When he had gone away to school, Jimmy Lu had been what seemed the last hope of an aging neighborhood. Large numbers of the other kids from the area went to college as well, of course—they were Asian, and it was expected. But, everyone knew their motives. The others, they were escaping, pure and simple. They were not about to return—not once their freedom had been gained—not to face the unstoppable menace that had ruled their world since it had been created.

No, none of the others would be of any help. Jimmy Lu was the one everyone was counting on—Jimmy was the one everyone knew was going to come back and do something about their troubles. There had been no doubts—not in anyone's mind. None whatsoever. And, as at least one someone out of all those involved should have realized, that was the problem.

Jimmy's enemies knew his intentions as thoroughly as every one else. How could they not? Certainly, some of these enemies had been amused, many indignant, others outraged. There were those among the Kwau Kuai, the ones he wished to stop, who almost welcomed an honest confrontation. They had been looking forward for some time to a struggle against a force that understood them—a test to prove their theories correct. It had been too long since such a glorious event had occurred, they protested.

Far too long.

They were bored. Others craved the delicious power such a confrontation would bring. Still others saw it as merely a stepping stone, a first action in a much larger, long-dreamed-after confrontation that would plunge the entire world into chaos, a chaos they firmly believed they could control.

In the end, however, the voices that finally prevailed in the multiple arguments over what to do about Jimmy Lu, were those that urged for the teaching of a lesson. The warmongers turned aside, it was agreed that what was truly needed was a return to the status quo. And that could be done simply enough. All they had to do was dispose of Jimmy Lu.

Of course, to merely kill him, it was decided, was not enough. The people needed to be re-educated—reintroduced to the past and to the names and faces of those whose rules were the real rules—whose powers were the strongest.

To just kill him would be a waste—they argued—and weak. Times had changed. No one believed that the Gaun Cee Qui even existed anymore . . . no one with the power to stop them, any way. There was no longer anything to fear, it was stated convincingly—no need to hide.

Jimmy Lu's death, it was decided, would be a reminder, a statement, something everyone would remember in trembling flashes for a very long time—when they were awake, when they slept, when they looked in on their children in their beds in the middle of the night, when they looked at their own faces in the morning mirror—up close, cold and small under the sun they had lived to see once more.

Thus Jimmy had been challenged to come to Hester Street in a way that had cleverly forced his young pride to forget what Pope had said about the "never failing vice of fools." Abandoning the near invincible weapon of common sense, he had walked into the trap laid for him—boldly, it is true, but stupidly, as well—as it had been planned. And, once there, he had been thrown down and torn into humiliatingly little pieces—made so small that his dream was lost to all who saw the frightful horror to which he had been reduced.

The Kwau Kuai left a piece of their carnage on the doorstep of everyone they wished to squeeze down under their thumbs. Shredded and drained bits and splatters were dropped through mail slots, hidden in rice barrels, smeared on bathroom mirrors, dropped in babies' milk bottles, hung in shop windows between the roasted ducks and chickens.

And then, as a last joke, for a final numbing humiliation, the severed tip of Jimmy Lu's penis was left in the jar on his mother's bedstand—the one that held her false teeth every night. Silent hate had slid into her sleeping room and stuffed her son into her mouth, giving her an undeserved vision of shame to torture herself with, forcing her to damn herself with curses for not raising her son smart enough to know that merely being good and decent was not enough.

When the morning after finally came, and the evening's darkness was lifted to reveal the horrible proof of what had happened, the Kwau Kuai laughed to itself in self-congratulations. Its point, all its members were sure, had been proved. They were in control, and everyone would know it. And, for the most part, they were correct.

Chinatown was subdued once more, back in the grip of the ancient terror, the Gaun Cee Qui, that had ruled it from its opening days. All of its citizens were humble—again. All of them once more quiet.

All, of course, but one.

CHAPTER ONE

Y OUNG FINGERS—STRONG, NIMBLE BONE and muscle—twisted
through the ancient hair for the ten thousandth time, still numb, still
amazed. Still uncomprehending. The man staring at himself in his mirror no longer noticed the burn-scarred frame surrounding the reflecting glass.
That much he comprehended. Now his face and form were the only thing he
saw, the reversed image in front of him showing only the man he was, leaving
him to search for the one he once had been.

He had never been a vain man in the past and, in truth, he had not become
one now, either. But, he had found that he could not pass a minor without
noticing his recently paled hair. Brown one day, white the next. If the mirror
that caught his attention happened to be the one he had had moved from his
office into his home he would stop automatically—staring—looking and remembering more than just his hair's former color. Drawn to its now-webbed,
lightning-fried silver, it had become a constant reminder of the horror that
had come and gone, leaving him strong but frail, young but weary.

Finally, when he tired of the wondering scrutiny, he let his eyes wander. He
checked his tie, straightened the already-perfect knot another time, smoothed
his crisp lapels. He looked himself up and down, searching for any imperfection that might delay his departure. Finding nothing, however, he turned at
last from the mirror, returning to the trek to his apartment's front door.

No fat, at least, he thought.

He smiled at himself sardonically. He had always been more lean than bulky
even before the great Conflagration. Now, however, he was gaunt—withered
and crippled and stricken with eyes that saw through the ages, instantly assessing every happening around him with the blinding speed of one with the
right to judge anything he wanted.

Ignoring the pain of motion, he pressed his weight down on the Blackthorn root walking stick he had been using as a cane, moving himself across
the length of his dining room. Grabbing his hat down from its usual peg, he
covered his white hair, then turned the knob of his apartment's front door,
opening it just as his former assistant's hand was rising to strike it.

"Jeez, boss. You get me every time."

"It's not conscious, Paul," the man apologized. "I don't do it on purpose."

"I know," responded Paul Morcey, a grin on his face. "That's what makes
it so interestin.'"

The smaller man, balding but sporting longish hair pulled back in a near-foot-long ponytail, stepped inside, shutting the door behind him. Spinning around within the small foyer of London's apartment, he presented his arms with an exuberant "ta da" flourish, showing off his new suit. It was black, simply cut, with the faintest of gray pinstripes—neat, but not overbearing; simple, not grand. His shoes were buffed but not shining, everything in his appearance designed for him to blend in, not stand out—all as his partner had instructed.

"Nice outfit," said the man with the cane appreciatively. "You're learning."

"No one's going to notice me now, right, Mr. London?"

"Just all those love-starved businesswomen hearing their biological clocks ticking, just dying to wrap your ponytail around their wrists."

"Yeah?" responded the balding man with calculated innocence. "Where are they?"

"Oh, out there somewhere."

"You sure about that?"

"Absolutely. I read about them in *Time* and *Newsweek.*"

"Ohhhhhh," answered Morcey with exaggeration. "Then it's gotta be true. Right, boss?"

"Oh, yes," agreed London, smiling. "Absolutely."

He was always cheered by the presence of his one-time assistant. Until recently, Paul Morcey had been a janitor. But that had been a lifetime ago—a short lifetime—one spanning only fifty-six days, but a lifetime nonetheless.

Not even two months, thought Theodore London.

He stood still for a moment, leaning heavily on his cane, his mind flashing over the events that had brought him to that present moment in time. Fifty-six days previous, he had had dark hair that curled when soaked by rain or the sea. He had been blessed with two good legs then, arms that could knock back any man, and a strong reserve of wind within him—enough to last through any run or climb or fight.

Now, more than a million and a half people were dead, all of them gone in one monstrous flash, half of him stolen away by the same horrific gale that had claimed the others. Not allowing himself to get lost in the thoughts constantly circling within the back of his brain, however, London told his assistant;

"What do you think, Paul? Will the first good breeze knock me over?" The ponytailed man laughed, not even half able to take his one-time employer's words seriously.

"Yeah, right, boss. Jeez." He laughed again, tilting his head to one side. "Hell itself didn't shake you once you got yourself planted. Call me an optimist, but somehow, I don't think a little May breeze is goin'ta do the trick."

As Morcey headed down the stairs from London's building to his car waiting double-parked below, London allowed himself a brief smile, answering quietly;

"Maybe you're right, Paul."

Then, he put weight on his leg and began the pain of hobbling his way to the street.

London pushed with his shoulder to open the door to Leo's, the diner around the corner from the building housing his office. It was just a hot dog and juice shop, but he had eaten breakfast there on an average of perhaps three days out of every seven for the preceding four years. It was a simple place—one that seemed to the detective to be open twenty-four hours a day—always manned by the same three silent men.

Morcey had gone to park the car in their spot at the local lot; London would see him again at their office—once, the detective realized, he managed to limp all the way there, the block and a half that now suddenly seemed like forever. Made his way there for the first time, he thought again, in fifty-six days.

He wondered at what it would be like—to walk through the door, to be just—*just*—a detective once more. Not the man who saved the entire world—who had rescued every man, woman, and child alive or ever to live in the future—a future that now had a chance to unfold only because Theodore London had been born.

No, he thought, that guy lived for a few days, and now he's gone. I don't think I get to be that guy anymore—I'm not sure I *want* to be that guy again—not ever again.

Theodore London had saved the world, and all its teeming billions, at a cost he could not help but doubt had come as a bargain. Fate had positioned him to be The One, the only person who would be in the right place at the right time to take advantage of the only split second of opportunity there was going to be when the world could be saved at all. Despite the staggering costs in both lives and the property they held—-despite the staggering costs as well to the man forced to make the decision—London had pulled the trigger that killed his best friend, along with a million plus other people, but also the impossible god demon from a decayed and hellish universe that would have destroyed not just the world, but everything in existence.

Teddy London had boldly cut a sickly, rotting tumor from the body of life known as The Earth, good cells sacrificed to save the whole. He had done it without debate, truly expecting to be one of the ones who perished. No one was more surprised at his survival than he was himself. But survive he did, however, and subsequently he was nursed back to a semblance of health by his friends, the only people alive who knew the following two secrets.

The first thing they knew was that their friend had saved the world around them—the galaxy, and from all they could tell, the entire universe—from a never-ending nightmare of torture and torment, one that would have consumed every person on their world, every molecule of life, and then spun on to every other star and planet in the nightly firmament, and all beyond, until everything that could possibly be touched, that held joy or life or even the barest glimmer of hope, was as husked and useless as twice-burnt coal.

The second thing they knew was that he still lived with the pain of a million and a half voices screaming in his head. Screaming in pain as they died in burning terror, the handful sacrificed so billions might live, but cursing their pain and howling with all the power of a million years of developed nerves, feeling every burn of all flesh that was ever seared.

His friends also knew that it was the mindless bellow of those voices, the hollow, screeching agony of them that went on for days before London finally came out of his coma, that had actually withered him. Not the weight that pinned his leg or, as the hospital report had listed them, the:

Eighty-nine lacerations;

Seventeen first-degree burns, 7% body surface damage;

Six two-degree burns, 24% body surface damage;

Twenty-eight third degree bums, 11% body surface damage;

Pneumonia;

Fifteen abrasions;

Seven broken bones; et cetera.

None of it. It was the guilt of his heroism that had crushed him into a smaller man, a white-haired oldster who had come to look on the end of his life as only a release—one of which to be dreamed. For, it was beginning to seem to the detective that he would limp and slouch through that crushing guilt until the end of his days because the nature of its weight was to cripple, and he already lacked the power to stand.

He knew those who loved him were worried, but he did not know what he could about it. He had played his part, and as far as he was concerned, he should have been finished by then. Retired. Given the chance to just roam the range before him in the days he had remaining. Indeed, after all he had done, all he had experienced, how could anyone expect him to just work a job now? What was he supposed to do . . . go back to the mindless pursuit of dollars? For what? So he could buy lottery tickets?

Why, he asked. So he could pay taxes, eat in restaurants, go to movies, hand tribute over to beggars?

Was that the rest of his life? Watching the news so he could see who died that day—what planes fell from the sky, which congressmen were not proven to be cheats or drunks or rapists— that week? Was there nothing more to the future except trying to remember to separate his plastics from his cans from his news papers from his metals? He had stepped up onto a stage where whim became reality, and now he was supposed to . . . supposed to . . . what? Fit in?

How, he wondered. How could anyone expect anything from him ever again? And yet, they did. Everyone expected the detective to simply go on living now. He had looked into the face of a god, an all-powerful monstrosity of hate and greed, a rapacious garble of energy and self that . . .

Annoyed, London silenced the part of his brain that could not stop yammering about what had happened. Life goes on, he told it. You survive, you do what has to be done. You take responsibility for what you can and see it through.

"That's all!" he hissed under his breath.

Staggering to the counter, drained by the effort it took to shut down his memory, he slid onto a stool and smiled weakly at the man who had taken his order—what—perhaps a thousand times over the years?—telling him;

"The usual Joseph."

"The usual 'what,' senor?" the man asked in earnest.

"Two eggs, scrambled, American cheese melted through, served with a lightly buttered, toasted bialy."

He could see that the counterman thought he knew at whom he was looking. Out of mercy, he summoned the energy to allow his old self to flood his eyes for a moment, adding, "Tea with lemon?"

"Senor London?" he asked, not believing what he was seeing. "Is it you? Truly you?"

"It's what's left of me," he answered, letting his eyes close over again.

"Was it . . . the nightmare?" asked another of the countermen.

London nodded, memory eating at the energy he was using to hold it at bay.

"I knew it. Everyone—you see," the one said to the other, the third working on London's order. "Everyone knows someone who suffered. Everyone in the city . . ."

"What do you expect?" answered his mate. "A million and a half people . . ."

"More."

All three turned toward London's voice.

"Excuse me . . .?" asked the first.

"It was more."

"More 'what,' senor?"

"More lives—screaming. Hundreds of thousands more." The detective pulled down a deep breath, tasting it, sucking the life from it. Then he finished, the death in his voice frightening the three countermen to the point where all they could do was stare at him numbly.

"One million . . . ," he told them, ". . . seven hundred and nineteen thousand, five hundred and sixty-two."

"How?" asked the one who had not yet spoken, the one carrying the then finished breakfast platter. "How . . . do you . . . know?"

"They told me," answered London.

His eyes passed over all of the men, shaking them with their assurance that he was neither mad nor lying. The one with the platter, fighting his nerves, had to use both his hands to keep the meal steady, afraid to spill it, afraid to drop it, afraid to approach his customer. As his fingers slid the hot plate toward London, the detective's eyes scanned the food, one of his favorite meals, in one of his favorite eateries.

His body started to tremble from the sight, his long-empty stomach rebelling, screeching for the food on the plate before him. The warm smells of it seized him, rocking the detective with agonizing rumbles of pain and desire. His hands, shaking with indecision, skittered toward the food like rats. His fingers slammed awkwardly against and through the surface of the eggs, the melting cheese burning him, releasing memory. Trailing hot strings of dripping food, he thrust his hands into his clothing in search of his wallet.

Finding it, he threw money at the countermen, neither knowing how much nor caring. He only knew he had to escape them before they realized just what he was. And then hated him as much as he hated himself.

CHAPTER TWO

L ONDON LIMPED THROUGH THE front doors of 132 Greeley Arcade, tired and shaken, wishing he were home, safe behind his fast-drawn curtains. It was too soon, too early for him to be back, he thought. Far too early. Shaking, he leaned against the long marble wall, grateful for the support. None of the others waiting with the detective recognized him, not even the front deskman who had watched London enter on a daily basis for years. To all of the others grumbling and fidgeting in the lobby, he was merely another tenant or tenant customer, waiting for the elevator. Easily ignored.

No one.

"I should have never tried to do this again," he told himself, feeling as though his mere presence outside his brownstone were enough in itself to certify him insane. "Not now. I should be home. This is just too soon—too soon . . ."

A moment away from limping back out to the street in search of a cab—from fleeing—one of the sets of elevator doors before him opened, forcing the detective to go up to his office. He stepped inside with the others all around him, ignoring their push and feel, closing his eyes as the doors slid shut again. He could feel them, the entire way up, smell them, hear their thoughts, feel their desires. The stench of their formidable presence was overwhelming. Intoxicating.

Exiting the metal coffin, the detective gasped, his back hitting the wall of the hallway as the doors slid closed behind him. He put the fingers of his left hand to his forehead, shutting his eyes at the same time. Sucking in the joyful emptiness of the hallway, he finally released the breath he was holding, then used his Blackthorn cane to maneuver himself the fifteen steps to the entrance to his office.

Once there, he stood before it for a moment, not going straight in. Gathering his breath, he calmed his nerves, using the moment to scrutinize the letters on the frosted glass embedded in the door of his office. He moved his eyes in a fashion indicating to no one in particular that he was somewhat please to see that his company notice had been repainted as per his orders.

"The London Agency."

He read the words aloud softly, under his breath. Now that he had a set of partners he had shortened the old wording, making it stuffier, more corporate, more businesslike. The agency was the only thing outside his home that he owned and, if it had been up to him, he would have closed the place down, happy at the thought of never having to see it again.

But, he had told himself, his friends had risked as much as he had and, like himself, had nothing else to show for it. For them the detective had kept the firm solvent—kept it intact as a base from which they could all anchor themselves. He felt it was the least he had owed them.

And what do you owe yourself?

The voice hissed softly in the back of his mind, a nudging curiosity, licking its lips over things he could not bring himself to consider.

Cracking the door finally, he peeked inside cautiously, throwing up shields against what he might find. The only thing he found was one of his partners, Lisa Hutchinson. Her back to the door, she was busy at her computer. Part of London's brain still stirred at the sight of her—thick chestnut curls cascading down over her shoulders, shimmering in the morning light. He remembered her face, high, striking cheek bones red with life, perfect nose and chin, and her eyes—blue as a lake reflecting violets—eyes old before their time, begging for youth. She was wearing a bright summer print, the pattern of which lightened the detective, easing his pains for a moment.

Who knows? he wondered. Maybe it's all for the best.

And, on the notion, he took the knob in his free hand and pushed open the door, finally stepping back into his old world.

"Teddy!" shouted Lisa.

Abandoning her computer, the woman came around her desk quickly, her arms taking London in a soft but rushing manner. She had not seen him since his first few weeks in the hospital. Once released from its greedy care, he had spent his time at home by himself, solitary except for occasional visits from Morcey, the only person of the many who tried whom he would allow entry.

"You're back!"

She had called him a hundred times, but he never answered the phone. When she came to the door, he told her to wait for him to heal, not wanting her to see him in his reduced state. Not wanting to see her at all. She had said she would wait, and had left him to his recuperation.

Now, her period of waiting finally over, Lisa hugged him to her fiercely, desperate to see him tall and solid once more. He had challenged the forces of Hell, braved every nightmare she had ever known, conquered the most terrible forces imaginable, simply because she had asked him to do so. When every hand had been turned against her, his had been there for her and nothing had been able to stop him. When force had been necessary, he had been stronger; when intellect was called for, his had been superior. No woman had ever had a greater champion and she loved him for it with every fiber of her being. A love, of course, that he was now not only unable to respond to, but of which he was actually afraid.

The woman, of course, sensed it immediately, hugging him for only a moment before she could feel it—his thunderous discomfort—and the distance it was generating. Releasing him from the embrace, still holding his sleeve, she asked him a quiet question.

"Teddy, what's wrong?"

"Just the strain, first day out and all."

She let his sleeve fall away, his arm dragged down helplessly by its weight.

"No it's not," she answered. "You've avoided everyone but Paul since you got out of the hospital. We were all so . . . so upset about what happened to you. Pa'sha's just been sick—he tries not to show it, but he's been really worried. And he's not the only one."

Lisa regretted the admission for a fraction, then damned the hesitation and pulled herself inward, telling him;

"I was really scared—terrified—that I might lose you, that, that . . ."

Then suddenly the woman stopped herself short, feeling her fear growing into anger instead of concern. "Please, let's not worry about this right now. Come on," she said, almost managing to laugh. "Get into a chair before you fall over."

Helping him along, treating the man she loved like a fragile grandfather, Lisa got London into his inner office, shutting the door behind them while he headed for his desk.

"Can I talk to you?" she asked, dreading his answer no matter what it might be. "Or should we wait?"

"We can talk," he answered passively. Not knowing what else to say. She stared at him, tracing the look of helpless acceptance in every line of his face. With no idea how to reach the man she remembered, she killed the silence with simpler things, trying to work her way up to that which really concerned her.

"I've got the computer system ready."

"Everything?"

"Yep'per," she answered proudly. "Between the records you sent from home, and the old files of yours that Paul brought up from the basement, I've gotten everything you lost—from back when we first met—onto disks and into your new system. The London Agency is actually open for business."

He nodded, letting her know he was pleased. She had quit her job to rebuild his firm, just as Morcey had quit his to follow London into the nightmare. When they had all survived, he had made them his partners. The division of labor was obvious enough. Lisa, with her programming skills, would operate the records and finance end. Morcey would take over the investigations, reporting back to London who, if all went well, would just sit back and oversee operations.

Unfortunately, it was also obvious that both of the Agency's new members had a lot to learn. Lisa was too inexperienced and, perhaps, too young to be an efficient business manager, especially a business as rough as London's. And Morcey, for all his eagerness, did not have the experience of his employer's years in the field.

They both had strong wills, however, and at first London had been pleased with the plan. It had allowed him to repay Morcey for his loyalty, and to keep Lisa near him. But, as the days of his recovery had stretched out, each one draining him more rather than making him stronger, he had come to think of the move as a horrible mistake. One he could not now see any way to rectify.

"Actually, you may have a little more information than you did before."

"How so?"

"Well," answered Lisa, the youth of her hope rising up against the growing truth that gnawed at her.

"Do you remember all your old friends in the business, like Sheila Harvey, and Dann Thornton over at American Protection, or Del Rehill at A.S.S., or everyone's favorite, Mark Russell?"

"Yes . . .?" he questioned her with a feeling bordering on interest.

"It's surprising how easy it was to crack their information nets and transfer it all here."

"Yes . . .?" he said again, barely changing his tone.

"It was easy. Once I back-doored into Allied Securities, I went through their system to crack American Protection. Then I double-duped all the files through one company to another, so, if they ever do catch on, they'll trace the thefts to each other."

He looked at her both skeptically and slightly shocked—wondering how the scared little girl from Vermont who had first come into his office could have wrought such changes within herself in so short a span. Understanding his expression, she told him;

"I do think you'll be pleased when you call up some of your files."

"You do, huh?"

"Yes, I do," she answered with a tone of accomplishment. "Go on," she ordered, coming around the desk to join him.

"Try one."

The last time London had sat behind his desk, there had been no terminal. The one he used to have had been smashed by his enemies. All his files—paper or electronic—had been destroyed. Along with his phone, his rug, his window, his life . . .

Dammit. *Goddammit*, shut up, he thought, cursing all the never long-silent voices in his brain. Stop it already! I've got a life to get on with. Okay dammit! So everything got destroyed. Well, what about . . . now?

What did he have now?

Curious, he keyed his initials onto the glowing screen before him. When the program asked for his password, his eyes flashed across to Lisa. Hers dropped for a second. She colored for a moment, then looked at him again, telling him;

"Hero."

Teeth biting his lip at the conspicuous label, he steadied his hands above the keyboard, pecking at it—at the word. Right index finger poised, shaking, finally slamming down . . .

"H."

Left hand, middle finger, automatic snap . . .

"E."

Same hand, index finger, already up to the correct row, hanging in hesitation . . .

"R."

Right hand, ring finger, trying, trying—

Lisa hit the key for him, her face trying to hang on to the mask of pride in her work, everything behind it falling into silent tears, mourning that which she knew she had lost.

As the computer granted London access to its secrets, Lisa said quietly;

"I'm sorry. I programmed it for you . . . a long while back, I guess. I'll change it for you later."

"It's all right," he told her, trying to be chipper. "It's just a word. Any word will do."

And that was when she left. He heard a sharp rush of her breath, felt the air go cold around them, and then she was gone, only the trailing echoes of her footsteps disappearing into and down the hall. He never tried to stand.

What was the point?

It was better if she got away from him—whispered the little voice inside—better for her. She was young, ten years London's junior—still a virgin. She needed someone who could take her and bring her along through all the stages of love, someone who could still love—indeed, someone who was still alive. Not some one three-quarters dead.

Not him.

And then the other voice in his head raged against his despair, boiling over into its pain. And why not you—you moron? Why not? Aren't you the man she fell in love with? You haven't changed—you idiot. You're the man she loves.

No, I'm not, he answered himself. He's done now. I'm what's left. All destroyed—finished. All I want to do is die.

The admission frightened parts of his brain—pleased others. And why can't I? Why *shouldn't* I? I paid my dues. I did my bit. It's someone else's turn now.

Shut up, he snarled back at himself, fighting for his life. Don't tell me you don't want her. I don't *care* if you want her or not. *I* want her! I deserve her and I'm going to have her!

Fuck you—he told his despair, roared at it—you want to die, go die. Be my guest. But leave me out of it. I want to live. Do you hear me . . .

"Goddammit! I want to live!"

"Glad to hear it, boss."

Morcey had come in while London had been lost within his own head. Staring up at the ex-maintenance man, the detective said;

"Did you see Lisa in the hall?"

"No, why?"

"I've done something stupid—I mean, part of me, I let her see, well, 'feel' actually . . . I mean . . ." London caught his breath, cutting off the rush of words jabbering out of him. Starting again, he said;

"Paul, I think I've lost my mind."

"Yeah, so?" asked Morcey, his words slurred by a mouthful of cream-cheesed bagel. The detective looked up at his partner, wondering what he meant. Morcey told him.

"Awww, hell, Mr. London. You think you're crazy, right? So what? I mean, me, too." Taking a long pull of coffee, he added, "It's like Doc Goward told us; we seen things beyond our comprehension. We can't help bein' crazy."

"It's not the same, Paul." He looked his friend in the eye, desperate to find words capable of explaining his torment. "I keep hearing the voices of all those who died. It used to be only in my sleep. Lately, I hear them all the time . . . I can hear them now."

"What are they sayin'?"

"What?"

"I mean, what do they want, boss? Are they asking you somethin', or tellin' you somethin', or what?"

"Screaming, mostly. Just screaming. So many of them died so horribly—all at the same time—I don't even think most of them even know they're dead. The only thing they share is a knowledge of who it was that killed them." London waved his hand weakly, a grim smile curling one side of his mouth.

"You remember who that was, don't you?"

"Boss, I'm tellin' you this for your own good. It ain't healthy for you to dwell on this stuff. You gotta get on with your life and all."

"Why?" The detective asked the question quietly—sincerely—honestly wondering if his friend could come up with some reason he had missed.

"Awwwww, boss, don't go gettin' yourself all upset. Nobody knows the answers to questions like that. After a tragedy, you just go on—you just *do*—that's all. Just lettin' yerself die ain't the answer to anything."

When London stared, the balding man told him;

"What? You think I don't know what's goin' on? You think I'm just some kind of goof or somethin'? I know yer not eatin'. I know. You think we're stupid? You think—"

"No, Paul," answered the detective. "No. I don't. I—I almost wish I did. I wish there was something about you, and Lisa, that I could latch on to, something I could ridicule or feel superior to, just so I could leave you both behind. But, I can't."

"Oh, jeez, boss," answered Morcey with obvious sincerity. "I'm glad to hear that."

London smiled, appreciating his friend's efforts. Then, remembering something he had wanted to say, he reminded the ex-maintenance man;

"Well, that's good, anyway. And while you're at it, would you like to keep in mind the fact that I'm not your boss anymore. We're partners now, remember?"

"Yeah, sure, Mr. London, I remember."

Smiling again at the balding man, never quite certain when his friend was joking and when he was in earnest, London said;

"Paul, go and see if you can catch up to Lisa, will you? Take her home if she wants, or bring her back, or, well, you know . . . whatever she wants. Just make sure she's okay."

"Sure thing. I'll take care of her. You relax, get your strength back. I know nine-to-fivin' it ain't exactly a thrill for a guy who's saved the world and all but, you know what they say 'Meat's meat, and a man's gotta eat.'"

Morcey departed from the office then, leaving London alone with his thoughts. The detective looked around the room, trying to spark some interest within himself in his surroundings. His new partners had done a good job in making the place look professional once again—more so, he had to admit, than he ever had. He realized that the majority of their ideas of what a private investigator's office should look like had mostly come from black-and-white motion pictures but, then again, he thought, what exactly was wrong with that?

Maybe we'll start a trend.

Or maybe, he listened to one of his more mature voices for a moment, maybe he could get back into the old groove. Security work, employee checks, child custody, all the rest.

It wasn't like it was horrible.

And, he thought, if when he had walked the dream plane, if he had been as close to the next stage of reality as he had felt he had been, had indeed actually touched the mantle of God, then maybe surviving was in his favor. From what he could remember from his early religious training, the Almighty was not supposed to be too keen on the idea of suicide.

At the least, London told himself, he could stay with the firm long enough to make sure Lisa and Paul would be all right, able to handle things on their own, and then he could just retire. Abandon the city, and its horrid crowds, leaving all the numbing, reeking madness of man's daily hatred behind him. It was true that what had happened to him fifty-six days earlier had been a nightmare. But, like all nightmares, it had ended. He woke up.

He had survived it.

Now, he told himself, hushing the howls of fear curling up out of the back of his mind, maybe it was time to learn something from what he had been through. If it was actually all real, reincarnation, the great circle of life—all of it—then every moment he wasted not preparing himself was just . . . what? Bad karma?

"At the least."

He had said it aloud as a joke and, it had made him smile but, there was a disturbingly large part of him that was absolutely convinced that he was right. Continuing his conversation with himself, he said;

"Okay. You survived. You actually got out of bed, put on clothes, and made it to work. Bully for you. It took all your courage, but, you actually managed to do what every average Joe and Josephine does every Monday through Friday of their lives."

Even though the dread of going home and then coming back, going home and coming back, going home and coming back again and again and again, raged through him, turning his skin cold with the thought of chaining himself behind his desk every day after day for who knew how long with no end in sight, he fought it down, trying with all the positive force he had left to lock it away—at least for a while—saying;

"Maybe . . . okay? Just 'maybe' we could stick it out. After all," he joked with himself, still talking aloud, "how much is anyone going to expect from a dried-up old man with a cane?"

And, as fate would have it, at that moment, Mrs. Xui Zeng Lu came through the front door of his office.

CHAPTER
THREE

T HE WOMAN CAME INTO London's inner office, staring at him as if waiting for the answer to a question. The detective had been aware of her presence since she had first passed through the agency's front door, of course but, he chose to say nothing—wearily hoping silence alone would be enough to send her away. It was not. The woman moved through the outer office, past the secretarial post, ignoring Morcey's room, walking straight into the back office.

London watched Mrs. Lu with a mixture of futility and curiosity as she moved forward and then sat in the largest of the three chairs in front of his desk. Tired of waiting for her to speak, he offered;

"Yes, can I help you?"

"We shall see."

The detective furrowed his brow. Pain shot through his abdomen, but whether it was the screams of hunger he was growing well used to or a warning of some other type, he could not tell. While the back of his mind debated the two possibilities, the old woman pulled a black silk pouch from her bag, then placed it on the desk halfway between London and herself.

What now? thought the detective, eyeing the long, thin pouch, guessing at its contents.

"Please," said the woman. "Reach inside. Pull out whichever of the *cheem* you feel is the one for you." Looking at the woman askance, feigning confusion, London asked her;

"What do you mean?"

"You are still so blind—after everything that has happened? After all you have done, the veil is still before you—keeping you from seeing clearly?" Her face flashed with an anger the detective could tell was only partly studied. Looking into London's eyes, she dismissed his coyness, saying;

"Or are you just another little boy who likes to waste time playing games with his elders?" A look that all sons understand crossed her face, giving London a small bit more of an idea of that with which he was dealing.

"I am a mother. Long time, more than one baby," she told him. "I understand the games children play. Reach into the bag—pick your *cheem*."

"You want to talk about not wanting to play games?" he said back to her. "You came to the right place." Sucking down enough wind to keep his rasping voice going, he continued.

"If there's anybody in this town that doesn't want to play games, ma'am . . . it's me. I don't know what you want but, I'll tell you plain—I do not have time for any nonsense. If you want to hire a detective, you came to the right place. If you want to work some kind of sideshow act, I'm asking you politely . . . please . . . some other time."

"I did not come here to hire a detective," answered Mrs. Lu. Grabbing up her *Kow Cheem* bag, she took it in both hands, shaking it toward London repeatedly. With a slow, steady rhythm she shook the sack levelly, the action of her practiced hands forcing one of the *cheem* to work its way forward. As the single stick bounced free, she said;

"I came to find the Destroyer."

The *cheem* stick hit the blotter in front of London. It bounced once, twirled on its end, then dropped in front of the detective, lying motionless before him. London stared at the woman. How could she know?

How?

Two months earlier, he had discovered that Fate had picked him for a duty. As events unfolded he learned that a number of men had been picked throughout the history of the world for the same duty—the title coined over the centuries for them being "the Destroyer." The voices in London's head were a continual reminder that he had indeed lived up to the name.

His choice had saved the world, but it had also killed over a million and a half people. No one but his friends knew of this, however, and for obvious reasons none of them had said a word to the world outside their little circle.

How, the detective wondered, had the woman before him discovered what had happened? And, the other side of his reason asked, how much did she really know? Had she, indeed, discovered his dark secret, or did she only know its name? As his eyes came back to hers, she told him;

"All of it, Mr. London. I know it all."

The detective blinked twice—hard—shocked, unbelieving. His mind raced—part of it looking for something to say, the other half trying to figure out the woman before him and whatever angle she might be playing. Desperation started setting off bells within London's mind, alarms he silenced as quickly as they began. Panic, he reminded himself, was not going to help anyone.

Starting to take the old woman seriously, he took her in on the physical level with a glance—height; weight; hair, eye, and skin coloration; body fat levels; age; strength; general appearance, make-up worn, the effect created by her manner of dress; mannerisms, hand gestures, eye movement; posture—

At the same time other parts of him, parts that had worked instinctively in the old days, suddenly flared up into his conscious mind, their debates frightening him as he listened. In the split second since the woman had announced that she knew London's terrible secret, his brain had begun to dissect her, reaching into her aura, working to determine the direction of her spiritual growth, how wise she was, how developed her soul might be–

What?

London's mind sputtered to a halt at that point, asking itself what it was talking about. Ever since he had come to in his hospital room after the Conflagration, his mind had been feeding him new kinds of input. Perhaps it was only what he thought it was, just a simple shifting of functions from the subconscious processing level to the conscious, but it was a disturbing phenomenon to which he had still not grown accustomed.

Now, in the part of his brain where he had previously spoken aloud to himself, worked out problems, debating with his various selves, like any other thinking person, suddenly he found himself sizing up others in ways he could not explain—watching the flow of blood through their surface veins, measuring the invisible electrical energy surrounding their skin, labeling them with moral considerations merely by the number of blood vessels broken within their eyeballs.

The detective's lashes parted after the second blink. As his attention focused on the external reality of the old woman once more, she told him;

"My name is Xui Zeng Lu. I am what you might call a 'witch woman.'"

"And why might I call you that?"

"It is as good a translation as any for what it is I do." The woman picked up the *cheem* and tucked it back in its bag. "Do you know the *Kow Cheem?*"

"We call it the *I Ching.*"

"Yes." She smiled thinly, like a spider at the first scent of fly wings outside its webbing. "Do you know what it says?"

"Whatever people want it to say," he answered roughly, half angry, half frightened. "Like any other kid's game, it's a con, a dodge, a translation of half-felt fears and hopes and sorrows that gives the suckers something to believe in."

"You are a blind and frightened man, Mr. London."

"It's a blind and frightened world, ma'am." Then, feeling himself coming alive, he took the initiative and asked, "Which makes me wonder, with all due respect, what is it that you want? Let's get to the point."

"My son was murdered. I want you to kill the things that killed him."

"'Things'?" asked London. Parts of him reawakening, thrilling to the possibility of *more*, he asked a question the majority of him did not want to have answered. "What kind of things?"

"Kwau Kuai," she informed him in a cold voice, snarling the words, then repeating them in English.

"The Ancient Evil."

"And," he asked sarcastically, "exactly *which* ancient evil are we talking here? There are so many, you know."

"The Gaun Cee Qui," she told him, following her words with an explaining translation . . .

"The vampires."

And then the detective's fears seemed to disappear like a popped soap bubble. Without missing a beat, London threw back his head and laughed. His body shook with the utter preposterousness of it all. Something akin to relief surged through him like a spring thunderstorm flooding the prairies. Now he understood, he told himself. It was all a joke, just a joke. Morcey would come around the corner any second, with the rest of his friends. Any second now, their laughter would join his and the cleanness of it would erase the tension that had been dogging him for so long. Any second, he knew . . .

Any second . . .

He opened his eyes, almost shocked that the woman was still the only one in the room in front of him. She sat through his laughter, unperturbed, as he called out;

"Paul? Lisa? Pa'sha? Somebody?" He said the words with little conviction—followed them with others sounding even more hollow. "I mean, enough's enough. Come on now. Joke's over."

He called out to the empty rooms beyond his, knowing the truth, but dreading the thought of facing it. Rational enough to admit defeat, however, he turned to the attack again.

"All right, lady, all right." The detective sighed heavily, folding in on himself slightly. "So this isn't a joke—at least—not one my friends are playing. So I guess I'll have to go all the way and ask, what's your game?"

Staring at the imperturbable Mrs. Lu from across his desk, he snarled, "I mean, on the whole, as I hope you can see, I'm not a really well person. I'm certainly not up for this kind of shenanigan so soon after what I've been through. So then, you tell me . . . why the hell should I believe in you and your vampires?"

Still sitting quiet and motionless before him, the old woman reached again into her bag, pulling forth a small, polished ivory box. It was carved on all sides, a never-ending trail of elephants following one another to the right, trunk to tail. Putting it on the desk before her, she said;

"Why is it you do not believe in vampires, Mr. London?"

The detective sighed, knowing his reasons, knowing she was as aware of them as he was. Not wishing to surrender the high ground, though, he told her;

"Since I doubt the reasons I don't believe are going to matter to you, why don't you go ahead and give me your spiel, so we can get through this faster—all right?"

"No!" Mrs. Lu spit the words at London, anger flashing, shattering the mask of calm in which she had disguised herself up until that point. She slapped her palm against his desk three times, each slap a cracking whip noise of fury, each one punctuated with another shouted;

"No! NO! NO!!"

Pulling herself inward, she caught London's eyes with her own, staring deep inside of him, giving the detective access to her soul at the same time.

"You cannot hide from me the strength of your convictions—puny, shriveled things that they are—and I will not allow you to hide them from yourself. You speak now—tell me . . . why is it you do not believe in Gaun Cee Qui?"

Slightly startled, fumbling for an explanation, London offered the best response he could make.

"Well, nobody be—nobody except you, of course—believes in vampires. That's just myths—stories from books and movies."

"No, Mr. London," she said sadly.

"Movies are what make you think the dead do not walk. Someone constructed a fantasy for you that you chose to believe. You sat in the dark as a child with your hands full of candy and butter corn, and when later you screamed in the night, your mother told you it was just a movie, giving you the illusion of safety by wrapping you in lies."

The woman leaned forward from her chair, moving her hands in front of the detective as she told her tale.

"The Kwau Kuai have been with us for a thousand thousand years. They are older than the oldest Chinese dynasty, which makes them older than all of civilization—older than all of history itself. No one outside of the Gaun Cee Qui themselves know where they came from, or why they are. Every land has known them, every age has had to deal with them.

"Now," she told him, "they have come again. They are here now, Mr. London, and they are ready to take the opportunity our new age of enlightenment has given them to strike out once more."

"Now wait a minute," snapped London, desperate to hang on to his safe beliefs. Mastering his warring impulses, not wanting to again step into the world beyond, he pulled his fragmenting resolve together and snapped;

"You can tell me how much *you* believe all you want but that's not proof. You talk about a million years of vampires—well, where are they? Where are they in history books? You make it sound like every thirty years a bunch of vampires get together and try and take over the world like it was the Super Bowl or something. How come nobody—and I mean, *no body*—has ever heard word one about this. Ever?"

"You have heard, you simply choose not to believe." As London snorted, Mrs. Lu told him;

"Why do you think the Roman Empire fell? What do you think your Inquisition was all about?" Passion consumed the old woman completely for the first time. Sweeping her hands through the air before her, she continued in the same vein, the depths of her voice growing in power with every breath.

"When the Mongols rode forth and carved most of the known world for their own, what do you think rode at their head? When the Dark Ages ruled Europe, when men dwelled in the ruins of previous dynasties as if they were caves, so regressed by their fall from intellect that they did not even recognize those structures as man-made objects—what do you think was behind it all?"

"Nothing," answered London, "not in any organized sense. I'm not a big believer in the brotherhood of evil mutants."

"Then you are as doomed as the rest."

London sighed, weary and aching, the pain in his guts and heart and withered leg tearing at him. Drawing what power he could from the atmosphere around him, he stared forward at Mrs. Lu, not even able to catalogue the questions flooding his brain. Then, knowing it was his turn to speak, he finally asked the words he had hoped to avoid, the ones from which he could not escape.

"Mrs. Lu, let's say for a minute, just for a minute, that there really are vampires. Now, you have no proof . . . you've got a good voice and a commanding presence, I'll give you that much. It's a great act, and you've got a terrific story to go with it. So, I'll give you a minute of belief.

"Even if there really are vampires out there somewhere, what makes you think I care? Why would I? Why *should* I? Just what in *Hell* made you come to me?"

"Because you are the Destroyer."

"So—so what?" London leaned forward across the top of his desk, shaking his hand angrily in Mrs. Lu's face.

"Maybe I'll even give you that one, too. Okay, for that same minute, let's say I am this Destroyer, the figure Fate named to face down the Q'talu. Well, even if I am the Destroyer, you've still got no business here because, lady, believe me, his work is finished."

London fell back roughly in his chair then, his fury past, his energy spent. Looking at Mrs. Lu, he gave her the rest in a weaker voice.

"That's all over now. The job's done. I played my role, did my duty. What's left of me is out of the Destroyer business."

Mrs. Lu, unmoving, unblinking, stared at the detective, summing him up. Then, without warning, she shut in on herself—closing her eyes, sitting back quietly—her hands folded in her lap, her breaths short and regular.

"Mr. London," she said, eyes still closed, hands still folded, "Destiny did not move you like the winter snows, did she, driving you as a tiger from the mountains? No—she did not force you to your role—she sheltered you for it."

And then, suddenly, Mrs. Xui Zeng Lu reached what she needed to understand. Somehow, something of the detective's past pain touched her through the air, forcing the old woman to abandon her hopes of bending him to her cause. Opening her eyes then, Mrs. Lu stood suddenly, blinking. She looked down at the detective, her mask breaking into pity. Reaching forward, touching his hand gently, she felt his sorrows, all of them. Contact with him told her much, the knowledge forcing her eyes to well with compassion as she said;

"I did not know it went back so far." Rising from her chair, she let her warmth flow from her fingers into his wrist, trading its balm for any sting her words might have caused.

"I did not know there had been . . ."

And then her eyes caught London's once more, and she could see that he was beginning to remember that first horror that Mrs. Lu had already seen.

". . . so many."

She broke the connection between them and headed for the door, moving as silently and as quickly as when she had first entered. Shutting the front office door behind her, she headed for a conveniently opening elevator, following in the pair of men from the furrier's in the office next to London's.

Some minutes later, Paul Morcey returned to The London Agency. Lisa had wanted to go to her apartment, so he had taken her there as ordered. The ex-maintenance man had then come back, expecting to find the detective busy in his office. He did find London in his office, but if he was busy, it was in no way that his partner could discern.

CHAPTER
FOUR

THE OLD, DARK GREEN truck moved along the dirt road in a jarring fashion—half the bouncing caused by the horrible rutting from the storm the day before, half by the driver's efforts to avoid it. On both sides of the roadway, the scrub grass and weeds shone from the storm's efforts, all of them still slick with water despite the sun's best efforts to bake it all into cloying humidity. Wildflowers pushed out from under and between—pinks and oranges, yellows, blues, and whites breaking up and dotting the greenery in all directions, puddles everywhere, unable to soak into the saturated ground.

The woman in the passenger seat, a lady who frowned back at those who looked down on the idea of "housewifing" as a career, moved her gaze from the scenery outside her window across the cab to steal a peek at her husband, then down to the baby in her lap. The noise of the two boys in the back of the battered pickup caught their mother's ear, pleasing her for once. It seemed like a good day ahead for the family. That would be a pleasant first, she thought for a moment, then admonishing herself;

Okay, maybe not a first ever—but the first in a long, longggg time.

She smiled at the sunlight collecting in and reflecting through the various blemishes in the windshield. Sparkling like gems, the collection of tiny cracks and gouges prismed the rays, flinging color in different directions with every jolt and turn of the truck, irritating the driver, but, pleasing his wife and dazzling their youngest son.

The boys in the back could not see the burning rainbows delighting their brother. Nor would they have cared if they had noticed. Such things, after all, were only for babies, or girls, or those other boys who wanted to be one of the former two. Not the London brothers, however. Rosie, Arkansas, had never seen a wilder pair. They were only ten and thirteen but, they were as tall as boys ten and thirteen can be, with heavy bones—solid frames raw from growth but flush with energy and the strength of boys far older.

The pair had done it all—the all that could be done by boys so young so long ago. In their short years, they had canoed the local lake and scaled the nearest cliffs, manned tree houses deep in the forest and once even rode in a hot air balloon. They had explored Blowing Cave and gone hunting with their father, killing rabbits and possums and one deer, though no one knew whose shot brought the unlucky beast down. They had even snuck away from

Cub Scout camp to spend the night in the creaking Macedonia Cemetery on the outskirts of town.

They were also the subject of many tales no one could prove one way or the other. Some said they stole pumpkins from old Turl Taylor's farm . . . others said they were the ones who burned down the old bleachers at the condemned school and everyone knew the eldest had already had sex. No matter what he said red-faced and flustered to the contrary—everyone just *knew*. It was, as the people of Rosie might say, a known fact.

Just like the fact that they were fighting terrors, either of them able to take on any other boy in their school—most in groups of two, sometimes three. Once, back to back, they had held off a snarling ring of their day-before friends, battering them as they came forward, young fists smashing faces, clubbing back their classmates because of an imagined trifle. They covered each other and held the line, neither of them injured more seriously than the least wounded of their foes. This defense, of course, coupled with their usual good natures, and the stories everyone told of their exploits, made them exactly the fellows that everyone wanted as friends.

As the ten-year-old grabbed his older brother around the neck, pulling him down into the bed of the truck, the move starting the two of them tussling anew, their father whacked his knuckles against the rear window of the cab, yelling out the driver's side window at the same time;

"Settle down, you heathens. Save some of that energy for the Tomahawks."

As the fight in the truck bay broke up into giggles, the father turned to his wife and said in mock pain, "God, woman—football players—you just had to give me football players. We couldn't have had some sweet baby girls. No, you had to provide this troupe of Vikings."

"Kevin Peter London," answered the woman with humor in her eyes, "if I had anything but this baby in my hands I'd hit you with it."

"Of course, Virginia, of course," answered her husband, feigning sorrowful resignation. "What else can I expect? Like mother, like sons."

"Ohhh—you're impossible," she told him, digging a finger into his side for emphasis. "Do you know that?"

"Owwwwwww," he howled, so loud both boys in the back heard him. They laughed at Dad, taking abuse from Mom again, knowing the truth that he could break most men in half . . . knowing it the same way the whole town did . . . either from having seen him take apart Curtis Wilson, or from having heard the swelling tale retold by those witnesses to the event.

Wilson had seen the boys with their arms around each other's shoulders, walking in a silly matched step. He had stumbled out of a local restaurant—one everyone in the dry county knew as a place to get a back-room bottle. His drunken state, matched with his natural cussedness, caused him to laugh at the sight of the boys. Unfortunately, it also caused him to fall over them as well.

Trying to cover his own stupidity, he blamed the pair for his faults, kicking at them, calling them "faggots," cursing them in front of their parents just a few feet behind.

Kevin London had extended his hand and pulled Wilson to his feet, then told him he was mistaken, and that he owed the boys an apology. Wilson pulled his hand from their father's, calling him a liar and a faggot breeder. London had let the alcohol talk, sighing that his family had to live in a world where drunks could do as they pleased in public. Then, Wilson called Virginia London the faggot breeder's whore.

No one had ever thought of teaching assistants as the kind to pack devastating lefts. Or rights. Or combinations of the two that could leave a man a hundred pounds heavier crumpled in the dust, heaving his dinner across the sidewalk, blinded by both his tears and a large quantity of newfound humility. They learned to on that dry night, however, as the Londons gained new respect throughout their community.

Such thoughts were far from Kevin's mind as he drove his family to the afternoon's game site, though. With the teacher's strike going into its sixth week, his thoughts were more on where the next week's groceries were going to come from than hotheaded triumphs of the past. Virginia's hospital time had eaten up a lot of their cash . . . nine months earlier they had both thought he was going to have a job when the baby came.

Then again, thought Kevin London wryly to himself, it's not like I don't have a job. I have a job—I'm just not permitted to work it, and, of course, those keeping me from working it won't pay me to not work it, and they won't allow me to work another one while I wait to get back to the one they won't let me work. Yeah, life is sure fun sometimes.

His wife had made a science of juggling their bills, an art of turning boxes of macaroni and a few vegetables into something that somehow seemed different from the last nine times they ate it. Kevin and Virginia London had been together a few weeks shy of fourteen years. In that time they had weathered far worse than their present situation. His face softening into a smile bigger than his current problems, he figured they could weather everything coming at them this time as well.

Then they turned the corner around the edge of Ron Gump's orchard, the turn that offered the view of the high school football field. As he urged his aging truck forward over the last half mile, working it carefully so as not to get stuck in the mud oozing its way up through the road's pitifully sparse red dog rock coating, Kevin told his wife;

"This is typical. We can't teach the kids, but God forbid they miss a game of the football season."

"Kevin, it's not the boys' fault the union's on strike."

"I know that, Ginny. I'm not blaming the boys—it's just the stinking hypocrisy of it all that I hate."

But, by then, the truck had reached the old wooden bridge, the one everyone in the township kept saying should be replaced. Of course, the township said it was the state's bridge, and the state said that technically it belonged to the corporation leasing the land to the township, and the corporation argued that the deeds clearly showed where their custodial responsibilities started and where they finished. Like any kind of politics, it all sounded right, but the result was that the usual nothing happened.

Until, also as usual, it was too late.

Kevin started the truck up over the wooden hump at the mouth of the bridge, the back of his brain noticing something strongly enough to stir his consciousness into commenting.

"You feel that, Ginn?"

"What?"

"That bump at the beginning of the bridge—it's like it's all smoothed out or something."

"Maybe they fixed it," she offered.

Kevin London laughed deeply at the notion that anyone in power might have done anything intelligent without having a gun pointed to their head. Then his laughter stopped. The bump was not the only thing different. The creaking he always heard as he approached the middle was louder—straining, crying—the bitter sounds of wood and metal divorcing in pain.

"Jesus, St. Mary, and Joe," cursed Kevin under his breath, his fingers shaking, hand debating going for a higher gear or maybe reverse. It mattered not, however. Too many cars had crossed the old bridge that day—too many people walking, coming on hikes, or in trucks and buses—just too many. The end of the bridge before them gave way, cracking sharply, its right side scraping its way down the loose and soggy wall of mud that was the other bank. It only gave by two, two and a half feet. But that was more than enough. The truck jerked, then swerved, brakes trying to grab the surface but only sliding on the water-logged pulp instead—crashing against and through the right-side wall, snapping the restraining timbers easily—falling awkwardly into the swollen waters below.

"Ginny? Ginny!?!"

"Kevin! Oh, God, Kevin! The boys!"

Kevin London had been thrown from the cab of the truck. Hanging on to the outside of the door, he fought the torrent pulling at him, praying for the strength to fight against the force trying to suck him away into the rage the river had become from the weeks of never-ending rain. Getting his feet into the mud on the bottom, he realized the side of the cab had caught on one of the small, flattish islands in the middle of the river—usually visible—now submerged. Being in the water, he could also tell the current was slowly pushing the truck forward—forward at a rate that would move it underwater in just a few minutes.

"Ginny, get out! Now, darlin'. Now!!"

"I can't, Kevin," she screamed back, water flashing over her face, working at drowning her, sucking at her arms holding the baby out of its deadly reach. "It's the door, it's crushed in—it's got the seat belt caught. I can't move!"

Not wasting time on further words, Kevin London moved around the front of the truck, holding on to it, pushing it back at the same time, working his way to his wife's side. Wedging himself in between the truck's crushed body and the next small island his feet could find, he put his legs into the sopping ground as braces, planting his back and arms against the door frame, holding the two tons of water-swept steel and iron back with clenched teeth and screaming muscles.

By this time several other vehicles had arrived at the town end of the bridge. People at the school had noticed the commotion as well, hurrying out to see what had happened. Without hesitation, Kevin London's neighbors and townsmen, many of them having no idea who it was they were trying to help, swarmed the banks of the flooded stream, cursing the rain and politicians, forming human chains against the water, working their way to those in need.

Kevin explained his problem in gasps and ragged pants of sorry breath. Men swarmed into the cab, tearing at the frozen seat belt, cutting with pocket knives, fumbling through the neck-high water, finally freeing the trapped woman, pulling her and the baby from the cab. The efforts of all the rescuers were noble to say the least, heroic in every case. They were also, unfortunately, a tragic handful of seconds too late.

Intent on their task, not able to hear the cries of those on the shore, the men working their rescue did not see the flood-propelled debris coming for them. Two logs, wreckage from some other disaster farther upriver, shot straight for the truck, one ramming it broadside, the other flipping upward and coming down on top of it. Kevin London's legs were broken instantly, his spine shattered as if made of glass. He disappeared from sight as the crumpled vehicle broke free of its perch, the island beneath it crumbling.

Virginia London was pulled upward onto the shore, choking and sputtering—screaming, hysterical—still holding her baby above her head, making her God offering as if she were still in the water. A total of eleven were swept away . . . eight of the sturdy, reckless volunteers along with Carl and Walter London, and their father Kevin.

In all the confusion, no one really noted that young Theodore never cried until taken from his mother's hands.

CHAPTER FIVE

"**B**OSS!" SHOUTED MORCEY, NOT knowing what else to do. "Sweet Bride of the Night—wake up!!"

London's eyelids fluttered, blinking away the pooled tears hanging from his lashes. As his mind slipped back into regular consciousness, a groaning sob broke forth from his lips, a burst of pain exploding outward from his soul. It was a poisonous knob that had grown there all his life but, which he had never felt until now. The detective's fingers wiped at his wet face, part of him marveling at the fact he still had juice enough within him to cry.

Turning to Morcey, he asked, "Where's Mrs. Lu?"

"Who's that, boss? There was nobody here when I got back except for you."

London glanced at the clock on his wall, realizing he had been lost within his own head for well over an hour. Wiping his cheeks and chin down with a tissue pulled from his top left desk drawer, he said to his partner;

"Well, Paul . . . I guess I'm not shaping up to be much like the hardboiled kind of guy you thought I was."

"You kiddin' or somethin', Mr. London?" asked the ponytailed man. "Jezz'ma'knees, how much more you gotta go through before you stop beatin' yourself up, anyway?" When the detective merely stared at his assistant, the smaller man continued.

"I mean, boss, believe it or not, everythin' in the world ain't yer responsibility. I know you been takin' things hard and all, and I ain't trying to minimize what happened. Yeah, sure—it was bad—we killed a lot of people . . ."

London looked sharply at his assistant, his eyes narrowing at the word "we." The reaction was not lost on Morcey.

"Yeah, I said 'we.' Did you think Pa'sha and me don't feel just as guilty as you? For that matter, whaddaya think was goin' through Doc Goward and Lai Wan's minds? Sure, I know you pulled the trigger, but we all helped get you there. And, boss, I'll tell ya . . ." added Morcey, his voice growing quiet.

"We, I mean, me and Pa'sha, you know . . . we talked about it—had to get like pretty drunk first actually but, we talked about it. And we both agree that we woulda done the same thing that you did."

The ex-maintenance man lowered his eyes for a moment, biting at his lip, then continued.

"But, just because we knew you did the right thing . . ." he hesitated, his already lowered voice shrinking to a whisper, "we was awful glad we weren't the one that had to do it."

"That includes me, too, Teddy."

Both men turned at the voice, finding Lisa framed in the doorway between the offices.

"Did you think it was any different for me? I started the whole business . . . remember? I'm the one that came to you looking for a detective to . . ."

"That's different," interrupted London. "You were in trouble. You really did need help."

"So did everybody," she responded. The detective motioned with his hands, but the woman cut him off.

"Teddy, the whole world needed help. You saved everyone but a small pocket that just couldn't be saved. You were ready to die with them—you just didn't. And I think that if you're still here, then there must be a reason." Brushing her chestnut curls out of her face, she squared her shoulders and then said;

"And if that's the way it is, then you're just going to have to make the best of it."

The detective stared at her with a slightly wounded look to his eyes, wondering how she could so trivialize what had happened, wondering why it was that neither she nor Morcey seemed to understand. Then, suddenly, it dawned on him that perhaps he was the one who did not understand.

"Lisa, I . . . I don't know what to say."

She came around the desk, going down on one knee next to him, placing her hand on his wrist. Warming him through the connection, she said;

"Teddy, you don't have to say anything. We all understand. We do. Don't you remember your own speech? You told everyone that if you pulled it off, if the bunch of us saved the world, that no one would know? That the next day life would go on, and that we'd all have to just go back to doing our jobs and pretend like nothing ever happened? Do you remember?"

He nodded his head, almost smiling, Lisa's sensible, calming words pushing back the horrible jumble of cursing noise buzzing in the crippling shadows of despair working in his brain. Seeing his agreement, she continued;

"It's that next day, Teddy. When Paul dropped me off at my apartment building, I just stood on the sidewalk for a minute and then I hailed a cab and came right back here. I couldn't leave you alone to face this all by yourself. I love you too much."

"I know," he told her.

"Do you know what I mean, though?" she asked.

"Yes," he responded. "I think so."

The young woman moved closer, putting her arm around the detective, hugging him, dropping her head to one side, resting it on his chest. As Morcey threw his interest into everything in the room except the couple, Lisa said;

"I know we won't be walking down the aisle—I know it's not that kind of love. But I feel it just the same and, I know you feel it, too."

"True enough," he said, his voice growing dark and cold. Lisa did not pull away from him, however, somehow knowing the change had nothing to do with her. As the dream he had had while sitting in the office by himself played before his eyes again, this time in just a flashing split second, Morcey asked;

"Boss . . . I hate to interrupt and all, but . . ." his hand pointed toward the front center edge of the detective's desk, "What's that?"

London and Lisa pulled away from each other slightly, staring forward in the direction Morcey was pointing, toward the carved ivory box left behind by Mrs. Lu. That scene replayed itself before the detective's eyes as well, his curiosity as peaked as that of his partner.

"A woman came in while you were gone to try and hire us," he told the others. "I got a little too caught up in myself and she left. I guess she forgot it."

"Jeez," answered Morcey. "Let's see what it is."

Picking up the carved ivory box, the smaller man studied the circling elephants for a moment, then slid the smoothly fitted lid from the main section of the box. After that, he looked inside, his eyes growing large at the sight of its contents.

"Sweet Bride of the Night."

"What is it, Paul?"

"Oh, nothin' much, boss," answered Morcey. Handing the box over to his partner, telling him, "Pretty much standard stuff for The London Agency."

The detective accepted the container, bringing it down to a level where both he and Lisa could view its contents. Both of them reacted in fairly much the same manner as Morcey.

"Teddy . . ."

"I see, I see," he answered.

The young woman took the box away from London, staring into it with wonder and confusion. "Who just leaves something like this behind?"

The detective took the box back, purposely spilling the scores of dazzling, multifaceted rubies and emeralds resting within it out across the top of his desk. As the three stared at them, wondering what their presence might mean, London said;

"I guess I should tell you two what's been happening here while you were gone."

"That would be nice," admitted Lisa, picking up one of the larger stones, bringing it to her eye to study more closely.

"Yeah," added Morcey, pulling up a chair, overjoyed to see his partner finally returning somewhat to his former self. "Tell us a story, Daddy."

♦ ♦ ♦

London told his two partners everything that had happened while they had been gone from the office. He gave them the entirety of his exchange with Mrs. Lu, and he told them the story of the death of his father and brothers. Then, he said;

"What's so strange to me about the . . . 'vision'—I guess that's what I should call it—is that I've never 'remembered' it before. I mean, it's bizarre enough for someone to flash back to something that happened to them when they were a baby, but as I told you, I was asleep the whole time. Exactly how could I remember something I never saw?"

"Maybe you should ask Lai Wan, boss," suggested Morcey.

"Are you still seeing her, Paul?"

"Awwwww, I wouldn't call it 'seeing each other,' Lisa," answered Morcey, slightly flustered, his ears going red. "I mean, we had tea together a few times is all, and we did go down to the aquarium out at Coney that one weekend but, you know . . ."

"We're getting away from the point," added Lisa.

"Well, but then," asked the detective, "what exactly is the point here, anyway? We've got an old Chinese woman who comes here claiming to be a witch. She says she wants to hire us to kill vampires, changes her mind, and then walks out, leaving behind what looks like a king's ransom in cut gems. Somehow her exit prompts me to have this dream, and then before I know it, Paul's shaking me awake, and here we are."

The detective looked back and forth between Lisa and Morcey, scanning their faces, then added, "Now, I'll be perfectly honest and be the first kid on my block to say that I don't have the faintest idea what's going on. So, partners, any ideas?"

"I got one, boss."

"Spill it."

"I don't wanta cause anyone any grief or anythin', but this Mrs. Lu said she was a witch, right?" London nodded, giving Morcey the go ahead. The balding man continued, saying;

"So, well, the way I figure it, the biggest question we got is, how did she know you were the Destroyer, right?"

Another nod.

"Without gettin' all mystic or nuthin', I mean, if you think about it . . . she ain't the only Chinese witch we know."

And suddenly, everything became clear to the detective. Pressing his back against the buttoned leather of his chair, London told Morcey, "Paul, would you see if you could get your tea-drinking partner on the phone. I'd like to get her here, as soon as possible, if it wouldn't be too much trouble. Tell her we'll pay for her time."

Morcey started to ask another question but looked over at London and cut himself off. The detective had closed his eyes, resting his head back against the top of his chair. His fingers bridged before his face, first tips just touching his nose, London had gone inside his own brain, leaving the rest of the world to those who belonged there. Lisa and Morcey left the room quietly, heading for their own areas of the suite.

"So," asked Lisa after she closed the door to the main office behind them. "What do you think?"

"About the boss?" When she nodded her head, Morcey answered, "I'll admit, I was gettin' a little worried, but I think he's goin' to be okay, now."

"I hope so."

"No, really, I mean it. Don't sweat it," answered Morcey, knocking his ponytail off of his shoulder and back behind him. "This is just what he needs." When Lisa eyed the balding man, he elaborated.

"He's got a lotta stuff to work through, I won't deny that or nuthin', but I think deep down, after ya get through all the guilt and everythin' and all, I think the biggest—the only—problem Mr. Theodore London had was just dealin' with havin' to go back to the old grind."

As Lisa sat behind her desk, her hands absently adjusting some of the papers there into neater piles, Morcey continued, "Way back when, a hundred years ago, when you went and found me in the hall and told me he needed help—back when we came in and saw that thing from Hell ready to finish him off—let's face it, the whole world changed for all of us.

"Now me," said the ex-maintenance man with a smile, "I killed a monster then—and I don't mean some creep who did things so horrible that the only thing you could call him was a monster—I mean a real horror movie-type monster. I cut it in two with an ax like I was Conan the Barbarian, or somethin'."

"I was there, Paul," said Lisa softly. "I remember."

"Well, sure you do. But, that's my point." Sitting down on the edge of the young woman's desk, the ex-maintenance man asked her,

"Did you think for a minute then—for a second even; when he asked me if I wanted to help him find out what was goin' on, that I would say anythin' but 'yes'?"

"I wasn't thinking much about anyone else but myself right, then," she confessed.

"Of course you weren't. I know that 'cause neither was I. I was so scared I was shakin', but I wasn't so scared that I dumped in my pants or anything . . . and that was 'cause I'd *won*. Yeah, I'd killed a monster but—you see—that's my point, I *killed* it. Me, Paul Morcey, regular guy. I killed a monster. For a guy that's heady stuff."

Lisa simply stared as the former maintenance man smiled. With a twinkle in his eye, he dropped his voice an octave, telling her;

"Now, I mean, what was I supposed to do after all that, just go back to makin' sure all the offices in my building got enough heat in the winter and AC in the summer? Fuck that—pardon my French—but, hey—suddenly, I wasn't just some regular schmoe any more—I was a monster killer. When he asked me if I wanted to help him find out what was goin' on, wild horses couldn't have stopped me from signin' on."

"I understand all that, Paul," interrupted Lisa. "But what does that have to do with Teddy?"

"He's changed, Lisa. Don'tcha get it? Lookit what we're talkin' about in there. We're talkin' about witches and vampires now like we woulda talked about who we was gonna vote for two months ago." Looking down at the company's youngest partner, its oldest told her;

"We're all different, now. It just ain't like it was. We believe in things now that a while ago we woulda called 'kid's stuff' if we saw it in a movie. What I mean by all this is, I've done things now I never even dreamed of doin' before. Big things. And, Mr. London, man, I mean, this might be too much a guy kinda thing, but what the boss has been through—how can we even hope to understand what's goin' on in his head now? It's like he killed Godzilla with his bare hands."

Then, suddenly the balding man's voice took on a quieter tone. Leaning down toward Lisa, he finished;

"And, I'll tell ya somethin' else. I know the boss' been upset about everyone that died and all, but, I'm tellin' ya, underneath all that, my bet is there's been this little voice askin' him what he's gonna do for an encore."

"And . . .?" asked Lisa, sensing the unspoken words in the balding man's voice. Sliding off the edge of the young woman's desk, Morcey straightened his tie, smiled, and then spread his arms wide as he said;

"And, well, what with carved elephant boxes filled with jewels showin' up, and the boss havin' visions, and some old Oriental woman who says she's a witch screamin' about gettin' revenge on the vampires that killed her son, my guess is, baby, it must be showtime."

Lisa considered Morcey's comments for a moment, then asked, "What are we going to do, then?"

"You, you're gonna get Lai Wan on the phone and tell her that Mr. London wants her here right away and that she'd better get her mystical little butt movin'."

"Teddy wanted you to call."

"Yeah," the ex-maintenance man said with a diplomatic drawl, "but she can be kinda, you know, moody. And, this is too important for an argument. I figure another woman tellin' her what's up will motivate her a little better."

"Okay," agreed Lisa, smiling to herself, remembering the balding man's embarrassment at being asked whether or not there was anything between himself and the psychometrist.

"But," she added, "what are you going to be doing?"

"Me?" answered Morcey, heading out the door. "I'm going shopping."

"Shopping? Now? What for?"

"What else?" answered the balding man, heading out through the door. "Crucifixes."

CHAPTER
SIX

"OKAY, FIRST OFF," ASKED London of the woman sitting across his desk from him, "I'd like to thank you for getting here on such short notice. I know you don't like to travel, especially without any prep time."

The woman nodded, almost imperceptibly, moving her eyes more than her head. The detective, leaning back in his chair, held up the carved ivory box, all of its gem stones once more safely stored back within its hidden chamber. Passing it across his desk, he asked, "can you tell me anything about this?"

"I will try," answered the woman.

Her name was Lai Wan; she was a psychometrist. The text book word for what she did was coined by a Professor Joseph Rodes Buchanan to label the paranormal ability known as soul measurement. In simpler terms, the woman had the power to "read" within her mind's eye the past history of any object or person merely by laying her hands upon them and sharing their experiences.

Her ability to interpret this state of heightened awareness had come to her after she had gone through an out-of-body experience while on the operating table. Her surgeons had not expected her to live and, indeed, she did not disappoint them. She died in surgery—for a time, anyway. Her death, as she had once put it in, for her, a rare moment of humor, "hadn't taken too well," however, and she had returned to life—greatly changed from the simple, pleasant young person she had been before the accident that had tried so hard to remove her from the world.

Before her death, she had been a woman given to gay colors and modern fashions, restaurant parties and fine living. In the days just before her experience, she had been dividing her time by working in real estate and counting the days to her marriage. All of that changed.

Within days of her release from the hospital after her ordeal, she gave away all her jewelry, stripped her closets of most of their possessions, keeping only a few long dresses—all of them dark, concealing things. She also gave up her share of Bifora, Mason, & Gleason Realtors, abandoning the little desk and its chains, seeing her modern career for the stupefying trap it was. She did not have to do anything about her fiancé—he left on his own, more than repulsed, terrified of the coldness that had seized the woman he had loved.

Now, draped in flowing black, her shoulders and head almost completely covered by a dark scarlet lace shawl, she held the box London had offered her in her left hand for only a few seconds before she announced;

"This was meant to be your retainer."

"But the woman that left it behind had decided she wasn't going to hire me."

"Not exactly," answered the psychometrist, setting the box in the middle of the detective's desk. "Apparently she made contact with some memory of yours that upset her. I cannot trace the memory from the box, however."

"I know which memory it was she hit. Let me ask you, though. Lai Wan"—London leaned forward slightly—"do you know this woman? I mean 'personally'?"

"Yes. Her name is Xui Zeng Lu." The detective caught a tiny spark in the psychic's normally cold voice. It was a warm note, but a conflicted one. The fact told him nothing except that the relationship between the two women had not been a casual one. Not allowing his face to make any physical note of the information, he simply waited, giving the woman the chance to tell him;

"She is the leading witch of Chinatown."

"Do you know where we can find her?"

"Her storefront is on Pell Street—between Mott and Mulberry."

"Paul," called London.

"Yeah, boss?"

"Take a drive down to Mrs. Lu's establishment and see if you can't find some way to persuade her to join us. Call in if she's not there or it looks like a long wait, but do whatever you have to to get her back up here."

"Whatever I have to, within reason, or otherwise?"

"Use your discretion."

"You got it, boss."

Then after Morcey had exited, the detective, still behind his desk, unmoved from his seat since he had first taken it hours earlier, returned his attention to Lai Wan. He regarded the psychometrist with an approving suspicion. She was a forceful and clever woman, used to being in command of whatever was going on around her. As when he had first met her, London could see he was going to have his hands full trying to deal with her. Speaking slowly so as to choose his words carefully, he asked;

"From your reading of the box, or even just from your own dealings with her, do you have any idea why I'm concerned about this woman?"

"Not really, Mr. London." The woman's voice took on a chiding tone, "I remind you once more—I am not a mind reader."

"All right," answered the detective with a nod, "we'll try a different tact. Can you explain your relationship with her?"

"Old Lu and I have a mutual understanding—we stay out of each other's way. She is one given to working the more primitive superstitions—reading palms, telling futures through the phases of the moon—we do not work the same side of the street."

The detective could easily see from the slow narrowing of Lai Wan's eyes that she was no friend of Mrs. Lu. Deciding to just jump ahead and see what effect his next question might have, he asked;

"Did you tell her about 'the Destroyer'?"

The woman stiffened, visible anger showing in her face. "That bitch!" shouted Lai Wan suddenly, startling Lisa sitting behind her in the back of the room. "I knew she couldn't be trusted. Ohhhh, I just knew it."

When the detective questioned Lai Wan's lack of faith in Mrs. Lu's trustworthiness, the psychometrist answered;

"She came to me about a week ago. She was greatly distraught, upset over the death of her son. She wanted to know if there was anyone I knew of that might avenge her—none of her regular connections would touch the assignment."

"The police weren't any help?"

Lai Wan did not dignify the question with any more of a response than the twin flashes of anger filling her eyes. Continuing, London asked her;

"Mrs. Lu seemed like a woman who might turn out to be fairly well connected. Even with the kind of money she was willing to throw around she couldn't find any takers?"

"People were hesitant. She is claiming her son was killed by . . . by vampires."

"You don't sound as if you agree."

Lai Wan snorted a sharp breath in disgust, her eyes focusing on London with a hostile fire.

"And do you agree?" she asked.

"It's your opinion that matters to me right now. After all, try to remember that I'm a little newer to the monster-chasing business than you are."

"And might I ask you to remember, and please to note that I am most urgent in this request, that besides not being a mind reader I am not a monster hunter, either." Lai Wan's answer was sharp and cold, her already straight figure seeming to grow slightly taller as she continued.

"I helped you as best I could in every way possible against the Q'talu because much was at stake," she reminded him. "But just because you have now faced one abnormal thing, do not suddenly believe there are ghosts behind every corner. Will you attempt to solve the puzzle of the Black Cat of Killakee next, or go to China to explain the Ch'iang Shich?"

London bridged his fingers so as to support the weight of his head with them. Elbows on his desk, he hid his eyes in his hands as he interrupted;

"Lai Wan, slow down. Take a break. All I'm trying to do is to get to the bottom of all this. Take a look at this thing from my point of view—

"Fact . . . a woman comes in here and asks me to kill vampires for her.

"Fact . . . she claims the reason she wants these vampires dead is because they killed her son.

"Fact . . . she claims to not want my help anymore but leaves behind a fortune in gems on my desk." Then, raising his head within his hands so he could see again, he talked into his fingers, saying;

"Final fact . . . she abandoned this considerable amount of wealth for one of two reasons. Either, 'A' because she was so consumed with grief that she did not remember it when she left, or 'B' because she still wants me to chase vampires for her."

Sitting back against the spine of his chair, London lowered his hands while pushing himself upward, straightening his frame so he met Lai Wan's eyes clearly.

"Now, I don't have a whole lot of people I can go to with this problem. You actually knew her—that makes you the best bet I have for getting some straight answers. If you simply don't want to help me—there's not much I can do about it. If you have some personal grudge against this woman and it just makes you so crazy you can't be of any help . . . well, there's not much I can do about that, either. But if you want to give us a hand here, I have to admit that we'd appreciate it."

The psychometrist eyed the detective with reservation, drumming the fingers of her right hand against her leg almost unconsciously. London waited quietly for an answer until a shift in the look on the woman's face told him he had one.

"Thank you," he told her. She nodded curtly, knowing she had no choice other than to help the detective, but showing her displeasure nonetheless. London acknowledged his appreciation by softening his tone as he asked his questions.

"Try and put aside whatever your differences with Mrs. Lu were and think about this objectively. Tell me, does anyone know who murdered her son?"

"No."

"How did he die?"

"His murderers tore him into little pieces. These small bits of flesh were left in places where people would find them—in their homes, their businesses, schools—all manner of public places. One is forced to think that whoever killed Jimmy Lu was out to intimidate most all of Chinatown."

"And," asked the detective, "who would want to do something like that?"

"I don't know," answered Lai Wan. "And I won't guess. Speculation isn't my line. Bring me a piece of Jimmy Lu's corpse and maybe I could tell you."

London sat back for a second, knowing the woman's tone was telling him something, but that he was missing whatever it was. Working at keeping the silence between them at bay, he followed up by asking;

"Why would Jimmy's mother say it was vampires who killed him? Does she really believe in them?"

"I . . ." Lai Wan hesitated, her usually careful words stumbling for a moment. "I don't know."

"Do you believe in them?"

"I," the words stumbled again, intriguing the detective. "I don't know that, either."

"Well," said London, shutting his eyes for a moment as he took a deep breath, opening them again as he let it go, "Mrs. Lu seemed as if she genuinely loved her son. I think her grief was real. Which means I'm also forced to believe that we have to accept the fact that she wouldn't call his murderers vampires if she didn't mean vampires. And so," finished the detective, laying his hands flat on his desk;

"I guess what we're going to have to figure out is, what exactly does she mean when she uses the term."

"Mr. London," answered the psychometrist, her tone suddenly growing far softer than the detective had ever heard it. "I wish I could help you more than I sense I can. You do not know how much I wish I could. But . . . I cannot. As I'm sure you can tell, there was no love lost between Xui Zeng Lu and myself. Our abilities are actually much the same in the end results, but our approaches to their uses are different.

"Mrs. Lu is of the old school. Parlor tricks performed for dollars. I know I take money for my services, but I do not pretend to be in touch with ghosts—speaking instead for dead relatives—outlining what lies around the next corner one might turn by the shuffling of cards or mathematics performed in accordance to the alignment of the stars."

Pursing her lips, the woman shrunk in on herself. Then, after a long moment, she added;

"Who knows? Maybe she really does believe in vampires. But," she snapped suddenly, "does that matter? Will that help you one way or the other? Will it settle anything? Solve anything?"

Then, her voice cracked slightly as she added, "Will it bring Jimmy back?"

Lisa made a small noise, one barely audible, but enough of one to catch the detective's attention. As London turned his vision to where his partner sat in the back of the room, Lai Wan turned as well. The two women's gazes locked for only an instant, but it was enough. Lisa could stare into the dark brown eyes of the woman before her for only a second before she said;

"I'm so sorry."

London narrowed his eyes, showing Lisa that he did not understand her apology. She ignored the look for the moment, leaving her chair to go to Lai Wan's side. Then, after she had put her arm around the Oriental woman's shoulders, she answered;

"Jimmy Lu . . . back before Lai Wan, ah, 'died,' he was her fiancé."

The psychometrist's silent tears confirmed Lisa's guess.

CHAPTER SEVEN

L ONDON SAT BEHIND HIS desk, watching Lisa comfort Lai Wan, cursing himself for not making what should have been for him an obvious connection.

You're slipping, pal, he told himself. Monsters aren't supposed to be your strong point but . . . people are. If you plan on actually solving this case, or any cases at all for that matter, you better get back to your own game.

"Lai," said the detective, softly, several times, finally catching the woman's attention. "You want to give us some of the details on this?"

"Why?" she sniffed, still crying. "What purpose will it serve?"

"I'm not actually certain, to be perfectly honest. But, I need to know why Mrs. Lu came to me—what she expected me to be able to do for her."

Loosening the knot of his tie, London changed his approach and asked, "Tell me about you and Jimmy."

Lai Wan dabbed at her cheeks with a handkerchief she had pulled from somewhere beneath her shawl. Returning it to its hiding place within the secret folds of her dress, she allowed herself to make one last tiny sniff, and then told her story.

"There is not all that much to tell. We grew up together in Chinatown, loved each other, always we knew we would marry someday. Jimmy was not like a lot of Chinese—he did not get along with his mother. He did not believe in the old ways—they fought over what she did."

The psychometrist's voice slipped back into the cold tones with which those in the office were most familiar. Continuing her tale without anger, she let her forced lack of emotion show her true feelings.

"Jimmy would not take anything from his mother. For several years after high school he worked in some of the local shops—'coolie work' some called it—to embarrass his mother, to show he would rather live as a dog in the gutter than follow her ways. After his point was made, he joined the army.

"It changed him some," she said in a lighter tone. "Maybe it was just being away from him for six years but, by the time he returned with his G.I. Bill money, ready for college, he was finally—absolutely—his own man, with nothing further to prove to his mother."

The Oriental woman shifted her body slightly in her seat, the look of the motion letting London know it was not the chair making her uncomfortable. "Of course, it was in his first year there that I had my accident. The change was too much for him. When he saw the 'shifts' which occurred within me, *to me*—saw the abilities I came away with—he declared that I had become too much like his mother, and that he could no longer marry me."

Her voice frosted over again. Lisa and London made eye contact briefly, then returned their attention to the psychometrist before the lack of it was noticed.

"He put in his four years, got his chemical engineering degree. I will admit that I kept myself . . . aware of his progress. I—I . . ."

Sensing the woman did not know how to continue, Lisa asked her, "Were you hoping he would come back to you?"

"Yes. I always made sure he knew how unlike his mother I was—that I was working with scholars and scientists to try and discover what my powers were, where they had come from, why it had happened to me . . . to us."

"It didn't work, though," added the detective gently. "Did it?"

"No," she told him. "He could see nothing beyond his own pride. The people I helped, the missing children I led the police to, the stolen properties I discovered—all with the hand of science—*his* science—documenting every movement, none of it made any impression on him. The last time we talked, the last time we saw each other, a little over a year ago . . . that was when he said he knew I would never change—that I was a witch and that I would drink from the night moon wells for the rest of my days."

Looking at London, Lai Wan told him;

"I answered him in kind. I took his hand and told him that he would die a fool. Then, suddenly, I knew I was not just speaking my anger, but that I had actually glimpsed ahead into his time line. And," her voice broke slightly as she finished;

"He knew it as well."

The woman's voice and demeanor took on a faraway aspect, as if she were no longer in London's office, but back at that last meeting. Continuing to speak without actually being conscious of others listening—the remembering of her pain all she could bear to concentrate on—she said;

"He pulled his hand out of mine and asked me to leave. I pleaded with him to listen to me, to let me help him. He screamed at me, laughed at me. When I begged him, he . . . he struck me, backhand across the face. He did it twice more. The first and third times he hit me I fell to the floor. I did not get up again until I saw he had turned his back on me. Then I reached up for the door and let myself out, crawling on my hands and knees.

"I have not seen him since that day."

"And," added London, "I guess the rest is pretty much easily explained. After her son's murder, she came to you, as another woman who cared about him, and as someone she could relate to on a professional level. She asked you if you knew anyone who might do her revenge number for her, and when my name and everything that had happened popped into your mind, she grabbed on to it."

"Oh, oh God, I am so sorry I . . ."

London put a finger to his lips, signaling the woman that she had nothing more to say.

"SSSSSSShhhhhhh—no. Don't worry about it. She didn't get to be the head witch in Chinatown by not having a few tricks up her sleeve. At least this explains how the word got out on me. Anyway . . ." But then, before anyone could say anything further, a voice called from the outer office in a deep Southern accent;

"Yoo hoo, is anybody to home?"

"Wally?" The detective's voice took on a note of warm surprise as he called out. "In the back, pal."

In response to London's call, a man entered the suite's main office. He was of average height, only a handful of pounds over weight, decked out in a dark but lightweight summer suit. He wore wire-rimmed, prescription sunglasses, a broad grin, and elegantly styled hair—something about him making all three accessories seem exceedingly natural. As he took the detective's outstretched hand, he said;

"It's been a while, babe. Very glad to see you in one piece," quietly adding as he assessed London's various inflictions, as well as his notice of the cane leaning against the back wall, "more or less."

"A little trouble in the Conflagration. Fine now . . . more or less. What's the story with you?"

"Business. What else—a deal here, a job there—just flitting from place to place like the magpie I am, trying to teach your type something about manners, as usual. Here—here's a good for instance."

Turning to the two women, the man introduced himself.

"Ladies, I am Wallace Daniel Barnes. If you tell me you like my hair, then you may call me Wally. And you two charming creatures, besides being stuck with the largest boor on the Eastern Seaboard, are . . . ?"

London sat back in his chair, smiling to himself as his old friend lightened the mood. After Wally, Lisa, and Lai Wan had finished their introductions, he clapped his hands together, rubbing their palms one against the other as he asked;

"Okay, I know you, Theodore. You didn't drag me downtown just to see my new suit. And, although a part of me dearly wishes you had, I won't debate the painful. No, instead I shall simply inquire as to what it is that you have for me?"

The detective pushed the elephant box across to him, saying, "Your theatrics aside, I do believe you'll find this worth the trip."

Wally picked up the box, studying the sides first, then flipping it over to check the bottom. As he did, London explained, "Ladies, I called Wally earlier, asking him here because I wanted his opinion of Mrs. Lu's box. Wally is an appraiser."

"Oh, isn't the dear boy just ever so genteel?" added Wally, his eyes never leaving the box as he rolled it around in his hands. "An 'appraiser.' Don't you just love him? Ladies, I'm a fence, the best in town."

"But, Wally," added London, teasing his old friend, "when you're the best, you get to choose your own titles."

"I will remind you, honey, that my mama taught me that the truth is the only thing that can set you free. That being the case, the title I chose is 'fence.' Now shut up and let me look over this wonderful little treat."

Pulling a small velvet pouch from his inside suit pocket, Wally withdrew a powerful magnifying glass from it, pushed his sun glasses up through his hair, and then checked the same areas again, closer.

"Shadow creme ivory. Very intriguing," he said under his breath, as much to himself as to the others. "Nice work, no power tool etches, no diamond gouges either. Wasn't done in this century, I'll tell you that much."

He flipped the box over, studying the bottom again.

"Bronze plate here says it's from some emperor's household, don't know which one. It's at least twelve hundred years old, just a beautiful thing, isn't it? I spotted only four breaks, two of the elephant's tusks, one trunk, one of the tails. Couldn't be helped, I'm sure."

"No, of course not," added London, teasing his friend.

"No, course," agreed Wally absently, not noticing the detective's joke, too absorbed in his studying of Mrs. Lu's box. "It's hard to keep detail work like that in one piece . . . especially as the old centuries go piling up on each other. But something tells me this is only the preliminary."

"Go ahead," said London. "Crack it."

Wally opened the box, the detective watching the fence's eyes then even more closely than he had been. He was not disappointed with the reaction he witnessed.

"Oh, you naughty man," said the appraiser. "You do know which toys make junior dance, don't you?"

"What do you think?"

Wally spilled the rubies and emeralds out across the desk, able to access half their worth just by watching how they caught the sunlight streaming in the windows. Running his hands across them, rolling them over the wooden surface below, he absorbed the quality of their cuts through their feel against his soft and educated palms. Picking up several of the larger stones one at a time, he examined them with his glass, first against the sunlight, then away from it. While he worked, the phones on Lisa's and London's desks rang. Lisa answered the central line from London's phone, then handed it to the detective, telling him;

"It's Paul."

London talked with his partner for a moment, then said, "There's a lot going on in my office right now, let me get out of everyone's way. Hold on,

I'll take the call on your line."

After that, the detective put Morcey on hold, pulled his cane toward him, and started for the door, saying, "My partner apparently has a lot for me. Play with your toys, Wally. And don't get cute. Lisa will be watching you."

As London left the room, Lisa apologized, "He didn't mean anything by that."

"What?" asked Wally, flashing the young woman a disarming grin. Cranking up the Georgia in his voice, he smiled wider as he asked;

"You sweet thing, you don't think I'm a thief? You don't think I could slide half of these darling babies up my sleeve without you noticing?"

"She never said that," interrupted Lai Wan, adding in her usual cold tone, "She merely informed you that Mr. London did not actually think you so stupid as to attempt to steal from him."

"Right on both counts, Ice Queen," replied Wally sharply, his head still bowed. Then, looking up suddenly, he added, "She never said that, and even I know that only stupid people try to steal from Theodore London. But since I asked her if she thought I was honest, and not an idiot, I'm not all that exactly sure what concern it is of yours."

Lai Wan sat back in silence, both she and Lisa watching Wally continue his analysis of the gems on the desk. By the time London returned, the appraiser had separated them into fourteen piles, most groupings all one type of gem or the other, with only a few piles a mixture of both. As the detective returned to his chair, Wally sat back in his own seat, pulling his sunglasses back down into place, pleased with his work.

"Well, you want it short or long?"

"Do I ever want it long?"

"Just asking," offered Wally. "It's all part of the service."

"Make your bid."

"I have always appreciated the fact that you have never come to me with anything less than the best. But this, I tell you now, su'r, this is some kind of quality. These stones would be valuable even without the history."

"I can't guarantee the jewels are as old as the box," admitted the detective.

"Don't worry, child, you'all don't have to. I can do that all on my own. There's enough age dust, those red and green flecks down in the bottom seal of the box, to tell me all I need to know. Anyway, I recognize that look—you must have got some interesting news on the phone—so I'll just get down to business now."

Wally put one hand over his face for a second, cutting himself off from the room, his eyes rolling up under their lids into the back of his head. He held the pose for only a moment, the broke it, saying;

"Five hundred eighty-five thousand for everything."

"You can't have the box—just the stones."

"Well now, and why can't I have the box?" asked Wally with genuine surprise.

"Because I want it," answered the detective. "How much for the stones?"

"Huuummmm, well, I hadn't been thinking along those lines, ah, but they are such beautiful toys . . . one hundred sixty-two—I can have a check to you by the end of business tomorrow."

"Make it cash in an hour and I'll take one hundred even."

Wally's eyes grew large behind his dark lenses. Knowing he had heard the best deal he was going to get, he said, "Oh, I think that can be arranged. You did say 'cash,' didn't you?"

"Glad to see your hearing still works." Without anything further, the appraiser rose from his seat and made a slight bow to the two women, saying;

"Ladies, it was a pleasure to meet you both, but since I am as sure he meant 'an hour' as he did 'cash,' I find I must be dashing off." Turning back to London, he pointed a finger at the detective, then said with a smile;

"See you'all in fifty-nine minutes."

Then, after the door closed behind the appraiser, Lisa asked, "Does this mean you're taking Mrs. Lu's case?"

"Yes, I guess it does." Even though he was answering Lisa, the detective looked at Lai Wan as he completed his answer.

"First off, the agency has been running a tab for almost two months without taking any income in. An infusion of tax-exempt cash should help nicely. Second, I let her walk out of this office leaving her retainer on my desk. There's no excuse for being sloppy. I let her hire me, now I have to do the work."

"If you are doing this just for me," said Lai Wan suddenly, "I would ask you to please leave things as they are. Jimmy meant a great deal to me at one time, but that is long past. More death will not help my grief."

"Well," drawled the detective, "maybe it will, and maybe it won't. That's not important anymore."

Both women looked at London, sensing his words were telling them more than they knew. Not wanting to be vague, the detective explained;

"Paul found Mrs. Lu. It was pretty easy. Half of Chinatown was outside her store. She was killed the same way her son was. Apparently right after she left this office. If I'd acted sooner, she might still be alive. I said no one else was going to die because of me and, the first day I set foot out of my apartment, people are getting torn limb from limb in the street."

London reached into his lower left-hand desk drawer, finding his .38 revolver Betty and his handmade combat knife Veronica exactly where he had asked Morcey to store them for him. Starting to break Betty down for cleaning, he asked;

"So, who's up for dinner in Chinatown tonight?"

CHAPTER EIGHT

CANAL STREET, ONE OF the straightest lines in all of lower Manhattan, is the more or less official dividing line between Little Italy and Chinatown. Whether coming up from the Holland Tunnel or down from the Manhattan Bridge, for most people the best way into the older parts of the neighborhood had always been to turn in at Mott Street and then work their way back and out from that point. There exists no particular geographic reason for this—it is just what most people do. Which, of course, was why London and those with him entered along Mulberry Street instead.

"Boss, I gotta tell ya," said Morcey, frustrated with the crawling bumper-to-bumper pace of the Chinatown streets, "I still gotta say it woulda been a heck of a lot easier to just come down Canal and turn at Mott."

"I know that, Paul."

"Then why'd we come all the way around the back end of the world like this?"

"Because," answered the detective from the rear seat, "if we actually have enemies here, there's no sense letting them know who we are and where we come from any sooner than we have to."

His head was against the back windowsill of the car, his eyes shut. Lisa, sitting next to him, had gone home to change into an evening dress—black, off one shoulder, gold jewelry to match her belt buckle—bow clasped, rectangular bag to match her black, bow-toed heels.

London was still in his same suit, unwrinkled, unstained. His hands rested on the knob of his Blackthorn, holding it in a vertical balance against the floor. Not thinking, leaving his mind a blank, the detective listened to the streets around him as they crawled through the usual gnarl of automobile and foot traffic. Despite the lateness of the hour, it was still New York City, and Chinatown at that. The crowds would not disappear for quite some time.

As the car continued to edge forward, London send his senses ranging, feeling out those eyes that paid their car any particular notice, giving close attention to what kind of notice they paid it. There were those who envied the car's smooth lines, those that wondered at the old man with the young woman in the back seat, those others that wondered at the Occidental driver with the Oriental woman next to him in the front seat.

Nobody seemed to be looking for them, though—at least, thought the detective, no one who had found them yet, anyway.

Good, a voice within his head whispered, we need every advantage we can get here.

London had added some facts to his knowledge of the case between the time he had learned of Mrs. Lu's death and when he and the others had finally left for dinner. Through a few phone calls he had confirmed the details of Jimmy Lu's death, and his mother's. He had also discovered that a great deal of pressure from all levels of the neighborhood had been brought to bear on the police—store owners, local assemblymen, underworld contacts from within the Chinese tongs, as well as from the Italian mobs across the Canal divide, old ladies in the street—all of them and more looking to keep the second murder as quiet as the first. He was also able to establish that Mrs. Lu was indeed known throughout the city as, at the least, "a highly unique and eccentric character with some undeniably powerful occult talents" as one newspaperman who wished to remain unnamed had put it.

Not psychic enough to know when there were vampires knocking on her door, though, thought the detective. And that, at least for the moment, was what London was willing to call whoever it was he was hunting.

Why not? People are getting clawed apart by beasts and everyone around them from near and far is afraid to let the media know anything about it. Of course, the police and city hall are willing to let it be covered up. What's that—cops and politicians draping their asses—big surprise . . .

Still, there was something about the attitudes of those he talked with that disturbed him. For many the fear gripping them was apparent—welded into the air surrounding their voices as their words spilled out of the phone. For others, it was hidden by smugness and ridicule—jokes their tellers laughed at to cue everyone that the notion they were talking about was something only meant to belittle the superstitious. Them, why no—they would never believe in such nonsense.

It was not going to be an easy case. London snorted under his breath at his mental understatement. No, it certainly did not look like an easy case.

Vampires.

God, he thought to himself, almost laughing, doesn't anyone want a cheating spouse tailed anymore? Whatever happened to background checks on employees or future wives? Don't people still steal enough from their employers and the shops they go to for someone to need security agencies? Do all the cases in this town now have to come from the Twilight Zone?

The detective listened to the thought with casual amusement. That morning he had been hoping for something that would keep him from having to go back to the ordinary world. Now that he had found something, he was clamoring for the safety of normality.

What was it Samuel Butler said, he asked himself, "Neither have they hearts to stay, Nor wit enough to run away." Better make up your mind, pal.

And at that moment, Morcey finally managed to get to the corner. Flipping on his turn signal, he threw over his shoulder;

"Pell Street, boss."

"Thank you, Paul."

London opened his eyes slightly, keeping them slits against the neon and reflected streetlights shining from every direction. Now suddenly the slow crawl of the traffic worked in their favor, the near motionlessness of the flow giving the detective time to get a good view of the area surrounding Mrs. Lu's parlor.

The police were gone, leaving trailing ribbons of bright yellow barrier tape strung over the shattered door and bay window. Large chunks of plate glass still littered the sidewalk, some stained dark with blood. The door hung in pieces from its hinges. London noted the size and quality of its locks, the thickness of its splintered timbers, impressed with the power it would have taken to shatter it. He also noted the wealth of forensic information left behind and knew there was no doubt this case was officially being swept as far under the rug as possible. The thought did not sit well with him. Then, as Morcey's car finally began to edge past the storefront, the detective ordered;

"All right, Paul, I'll be getting out here."

"But there's no place to park," answered his partner. "I can't even double-park here. It's too narrow."

"No problem," answered London. "You take the ladies on to the Silver Palace. It's just up around the next corner to the left. Get parked and join them. I'll be there after I look things over."

"Okay, yer the boss."

The balding man stopped the car in the middle of traffic, instantly calling down a cacophony of horn blasts from behind them. The detective exited as quickly as he could, shutting his door firmly behind him, allowing the car to move off. As it did, he observed that he was not the only one who had gotten out.

"Anything you'd like to tell me?"

"Mr. London," answered Lai Wan, "you are not the only one who wishes to discover the truth at the bottom of all this. Unless your powers of observation are such that you have no need of my skills, I would like to see what I might be able to contribute."

"Fine by me," answered the detective honestly, crossing over to the other side of the street through the again stopped cars. "Let's see just how much the police left behind."

Stretching the barrier tape upward with his cane, London allowed Lai Wan to precede him, then followed her through the gaping doorway. In most cases, someone would have covered such damage by now, relatives or friends would have nailed plywood into place, called repair people, gotten about the business of life by putting things back together. Such was not the case at Mrs. Lu's, however. There were no relatives left to come forward, no friends with nerve enough to defy the implication of the destruction. Pulling a high intensity pocket flash from inside his jacket, the detective followed the lines of damage—tracing it with his eyes, reconstructing the events passed through the experience of years of similar sights.

He could tell from the path of destruction he was following that, amazingly, there had been only one assailant. He had come directly through the front door. A tiny shred of torn flesh hung from splinters high along the wood marking where he had shattered it, giving the detective a fair idea of the invader's proportions.

London could see where someone from the police had scraped away their share for analysis, but more than enough remained to allow the detective to determine the man's size. Knuckle skin—hairless, mottled with back-of-the-hand wrinkles, no finger or palm lines.

"Goddamned big son of a bitch," said London aloud. "I'll give him that much."

Mrs. Lu's murderer—Jimmy's as well? wondered the detective—had smashed down the door and gone straight through to the back rooms—to the kitchen. Angling on his cane, the detective followed the killer's path, stepping over the debris of the previous struggle. He noted the trappings the old woman had chosen to surround herself with as he moved through her business, playing his light about—beaded curtains, large pillows, tapestries of goddesses granting favors, potted plants—all the regular trimmings one could find in every one of the city's thousands of tarot parlors.

I guess some things never change, thought the detective.

Making his way through the building, still following the murderer's path, his eye was suddenly caught by an odd crack in the wall of the kitchen's entrance. Judging from the angle, the killer had swung at something but missed. Why such an erratic swing, though? And why had he missed? On the opposite side of the doorway jamb London suddenly spotted an arcing smear of a bright liquid, almost a grease.

He ran an index finger over it—through it—drying but not yet dried. Bringing the finger to his nose, he sniffed, straining for recognition. The slight odor on his fingertip was pungent, burning. He looked around the overturned kitchen, spotting a bottle of Chinese hot pepper & garlic sauce. The detective worked it up off the ground suspended on the end of his cane, seeing no need to add any new prints to the crime scene. Taking a deep, choking whiff from the now nearly empty jar, he staggered several steps backward from the power of the smell. Letting the jar slide off the end of his cane, he thought;

Well, if the old girl got him in the eyes with that stuff, I'm surprised she didn't get away completely.

He knew that was not the case, though. The evidence was far too clear. Mrs. Lu had been beaten into submission in the kitchen, her heel marks against the side cupboards growing weaker with each kick, showing that she had not lasted long against her attacker. After that, she had been dragged, most likely unconscious, back out through the front. Why and how the front window had been smashed, the detective could not tell. Some how, though, it did not seem important.

Weary of his surroundings, weary actually from the effort it took to stand, London called out to Lai Wan.

"Ready to give your way a shot?"

"Yes," she answered from another room. "Any time."

"Now's a good one."

Slowly limping back down the hall from the kitchen to the front door, he found the psychometrist in the forward sitting room, standing quietly. A glass ball the size of a cantaloupe rested in her hands, cradled in a red silk cloth. The sphere was a deep black, shot through with faceted crystal bursts—one that caught the available light, but instead of reflecting it outward, bent it from one internal spot to another. Not knowing anywhere near enough about what he was looking at to even hazard a guess, the detective asked;

"Souvenir?"

"It was her reading crystal."

"Part of the hocus-pocus setup you and Jimmy disliked so much?"

Lai Wan remained unmoving, her shawl and skirt enveloping her more than the darkness around her. She ignored London's remark, holding the crystal ball, eyes closed, her breathing going shallow. Concentrating on those memories she could read from the sphere, she finally intoned;

"A large man of a great size, Asian, with extremely large ears, his face scarred down the left side. It is a jagged cut, one that has healed over and been opened again. He is filled with . . . with power, with energy—he smashes the door with a single blow of his hand. He enters the apartment like a runaway horse—silent, fury boiling off him like steam. Ma'ma Lu is in the kitchen. She has time to turn—something in her hand, she hurls it—no—just its contents. They strike his face. His eyes are burning. He screams—grabs his eyes and screams."

London listened to the words, but also to the woman's tone. Her voice was more emotional than he was used to—more involved. Moving into the living room, he set his cane in each new position cautiously, mindful of the loose bits of glass and furniture everywhere. Reaching Lai Wan's side, he was not sure what to do but he stood there nonetheless, listening, waiting.

"She cannot get by. He catches her arm in one hand as she tries. Her upper arm is crushed as his fingers simply close around it. She screams—the pain bursts out of her with force, like the yoke from a dropped egg—he tosses her back into the kitchen. The table overturns as she hits it . . . two of its legs snap. She tries to stand but it is already too late. He crosses to her side, still blind. He hits her—once—again—again—again—again—she stops moving—again— again—again—she stops breathing—again—again—again—again—"

London took the woman's shoulders in his hands, shaking her gently, telling her as softly as he could;

"That's enough."

She opened her eyes, the water clinging to her lashes, bobbing, then dropping away.

"He killed her," she said. "He tore her apart in her own kitchen, with his bare hands. He stuck his hands into her and ripped out her insides. He tore the flesh from her bones, broke the bones into pieces—he—he—he . . ."

As the woman pressed against the detective he folded his arms around her, sending all the strength he had to his failing legs so he might be of some support. As she cried, he told her;

"It's all right. We're going to get to the bottom of this. We'll stop these people."

And then, London's gaze hit the street. The figure he saw caught his attention instantly. As he reacted to what he had seen unconsciously, Lai Wan, sensing his distress, made her link with the detective stronger, suddenly seeing through his eyes.

London let go of the psychometrist, practically pushing her away. Then he rebalanced himself with his cane, his free hand disappearing underneath his jacket as a very large Oriental man with extremely large ears and a jagged scar down the left side of his face began to tear away the yellow police barrier tape stuck up over the broken front window.

CHAPTER NINE

L ONDON DROPPED HIS BLACKTHORN and then shoved Lai Wan away roughly with his free hand.

"Run!" he ordered. "Get Paul! Cops—anybody. Go!!"

As she began to move, the detective shifted his weight, putting himself between the massive form climbing over the sill and the retreating psychometrist. As the terrified woman made her way stumbling in the darkness toward the front doorway, London got his .38 free of its shoulder holster, pointing it at the fearsome giant pulling himself up and into the room. His free hand came over the snub-nosed barrel, stroking it as he moved his fingers down its length, over his other hand, to where they could encircle and brace his wrist.

"Okay, Betty," he whispered to the revolver, "we'll give him one little chance."

Grinding his feet into the glass and splinter-covered rug, the detective barked, "Freeze it, Gorgo! Believe me—one warning's all that's being offered today."

The massive man with the large ears stopped long enough to look London squarely in the eyes. He smiled at the detective, stretching his grin from ear to ear. Showing his teeth as he made a short, chuckling sound, he said;

"Little man . . . little gun . . . little sense."

And then he began to move again, his intentions made quite clear by both his clenching fists and the low growling noises churning out of him. Coming up through the window, he had not unbent both knees before London fired. The gun roared, spitting flame and lead, once, then again, planting two splattering hunks of lead in the giant's chest. The man staggered backward several steps, moved but not shaken.

The detective blinked, not willing to believe for a moment that his shells had had so little effect. His target should have been crippled and howling, if not just plain dead. London had abandoned normal street ammunition early on during his last case. When the detective had strapped Betty on earlier in the day, she had still been carrying the deadly dumdum hot loads he had begun using two months earlier when he had been facing flying monstrosities whose skin could turn standard bullets. These were serious weapons, bullets which shattered within a target, sending metal flying in all directions, shredding organs. Two such shots could have stopped a charging alligator, or a buffalo.

Leveling his .38 again, London shouted, "Jesus H. Christ but I'm getting sick and tired of this!"

And then he fired again. And again and again and again and again—all four shots striking in a perfect chest pattern—each one blowing sizable chunks out of their target. Every shot slammed the giant back another step, step and a half, until the last one provided the momentum to knock him back out through the shattered front window.

The giant hit the sidewalk with a smashing thud—one which shot the air out of him in a sickeningly wheezing huff. The detective—not willing to risk faith in the usually reliable notion that six shells cut to blow apart inside their target, propelled by a disproportionate amount of gunpowder, might have actually killed somebody—scooped up his cane from the floor and then quickly hobbled to the back of the room where he started reloading his .38 immediately. Unsnapping half-moon clips from the back of his belt, he was slotting the second set in when he heard a scrambling noise from outside the window where his attacker had fallen. He snapped the refilled cylinder closed, cursing;

"Shit."

Gritting his teeth together, he aimed at the area of the empty window, waiting for his foe. A large, blood-drenched hand came over the sill, groping, clawing, struggling for some kind of hand hold. Its rod-like fingers dug into the carpet, stretching it, pulling it upward just enough so as to be able to have something to grip. And with that minimal amount of leverage gained, thickly corded muscles strained beneath the thin leather of the sleeve around them, pulling the bleeding, hulking body attached upward—back into Mrs. Lu's parlor.

London shuddered to see the monstrous form of his attacker dragging itself up over the sill again. Somehow, despite the blood still pouring from the gaping wounds in his chest, the giant was making his way back into the room. London watched as the man trembled his way to his feet again, standing before him, arms outstretched for balance, the effect rendered that of some black-and-white Frankenstein movie. Staring in disbelief, the detective waited for the man to take his first step within the room and then screamed;

"Eat lead, Dracula!!"

The trigger recessed once—twice—three times. Betty's muzzle erupted, spitting flame and metal across the room. The first slug splattered through the open meat of the man's chest, sections of it burying itself deep in the giant's heart, bursting a ventricle and releasing arcing sprays of blood. The second blew a ragged two-pound section of lung and kidney and muscle outward like moist shrapnel. The third shell found its way to the giant's spine, shattering two vertebrae.

The three dead-on hits spun the man twice around before their momentum faded—bouncing him off the wall to London's left, finally throwing him facedown at the detective's feet. The massive body twitched in disjointed spasm, trying to assess the damage done to it. Backing away from the giant, London watched as once again the hulk tried to stand.

The detective's eyes widened, half in horror, half in curiosity, as he watched the hands working their way across the floor, back toward the shoulders, trying to find the proper place from which they could lever upward the body to which they were attached. The elbows, responding, made flapping chicken-wing motions at the same time, shaking to stabilize.

What does it take, thought the detective. Nine bullets, nine hits—dumdums, for Christ's sake. What the hell does it take anymore to kill somebody?

Getting his cane, finally able to again rest his weight on it, London caught his breath as best he could, trembling from the effort of holding Betty steady through the nine shots. He had spent over a month in bed—two more weeks just learning to walk again. His shooting arm was paralyzed with pain now, numb from the nine recoils. His breath chugging out of him in short bunches, his eyes stayed with the horror before him—the slowly rising form of the giant.

It made no sense, the facts before his eyes following no logic the detective could rationalize. By all rights the thing before him should have been long dead—chest gone, heart pierced, lungs broken, spine halved. Staring in wonder as the giant's knees began to draw up under it, London shouted at him;

"What's keeping you up? What could possibly be keeping you going?"

Then, suddenly, he stepped forward, ramming Betty against the man's skull. Pulling the trigger three more times, he screamed over the roar of the bullets;

"Then again, who cares?!"

The giant's brain exploded into fragments, skull-splintered bits of gray matter splattering the far wall. London fell in a heap, nearly crippled by his effort, his cane flying away from him across the room. The giant collapsed into a mound of bloody flesh—one badly folded in on itself. London lay where he had fallen, panting, his mind putting everything he had seen in order, working at getting him back on his feet and out of Mrs. Lu's before anyone could arrive on the scene. He knew it would not be good to be observed by any spectators, let alone to stay long enough for the police to arrive. He could hear their questions in his head.

Just what were you doing at the scene of a murder behind the police barriers? Oh—your client is a dead woman . . . how melodramatic. And why did you feel compelled to shoot an unarmed man? Before he had done anything whatsoever to you? And why did you feel it necessary to shoot him twelve times? And what made you think you could do it with illegal ammunition? Oh . . . he was a vampire—the vampire that killed Mrs. Lu. Oh, the one who killed both Mrs. Lu and her son. And you're sure because your psychic looked in the dead woman's crystal ball and then told you so. AAAAAhhhhhhhhhhh—

No, he told himself, pushing his back upward against the wall, it would not do to still be there wheezing on the floor, murder weapon in hand when the police arrived. Staggering forward the several steps to where his cane had fallen, he stooped to pick it up, ready to hobble off into the night when suddenly he sensed the shadows of others coming over the shattered windowsill toward him.

Looking up, he saw a trio of smiling Oriental men closing on Mrs. Lu's storefront, all staring at him intently. They were all of a kind—young faces, stylish haircuts, well-muscled bodies, finely cut clothes, faces shaped by a lifetime of sneering. The one in the middle said;

"I don't believe it—he's put the good-bye to the Muzz."

"He has," said the one to his left, wonder in his voice. "He has indeed."

"What are we going to do about this?" asked the first.

"Obviously," answered the last, "we kill him."

The three men came over the sill, unafraid as if oblivious to the fact that what had killed the Muzz might also kill them. London watched them approach, knowing he had no time to reload before they would all be upon him, in too much pain to load and fire the smoking revolver in his hand even if he had all the time in the world. As he moved his hand down his leg, casually, trying to reach his knife, Veronica, the middle one studied the carnage that had taken down the Muzz, saying;

"Bullets. I always seem to forget that they can kill."

"Only a lot of them, in the right places," said the second one. He looked at the corpse for a moment, then turned to the detective, asking;

"You . . . how many?"

"How many what?" asked London.

"Bullets. How many bullets did you use on the Muzz?"

"It took twelve," he answered.

"You see," said the last of them smugly. "The Muzzer just got too confident. Always bad."

"Twelve dumdum hot loads," continued the detective. "Bad-assed ammo. I mean really serious stuff. Tell me—how'd he do it? How'd he take twelve of them?"

"The Gaun Cee Qui are tough, Qua'lo."

"You're telling me the Muzz was a vampire?"

The middle one's interest peeked suddenly. "You speak Cantonese, Qua'lo?"

"No," answered London, stalling, praying for the police now, for Lai Wan to have reached some kind of help—for anybody. "It's just a word I picked up from my client."

"And who's that?" asked the third one.

"Mrs. Xui Zeng Lu."

The three laughed among themselves, the middle one hitting a deeper chuckle than the tittering of the other two. The first one, unable to contain himself, told the detective;

"Your client's dead, Qua'lo."

"I know," answered London calmly. "So's the guy who killed her."

The trio eyed the detective. He could feel their confusion through the darkness. The three before him were used to being feared. People simply did not talk back to them—people were not supposed to even be able to look them in the eye, let alone make veiled threats to them. Looking to wipe away their confusion, the first asked;

"And does that mean you now think things are even? That you can just totter off to home now?"

"No, not really."

"And why not?" asked the middle one, his curiosity bordering on real interest.

"Because," answered the detective, "I was hired to track down the killers of Jimmy Lu. They're the ones I was after in the first place. This sap," London indicated the still-bleeding corpse on the floor, "he just got in the way."

The three laughed out loud then—raucously—slapping each other, unable to believe London's brazen front. The middle one finally silenced his partners, telling the detective;

"Oh, little fella, you're good—you know—I'll give you that. You're really good. It's rare one gets to see someone as tough as you who's still crawling around in their own generation." A sad smile crossing the man's face, he said;

"Still, admiration for your audacity aside, I'm afraid as much fun as it is to listen to your bravery, we must be on our way. You've got a good sharp tone—smooth voice—very controlled. Really good. Hell, it's almost a shame to kill you." Turning to the young man on his left, he ordered;

"You do it, Li. We've got to get going."

The first man stepped forward, fingers curling into fists, ready to finish London off. The detective pulled Veronica free, hoping to be able to take at least his first attacker with him. Flipping the knife in his hand, London pulled back to make his first swing when suddenly the one coming for him lost his balance, flying end over end into the wall across the room from the detective. Not knowing what had happened, the two remaining men wheeled around, scanning the room to find the source of their companion's troubles.

The source was an older Oriental man, one who took the hand of the middle attacker into his own and then twisted, shattering half the bones in the man's palm and fingers. As the third moved forward, his hand raised to strike the older man down, London's defender raised his arm to meet the other's, then struck forward with the blocking hand, smashing the man's bridgework and nose. As the detective watched from his place on the floor, the older man shot one of his feet into the back of the one called Li, shooting it forward again and then again. London could hear the snapping of ribs and vertebrae with each kick.

As the two still standing went for the older man, all three moved about each other in silence, all of them looking for an opening. Suddenly, the middle man, thinking he had found one, threw his open fist forward, shooting for their assailant's head. The motion caused the older man to duck, once, twice, then a third time. After the third retreat, however, he caught the arm flying for his face at the elbow from underneath. His fingers pinching inward, he dug into the nerves and joint of the elbow, causing his victim to howl in ungodly agony.

The other still capable of moving came forward, hoping to take London's defender while he was occupied. The older man kicked out toward him—almost a casual gesture—a lightning blow that shattered the connection between the man's skull and neck. The head topped over obscenely, rolling around the shattered spine top, unable to steady itself. Returning his attention to the man he had by the elbow, the older man pulled back with his other hand and then shot his fist forward into the man's chest, shattering all its ribs and the sternum. Then, he released the one in his grasp and delivered a series of kicks to the now fallen trio, breaking all of their legs in several places each.

A sour smile twisting his mouth, the victor addressed the vanquished as a group, saying;

"It takes a long time to heal so many breaks, doesn't it?"

As the three rolled on the floor in pain, stunned from the swift and unexpected attack, the older man pulled a samurai short sword from inside his jacket. Going down on one knee, he bent over the middle man, grabbing his head by the hair. Holding the blade before the fallen man's face, he said;

"Far too long."

And with that, the older man drew the blade across and through the middle man's throat. Blood arced about the room, pumping free by the gallon. As the older man repeated the stroke on his other two opponents, London watched in fascination as the first of them began crawling forward. The detective made to warn the older man, but the other shrugged off London's efforts almost with contempt. Then, standing away from the trio, the older man addressed them once more.

"If any of you do survive, tell your lord his time is numbered."

Then the older man crossed the room, headed for the window. The three on the floor before him dying by inches, London made his way to his feet, shoving Veronica awkwardly into his pocket. Reholstering Betty, he pushed off with his cane, agony still throbbing throughout his body as he called to the older man;

"Sir, hey—wait. You saved my life."

The man stopped before the window. He stared outward for only a moment, then turned and faced the detective. Anger growing red in his eyes, he pointed a hand at London's face, growling from deep within him;

"You are a miserable, puny excuse for a man. You are nothing. How could

Fate have ever picked such bastard scum as you?"

London stood back, slightly shocked. Of all the reactions he had thought possible from someone who had just risked life and limb against impossible odds to save him, anger and curses were not two of them. Startled into silence, he did nothing other than watch as his rescuer continued on and through the window, dropping to the street as quietly as he had entered. Then, suddenly, the older man turned and stared into the detective's eyes, telling him;

"I am the one that should have been picked. I should have been the Destroyer."

And then his rescuer disappeared as London stood staring at the space in which he had been, his mouth hanging open in total surprise, the bodies of the dead and the dying forgotten behind him.

CHAPTER TEN

PAUL MORCEY TURNED OVER the last of the corpses, jerking its pants pockets inside out. Finding little of consequence, he announced; "That's it, boss. That's all of it."

"All right, fine," answered London. Sucking down a deep breath, he braced himself for the titanic effort of moving and then added, "Let's get out of here."

Limping awkwardly for the doorway, the detective hurried his steps as best he could. The worst of the pain in his shooting arm had almost dissipated. Even with his slight head start, however, he made it to the street only seconds before Morcey. Catching up to and falling in step with his partner, his suit jacket's side pocket stuffed with the belongings he had stripped from the four bodies inside, the balding man said;

"Sweet Bride of the Night—I'll tell ya, boss—things are never dull on this job."

Almost as if he had not heard his friend, London said, "I can't believe that no one—no one—has come around to see what was going on in there."

The detective spoke to his partner in guarded whispers as they made their way through the nighttime crowds, up Pell Street to the Silver Palace.

"I shot off a dozen hot loaded rounds in there. In case you weren't aware, that makes a lot of noise. The man who came in through the window, the one who killed the other three . . ."

"You didn't wipe them all?" Morcey spilled over with questions. "The man who came through the window? What man who came through the window?"

"The one," answered London, "who thought he should have become the Destroyer."

"Huh?"

The ex-maintenance man glanced over at his partner, shaking his head, half in puzzlement, half in astonishment. The detective, realizing he was relating the events that had taken place since he and Lai Wan had left the car a little too much out of order, apologized, saying;

"Sorry, I guess I should start at the beginning."

The two turned left onto Bowery Street, making their way through the jostling crowd on the sidewalk. With the Silver Palace now in sight, the balding man told his partner;

"Boss, no offense or nuthin', but why don't you save your breath until we get back to the girls? After all, I mean, we're gonna be there in a minute anyway and, you know you're gonna have ta tell 'em all about this one."

"Yes," answered the detective with a sigh, pushing off each step with a renewed vigor, ignoring the pain in his leg. "I imagine I do."

As they continued their march up Bowery, suddenly Morcey started laughing to himself. When London asked him what was so amusing, he answered;

"I was just thinkin', boss, when we get down to checkin' out the wallets we boosted from those guys . . . I bet I know one card none of 'em will have."

"What's that?" asked the detective.

"Ahhh, easy—blood donor cards."

London rolled his eyes, chuckling in spite of himself.

Once the pair arrived at the table where Morcey had left Lisa and Lai Wan after the psychometrist had sent him out to London's aid, the detective told them everything that had happened. At first Lisa had been overjoyed to see the pair of them come in unscathed. As London related what had happened to him since he had covered Lai Wan's run for safety, however, the young woman's composure shrank away, folding in on itself until only the tiniest square of it remained. By the time he had finished, her frayed nerves had wrung her napkin into a sorry rag.

Her fingers played at the stitching running up its side, pulling and tearing, slowly wrenching the cloth into pieces. Trying to get a hold on the strain she could feel in her throat before she spoke, she cleared it several times, embarrassed at each new noise. Finally, when she felt confident her voice would not crack, she asked;

"So, there really are vampires in the world?"

"There's something at work out there," answered London. "I'll give Mrs. Lu that much."

"So, what're we gonna do, boss?"

The detective looked at his partner, answering, "I know it's not very dramatic, but we're going to proceed as we would in any other instance. We're going to track these things down, find out what they're up to, and then decide our best course of action based on what we learn."

The psychometrist ran the fingers of one hand along her chop sticks as she asked, "Do you have any idea who this person might have been who came to your rescue?"

"No, and I wish I did. Obviously I'd like to talk to him for a number of reasons."

"'Cause he knows you're the Destroyer?"

"Certainly one reason, Paul," answered the detective.

"The question there is, though, did he get that information on his own, or did he get it from Mrs. Lu? It would seem that there would have to be some sort of a connection between them—I'm hard pressed to believe he just happened to be going by her storefront when those things attacked me. He also apparently knows about vampires . . . more than we do, at least. So, what's the connection? Did she try to hire him to avenge her son's death? And if she did, did she try to hire him before or after she tried us?"

"What do you think he meant?" asked Lisa, changing the subject.

"About him deserving to be the Destroyer?"

The young woman nodded. London sat back in his chair. Suddenly, though, before he could answer, a waiter arrived with the orders Paul and Lisa had given when they had first arrived. The young man placed all the dishes on the Lazy Susan in the center of the table—Chinese family style—four bowls of white rice, crisp roast pork with onions and both red and green peppers, curried chicken and potatoes, bamboo shoots with beef, cauliflower with scallions, a platter of fried rice noodles, and a large tureen of vegetable beef broth. After the waiter departed, as the others slid the paper wraps off of their chopsticks, the detective answered Lisa's question.

"I'm not sure. Anyone's guess is probably as good as mine on that one. But," he said, his voice taking on a joking tone, "here's something I thought I'd never see."

All eyes turned toward Morcey as he grabbed up a large, black-crisped end piece of pork, sticky with onions, using his chopsticks.

"What? What now?"

"You," answered London. "Using chopsticks."

A tiny trace of a smile passed over Lai Wan's face for only a moment. Cranking his head to the side, letting it bob up and down slightly, the ex-maintenance man answered;

"Boy, mother of mercy, a guy picks up a new skill and all of a sudden he's gotta take the raspberry from everybody."

"My apologies," replied the detective, his smile not fading. "I guess I'm just too used to thinking of you with a Twinkie in one hand and a Yoo-Hoo in the other."

"Hey," answered Paul seriously, "that's what I had for lunch."

Lai Wan smiled again; Lisa laughed out loud. Not allowing himself to be affected, Morcey popped the large slice of vegetable-coated meat into his mouth, talking while he chewed.

"Women. Everything's sooooooooo funny."

London said "good-night" to the others at Morcey's car, pledging his partner to see the two women home safely. The balding man leaned out of the driver's window, asking the detective;

"What're you going to do, boss?"

"I think I'll stay down here for a while . . . do a little looking around."

"Like the lookin' around you was doin' at Mrs. Lu's place?" he asked, concern coloring his voice.

"Well," answered London honestly, his smile not quite exposing his teeth, "let's hope I can keep it to just the looking part."

Morcey's right hand reached up for his keys, turning the one in the ignition slowly, his eyes never leaving his partner's. Finally, as the motor turned over with only two rattling kicks before dropping down into its usual comfortable hum, the ex-maintenance man conceded;

"Ahhh, I guess yer a big boy. You know what yer doin'—usually, anyway."

"Thanks for the vote of confidence."

"You know what I mean," responded Morcey. "Just take care of yerself, that's all." He pulled away from the curb slowly, calling out at the detective;

"I ain't ready to start runnin' the agency by myself, yet. You know?"

"Don't worry," said London to the air, watching the car disappear into the traffic. "I think I can manage to stick around for a while longer."

So saying, the detective started making his way back down Bowery, turning on Pell, heading for Mrs. Lu's. The contents of the vampires' pockets that he and Morcey had studied in the restaurant had told them nothing. Each had carried some basic identification—one out-of-state driver's license, some credit cards, a gymnasium membership—but there had been nothing that gave London anything with which he could work. There were no business cards, no photo IDs, no handwritten bits or pieces, and, as Morcey had predicted, no cards for any blood banks.

"Maybe if they allowed withdrawals," mused the detective, his eyes glued to Mrs. Lu's shattered window as he approached her former residence.

He stopped across the street from the storefront, looking to see if there had been any changes in the two hours since he had limped away with Morcey's help. He noted several important ones. The body of his massive attacker was gone. So was all of the blood his dozen bullets had splattered about the front room. So also were the bodies of the detective's three smaller attackers, the ones killed by his savior. There was no evidence the police had returned, however.

Besides, even if they had, he thought to himself, cops don't scrub up blood.

As a delivery van passed the storefront, London noted a flash of light inside the shattered living room. He waited for another car to go by, watching to see if its headlights were caught in the same manner. They were. So were those of the next. And the next.

Not sensing anyone near, no one interested in either himself or the building he was watching, he crossed the street, re-entering Mrs. Lu's shattered home. Once inside, he headed directly for the reflecting spot. Going down on both knees slowly, he reached under one of the room's wrecked chairs, straining his arm until his fingers came up against a cold, smooth object. Pulling it forward, he discovered Mrs. Lu's reading crystal. Dragging it forward, he realized Lai Wan must have dropped it when he sent her packing. Looking around, he noticed the red silk cloth in which it had been wrapped.

London pulled the ball and the cloth over toward himself, and then, pushing himself upward with effort, recovered his feet while maintaining his grip on both the cantaloupe-sized crystal ball and the silk. He began re-covering the one with the other when suddenly he was struck with the notion that he should leave. At once.

It was the same kind of gut feeling that had guided him through a thousand moments of more mundane types of detective work in the past, but now it seemed stronger, more strident. He felt as if fate had offered him a small window of safety through time so he could retrieve the crystal, but that was all. Now that it was in his hands, he was suddenly "sure" that there was nothing remaining to be gained within the storefront except trouble if he did not vacate the premises immediately.

One hand around the silk-wrapped globe, the other tight about the top of his Blackthorn, London shoved himself off toward the street. He came back out onto Pell at a brisk pace, moving as quickly as he could down toward the next cross block, not quite ready to vacate the area but, certain he did not want to spend any more time in Mrs. Lu's.

Finally, around the corner from the storefront, he paused for a moment, leaning back against the plate-glass front of a Mott Street restaurant. As whole roasted chickens and ducks peered over his shoulder from their places hanging in between the red-glazed racks of ribs, the detective pulled back a corner of the scarlet cloth to study his prize. The crystal facets within the sphere still caught any light that struck them, bending it inward, reflecting it from one internal spot to another.

Wait a minute, thought London, confused by what he had noticed. Experimenting, he turned the ball over and over in his hands, moving it at different angles away from and toward the different light sources around him. No matter what he tried, however, the light still reacted the same. Stopping his experimenting for a moment, he held the crystal steady, staring at it with one puzzling question eating at him.

How, wondered the detective, if the ball absorbed all the light that it came in contact with, had it reflected the headlights of the cars going by so he could spot it in the first place? He was still absorbed by the same line of questioning when the woman in the red leather dress came over to him.

CHAPTER ELEVEN

THE WOMAN MOVED WITH the strong, fluid motions natural to those raised in the tropics. They were not the exaggerated, cheap movements of an urban teenager, trying hard to imitate some rock video star's tightly dressed backup singers—the woman moved like water down a pebbled hillside, filling every empty space, caressing every curve.

London, aware of her since she had started across the street in her intersecting line toward him, gave the woman marks for form, even as he wondered what she might possibly want. She stopped in front of him, saying;

"I'm sorry to be so forward but, I'm afraid you're forcing me to do it."

"Oh? I am, am I." responded the detective. "Now why's that?"

"Because if I didn't stop you and talk to you now, I'd probably never get another chance."

"And if I can ask without being rude, or forward, what is it that you wanted to talk about?"

London studied the air around him as he talked, looking for any threats. Was the woman setting him up for yet more attackers? Was she a threat herself? Her eyes mirrored no duplicity, but he was beginning to wonder about what could be hidden and what could not anymore. Trying not to be obvious, he studied her movements carefully as she answered;

"Your crystal. It's extremely lovely."

"Thanks," he offered. "I just picked it up."

London took the woman in at a glance. His years on the street refused for even a second to think of her in any way except as some part of what was going on around him. Swiftly, he catalogued her features for future reference: black hair, long and straight, bangs cut across the forehead; skin, rich, deeply tanned; eyes, dark brown, large and sharply intelligent; height, five feet nine or ten inches, depending on exactly how much was coming from her red, extremely high-heeled boots; weight, 105, maybe 110.

Her face was beautiful, all of its features striking, not in any classic sense, but still in a way that worked perfectly—the kind of arrangement that held its perfection no matter into what look their owner might mold them.

"I'll buy it from you."

"I don't think I really want to sell it."

"You don't know what I'm willing to offer."

"You don't know what I had to go through to get it."

The detective noted through the slits up both sides of her leather skirt that the woman's legs were somewhat better muscled than her upper body—which made her a what, he wondered, dancer? Jogger? Skier? Skater? Her attitude impressed the detective. She stood in front of him comfortably, not seeming very afraid to hold a conversation with a total stranger on a dark street in a sometimes unsavory neighborhood. London tried to get a handle on the woman, looking to figure out what she wanted, how she fit into things, the defensive part of his brain hoping to turn whatever she was after against her before she could use it against him.

"Why don't we go somewhere and talk about it?" she asked, giving him a smile bright enough to light up the street or blind a minister.

"Well, I'll tell you. I've had a long day and I'm tired. I'm also mixed up in a situation that not only do I not want to talk about, but I doubt you would want anything to do with unless you're already a part of it."

The detective watched the woman while he talked, looking for some clue as to what her real motivation was. Her face gave away no reactions to anything he said, however, save to tell him with its look that she was both slightly intrigued and insulted.

Well, he thought, if she *is* setting me up for the next round of assassins, she's awfully cool about it.

"Look," she told him, half touching his wrist, half the crystal ball, "I would really like to talk to you about this piece. If I can't get you to sell it or trade it to me, I'd at least like a chance to study it. Come on," she urged, flashing him the high wattage smile again, "what have you got to lose?"

"Hummmm, now isn't that just what I'm always asking myself?" he answered, giving her a smile of his own. "Okay, you win. Let's go somewhere and sit down and you can study my toy here to your heart's content. Good enough?"

"Perfect."

The pair walked down the street together toward a bar the woman suggested that London both knew of and agreed to. Along the way they traded the usual pleasantries. Within them, she managed to assure him that she really was only interested in the crystal while he was able to let her know that he was only interested in letting her pursue her interest.

When they reached the bar, London cradled the sphere under his arm, shifting his walking stick from one hand to the other. The woman opened the door, letting him step first into the sharp blare of hard noise—wired music, shrill voices, shouts, screams, and bitter false laughs—pouring out through the entrance over them both. After fighting their way through the assault of noise and the throng clustered toward the front of the place, the pair considered themselves lucky to find a small table right away, one not only in the non-smoking section but also under a fairly strong light as well. Indicating the light, the woman said;

"It's probably why no one's sitting here."

"Why's that?" asked London, curious to hear her answer. The woman hunched her head down low on her shoulders, peering into the sphere resting on its red silk wrap. Not taking her eyes from the crystal, she told the detective;

"People come to places like this to be a mystery. They don't want anyone to be able to look into their eyes—into their souls, to catch them in whatever lies they're going to be telling. I mean, it's a mutual thing—whether it's men after women or women after men, men after men, women after women—whatever—you know how it goes, I mean, it's not like all the hunters aren't being hunted at the same time . . .

"Anyway, what I meant was both sides agree to listen to those things that the other wants to dish up. Then they pass judgment on what they've heard and take it from there. And, let's face it, since, deep down, both sides really want to be tricked in the first place, the darkness is a big help. After all, lies are born in darkness . . ."

And then, suddenly, the woman looked up with an embarrassed, almost guilty look on her face. The shock of it surprised the detective, making him wonder at its source. But then, before he could ask anything, however, the woman straightened her shoulders and said;

"I'm sorry. I should be ashamed of myself. I've been so intent on separating you from your property I've just been blathering. I haven't even introduced myself."

Cupping the fingers of one hand around the other, her wrists resting on the table, the woman took a short breath and then looked up again, saying;

"Please forgive me. I'm Karen Tezzler."

"Forget about it. I'm Theodore London. But you can call me Ted."

Tezzler stuck out her hand, giving it to the detective along with her apology. London took it, shaking it gently, his hand relaxing against the softness and warmth of hers. Their grasps broke as a waitress came to their table. The ordering of a set of drinks sent the waitress off to the bar, giving the woman a chance to resume her studies of the black sphere and London a chance to continue to study her.

"So, tell me . . ." he asked, "why is it you're so interested in my little trinket, anyway?" Without raising her head, Karen answered;

"Ted, this wonder of yours is by no means a trinket. This is one of the most beautiful crystal balls I've ever seen. I could tell that much from across the street when I spotted it in your hands. It looks to have properties that . . ." Then, looking up, she asked;

"You really don't know what you have here, do you?" Before the detective could say anything, she pulled the answer from his eyes and laughed.

"No, I didn't think so." Taking his hands in hers, the woman wrapped his fingers around the crystal, telling him;

"There now, feel it. Really *feel* it. Can you see how smooth it is, how almost perfectly round it is?"

"Almost . . .?"

"Ummmhumm. There are some slight warps in its curve—it's not a machine-worked piece. This solid lump, all five, six pounds of it, this thing was hand-blown. I've never seen a ball like it before—anywhere. For the life of me I can't figure out how they did it—the way it catches the light—the colors that flash inside it whenever you turn it. Close your eyes . . ."

"Excuse me?"

"Keep your hands on the ball, cover as much of its surface as you can, and close your eyes."

Playing along, the detective did as the woman asked. As he laid his hands on the crystal, feeling its cold smoothness, the woman continued to speak. Her voice becoming an urgent whisper, low and coaxing but somehow perfectly clear to London over the pounding noise of the bar.

"The crystal itself is cold, but can you feel the warmth that's inside of it? Can you feel it coming to the surface? Hold on to that feeling and call to it. Focus your consciousness on that heat—picture it in your mind, see the color of it, taste it, let it dry your throat, let it into your fingers . . . call to it, call to it . . ."

And while the woman continued to talk, London followed her instructions, urging the energy within the crystal to come to him. Remembering the things told him by the professors and mystics he had met fifty-six days earlier, he abandoned all his disruptive or negative thoughts, throwing them off—relaxing his way out of their chains. For the moment, without even wondering why, he filed away the vampires and Mrs. Lu, Lisa's pain, Morcey's concern, Karen's possible ulterior motives, and his own guilt, even the bar itself—forgetting its drubbing noise and empty people, blotting them out.

Ignoring the side of his brain questioning the rationality of what he was doing, he set about giving his companion's request an honest try. His mind focused only on the crystal and whatever power might be within it, he called it to him, startled when it suddenly touched him. The brush of it broke his concentration for a second, but he refocused himself, tracing the retreating heat back to the center of the sphere.

Finding it, he called it to him once more, this time not allowing the connection to break away when he felt its touch. The warmth flowed up both his arms, traveling not like light, but like heat, slowly, reassuringly. It wrapped up and over his shoulders, spreading down his breastbone and into his abdomen as it simultaneously moved up his spine and into his head. Then, working its way through the bones of his skull, it flooded into his brain and groin at the same moment.

Images filled his closed eyes, frozen seconds out of time, some unknown to him but most recognizable. He flashed on the scene Mrs. Lu's visit had brought to him, saw his father and brothers and neighbors again swept away, boiling brown water swirling their shattered, drowning bodies away along with all the other debris. Then he saw the giant again, and his other three attackers, saw himself kill the first, rewatched the deaths of the others, replayed the face of his condemning savior.

More faces filled his mental field of vision after that, each one coming and leaving faster than the one before it . . . Fred Wayne, his childhood best friend; his partner, Paul; Elizabeth, the woman he had almost married; Jenny, the one he did; Zachary Goward; Pa'sha Lowe; Lai Wan; Lisa . . . the Spud—He saw the Spud once more, waving his arms atop the fuel tank—begging for a private death in the hopes it could prevent billions. He relived the scene from all angles, seeing not only his pulling of the trigger that killed so many but also the tears in his eyes as he did it.

Then the memory was gone, replaced by a blurringly fast cavalcade of others. His first car, the day he punched out Del Rehill and went to work for himself, the choking blob of gristle and fat that had so disgusted him he had never eaten red meat again, the drunken night he discovered too much alcohol could rob him of his legs . . . others.

Half of his brain lived the flashes of reality crashing around him one against the next, the other voiced its concern, asking what was happening in the physical world outside of him. It recognized a pattern to the images assaulting the detective, each one more personal than the last, getting closer and closer to those moments that had made him the man he was.

Growing concerned over the amount of time he was spending inside the electrical loops within his own mind, his brain screamed at him to wake up and at least give the real world a cursory glance. Reluctantly, his hands began to release the crystal. But then he saw a familiar face wearing an expression he could not remember it ever wearing and, he had to see more.

CHAPTER TWELVE

M RS. LONDON SAT AT her place at the dining-room table, blowing smoke into the air from her cigarette, drumming the fingers of one hand anxiously against the bare, hardwood surface of the table. This, she told herself, was no way to spend her vacation time. Both her hands, the one holding her cigarette and the one tapping away unconsciously, were shaking slightly. Eight, possibly nine, fresh butts lay crumpled in the Souvenir of Orlando ashtray, each of them shredded and broken from having been crushed out with an exaggerated amount of force.

The woman brushed a handful of stray curls away from her eyes and looked up toward the clock built into the oven, frowning at the lateness of the hour.

Where could he be? she wondered to herself.

Her gaze strayed to the window, her eyes straining to determine if the darkness outside had grown any deeper since the last time she had looked—less than a minute earlier. Rationally, she knew it could not be, and yet, somehow, the scene outside seemed to her to have grown far darker. Taking a deep pull on her cigarette, she held the air in for a moment, feeling the nicotine pacify her brain.

She took another deep drag, held it down, then let it out and took one more. Suddenly, however, she began to sputter. The smoke she coughed out reeked of bitter chemicals. Without looking she knew she had let the cigarette burn down to the filter again, the smoldering fibers filling her lungs with such a blistering gas she found it impossible to breathe for a moment.

Once she finished coughing, she looked at the table before her. Without knowing it she had knocked her ashtray over while she was thrashing. Butts, ashes, and the tiny pieces of the spent wooden matches that she had snapped and resnapped were now spread across the shining wood of her tabletop, some of it on the floor as well. Spittle and snot veined with traces of blood that she had hacked up during her coughing fit lay in the middle of it all.

"E'uuuuu," she sighed, disgusted with the sight, "that's attractive."

Wearily, Mrs. London stood and crossed her kitchen to the sink where she got a washrag. She had meant to go back to the table but, before she could she caught a look at her face reflected in the large framed mirror hanging next to the refrigerator. Shock at what she saw drew her in toward the glass.

Her eyes were darkly circled, red, and puffy—her once freely curling hair tangled and wild. A longish strand of mucus swung bobbingly from one nostril. Tears started to roll down her cheeks, the look of her face embarrassing her even though no one else was there to see it. Forgetting the table, she threw the washrag back into the dishwater and then turned toward the bathroom, tears hitting the carpet beneath her feet as she ran.

Closing the door behind her, shutting herself off from the empty house, she turned the hot tap on full, splashing her face with the steadily heating water. She cleaned her nose and rubbed out her eyes, then splashed water over her head. She could feel it running down her neck, soaking the back of her cotton shirt. Ignoring the warm rivulets dripping their way down the curve of her spine, she combed out her damp hair and then, gathering it into one thick handful, she did it all up with a rubber band she found in the medicine cupboard.

Turning off the water finally, she looked at herself in the bathroom mirror, liking what she saw somewhat better, almost amused at her hairstyle.

"It's been a few years for ponytails, Ginny, old girl," she told herself, not able to ignore the gray streaks in her hair, none of which had been there the last time she had worn her hair in the same fashion.

Leaving the bathroom, she headed back for the kitchen. Rearming herself with the previously abandoned washrag, she wrung it out with determination. Then she crossed to the dining room, shuddering at the sight of the debris she had left behind.

With a sigh, she picked her cigarette pack up and then slid it into the pocket of her shirt. That taken care of, she began the task of cleaning the table and the floor. She was just finishing when she heard Teddy at the front door.

"Hey, Mom . . . I'm home."

"I'm in the kitchen."

Teddy London came into the dining room, dropping his school books on the freshly cleaned table, maintaining his hold on the football under his arm. Taking a sniff at the air, he teased his mother.

"Smoking up a storm tonight, huh?"

She had put on a more tranquil face before he had entered, forcing herself to remain calm. She had told herself a thousand times as the night had dragged on, her mind filled with dread, not to scream, not to overreact.

"What if I have?!" she snapped.

For years Virginia London had cared for her son on her own, a woman with no marketable skills, a woman who found that even the charity of a community as old-fashioned as Rosie, Arkansas, had its limits. She had managed for seventeen years, though, pushing herself from job to job, keeping their house around them and food on the table. Something inside had worked her, had driven her even when there seemed to be no way possible to meet the next truck payment, or repair bill, or . . .

"What if I have," she practically screamed. "What would you care? What does anyone care?"

She had been more than a good mother—she had been perfect. Stepping back from any life of her own she had worked only to raise her last remaining son. Three men stripped from her, she was fierce in her protection of him. She had let him find his own way in life, let others bloody his nose and break his heart, caring for him, but not smothering him.

Now, however, for the first time, the wall damming the years of frustration she felt over what fate had given her for a life snapped, spewing her anger like buckshot.

"You don't care! You don't give a damn about me."

Some terrible strength inside her had forced her up out of sick beds, dragged her from chore to chore, had always been there like a secret well she could drink from whenever she needed one more ounce of energy, or courage, or even just faith in the notion she could make it through another miserable, black-clouded day. Now, through the haze of her anger, she could hear it talking to her in the back of her mind, telling her to look at her son.

As Virginia London suddenly focused on Teddy's face, she saw him clearly—confusion and anger fighting for room in his features. She knew her words were hurting him but, for once she could not make herself care. Understanding the situation was not what she had in mind. Holding back from actually striking him, she moved forward on him, though, demanding;

"You're supposed to be home by six o'clock. If you're not going to be home you're supposed to call! That's all I ask, that you let me know where you are."

"But, Mom," pleaded Teddy, "I was at football practice. You know that."

"Don't give me any of that," she shouted. "Football practice is on Thursday nights."

"Mom," insisted Teddy. "This is Thursday."

And then, suddenly, the fury left her, the little voice inside telling her that he was right. She had forgotten, mixed up her days. It had been so many years since she had had any time off, she had simply gotten confused, had simply . . .

"Oh, my God," she sputtered, ashamed of herself for not only losing her temper, but for losing it for no good reason.

"Oh, Teddy, I'm so sorry. Oh, baby, oh please, I'm so sorry, honey . . ."

She hugged him to her, her sudden action forcing the football from his hands. He hugged her back tentatively, no longer angry but still confused. He patted her on the back, offering what comfort he could.

"Jeez, take it easy, Mom. I'm okay. But I'm telling you, you've been working too hard."

She gently released him from her grasp, pulling in breath through her nose and mouth—gulping it—trying not to cry again. Smiling, relief flooding through her, she answered;

"You may be right about that, son."

"I thought you were supposed to be on vacation? You only have one more day left, but you haven't done anything yet. Don't you want to get out of the house, or something?"

"Maybe—I don't know."

Walking over to the dining-room table, Virginia took her usual seat. Pulling out her cigarettes, she lit one quickly, using the motion to avoid the territory where their discussion was leading—the area holding truths like "leaving the house takes money we don't have."

Instead, she exhaled a large white-gray cloud and told Teddy, "Your dinner's in the refrigerator."

"Whatta we got?" he asked as he pulled open the door, scanning the inside.

"Macaroni and cheese. It's in the little pot. When I thought you were out horsing around or something I just took it off the stove and stuck it in the fridge. I'm sorry," she said again, starting to get up. "Here, let me heat it up for you."

"No. Sit down, Mom," ordered Teddy. "This is one Son of the South who can reheat his own pot of cheese noodles."

Grabbing the milk out of the refrigerator along with his dinner, he splashed some in with the now-crusty macaroni, stirring the solid mass of noodles and cheese to break it up as he turned on the fire.

"See?" he beamed. "Just like a New York City chef."

Virginia let another breath of smoke escape into the room, relaxing in the grasp of the burning nicotine, smiling at her son. As she did, she choked down a growling cough, thinking to herself;

Well, he's intelligent, strong, and not bad-looking. His teachers like him, the neighbors like him—all the boys want to be his best friend and every girl in town is crazy for him. And he can cook.

Her smile grew broader, and just a trifle wicked as she teased herself, adding, Well, he can reheat, anyway.

Blowing another gray plume into the air, her face broke into an honest smile as she thought;

Maybe I haven't done such a bad job after all.

Cigarette smoke blowing toward him, Teddy made a production of covering his food, joking with his mother;

"Hey, watch it, will you?"

"Oh, sorry, Mssssss. Childe. Please continue." Turning back to his stirring, Teddy chided;

"You better watch those things, Mom. They'll kill you, you know."

She stared at his back, comparing the size of his shoulders and the cut of his hair to the memories she had of his father. He measured up well in her eyes. She sat back—happy—pleased with herself at the way their lives had turned out despite the hardness of them at times. Taking what would be her last drag of the cigarette she was holding—of any cigarette, ever again—she told him;

"I know, son."

Then she coughed one final time, adding, "I know."

CHAPTER
THIRTREEN

L ONDON'S EYES OPENED SHARPLY, his head shaking from the violence of the movement. His hands were still gripping Mrs. Lu's crystal ball—Karen Tezzler was still sitting across from him. As he took in his surroundings, he realized the voice coming through the speakers, singing something insipid about the evils of the middle class, was still on the same sentence; perhaps three or four words since London had spotted his mother's face in the back of his mind and paused to relive a moment in time.

"You saw something, didn't you?"

The detective eyed the woman differently, wondering just what her concept was of her role in the events around him. Despite the innocent readings he got from her, some part of him found it impossible to believe she was as uninvolved as she seemed to appear. Looking at her once again with the idea of trying to discern her intentions, he shouted to her over the blare of the music and the voices all around them.

"Yes. I saw my mother."

"Good? Bad? What?" She asked her questions in an excited jumble, then suddenly calmed herself enough to sort them out. "What I mean is, what did you see? Was it your mother as she is now, or in the past, or . . ."

"It was the past. My mother's dead."

"Oh, sorry." Karen touched London's arm.

"Yeah," answered the detective, "so am I. I flashed on the night she died. It's nothing to apologize about. She died of lung cancer—about fifteen years ago. It's just that it's the second time today and . . ."

"You saw her in the crystal twice today?"

"No . . . not in the crystal. I had the first experience in my office when . . ."

And then; London suddenly wearied of trying to be heard over the noxious noise levels of the bar any longer. He found himself sweating profusely, his temples aching, eyes burning. Motioning to Karen to stand, he threw some money on the table to cover their drinks and then rose himself, his throbbing head almost spinning from the exertion. Getting his Blackthorn cane in hand, he pulled the corners of the red silk together around the crystal, then hefted it and headed for the front door. Karen joined him on the sidewalk, showing him more than a casual stranger's concern.

"What's the matter?" she asked, genuine concern coloring her voice. "You're all pale, and sweating. Are you all right?"

"Yes," he answered, assuring both Karen and himself. "I'm fine. It was just the noise in there—that and the heat from all the people."

"Oh, I know what you mean," she agreed. "I always feel the same way. Big crowds are hard to handle sometimes. I mean, all that free energy in the air is exciting, but sometimes it is hard to focus through it."

London, leaning against a relatively clean storefront, mopped at his brow with his sleeve. He ran his hand over his neck and behind his ears, gathering up what sweat he could. Wiping it on his suit pants, he said;

"Well, I hate to be the one to cut the evening short, but I'm starting to feel a little under it all. I think I'd best be shoving off."

"Oh, please," Karen protested, "this is all my fault. I shouldn't have rushed you so fast." Smiling at London, she took his arm gently, saying;

"Let me make it up to you. I promise I won't even try to separate you from your crystal again tonight."

"What did you have in mind?"

"My apartment is only a few blocks from here. Let me take you there. We can relax and really talk. I'll put on some music, the kind people used to put on when they wanted something to enjoy listening to, not hide behind."

London smiled at her words despite himself. Encouraged, she continued, promising him;

"And then I'll make you some orange-green tea that will perk you right up. You can see my crystal collection and then you'll know why I'm so fascinated by yours. Com'on—you'll enjoy it. We'll both enjoy it."

"We will, huh?" answered London.

"Sure, we're both all grown up. I'm sure we can find some way to amuse ourselves."

At this hint, the detective looked again into the woman's eyes, searching for any possible sort of duplicity one last time. Finding nothing, he decided to put aside his suspicions. Handing her his silken bundle, he said;

"Why not? Frankly, I'd love to put my hands on everything in your collection." Taking his arm again, she leaned over and rubbed her head against his shoulder, telling him;

"It's a big collection."

"I've got big hands."

Entwining the fingers of her left hand in those of his right, she told him;

"You certainly do."

Stretched out on Karen's sofa, London tried to assemble what he knew while waiting for her to come back from her bedroom. She had made a pot of tea first, then left him—"just for a minute, I promise"—to change clothes. Deciding to relax a bit himself, the detective had taken off his tie and shoulder holster. Wrapping them in his jacket, he laid them along with his Blackthorn on a nearby over-stuffed armchair, and then loosened his top two shirt buttons while settling in on the couch.

Pouring himself some tea, he held the cup to his nose, letting the steam roll up into and through his sinuses. As the heat penetrated throughout, soothing his headache, he laid out the meager pieces he had to his puzzle neatly, but found he was still not able to make any sense of them. He also could neither fit Karen into the picture, nor definitely rule her out.

"I just don't know enough yet," he admitted.

Sipping his tea, he looked from point to point in the room, wishing he had Wally with him. Although he was no expert, he was certain that a number of the things he was staring at were worth a great deal. Even without the appraiser's assistance, the detective could tell that, at the least, Ms. Karen Tezzler had very good taste.

As he inspected the room from his seat, he started making mental notes on the cost of the things around him. None of the art on the walls appeared to be prints. There was nothing of the extremely modern to be seen, either. The works were by artists from older times, confident in their realities—the most recent craftsman he recognized being Maxfield Parrish.

"I don't know what line you're in, Ms. Tezzler," the detective muttered to himself, "but whatever it is, you must make a hell of a lot doing it."

London stood at that point, fetching his walking stick, then crossing the room to inspect a shelf of well-dusted curios. Some of them were functional craft objects, tea pots, mirrors, knives, goblets, et cetera, but most of them were natural—minerals or crystals—quite a number of them carved into distinctive shapes. The detective went up and down the shelves, taking each piece in in its turn—a Buddha, two tigers at play, several warrior figures, several dancers, groups of running horses, nine intertwined dragons all happily chasing and fighting over the same sphere, elephants, one corner given over to twelve animals all intricately carved as one set that London eventually recognized as the symbols of the Chinese zodiac.

Of the scores to choose from, one carving in particular impressed him enough to stop him in his tracks. It was light green in color, almost translucent, the detective assuming it to be jade. A little over a foot in height, it depicted a half-dozen exotic goldfish swimming in and out of a willowy bed of seaweed. Closer inspection showed him a pair of frogs peeking at the fish from their hiding places on the bottom. He was still staring at it when the woman returned.

"Oh, isn't that one beautiful?"

London turned, the answer ready in his mind but not able to make its way to his lips. Karen entered the room, the sight of her stealing the detective's breath, his reason, and a good portion of his wits. The woman had peeled out of her red leather, trading it for richly embroidered silk. It was a large robe-like affair, shot through with gold threads, enveloping her from her neck on down. Part of the detective's brain was willing to bet the gold was real. Another part, the part he relied upon to keep him alive, realized that a change of clothes was not spectacular enough to account for his extreme reactions. At a loss for words, stumbling for something—anything—to say, London managed to ask;

"How . . . how did you, ah, get such a collection together?"

"Ahhh, you know, time and money. What else are you going to do with them? Come on," she said, heading for the couch. "Sit down, talk to me. Let's dig into each other."

"Sure," answered London, easing himself back down into the cushions. "Sure."

"So, ask away—what do you want to know?"

Again the detective tried to speak and again he found himself unable to form a coherent sentence. Even as panic spread through his consciousness, warning him that something was wrong, he continued to fumble for an answer to her question, finally just spreading his hands in helpless defeat. Smiling good-naturedly, as if she had seen the same reaction in men ten thousand times in the past, the woman said softly;

"Okay, okay, I guess I know the question that you want answered . . . don't I?"

London knew what she meant, but did not know how to tell her the bedroom was not on his mind. No part of him had any serious carnal interest in Karen Tezzler. But a dulling curtain had somehow settled over his brain, slowing his powers of decision to where he had no real will of his own. Indeed, when the detective looked up into her smile, he found all he could do was smile back. With that as her cue, Karen took his hand, telling him;

"I must admit I'm surprised to see my 'charms' working so quickly, especially on a big, powerful boy like yourself. They must be more devastating than I thought."

After her glib comment, however, the woman furrowed her brow, entertaining a thought for a moment. It gave her a second's pause, but in the end, it merely made her laugh. Dismissing it out of hand, she said;

"Come on, now, I think we can find a slightly better place than this."

And with that, the woman entwined the detective's fingers in her own, bidding him rise, and then led him down the hall to her bedroom.

CHAPTER FOURTREEN

THE DETECTIVE'S EYES OPENED, straining against the surrounding darkness. Touch was the first sense to respond with useful information, letting him know that there was a body next to him—Karen's. He ran one hand gently over her form, gathering what facts he could. She was asleep, breathing peacefully, warm to the touch, only half-clothed. Her silk robe was ripped in a score of places. A touch of his fingertips to his tongue revealing gold filigree under his nails.

As his eyes began to pick out the features of the bedroom, London's memory flooded back to him. As he shrugged off the befuddlement of some thing heavier than sleep in his mind, he began to remember their passion. Thoughts of Lisa filled his mind. He questioned what it was that could have possessed him? In the morning he had been cursing his inability to bring himself to the threshold of even simple mental love anymore. Now, he had allowed himself to be led to a stranger's bed where he had indulged, and been indulged, in every whim that had come to his mind.

The barking dogs of conscience, usually calm-toned voices of question, were now howling maniacs, baying incessantly, their message lost in the level of their fury. Slipping himself out of the foreign bed, London arched his back, surprised to find that he was not in the least stiff or sore. A carnal smile played across his face, a bit of swelling ego, mixed with surprise, laughing that he could have indulged in the marathon in which he had and feel no effects whatsoever.

Well, he thought, half his brain curious as to where his clothes were, half of it not, if someone will just explain what's going on to me, then we'll both know.

He wandered the apartment, searching for answers without having any tangible questions. He did not know who Karen Tezzler was but, he wondered, did it actually matter? If she was a vampire or their tool, why was he still alive? A small voice within his instincts still insisted she was after something other than just Mrs. Lu's crystal ball, but he had no idea what it could be, or how it could possibly tie in with his own mission.

And besides that, he was forced to ask himself, why had he slept with her? Indeed, how had it even been possible? That morning he had not even thought himself capable of an erection. Now, the spent form curled up in the bed behind him gave silent testimony to the fact that he had been wrong on that count—more than once. Their sex—only a schoolgirl would have called it "lovemaking"—had been violent and brutal, a clawing, biting, forceful encounter. They had both battered and smothered—forcing sweat and drawing blood that they had fought to lick from each other's bodies.

As he walked her room in what seemed like a dream haze, more and more of their time together came back to him. He remembered choking her at one point, as well as the sensation of her hands piercing his skin, her knuckles bent around his rib cage, shaking him like a bell. What it all meant, he was not certain. But he was determined to try to find out. Moving quietly, he began an inspection of the apartment while its exhausted owner continued to lightly snore.

He thumbed through the papers in the antique desk in Karen's bedroom, reviewed the contents of her closets, dressers, and various shelves, hoping to find something that might link her to the mystery he was trying to unravel. Nothing he found moved him any closer to a solution—until the globes of light began to flicker in the living room.

At first they seemed almost an illusion—a trick in the corner of his eye he was not even sure he had seen. Intrigued, though, he went to them—curious but without the slightest guess as to what he was looking at. They appeared to be some unsubstantial form of energy. They glowed softly, giving off only light, not heat, most of them roughly the size of golf balls.

Floating throughout the apartment, they multiplied rapidly, seeming to double their number every few seconds. London watched them intently. Sometimes they would go around each other, sometimes they would collide. Some would stop moving and merely hang in space; others would speed up and shoot off—some in a straight line, some in a curve, others in precise angles—disappearing through the walls or floor or ceiling. All of it happening for no reason the detective could discern.

Then, suddenly, they all began to grow. Each of the pale round lights started mutating in form, sometimes overlapping, some times existing one within the other like Chinese boxes. As they grew larger, they pushed against one another for space, gaining something akin to substance, beginning to crowd each other out of the room.

Then, as the detective continued to watch, he realized the spheres were taking humanoid form, stretching themselves heads and legs and arms. He wondered at the fact he felt no panic. Before he could explore the notion, though, one of the lights substantialized into a generally recognizable form.

Before London's eyes it took on the shape of a mariner—knotted rope in hand, girdled and skirted, a look of the Mediterranean to its face. Another crystallized, taking the form of a frightened Victorian workman. Another, a dying monk—another, a crying stockyard man—another, a blank-eyed soldier, dressed in desert gear fifteen centuries out-of-date.

They filled the room, blurring each other as they surrounded London, all of their faces staring at the detective. Craning his neck in a circular motion,

London realized that he was indeed the focus of their attention. He noted other facts as well—that all of them were men, that all of them were from different eras, different lands, different races. They did not complain as he studied them; they merely stared at him with hollow looks, no souls reflected in their empty, lifeless eyes.

And then, suddenly, London's mind jolted awake. Wake up—the protective sections of his brain screamed—start thinking!

Why, it asked, aren't you tired? Why aren't there any bruises on your body? Any scratches?

The detective had walked from the bedroom without his cane, without feeling the throbbing ache of his half-dead leg. How? What was happening to him? And, most importantly, why was he not more than only mildly curious about the multitude of phantoms surrounding him?

And then, the ancient shades parted, making room for more modern figures. Before London could begin to attempt answers to all of his other questions, he found himself confronted by a never-ending procession of twentieth-century forms. Men, women, and children this time, most in bedclothes. They all wore tortured faces filled with pain, and all of them stared at the detective, hating him. It only took a minute before he realized who they were. When he finally awoke, back in Karen Tezzler's bed room, he was screaming.

◆　◆　◆

"What's the matter, lover?"

The woman hung on to London's arm, holding him in the bed, afraid he might go crashing to the floor. The detective got hold of himself after a moment, able to control his voice but not his body. He found himself shaking with fear, a fear born of the knowledge of where he had been and what had happened to him there. As Karen tried to comfort him, he swallowed several great breaths, forcing himself to calm down. Once he had finally eliminated the violent spasms racking his body, he said;

"I'm all right now. Thanks."

Karen pushed up against him, closing her eyes, hugging him tightly. As he continued to breathe deeply, she asked;

"Bad dream?"

"You might say that."

"What would you call it?"

"I was more than dreaming . . . I was . . . in a place, what a 'friend' of mine calls the dreamplane. It's an area beyond one's mind—outside the level of normal dreaming. I don't know how to explain it. I really don't even know much more about it than that."

"Well," she asked, "what did you see there that got you so upset?"

"People," he told her. "Nearly two million of them. Some I didn't know, but . . . most of them I did."

"But why were they so upsetting to you?"

"Because," he told her, "I killed most of them."

Still hugging him, the woman went a bit stiff, a reaction for which the detective did not fault her. Hugging her back mechanically, mostly as a reassuring gesture, he told her;

"Hey—you know what I'm talking about. You know how dreams are. Don't worry about it. Let's just get, ahhh, a little cleaned up. I think all I really need is some cold water on my face and I'll be fine."

Karen let go of the detective, nodding in agreement. Holding her arms out from her sides, she showed off her shredded robe, saying;

"You might have a point there. You've got me looking like somebody's old rag doll." Pointing to the left, she said, "The bathroom's through there. You pull yourself together and I'll do the same and I'll meet you in the living room for a drink."

Having no better answer, the detective smiled, telling her, "Deal."

Minutes later, half dressed, inspecting himself in the bathroom mirror, London began to finally piece his wits together. He had somehow slipped onto the dreamplane after his romp with Karen. How that had happened, he was not certain. During his struggles with the Q'talu, he had been pulled there twice by a need to find Lisa. Although he did not understand the properties of the dimension, or how they worked, he did know that dying there meant one would die in the "real" world as well. Which was the main reason he had avoided traveling there since his struggles two months earlier. But, he wondered, what had dragged him there this time?

"Just another question," he told his reflection in the mirror, "As if I don't have enough already."

Struggling into his shirt, he winced at the pain his real body was in. Sex with Karen Tezzler was a strenuous proposition. A thought that made him wonder again—why had he done it? At that point he was perfectly willing to accept any reason—that he wanted to win her confidence so he might discover her involvement in what was happening, that he was desperate to break away from Lisa and wanted to use Karen to drive her away, that he had just suddenly been in the mood for raw sex and had taken it when offered—any answer whatsoever that even half rang of the truth he would have welcomed like a long lost lover.

But London's mind had nothing to offer him. As he thought back on what had happened, he had to admit that all he remembered was Karen suggesting they bed down . . . period. He had not agreed or disagreed—he had simply . . . performed.

Why? he wondered again. Why?

Making his way to the living room, this time in greater need of his walking stick than he had been all day, he again noted the multitude of dazzling pieces of art all around him. Dropping himself onto the welcome cushions of the couch, he studied a piece of bamboo, intricately carved in the shape of a basket of fruit, sitting next to him on an end table. As he looked at it closely, he could see that the artist had worked several mice into his design, all of them stealing grapes from the basket.

Karen returned while he was still studying the bamboo, carrying two glasses of sparkling water, each with fruit slices bobbing within them. As she approached, the detective thanked her for the drink. Placing it on the end table next to the basket, he asked;

"Tell me"—his hands indicated the pieces all about him—"how did you gather all of this? I mean, I've seen museums that didn't have this good a selection."

"Please, you'll make me blush."

"No," asked London, beginning to wonder just how anyone could have amassed such an amazing private collection. "I'm serious."

"Oh, come on," answered the woman in earnest, acting as if she really did not understand the detective's question. "You know how it is, it just takes time. I've lugged some of this junk around for centuries. Haven't you hung on to bits and pieces as the years have gone by?"

London let his mind's eye wander through his apartment. Out side of the mirror in his front room, he could not think of a thing that he had bothered to lug around with him in the way Karen apparently had. He told her;

"I don't know, not really. I guess life just seems too short to me."

"'Life just seems too short?'" she repeated his words as if she had never contemplated the thought before.

"Life seems too short."

She said it again, without the questioning tone to her voice, and then suddenly began to chuckle. As the detective stared at her, she threw her head back and laughed full and hard, as if he could not have possibly said anything funnier.

"Oh," she told him, gasping for air. "You are a riot. Oh, I have to tell that one to Jorhsa. Oh, my ... oh ..."

And then, Karen noticed the look on London's face. She had expected to see a satisfied expression, one that told her London was pleased at having made her laugh. Instead, however, she saw puzzlement, a baffled expression that let her know the detective had been perfectly serious.

"I don't understand," she told him. "I thought you were joking ... I thought ..."

London's brain raced, completing the sentence she had started to speak. He knew she had thought him privy to some secret. For some reason she had believed him to be someone who thought, like her, that the concept of life being short was a joke—the funniest one in the world.

"Oh, no," came the woman's voice, now reduced to the barest of whispers.

Of course, it had only been seconds but, by the time the word "vampire" had formed in the detective's mind, Karen Tezzler had secured a vicious blade from her collection and was already half way across the room.

CHAPTER FIFTEEN

T HE WOMAN LEAPT FROM ten feet away, the blade in her hand aimed at London's midsection. Instinctively, the detective hefted his Blackthorn and swung it with all his might, dealing the woman a vicious blow to the head. The hardwood knob of the cane connected solidly, sending her spinning off course. Standing erect, London went for Veronica, pulling the blade free from his boot with a quick, snapping motion seconds before Karen regained her footing.

"Miserable scum," she growled under her breath. "Fucking miserable wink scum."

London did not answer her, saving his energy for the struggle to come, wishing Betty were not tangled in the folds of his jacket, a lifetime away across the room. Karen came in slower the second time, her blade in front of her.

She slashed viciously but London managed to block, sparks jumping as their weapons' concaves crashed against each other. The detective stepped up onto and over the back of the couch, putting the large piece between the two of them. Sneering at his efforts, Karen backed off several steps herself, then bounded forward and leapt upward, heading straight for the detective. London stumbled backward awkwardly out of the way of her attack. He avoided the vampire's blade by a hair's breadth but dropped his cane while doing so.

Circling around to the front of the couch, he grabbed for his jacket, getting a firm grip on it but losing Betty, the .38 falling free of his grip and bouncing out of reach. Making the best of things, though, he whipped his jacket in a circular motion, quickly balling it around his free hand. As Karen circled the couch, he feigned another retreat, only to then suddenly step forward into her attack. Catching the edge of her blade in his weapon's quillon, he snapped his wrist sharply, bending her knife back toward her. Karen's free hand came down in a fist on his back—once—twice—twice more. London staggered from the blows, tears welling in both his eyes. Somehow ignoring the pain, however, the detective pushed forward with his padded hand, shoving Karen's blade deep into her body.

"Son of a bitch!"

Swinging with all her might, the woman caught London on the side of the head. The blow sent him reeling off balance, crashing into one of the display cases of crystal. Hundreds of thousands of dollars' worth shattered noisily against the wall and floor. Across the room, Karen stood shaking her head, chuckling at her own stupidity.

"Thirty centuries of gathering . . . well, it's not like I didn't deserve that."

"Deserve 'what'?" gasped London, dragging himself up from the floor. "What are you talking about?"

Karen pulled at her knife, wincing slightly at the pain as she worked it from between her ribs. Caught at a bad angle, the blade scraped along one of the bones the entire way, causing her to shudder as she worked it back out of her body.

"I thought you were one of us. The look of you—the smell of you. Where does a wink get all that power?"

"What power?" asked London desperately. "What's a 'wink?' What are you talking about?!"

Blood sluiced out of the vampire's side, spilling down her robe, coating her legs, soaking her rug. She ignored the sopping outpour as if it were inconsequential, smiling ruefully and shaking her head.

"You, you bastard—you're a wink."

"What?"

"A wink!" she screamed. "A drop in the bucket, a moment in time—a blink of the eye—*a wink!*"

And then suddenly she was moving again, coming at the panting detective with her bloodied weapon. London stepped wide of her attack, savagely kicking her in the side as she went by. The woman struggled to keep her balance but lost the battle, slipping on her own blood as a large fragment broken off from one of her shattered antiques dug into her foot. She landed badly on her side, several more pointed shards piercing her when she hit.

London, tiring rapidly, moved forward as quickly as he could, bringing his heel down on Karen's ankle with all the force he could muster. The woman screamed in pain, the end of her howl curling into a gutter dog's snarl. Ignoring her noises, the detective raised his foot and then brought it down again—hard—this time shattering her femur. The vampire cried out sharply, her knife dropping out of her hand as she swung her arms about wildly, clutching at the air in pain.

Using the last of the adrenal burst flashing through him, London raised his foot and brought it down again—higher—this time shattering the tibia of her other leg. Flashing white bone broke through the deeply tanned skin in two places, sending racking pain throughout the woman's body.

Bloody spittle foamed up through the vampire's tightly clenched teeth. London staggered across the room, both to retrieve his Blackthorn and to put some distance between himself and the hissing monster writhing on the floor. Sitting on the arm of the couch the farthest away from her, the detective gulped down a few deep breaths and then asked;

"So, now that I have your attention, tell me, what put you on to me?"

The woman gave no answer, merely fixing London with a hateful stare.

Not impressed, the detective took his walking stick in hand and then swung it from behind his back over his head with all the force he could, bringing it down on the vampire's ruined legs. The blow caused her to shriek and sputter. Her nails dug into the carpeting as she tried to quiet herself. As her body shook from her efforts to control her pain, London told her;

"Yes, you better be quiet. I'm sure you don't want the police here any more than I do. In your condition, they'll take you to the hospital. Wouldn't they? And my bet is you wouldn't want a group of doctors poking around your insides. Any more than you'd want the police asking me a lot of questions. No, Ms. Tezzler, my guess is that you wouldn't want that. Would you?"

When the vampire did not answer, London, almost too tired to do so, raised his cane, secretly hoping he would not have to use it again. The bluff worked.

"No," came the woman's croaking voice. "No, I wouldn't want that."

"There. I knew you could be reasonable. Now, let's try this all over again. What put you on to me? Why'd you come after me in the street?"

"I wanted your crystal, just like I told you."

"Something tells me there's a bit more to the story than that." Swallowing her pain, working to get her breathing under control, the woman asked London;

"Why are you playing this game? You know what's been going on as well as I do." The vampire stared up at the detective, looking for the signs of a reprieve in his face. Finding nothing, she continued;

"Great, a tough guy. All right, fine. We'll do this your way. I saw you at the old woman's shop—watched you retrieve her ball. I wanted it, but I hadn't wanted to go in after it. Not after what had happened earlier. Four of us dead in one night . . . I wanted that fucking crystal, but not enough to risk running into whatever had done in the Muzz."

At that point she looked up at London again, her expression asking if she had said enough. The detective gave her one back that let her know she had not. A menacing heft of his stick goaded her into continuing.

"I was willing to wait, though. I was hoping someone would bring it out—a cop, a relative . . . somebody. When I saw you with it, I thought—look at that . . . one of us—tall and dark and filled with tasty—it's my lucky day.

"My lucky day."

The woman repeated the words with an angry sneer, and then, she started to laugh. It was a painful, self-mocking sound, filled with bitterness and self-recrimination. Eventually, the harshness of it set her to coughing, blood-soaked phlegm bubbling over her chin, spilling down her neck and into her robe. Eventually getting her hysteria under control, though, she caught her breath and then continued.

"Forgive me my little joke. So, tell me, are you what killed the Muzz?" London nodded. The woman whistled weakly.

"Of all the people I thought would never die . . . ," she said in a hollow voice that trailed off into a whisper, more to herself than to him. The detective watched her face register the fact that he had been the one to kill the Muzz. She seemed as incredulous as the three he had confronted at Mrs. Lu's. Seeing Tezzler's near inability to accept the fact, London wondered to himself;

Jesus—who was that guy, anyway?

He thought to ask the vampire why everyone regarded the Muzz so highly, but held off.

One thing at a time, he told himself.

Then, Tezzler asked him, "So? What now?"

"Now? Now you spill your guts and I listen. You tell me why Mrs. Lu was killed. You tell me whose idea it was. You tell me what vampires are and where they come from. You tell me why you thought I was one of you at first, and then how you figured out I wasn't."

"Small order."

"I try to be accommodating."

"I was being sarcastic," the woman growled.

"So was I," answered London. "Now get busy and tell me what I want to know. You're not the only parasite on my list tonight."

The vampire started to breathe rapidly, short, shallow gulps of air, filling her bloodstream with oxygen. In between gasps, she choked out;

"I'm sorry . . . I won't . . . be able to . . . help you much . . . Oh, I can . . . give you a few . . ."

The detective listened to the woman, watching her as she continued her rapid breathing. He knew something was happening that he did not understand, but saw no alternative to simply waiting and listening.

"The Lu bitch . . . had to go . . . too much trouble . . . like her son . . . had to go . . ."

The vampire's body began to shake, legs trembling, fists clenched, teeth chattering in between breaths. Sweat rolled off the woman's forehead, glistening her cheeks, pouring over her chin, thinning the blood coating her throat.

"Council said they had to die . . . pain in . . . the ass . . . bastards . . . trying to get . . . people stirred up . . . as if anyone could stop us . . . anyone . . .

"Anyone at all."

And then, suddenly, the shattered body on the floor started to make its way to its knees. The detective's eyes grew wide—his mouth hanging open. The woman hissed through clenched teeth, ignoring the pain screaming through every part of her as she dragged her way across the floor. London snapped out of his amazement and hurled himself to the side. He came up against the arm of the couch and simply threw himself upward over it, seconds before the woman's nails tore open the cushion on which he had been sitting.

"You want to know what vampires are, you wink?" screamed the woman as she clawed her way up the couch. "We're your fucking death, you scumlick!"

London stared down the vampire's body as she crawled up over the back of the couch. He looked at her legs—blood stanched, bones knitting, flesh growing together right before his eyes. Somewhere in the back of the detective's brain, calm realizations were pointing out to him the differences in the kinds of damage he did to the Muzz and the kinds he had done to Karen. The front of his brain, however, was fixating on her claw-like nails and the distance between them and himself.

"That's it," she whispered, her voice now soft—filled with a seductive mix of sultry whisper and little girl giggle. "You just stay right there and wait for Karen. I want to show you some thing."

London's back hit the corner. The feel of the walls broke his retreat, surprising him with the fact that he had nowhere else to go. He fumbled Veronica free from his pocket, but before he could grab it securely, the knife slipped through the sweat coating his left hand, bouncing away from him. Grabbing awkwardly at his Blackthorn with both hands, he straightened himself up, telling the vampire;

"Well, darlin', I sure hope it's something special."

The woman kept moving forward, halfway over the couch. As she gingerly tested her feet against the floor, her expression shook her face violently, half of it pain, half of it relief that the pain was not as bad as she had expected.

"Ohhhhhhhhh," she answered, her voice still soft, gently mesmerizing. "It's special, all right. You know what I'm going to do to you, my sweet Ted? I'm going to drag your heart out of your chest and show it to you. Right through your breastbone. With my bare hands."

She snapped her fingers.

"Just like that."

Then, nodding her head impishly, she grinned at him, saying, "Oh, yes I am. In fact, the last thing you're going to see before you die is me taking a big bite out of it."

Her hands came up slowly, reaching for the detective.

"But then, maybe, if you're as strong as you look, and you live just long enough, the last thing you'll see is me spitting it in your face."

"Well," said London, "I'll grant you—that's special, all right."

And then, as the vampire moved toward him, the detective brought his walking stick up with all his might, ramming the contact end of the stick through her chest. Her eyes burst wide open. She made to scream, but nothing came forward. Wasting no time, London moved the cane back and forth, levering open the monster's chest. Blood sprayed forth in massive arcs, soaking him and the wall behind him. The detective ignored the mess, reaching down to the floor for Veronica. Copying the actions of the old man he had encountered at Mrs. Lu's, he drew the blade across Karen Tezzler's throat, savagely spilling the life from her without a moment's hesitation.

More blood splattered free from the vampire's body with the action. London staggered back from the carnage he had wrought, stunned at the horror of it, his chest and hands, his face and hair drenched in scarlet. He fell into a heap on the floor, panting with exhaustion and relief. He took in what air he could in ragged gasps, his head and back to the wall, eyes closed. They opened again at the sound of the vampire's voice.

"How . . .?" she asked in dying surprise. "Howwwwww?"

Her voice was a fading whisper, the sound of wind-driven sand moving across the dunes at night. London started at the creature, watching the confusion stretched across its face. He could see it deep in the reflection of its eyes, the knowledge that it was dying—dying without the ability to believe it was possible. And then, suddenly, the eyes that had blazed so intently only moments earlier glazed over dumbly—inert—cold.

Karen Tezzler was dead—finally.

CHAPTER
SIXTEEN

L ONDON SHUT HIS EYES again, hoping for a moment's respite. Trying to calm the rapid pace of his heart, ignoring his trembling hands,
he busied himself with simple tasks—straightening his collar, tracking
down Betty, cleaning Veronica, then sliding her back within her sheath. Finished, he sat on the couch gulping down great lungsful of air. He clutched his
walking stick to his chest as he did so, holding onto the solid length of root
as if it were a life line.

Before a handful of seconds could pass, however, a tingling sensation
pricked at him, interrupting his panic. The detective's eyes opened sharply.
His head turned from side to side, looking about as he actually expected to
find something touching him. He saw nothing.

Nothing looked different anywhere in the apartment, and yet, the uncomfortable feeling continued, traveling up and down his body. Electrical in
nature, it stabbed at his eyes and ears, his nose, throat, mouth, and fingertips.
It rolled over him, burning its way up his rectal passage, filling his intestines,
his stomach, liver, lungs, his heart, and then his brain, exploding out of him
only to settle on his skin and seep back into him through his pores. The sensation grew in intensity for a half minute that seemed like forever and then
disappeared, leaving the detective confused and burning.

Wiping at his sweating brow, London fought at the voices once more raging
within his brain, stirred up by the unidentifiable sensation. He had escaped
them for—so long—almost an entire day. Now, seeing the faces of the dead,
hearing them again, was almost enough to push him over into madness. Of
course, he now recognized many of the screams wailing inside his head, having
heard them so often since the Conflagration. But suddenly it seemed as if he
could hear new ones, older voices in unrecognizable tongues, bleating at him
for release in the same wearying tones. Cursing them all, with a harshness of
will he did not think he had within him, he drove all of the voices away with
a single, overpowering thought, slamming them backward once more into
dark silence.

Then, when finally he could again open his eyes, he looked toward the
mangled corpse stretched out a few feet away from him. It still lay where it
had fallen, the rush of blood finally reducing to a trickle.

What had happened to him did not seem to have been caused by it. Nor,
as in some uninspired motion picture, had it been replaced by a heap of de-

composing ashes, surrounded by a swirling fog. It was solid and, the detective knew—remembering the rest of the world through the haze of bizarreness that had assaulted him throughout the evening—proof positive to anyone that might respond to the noise he and the deceased had made that he was a murderer. In fact, everything around and about him was proof.

"Not bad," he said to himself. "Everything in the place is smashed, half of it with your fingerprints on it. You've left behind hair in the sink and sperm on the sheets. And if the police don't get to those mundane clues, we've got a savagely mutilated body—of a beautiful young woman, no less—and a suspect covered from head to toe in her blood type. A tired, battered suspect who looks like he just got done beating someone to death."

The detective laughed sardonically, almost amused at his situation. "Yeah," he concluded. "Not bad at all."

With that, he pushed his way up from the floor, using his Blackthorn for support. Making his way across the room, he strapped on his shoulder harness and stored Betty within it. Then he stooped to pick up Mrs. Lu's crystal ball when a sound coming from the front of the apartment made him stop—the sound of a key opening a deadbolt lock.

What now?

The question formed silently in the detective's brain, the thought of someone else coming in then, after all that had happened, striking him as almost comical. In no mood to laugh, however, London moved forward to the door, jerking it open with a harsh yank the instant both its locks had cleared. A man of average build and appearance came tumbling in, stumbling off balance from the detective's motion. As he fell, London slammed the door shut and then moved over top of the fallen figure.

"What are you doing here?" he snapped.

"I—I," the man stuttered badly, trying to regain his composure. "I was—was supposed to meet Karen tonight—we had a hunt date."

The man's line of vision circled the room, taking in the incredible damage. His eyes grew wide at the sight of the destruction of the dead woman's collection. They began to tear when he saw her body.

"How? Who?"

"I don't know anything about any hunt date," said the detective, ignoring the man's questions. Shaking him by the collar, London worked to keep his advantage, steamrolling the man with questions.

"Who are you?"

"T-Tabor. Martin Tabor. I really was supposed to be here. Oh, pulse and breath and sweet, sweet life. What happened to Karen? What happened?" Praying for luck, the detective answered;

"She tricked that wink into coming up here—you know, the one who killed Muzz."

Martin Tabor's breath rushed in sharply.

"It's a wink? A *wink?!*"

London nodded slightly, his eyes riveted to the man's face.

"Who is this maniac?" demanded Tabor, his arms shaking, eyes tearing. "That . . . that's five now! Five of us—in just one night! This is madness—some sort of horrible madness. I—I—I can't deal with this."

London helped the man up off the floor, even brushing him off. Working at lulling him into a false sense of friendship, he continued telling his story.

"She thought we could handle him—figured that would impress everybody. I tried to talk her out of it but, her mind was made up. You know, ah," the detective gauged the length of his pause for sincerity, then finished, "... *knew* Karen."

Martin sobbed again, nodding his head in agreement. His single tears expanded, now rushing in torrents down both his cheeks. Try as he might to look around the room he could not steer his eyes for long from the bloodied corpse near the windows. London marveled that he was getting away with his tactic until a voice within his head reminded him that Tezzler had thought him a vampire.

I don't know why, he mused, but if she thought I was one of them, maybe it makes sense this guy does, too.

Taking advantage of Tabor's rattled state, the detective kept going, twisting the truth into a story designed to push the smaller man to the breaking point.

"He was just too strong for us. I couldn't believe it. He threw us both around as if we were bags of feathers—as if all our power was nothing to him—broke our legs. We screamed our lungs out—both of us. Nobody came. He tortured Karen for hours, smashing her treasures, and, and . . ." the detective hesitated just long enough to sound contrite, then finished in an angry tone, "and then he abused her—over and over."

London went silent for a moment after that, sharing in Martin's grief. He maneuvered him into the overstuffed chair, brushing at imaginary dirt on the smaller man's suit. Then, before he gave Martin time enough to think, he told him;

"I'm sorry I jumped you when you came in. I should have realized that you were opening the door with a key—but I just didn't think. I was afraid it was him come back to finish me off. I didn't know what else to do." London sat next to Martin, confiding in him.

"Karen wounded the wink just as he killed her. He had crippled me, was going to finish me after her. But she managed to tear a piece of his chest out when he stabbed her. I watched his face—his pain—he really is just a . . ." The detective searched for Karen's words to him.

"Just a drop in the bucket."

"A mortal," said Martin with a helpless shudder, "killing the Blessed. No, not killing, slaughtering—slaughtering us, as if we were sheep."

The smaller man turned to London, grabbing at his shoulders, shaking him. Unable to control the hysteria mounting within himself any longer, Martin cried;

"She thought she was so smart—that she had all the answers—sound-proofed this place so no one would be able to hear when she brought home a snack. But you said it. No one heard you. No one came. Oh, what will we do? What can we do against this monster?"

London shook his head, half his brain working on maintaining his charade, the other half looking for some way to get himself out the door. From what he had heard so far, the detective was certain Martin was another vampire—one of the "Blessed," as he had put it—and London was in no shape to fight another superpowerful being, even one as cringing as the one next to him. He would have liked to search the dead woman's apartment but, he knew at that point that the most sensible thing was for him to get out as quickly as possible. Finally, he said;

"Look. We have to do something. We've got to tell someone about this, let the . . . council know what's happened." As Martin started to calm down, listening to London, the detective continued;

"I want you to stay here—guard . . . Karen . . . until someone can come to get her."

"But where are you going to go?" asked the vampire. London gambled, using the last scrap he had picked up from his conversation with the dead woman.

"I'm going to get the news to Jorhsa," he said. "We've got to get someone on this wink's trail while he's still wounded. We've got to stop this thing before it goes any further."

Martin looked at the detective nervously. London knew the idea of staying alone in the apartment did not sit easily with him. Reminding himself what would happen if the man on the couch next to him realized who he really was, the detective stood up, grabbing his jacket from where he had dropped it. Sliding it on in the hopes it would hide most of the blood coating his clothes, he increased his tone, ordering Martin;

"You stay and wait for the others. The monster knows this place and may have managed to tie into the phone lines."

"Oh," protested the smaller man. "He—he . . . couldn't. Could he?"

"I wouldn't have thought so before tonight, but then, I wouldn't have thought anyone could kill so many of us in one night, either. I don't think we should jump to far into paranoia but, then again, I don't think we should be taking chances, either. I'm going to go down to the street, find a pay phone and call the council. They'll take care of things. Then I'll come back—just as soon as I get though to somebody."

Finding the courage from somewhere within himself to agree to London's sensible-sounding plan, the crying vampire nodded weakly, saying;

"Yes, you go. I'll wait here." He turned then, staring over the back of the couch, looking again at the corpse on the floor. "I'll wait here. I'll be all right. You go. Yes, you've suffered enough. You should go."

London crossed the room silently, trying not to draw attention to his cane, just in case there was no such thing as a limping vampire. Then he picked up Mrs. Lu's crystal and slipped into the hall as quietly as he could, listening to Martin's pitiful sobs until the soundproofed door finally closed behind him.

CHAPTER
SEVENTEEN

"I DON'T UNDERSTAND IT, PAUL," said the detective in a fragile, tired voice. "But for some reason I can't explain, they both thought I was a vampire."

"All of 'em, boss?"

"Well, I'm not actually sure," admitted London, still trying to determine whether or not he was correct even as he continued. "Maybe not the Muzz, or the three that tried to avenge him. But the girl, and the little one I left in her apartment . . . there's no doubt they both thought that I was one of them."

It was late in the afternoon of the next day—one Theodore London had thought for a while he might not get to see. On the night before, once the detective had escaped Karen Tezzler's apartment, he had switched his way through a series of cabs, leading anyone who might be following him on a dizzying chase. Then, finally deciding it was safe to do so, he took the last cab directly to his partner's neighborhood. There he stripped away his blood-soaked clothes, leaving it to Paul to dispose of them permanently. And while the ex-maintenance man did so, London steamed away his tension in a hot shower.

He stayed under the burning water a long time, working at calming his nerves. Soaping himself all over for the third time, scrubbing at the blood that was no longer there, he ran the happenings of the day over in his head, trying to make sense of them. Coming up with no answers that could explain everything that had happened to him, he was forced to admit that he was just too tired to reason it all out.

Once having made that admission, however, he toweled off and then stumbled out of the bathroom through the clouds of steam pouring out all around him. Watching the hot billow filter through the apartment, he remembered the first monster he had battled, before he had ever thought such things existed anywhere beyond movie screens and horror novels. He had taken two showers that night—longer, hotter ones.

"Didn't come up with any answers then, either," he said quietly, chuckling hollowly in the back of his throat.

Making his way to his partner's blocky, oversize living-room couch, without any consideration over clothing, he lay down and curled up, falling into a deep sleep almost before his head touched the cushions. When Paul finally returned from his errand, he covered the detective with an extra sheet and then called

Lisa, leaving a message on her machine, letting her know that London was at his place. Then he went to sleep himself, not bothering to set any alarms.

♦ ♦ ♦

"Pretty strange, boss."

"Well, of course, it's not the strangest thing that's ever happened to me . . ."

"Amen to that," interrupted Paul.

"Yeah. But, strange enough."

"Well, anyway, what'da we do next?"

London looked up from his seat. He and his partner had driven down to the Lower East Side, what the residents of the area now called the Black City. The Conflagration that had killed so many there fifty-seven days earlier had done massive amounts of damage of all kinds. While the oil and chemical refineries of Elizabeth, New Jersey, had burned, the wind had pulled the flaming soot and crude out over the ocean, cutting a straight line across the bottom of Manhattan. From roughly Delancey Street in the north to St. James in the south, the heavy black clouds had been pushed over and around the city blocks on the wind currents created by the insane heat.

All of the buildings in the area had been coated with a thick, almost rubbery coal paste, a black filth that smeared its way from one shore to the other and then beyond, filling the rivers and streaking the ocean. It was a disaster beyond compare with any in the city's memory—the nation's. Fish had died by the thousands. The bodies of birds and small land animals had rotted everywhere on the island for weeks. The homeless had choked to death in the streets, their bodies black in the tar, heaped with the other uncomprehending creatures. Babies were found in their cribs, mouths filled with sludge, tiny hearts stopped by a fate that had condemned them to the wrong place at the wrong time.

London sat on a chair in the middle of an open field, a fenced-in block of rubble and weeds. Although a mile up the road you could sell land by the foot for twenty thousand a square foot, on the Lower East Side you literally could not give it away. Over the years, the corner of Broome and Suffolk had become a garbage dump—one littered with every useless bit of trash imaginable; sheets of nylon, soggy cardboard, broken bricks, used tires, liquor and beer bottles by the hundreds, plastic tubes, an old toaster, pieces of metal so rusted one could not begin to determine what their one-time function had been. In a few more years, lying in the same spot, they would not even be recognizable as the handiwork of man. And the detective was sure they would sit there undisturbed for a few more years. At least.

London had wanted to see what his actions had caused so they had driven over and stopped there. Morcey and he had walked across the field from the other side, ducking through one of the dozens of holes torn in the cyclone fencing the city had put up at some time in the past when it still cared about such things. Passing an abandoned taxi on the way, the ex-maintenance man had noted that the rear seat had been broken down and stuffed into the flooring, most likely used by the feeble whores still left in the area. London said nothing, noting instead the rat warren based from under the rusting cab. He could see their prints in the blackened mud, hundreds dug in here and there between the weeds and rocks and garbage.

He saw the prints of dogs and cats as well, the sight of it bringing forth some ancient, unnamed ancestor from the back of his mind. The scene triggered a release of information from the detective's racial memory, the long-dead elder taking control of one of the voices within London's mind just long enough to explain the tracks. Before he knew it, the detective understood everything about the chaotic jumble of claw marks and paw prints before him.

The ancestor voice pointed out the differences in the patterns of the dogs' tracks, showing the detective how many there had been in total, their sizes and weights. It noted that they had descended on the cats who had been lying in wait for the rats. When the rodents had returned to their den, the cats had sprung on them. And in the middle of that battle when their prey was occupied, the dogs had descended, tearing into both the cats and the rats like demons.

What amazed London even more than the sudden rush of information, however, was the fact that it did not worry him. With the first voice had come an understanding of who was speaking. In fact, the more the detective tried to identify within him whose voice was resounding in his head, the more he discovered. As the seconds had ticked by, Morcey talking, London staring, he had begun to assemble a picture of the man speaking to him, some great grandfather a hundred times removed.

He saw a man shorter than himself, rounder with blocky, hard shoulders. The man had thick, matted hair, a dark complexion and darker eyes—eyes filled with blood and a cold weariness. The man was a hunter—a raw kind of scout for some "civilized" army or another. The detective could tell that the man knew much of tracking and killing and that everything he knew was now at London's disposal. The detective also knew that there were now a thousand more voices just like his, waiting to be called on by London for their expertise.

How? wondered the detective. How did this happen? I'm not knocking it, but why now? What's different now? First that burning energy the night before, almost crippling him in the vampire's apartment. Now this. Doesn't it ever end?

Not able to devote any more time to that problem, London focused his attention on his partner, finally responding to him, asking;

"Next? Well, what do you think, Paul?"

"Me?" answered the balding man. "Jeez—lemme think."

The ex-maintenance man sat back in his seat, a throne some previous squatter had put together from old television sets. Cocking his head to one side, he told the detective;

"I guess next we should try and find this Jorhsa character."

"That was my thought."

"And how do we do that?"

"Now there," answered London with a grin, "is a harder question to answer."

The detective pushed back on his chair—not a chair, really, but only the frame of a chair to which someone had attached an old board—in some spots with nails, some with wire. Feeling the shabby construct shudder when he did so, London stopped putting pressure on the seat, standing up instead.

"I'm not sure but, I have a few ideas."

And then, suddenly, the detective drifted off, staring into the weeds behind him. From outside of him—from across the over grown lengths of the field—from every corner of the Black City—the cries of the long dead reached for him. Shoving past his defenses, their sound touched the souls of the smothered and the choked screaming again in the back of his head, drawing him toward the weeds.

He had brought too many of them close to their former homes, giving them the strength to break through his barriers. Closing his eyes tightly, he cursed them back into place, screeching them away into the shadows of his brain until finally only one voice remained.

And, somehow, the detective realized that, for some reason, this voice deserved his attention and would not be quieted like the others. Giving it the notice all the others had begged for, he felt himself suddenly pulled away from the small cluster of seats he and his partner had taken over. Following the urging of the chatter—the pleading—inside his head, the detective grabbed up his Blackthorn and moved further into the weeds.

"Boss? Where ya goin'?"

When London did not respond, the ex-maintenance man left his seat and moved off into the brush as well, tailing his partner at a covering distance. In the lead, London tramped his way across the field until coming finally to what he had been pulled toward. Most of an adult male skeleton lay hidden in the over growth, the bones remaining gnawed completely clean. The detective stooped, putting a hand to its skull. He brushed his fingers against the scratches left by cats and dogs and squirrels and rats and mice—by both their claws and their teeth.

The voice had found its remains, left crumpled in the field when the blowing, superheated smog had choked it to death. Its gibber turned into a scream, one that filled London's mind. It was a rage of shocked denial that spun itself into sad acceptance after a moment's noise—a final act silencing it forever.

London, however, had for the most part this time ignored the horrific noise generated by one of the dead living within him. His concentration had suddenly centered on the green all around him instead. Even as he had bent to examine the skull, it was dawning on him that despite the black tar resins smeared across the field, the weeds had grown back. They had cracked the oil-sealed ground as far as the eye could see, much of the field having already reached a five-foot height. Some of the older weeds, really bushes and small trees now, had not been bothered at all. When all their blackened leaves had fallen off they had sprouted new ones, refusing to die.

The detective was instantly flooded with comfort, and more. An epiphanous rapture warmed him, a raging swell of understanding making the larger picture he had been missing for the past fifty-seven days suddenly clear. Leaving the bones where they lay, food for the bugs and weeds, he turned to his partner, smiling.

"Boss," asked Morcey again, "are you okay?"

"Yes," answered the detective, stretching his arms out, flexing his cramped shoulders, feeling the blood coursing through his muscles. "I'm o-kay."

Turning then, unable to contain his joy, London put his hands on his partner's upper arms and then pulled his friend to him, hugging him tightly.

"I've been driving everybody a little bit crazy," he admitted, releasing his grip. "Haven't I?"

"Well, jeez," answered the balding man, somewhat embarrassed. "It's not like you didn't have good reasons."

"Oh, Paul," responded the detective, "people can find reasons for anything and everything they do. I could have used the same reasons to justify an entirely different set—hell—any set of reactions. And so, given all the possible choices in the world, what did I choose to do? I chose to whine and moan and baby myself and hide from reality—as if that were actually possible for very long."

"Oh, I don't know," answered Morcey, not really following his partner's logic. "I've seen an awful lotta people who could hide from reality for years at a time."

"I'm not talking about politicians and lawyers and talk-show hosts, Paul," answered London with a wide smile, punching his friend lightly on the shoulder at the same time. "I meant real people."

"Boss," said Morcey, feeling a bit foolish, "is it all right if I don't know exactly what it is you're talkin' about?"

"Sure," replied the detective, still smiling. "What makes you think I do?"

And then, suddenly, the ex-maintenance man laughed, a loud cleansing laugh that shook his beefy sides. Tears formed in both his eyes while he howled, the effect of both emotions making him too dizzy to stand. London caught him, laughing and crying as well. The pair held on to each other for a long moment, relief flooding them both for different reasons.

Finally, though, they pulled apart, brushing themselves off—wiping at their wet cheeks—still laughing. Then, without word or signal, the two fell into step, walking toward an opening in the fence leading out onto Broome.

"Sweet Bride of the Night," said Paul. "It's really good ta have you back,

Mr. London. And, since I gotcha back, I'll ask again . . . what'da we do now?"

"Now?" answered London, using his Blackthorn machete-like on the towering weeds in his way.

"Now, we go see about earning Mrs. Lu's retainer."

Chapter Eighteen

THEODORE LONDON SAT BEHIND the desk in his office, cleaning Betty. The action felt good—familiar. Lisa and Morcey had gone to dinner, not only to have a meal, but also to meet several of their friends. The detective glanced at his watch, confirming the whisper in the back of his mind that the others would be back soon. Reluctantly, he gathered up his bore oil, cotton patches, and cleaning rod, packing them all away in their special place in his filing cabinet. Then, with his desktop once again in reasonable order, he crossed to the window behind his chair.

Leaning against the wall, he looked out over the city. His view was one of midtown, stretching down all the way to where the old World Trade Center had once stood, an expanse, it seemed to London, containing all the water towers in Manhattan. He was not actually looking for anything in particular. Rather he was just passing time, giving his eyes a field to rest upon while waiting for the others to arrive. As usual, his instincts were correct. The first of the friends he was expecting arrived only seconds after he paused to take in the view.

"Little brother," came a booming voice from the detective's outer office, "I am very upset with you."

"Well," answered London, smiling as he did so, "it's not like you don't have good reasons."

The speaker entered the inner office. He was an enormous black man, standing six and a half feet tall, weighing close to three hundred fifty pounds. Coming around the detective's desk, he lifted London up off the floor in a smothering bear hug, greeting him;

"Bang bang, little brother."

"Bang bang to you, too, Pa'sha," answered the detective in a groaning voice. "Take it easy, will you. I'm not all that healed, you know." The large man put London back on the floor, telling him, in a stern, humorless voice;

"I should do more than bruise your ribs. I have been most concerned deeply. I come to your house and you turn me away. Flesh and blood to you when the world wanted you dead. Is there perhaps a good reason you make me nothing, breaking my face and throwing the pieces in the dust?"

London hung his head slightly, not knowing where to begin. Pa'sha Lowe was a weaponeer, an entrepreneur who sold quietly to a very select clientele. The two men had been friends for a dozen years. They had saved each other's lives several times. Fifty-seven days earlier, they had saved the world. Pa'sha had passed through the conflict without a scratch, as had Paul Morcey. It had weighed on him quite heavily that London, who had been injured almost unto death, had refused the weaponeer entry to his home while he convalesced.

Yes, Pa'sha had known that London was refusing entry to everyone but Morcey and, yes again, he knew that even the ponytailed little man did not know why the detective was hiding himself from everyone and everything. But Morcey had begged the others to give London time. He had assured them the detective would eventually be ready to face the world and that he would come back to them all ready to justify his behavior with a simple explanation. Pa'sha, the closest thing to family London had left in the world, had arrived first, ready for a good one.

"So, little Theodore, friend Paul says we should not be as angry as dogs without meat at the way you treat us all. What do you think?"

"Pa'sha," answered the detective humbly. "All I can say is that I'm sorry."

"Sorry? What is this 'sorry?' Weak and stupid nothings is this 'sorry.' What do I care for such things? Tell me true things, little brother," said the large man, his words dropping into a thick whisper.

"Tell me why?" he asked, his voice filled with sorrow. "*Why?*"

London collapsed into his desk chair. Pushing his spine into the chair's leather backing, he said;

"You saw me in the hospital. You know what kind of shape the Conflagration left me in—me and everyone else. Everywhere so many dead, so many more injured . . . dying. They sent anyone who could get out of bed home as soon as they could so they could slide another burned, broken body into their bed. When I got home, I—I was sure I was going to die. I didn't want you or Lisa to see me like that . . . see me die all twisted and shriveled."

"But you did not."

"That was a mistake," answered the detective quietly, his voice trailing off to where it almost could not be heard. "It sure isn't because I didn't want to."

"Why do you say this, my brother?"

"Why? Because it's true, goddammit to hell!" And then, London suddenly snapped. Furious and mean, he lost control of his bottled-up anger, spilling it out into the room. Staring at Pa'sha with cold eyes, he screamed bitterly;

"What do you know? You didn't wander around in your own dreams with maniacs tearing the skin off your body—did you?! You didn't have cardinals begging you to kill them—you didn't send anyone to their deaths. You didn't have that fucking thing from Hell crawling around inside your head, laughing at you, letting you know how it was going to eat the whole fucking *universe* and that there was nothing you could do to stop it! Nothing except kill nearly two million people! When's the last time you killed two million people? Anytime recent?"

"Teddy . . ."

"What? *What?!* What do you think you can say that I haven't told myself?

That it had to be done? That Fate did what it was going to do and I just have to live with it? That there's no sense in whining about things now—that I just have to face up to reality and get on with my life? Why? Why should I? Who threw the dice that named me the Destroyer? Why me?! *Why me?!!*"

And then, as quickly as the rage had come over him, it disappeared. The howling burst of energy fled his body, leaving him drained and empty. The detective sagged in his chair, flopping into its arms carelessly, feeling almost silly over his outburst. He had put such feelings behind himself earlier in the day. Unleashing them now, he told himself, was just self-indulgent sport—and cruel sport at that. Lifting his hand weakly from his side, he held it out to his friend, saying;

"I'm sorry, big brother." Then he laughed softly, adding, "There's that word again. But, well, at least you can see why I didn't want anybody around."

The larger man reached across the desk between them, taking London's hand in his own. Closing his massive fist over the detective's much smaller hand, he held it gently, telling him;

"No. I am the sorry one. Forgive me, my brother. I was too worried about the man you were. I should have realized that he would be gone. I hope the one who has taken his place can still find love in his heart for one such as me."

"Oh . . ." answered London, smiling weakly, "I think I can manage it."

Finding the strength to lift his other hand, he clasped it over top of Pa'sha's, squeezing it with what feeble pressure he could muster. The weaponeer brought his other hand up as well, joining it to the other three. After they shook hands for a second, the detective broke the hold, pleading weakness. Pa'sha understood and sat back in his chair, satisfied and relieved. The pair looked at each other for a moment, not having any more words for each other—not needing any.

Then, suddenly, the sound of the outer office door opening announced that the others had arrived. Pa'sha swiveled his head for a view. In seconds, Lisa, Morcey, Lai Wan, Wally, and an older, bearded gentleman in a dark tweed suit entered the inner office. As they all took the seating they preferred, the older man extended his hand to London, saying;

"Good to see you ambulatory again, Theodore." The detective shook the man's hand, answering;

"It's good to be ambling again, Doc." Turning toward Wally, London made a hand motion indicating he wanted the appraiser to join them. Once he had the two together, he said;

"You two are the only ones here who don't know each other. Wallace Daniel Barnes, Dr. Zachary Goward." As the two shook hands, exchanging pleasantries, the detective continued;

"Wally, and I use his own words here, is the best fence in town . . ."

"Damn straight," agreed Wally.

"And the Doc here works out of Columbia University. He's their top dog in the philosophy and theology department."

"Damn straight here, as well," added Goward with a smile.

The two sized each other up in a glance, each making quick mental notes about the other. As they both settled into chairs, London moved behind his desk, grateful to be able to get off his feet. He eased into his seat, sighing with relief as it took up the burden of his weight.

Settling in, he thought about the constant weariness that had plagued him lately. Physically he felt more tired than ever before in his life, drained to the point of exhaustion. But, whenever he would decide that he just could not go on any longer, somehow a burst of energy would come along from out of nowhere—not much—just enough to keep him going. And then, suddenly, he remembered; in Karen Tezzler's apartment he had had all the energy he needed—both when in bed and when fighting for his life. How could that be? He wondered, where was it coming from?

Then, feeling everyone's eyes on him, he said;

"Folks, I'd hate to think that every time we get together in the same room it's going to be to fight things from Hell but, that seems to be the case at the moment."

Wally raised his hand, grade-school fashion. London gave him a nod, asking;

"Yes, Wally?"

"Permission to be excused?" Everyone chuckled, or at least smiled. Knowing he had to address the appraiser's concerns, the detective said;

"I expect you'd like a little explanation?"

"No," answered Wally, "I'd like a great big fat one. You can start with 'fight' and wrap up somewhere around 'things from Hell.' Take as long as you'all need."

"Well," started London, "I could have gotten the information I needed from you without telling you any of this, but it might have left you in jeopardy. I couldn't do that."

"How obliging," offered Wally. "Courtesy always ranks high with an old country boy like myself, honest and true. But there's a tension so thick in here you could slice it down and serve it up with gravy. It was like that yesterday and it's worse today. So, why don't you get on with these explanations of yours? I'd like to know what you and yours and Pa'sha and the Dragon Lady there and Columbia University and the best fence in the city have to do with 'things from Hell?' Did I mention I was mostly interested in that 'things from Hell' part?"

As Wally dabbed at his temples with a handkerchief, London closed his eyes and pursed his lips, making a slight nodding motion with his head. Then, opening his eyes, he asked;

"Wally, that big fire over in Jersey about two months back, you remember that . . . don't you?"

CHAPTER
NINETEEN

WALLY SAT IN HIS chair, staring forward. First, London had told them all the story of the previous day. Most of them, after what they had gone through at the detective's side two months earlier, had no trouble listening to and believing a tale about something as ordinary, by comparison, as vampires. After that, London told the story of their struggle with the Q'talu to Wally, both to let the appraiser know that they were all serious, and to make certain the man knew exactly what he was getting into if he were to help them.

On occasion, Wally had looked from side to side, searching the faces of the others around him to see if he could find any thing that would allow him to believe he was being made sport of—anything at all. Long before the detective was finished, though, the appraiser knew the tales he was being told were true.

"Damn you, Teddy. What did you think you were doing? What do you mean—bringing me into this?"

"You're not in anything yet, Wally," London reminded him.

"Oh, yeah. Oh, sure. As we use to say back home, fuck me runnin', pal. You drop an atomic bomb on New Jersey to kill some blob from outer space and wipe out half the Eastern sea board, and now you want me to get a bag of garlic and help you chase vampires? Let me tell you . . ."

As the appraiser began to rise, Lai Wan reached out, touching his sleeve. Maintaining her contact, she plunged down through the layers of his anger, searching for its vital center. His true pain screamed out to her, begging for notice—the notice Wally himself had not yet given it. The psychometrist made note of it and then exited, telling the appraiser;

"Mr. Barnes, Mr. London did not kill Barry."

Wally spun around as if slapped, glaring at the psychometrist with hate flashing in his eyes.

"How the fuck do you . . ." Then, remembering the details of the stories just told to him, he shook Lai Wan's touch away, screaming at her;

"What do you know?! What could you know?!"

Lai Wan, her eyes betraying a pity the others had not thought her capable of, reached out to Wally again. As her fingers touched his arm, she offered;

"You are not the only one who has lost someone to the evils that stalk this world. You are not the only one who suffered in the Conflagration. Hundreds upon hundreds of thousands died but, because of their deaths, billions were spared. Yes, still now millions of the survivors live on in grief, dying inside, robbed of their fathers, their daughters and sons, their wives, friends—cursing themselves for being alive—asking '*why me?*' Yours is not the only dead lover. Everyone lost someone, Mr. Barnes."

"But," said the appraiser feebly, fighting the splintering cracks working their way into his voice, as well as the tears, begging for release.

"It wa . . . wasn't some, some evil thing . . ." His hand lifted, two fingers stabbing across the room, pointing at the detective.

"It was him. It was him. He murdered them all."

"No, Wally," answered Lai Wan, "Mr. London did not murder anyone. He and his friend the Spud thought they were sacrificing themselves for the good of everyone—for the whole world. Mr. London never thought he was going to live. I doubt he even wanted to."

And then, her voice grew quiet. Wally dropped his hand, wanting to hate the detective, wanting to be convinced not to. Dr. Goward broke the silence, doing his best to achieve the latter.

"Mr. Barnes, I understand that you're being asked to accept quite a lot in a great hurry here, but you have to realize why. If Mr. London is correct about these, ah, 'vampires,' then you must understand that if you aid us, your life will be in great danger. It would have been quite simple to get whatever information was necessary without letting you know a thing. That wasn't done, though, was it?"

When Wally shook his head in silent response, Goward continued;

"No. In fact, what has happened here is that you've been given the information necessary to extract whatever revenge you might desire over your lover's death. Mr. London has put his freedom, his life, his entire future into your hands, sir, simply because he refuses to take yours into his. I won't belabor the point, Mr. Barnes. I'll just add that I don't think men do such things unless they feel the stakes have gotten as high as they can."

Wally sat back down, his head hung low and to an angle, eyes shut tight, mouth pursed. His hands were balled and rigid, shaking from the strain of keeping them clenched. He lifted them off his legs, one after another, picking them up and putting them down, his body knowing fists were what he wanted, his brain not knowing what to do with them. Finally, though, his fingers uncurled, first shaking, then rising slowly to cover his face.

Wallace Daniel Barnes had not yet mourned his lover. The horror of the Conflagration, the newspapers and the television screens filled with repellent images—smoke and flames from burning cities flying upward to fill the sky; the charred remains of a thousand cars and trucks crashed up against each other, some deserted, some manned by corpses; the lines of now-homeless victims, waiting in stunned and broken silence for whatever scraps could be got to them by governments and charities; the mountains of bodies, piled like autumn leaves just to get them out of the way—all of it had seemed too large, too overpowering for him to justify feeling any personal grief when the whole world around him was mourning the insanity its survivors had lived to reach.

Now, however, now he cried. Long-silent tears that leaked through his fingers like the cold of winter through a cracked wall. Everyone in the room understood and allowed him his time.

Eventually Wally regained his composure. Begging off for the chance to have a cigarette, Lisa had accompanied him to the hall so he could have a moment away from the group without being totally alone. London had nodded when she suggested going with the appraiser, pleased to see his small team working so well together. Once they had left the office, the detective turned to Goward and asked;

"Well, give it to me. Are there such things as vampires or not?"

"At the moment," answered the professor, stroking his beard, "I'd say you know more about that particular subject than I do, Theodore. Before tonight I wouldn't have given someone trying to convince me of such things the time of day. But if you say so, I don't see how I have much choice other than to believe, as you put it, that there are some fairly peculiar characters running around this city who, at the very least, seem to *think* they are vampires."

"Then," asked the detective, "there's never been any evidence to support the existence of vampires?"

"Not much, really," answered the doctor. "My best guess has always been that the superstition rose up over the years in connection with porphyria victims."

"What're they, doc?" asked Morcey.

"Porphyria sufferers have an absence of an oxygen-carrying component in their red blood cells. It makes them sensitive to light and also shrinks the gum, making the teeth seem enlarged. Not that they would explain all the legends, of course." Reaching inside his jacket, the doctor continued, saying;

"Some sort or another of bloodsucking demon or monster, sometimes spirits, is part of the mythology of most civilizations. Our own vision of tuxedo-clad, erotically evil gentlemen preying on virginal barmaids seems borne mostly from the fiction and movies of the last hundred and fifty years."

Goward wrestled his pipe from his jacket pocket. As he began stuffing its bowl with tobacco, he continued;

"Of course, there have been a number of celebrated cases of both men and women, quite mad, who found erotic gratification in vicious acts of murder that would end with the drinking of their victim's blood. History records a number of ghouls who unearthed graves to eat the flesh of the recently deceased—the same kind of frenzies that caused the Leopard cults of West Africa to terrorize entire generations."

Striking a blue-tipped match on the bottom of his shoe, the doctor set the flame to his pipe. After a second, he dropped the spent match in the ashtray on London's desk and then exhaled a rich cloud of smoke smelling of cherry wood.

"Then," he added, "there is a twelfth-century English story about an evil personage who was given a proper Christian burial even though he went to his grave unrepentant of his numerous sins. This, of course . . ."

"Doc," interrupted London, "could I hazard a guess that we're getting off the subject here?"

"Hummm? Oh, yes. Sorry. Anyway, as I was saying, Central Europe abounds in tales of corpses being dug up and discovered to be fat, and ruddy complex-ioned, drippingly stuffed with the blood of the local countryside. How much of it is true . . . ? I couldn't say. No one could, really. Serious students of the occult give the notion of vampires little notice. Lord, the word didn't even exist in the English language until 1730 or '40."

"Then dragging you down here has just been pretty much a waste of your time," concluded the detective. "My apologies, Zachary."

"Tusshhh," added the doctor. "Aside from the fact that you couldn't drag me away from something like this with wild horses, in all honesty it is a relief to be here—just to finally see you again, fit and hale. What you went through against the Q'talu would have killed most men—left the rest insane."

"Thanks for the kind words."

"Not at all," added Goward, modestly. "Thanks for saving the known uni-verse. Now that you're out and about, anytime you'd like to fill a few dozen tapes for my records, I'll be happy to foot a few dinner bills."

"Well," answered the detective, "let's see if I live through this little party first."

"If there's anything I can do to help that along," came Wally's voice from the doorway, "and I assume there must be or you wouldn't have dragged me down here—why don't we get to it, before I forget my good manners."

"Love to," answered London. Greatly relieved, he added quietly, "Thanks, Wally."

The appraiser took his seat again, making no response. Lisa slid back into her own chair, moving her eyes in a way to suggest she felt Wally more or less stable. London took the subtle clue and started in.

"Have you ever sold any pieces to, or bought any from, the woman I men-tioned before . . . Karen Tezzler?"

"That name did ring a bell. What was her address?" After the detective gave the appraiser the information, the latter said;

"Yessss—I do hear a small gong. My God, I think I know the collection you were talking about . . . the one you said you smashed. Was there a piece, a jade piece, all seaweed and goldfish and frogs?"

When London confirmed his guess, the appraiser said;

"Oh, the Lord in church on Sunday—did I know Karen Tezzler. You wrecked that collection? You wiped out *that* living room? Teddy, if you wrecked that place you did . . ." the appraiser closed his eyes for just a second, then finished;

"I don't know—what? I'd have to guess at least a good fourteen million dollars' worth of damage."

"What . . .?"

"Oh, yes," confirmed Wally. "I was only in there once. I delivered a piece to her . . . minor stuff, just a couple of thousand, for somebody's birthday or something. Anyway, when I looked around, I told her she should get some more security. She just laughed."

"Do you remember who the birthday present was for?" asked the detective.

"Yes, yes. I think I do. I remember it because it was such an unusual name." Putting one finger on his forehead, the appraiser closed his eyes and thought for just a second before saying;

"Jorhsa."

Holding back his excitement, betraying the burning interest within him over the name in question by only the raising of one eyebrow, the detective asked;

"You wouldn't remember any other details about this Jorhsa, would you?"

Wally gave his memory another try, but was forced to answer in the negative. Before the group could fall into discouragement, however, Lai Wan asked;

"Mr. Barnes, if you would not mind, I would like to try to see if you have more knowledge of this person stored away within your subconscious than you can access on your own."

The appraiser hesitated for only a second before agreeing. When he did, Lai Wan closed her eyes for a moment, taking a short breath that she exhaled rapidly. Then she opened her eyes again and took Wally's left hand in between both of hers and concentrated, searching through all the history within his brain for the fleeting millisecond when his path had overlapped with Karen Tezzler's.

Since she had been inside the appraiser's consciousness just a few minutes earlier, it took the psychometrist only a handful of seconds to find the correct stream of thought. Plunging into it, she immersed herself within the moment of past-time she desired, forging her way forward until suddenly she was in Karen Tezzler's apartment, witnessing the scene through Wally's eyes, hearing the sound of it through his ears, becoming as much a part of him in that past time as he was himself.

She saw the piece Wally/she had brought, a silver statue of an idealized male American Indian, war shield and spear in hand, fearsome and fearless in both facial expression and body language.

"You were right," came Karen's words through Lai Wan's mouth. "It is perfect. Jorhsa will love it. His office at the club is so barren. It's been waiting for something just like this."

"Club?" asked London. "What club? What club?!"

"Do you want it delivered?" Wally had asked/Lai Wan repeated.

"No—no need. I'll be there myself, tonight. It's a birthday present."

"He's throwing himself a party?" Wally had asked.

"No," Karen/Lai Wan said. Karen spoke while she made out a check. Lai Wan watched her. "No; he never remembers his birthday. But a group of us always does. He just thinks it's another normal night. We'll show him different, though. Food and fun and human sacrifice—that's us."

"Dammit!" muttered London loudly—irritated—impatient. "What's the name of the goddamned place?"

"Sounds like fun," Wally had said, not knowing his customer was not exaggerating, now growing pale as he remembered the scene from his new vantage point. "Room for one more?"

Karen had looked at Wally as Lai Wan did now. The vampire's measuring glare came back at him through the psychometrist's eyes, letting him know for what he had actually been unwittingly volunteering. As a chill ran through the appraiser, Lai Wan repeated Karen's words.

"Sorry, I'm sure we'd have a few there that would just love to eat you up, but we've already filled the place to the limit. The end of the pier is pretty strict about such things."

And then London interrupted the proceedings.

"That's enough," he ordered.

Lai Wan opened her eyes. Everyone save Pa'sha stared forward at the detective, wondering what he might have picked up on that they had not. Sensing their curiosity, London said;

"Sorry to be so abrupt but, we've got what we need."

"What was that, boss?" asked Morcey.

"The End of the Pier, Paul," answered London. "It's a night club."

"The kind of place a vampire would own?" asked the ex-maintenance man.

"It just might be," hazarded the detective. Turning to Pa'sha, he asked;

"What do you think, big brother?"

The large weaponeer stood and then reached forward, pulling Betty out from underneath London's jacket. Holding the .38 up before his face as if inspecting it, he answered;

"I think, Theodore, that I had better fit you for something just a little bit bigger."

CHAPTER TWENTY

"A ND," ASKED LONDON, KNOWING his friend's taste in personal armament, "what exactly did you have in mind?"

"I was thinking more along these lines."

So saying, Pa'sha reached under his own jacket and pulled forth one of the largest handguns the detective had ever seen. The weaponeer passed it over to his friend, the weight of it catching London off guard, pulling his hand down almost to the desktop beneath it. Dragging the stainless-steel piece upward through the air, the detective said;

"This thing must weigh ten pounds. What the hell is it, any way?"

"It is the king of weapons, my friend. It is the Auto-Mag," answered Pa'sha proudly, "the most powerful handgun in all the world." London slid the clip out, inspecting the ammunition it held. The weaponeer told him;

"When first it was given birth, it took a 240 grain bullet. Do you know why? I will tell you. When this pistol was designed, its creator started with a cut-down .308 Winchester rifle case. And let me tell you, little brother, *that* is how you design a thing of true delight. He eventually necked the case down to accept the .357s you see nestled before you."

The detective stared at the weapon for a moment longer, smiling as he asked;

"Boom boom?"

"Oh, my yes, very sweet boom boom. The kind that makes the clouds weep that their thunder is so pale in the shadow of that which comes from this magnificent lady."

"Could I see that," asked Morcey. London handed the Auto-Mag to his partner, grateful to be relieved of its weight. Delight lighting his face from the feel of the weapon alone, the ponytailed man asked;

"Ooooooooouuue; pretty, pretty. Buy me a toy, Daddy." The detective smiled at his partner, then said to Pa'sha;

"Okay, you win. Not that I'm expecting any trouble tonight but, maybe you should dig up two of those for Paul and me."

"We up to fun and games tonight, boss?" asked Morcey, still inspecting the Auto-Mag.

"Just a little reconnaissance, is all."

"But," said Wally, "when are you going to take care of these things?" As all eyes fell on the appraiser, he said;

"I mean, okay, I'm convinced. There are vampires walking the streets, making meals out of whomever they choose. If the guest list hadn't been filled I'd have been an hors d'oeuvre myself. Okay, fine—you blew up half of New Jersey without worrying about it too much—what're you going to do about this?!"

London closed his eyes for a second, silencing the growling anger he felt rising throughout his system. Then, opening his eyes again, he stared forward at Wally, telling him;

"Please—try and get something straight here, will you? This isn't some comic book. We're not sitting in some Hollywood sound set play-acting our way through some stupid horror movie. This is real. We're in New York City. They do still have laws against things like what you're talking about. Hell, they have laws against everything."

London pushed back with his feet, moving his massive leather-bound chair on its ancient wheels. Standing, he came around the chair, shoving it into its space under the desk at the same time. Then, limping back and forth in the area behind it, he said;

"I understand what you're saying and why. But that doesn't change the facts. First, we don't have a client. Mrs. Lu is dead. But she's been avenged. We've already killed her murderer. On top of that, we've earned our retainer. She wanted the death of her son avenged. Those murderers are dead, too. In fact, having killed Karen Tezzler, we're one up on their team. But what the hell, we're the good guys, right? We've got right on our side—we can do whatever we want."

The detective turned his back for a moment on those assembled in his office, looking out the window behind his desk. Shielding his eyes against the sunlight working its way through the filter lace, he said;

"What would you like, Wally? Tell me, please. Shall we just go downtown to the End of the Pier and shoot it up? And then, when the police arrive, what'll we say . . . 'Don't worry, officer. It's okay. You see, they were all vampires.' Or shall we do the talk-show circuit first? 'Yes, we have proof. Do you remember the Conflagration? To tell the truth, it was actually brought about by a thing from Hell trying to gain access to our dimension, and, oh yes, did you know vampires were real?'"

London spun around then, feeling the motion in his bad leg, planting his palms on the top of his desk. Staring again at the appraiser, he continued;

"Don't get me wrong—I'm not going to ignore all this . . . if for no other reason than the fact that by now this bunch is probably looking for us—me, anyway. But try and remember, you just can't go around shooting people down in the streets and expect to get away with it for very long in this town."

The detective shook his head slightly, and then squinted his eyes, asking;

"Do you understand? They won't even have to find us guilty of murder—they'll either just put us away for being lunatics or, if they do believe us, then they'll lock us up for being racists. And if you don't think the brain-dead liberal intelligentsia of this town won't come out to champion the poor, misunderstood, downtrodden vampires against a miserable pack of genocidists like us, then you've got another think coming."

While London took a breath, Wally said;

"I'm sorry, Ted. Really, I guess I'm just—I don't know—confused, I guess. About . . . all this . . . about Barry. I'm just all churned up inside."

"I understand," answered London, earnestly. "I just have to make sure that no one gets carried away here. What's coming our way is damn dangerous. And," the detective's voice caught, choking his words in his throat for a fraction of a second;

"I just don't want anyone getting caught up in this before they fully realize exactly how alone we are. This city, maybe the whole world anymore, I don't know, just doesn't want people defending themselves, standing up for themselves, helping anybody. It's like a—a, I don't know, some kind of sickness, where everybody hides from taking responsibility for their actions, willing to turn the direction of their lives over to whoever's willing to take the reins. I don't want anyone getting in over their heads. I—I, hell, I guess it's like Dr. Goward here said before.

"I've got enough blood on my hands right now. I don't need any more."

London turned back to the window then, staring out through the sunlight, past the buildings beyond, past the limits of the horizon. The voices in his head were quiet. He had learned how to still them once and for all in the ruined meadow where he and Morcey had stopped earlier in the day. Even when they had begun to flood the dreamplane the night previous while he had lain exhausted in Tezzler's bed, they had only been able to appear as solemn figures, cold and silent.

He knew they could not bother him further. But that, he told himself, was not the point. What was really bothering him was not the fact that he had *their* blood on his hands, but rather that he had *enough* blood on his hands. The taste of death was so thick on his tongue that he could not taste anything else, leaving the simple truth that he simply could not contemplate the thought of another bite from that same bitter meal.

But then, before he could voice any further hesitations, he heard small murmurings behind him, followed by Wally's voice;

"I think everyone here wants to do whatever you think is best, Ted."

"He's right, boss," added Morcey. "Just tell us what you want us to do."

Calling on more strength than he thought he had within himself, the detective turned from the warmth streaming through the window and returned to his chair. Then, cut off from the sun, he outlined what each person in the room could do if they really were determined to make targets of themselves.

CHAPTER
TWENTY-ONE

I T DID NOT TAKE long for London to come up with a task for everyone. Lai Wan was given the first assignment. The detective wanted the psychometrist to reach into the crystal ball he had brought back from Mrs. Lu's apartment. He wanted her to study it—probe it from all angles—looking for any memories she might find that could tell them more about their enemies. His hopes were that Mrs. Lu might have known of some weakness Lai Wan could find within the globe, or even that there might be more to the globe than he had already learned.

Wally he asked to check his other connections, looking for anyone in his circle who also might have sold any pieces to the vampire. Perhaps they might have a friend list, London suggested, something that might link them more solidly to the unknown "Jorhsa," the only other name they had.

Dr. Goward was put to the task of pure research. Not having had any reason to give the notion of vampires any credence in the past, it was possible he might have things in his files that could match up with the newer information the detective had given him. It was a thankless task, one almost certain to produce little to no results. As London told the professor;

"As thoroughly as you do your research, I'm not expecting you to find much you overlooked. It's just that, well, being desperate and all, I'll grasp at any straws I see floating by."

"Don't worry yourself, my boy," Goward responded. "If you think this is anything for me but a holiday, then you really do have no understanding of the academic mind. I won't promise you anything—obviously that would be foolish. But I will do what I can."

Goward took a deep, satisfying drag on his pipe, saying, "And all the while I'm sitting hunched over my desk, I'll be imagining myself a full-fledged participant in a death-defying adventure. The life of an armchair detective does have its rewards."

After that, the detective turned to his partners. Morcey, of course, would be accompanying him that night. Lisa, the detective set to coordinating everyone else's efforts. First, she would have to take Lai Wan to London's apartment to secure the crystal ball. After that he wanted her to return to the office to enter in the company computer anything either Wally or the doctor came up with so the detective would have it all in one place. And, London told her, while she was waiting for any tidbits they might find, she was to do an ownership check of the End of the Pier. On top of that, if she could also find out when it was built, how often it had been sold—and when, names, dates, blueprints . . . ?

Pa'sha was asked to get together the weapons and ammunition he had offered. The relative unimportance of his assignment did not sit well with the larger man who wanted to accompany his friend to the End of the Pier.

The detective was adamant, however. Considering the group's inability to discern who was a vampire and who was not, the detective insisted Pa'sha stay behind as a next line of defense. London promised to check in with the weaponeer as soon as he and Morcey emerged from the club. And, the detective told his friend, if he had not heard anything from them by the next night, then he would be on his own, and London's opinion would not count for anything anymore.

Several hours later as he made his way down the street toward the End of the Pier, the detective wondered what his opinion was worth at that moment. The contradictory impulses he had been feeling all day were still working on him, making him wonder exactly what he hoped to accomplish. In many ways he felt like a fool. He had been correct in telling his friends that there was little logic in what they were doing.

But, a voice within him pointed out, to whose logic was he referring? London had met creatures who considered him as unimportant as he would a mayfly.

Is that all we are to them, he wondered. Bugs who experience their entire life cycle in a single day?

The detective had discovered a race of beings hidden from all mankind, who, if his information was correct, had been in the vanguard of every major downfall humanity had suffered. As he walked down the last block before the club, the only sound around him that of his Blackthorn striking against the pavement, he worked at how impossible his position was. Apparently some people had always known about vampires. But, as he was well aware, there is often a vast difference between knowledge and the ability to act upon it.

Goward had known that Q'talu had been close to breaking through to our dimension. The professor and his colleague had been able to study the ancient records of past civilizations and through mathematics accurately predict the moment of the monstrosity's return. But, as Goward had explained to the detective, two months previous, whom could he have told about what he knew? Who would have listened outside of someone like the detective who had stumbled onto the truth by himself?

Nagging doubt battled against vengeful certainty, creating a never-ending stream of conflict within London's brain, the bickering voices of his mind driving him to distraction. The detective knew he was going to have to make a decision soon. But, he wondered, how could he? The last time he had made a decision on a similar matter, well over a million—almost two million—people had died. And now, he had only his own sense of righteousness to tell him he had made the proper choice—to keep him on this side of sanity.

Pushing all debate aside for the moment, though, the detective took one last look around the Lower West Side waterfront area. The West Side Highway traffic downhill from the club was moving somewhat faster than its usual crawl. London took in the ruined look of the area one last time—before approaching the front door of the End of the Pier.

The club, unlike so many in Manhattan, had been a permanent fixture of the city for years—decades, if you counted the name changes. Most people living on the island had not heard of it, but those closer to the city's underbelly were all too well aware of both it and its reputation.

The club had generated many stories over the years. Tales of barroom brawls, murders, disappearances, bizarre rites held in back rooms, orgies, hidden opium dens, secret organizations holding sinister meetings—every type of unsubstantiated lurid tale that can be told had been circulated about the End of the Pier. Now, London found himself wondering just how many of the stories he had heard were true and, he added, more importantly, which ones?

He had never thought about them before, of course—why would he? But now, they all seemed to blend together making a sinister type of sense. Resisting the urge to shudder, the detective moved forward again, heading for the front door. He held himself in from reaching around to check the weight of his weapon as he passed by the doorman. It was a common, unconscious human habit, one for which any good security person would be trained to watch. London had sternly warned Morcey against it and was now glad he had. The security man on door duty that night seemed like a good one.

As the detective wandered into the body of the club, he assumed the guise of any first-timer, looking in all directions, casually, but inquisitively. Hoping he appeared to be just another lonely man looking for a night's companion, he studied the doors and windows, the back of his mind automatically recording all of the possible entrances and exits as a routine matter of course. The place's main room was a monstrously large affair, more than big enough for a partial pseudo-second floor made up of balcony-like runways jutting out at odd angles from just above door-top level all the way to the ceiling.

The entire club was shrouded in overlapping layers of shadow, every visible inch painted in only two colors—the brightest whites and the glossiest blacks. The tables, the bar, the doorways, and even the light fixtures followed the same design. Some of the effects were done in stripes, some in checkerboard, still other sections took on a polka-dot-on-flat-background effect. No matter where one looked, black-and-white was all they could see.

Searching for a central spot from which he could wait for his partner to arrive, the detective moved through the black-and-white tables and chairs, heading toward the bar. He ordered a seltzer with a twist of lime and then began to study the help. They were a trim group, good-looking and sturdy, all muscular to a point, all possessed of the same surly Manhattanite sneer. They might be vampires, thought the detective, but then again, on the evidence of bad dispositions alone, he could convict most of those people holding menial positions throughout New York City of the same crime.

Oppps, he thought, better watch your phraseology, detective. Mustn't be judgmental. It's not a crime to *be* a vampire—just to *act* like one.

Then, suddenly, before he could scan the bartenders or table hoppers further, a piercing gold spotlight shot down from some point out of the back ceiling, flooding the stage. Not waiting for an introduction or applause, the band it illuminated began playing immediately upon its eruption. Four pieces—two guitars, one bass, and a drum set were all that made up the ensemble—parts which in this case created a whole most club-goers would approve of immediately. The three men and one woman on stage set up a beat riveted together from an explosion of driving, burning thrash metal sounds tied together into a sinister background of modernistic tribal rhythms.

London noted the band's name, *Kill By Inches*, stenciled on the side of their bass drum. The detective smiled at the reference, the medieval term for killing a victim slowly through torture. Then, as if taking his cue from London, the lead singer, a tall, well-built man, mean and angry, appeared from behind the four musicians and took the center mike. Whipping his long red hair back out of his face, he started his solo.

"I can't dance,
I can't sing,
Lord knows I can't
Do anything.

"But you all came here,
Just to watch me,
When you could have stayed home,
And watched TV.

"Why you do it,
I don't know,
I thought only the homeless
Had nowhere to go."

Whoever they were, the detective gave them points for jumping in and starting without introduction. The lead kept hammering away at his song, beating the audience with the opening number, just as London spotted Morcey making his way casually to the bar.

"Drinking your booze,
And doing your dope,
Leading your cold lives
Divorced of all hope.

"Burning your money,
Just to see the flash,
Throwing each other away
Like the rest of the trash.

"Why you do it,
I don't know.
When did ennui
Become the in way to go?"

Morcey ordered a beer while the band continued to crank, wandering past London, allowing his partner the chance to pass him a message if he wanted to while maintaining his air of non-recognition. The detective let the ponytailed man continue on by, not having discovered anything that he needed to pass on as of yet.

Morcey set up shop at the other end of the bar, taking one of the unclaimed stools for his own. He leaned back, propping one elbow on the highly polished wood, working at appearing as bored as he possibly could. London had warned him slumping too far forward would show off the outline of his Auto-Mag. The detective scanned his partner discreetly, checking to see if the balding man was giving himself away. From the best he could tell, there were no problems.

Satisfied everything was all right, London started to turn back to looking over the hired help when suddenly it occurred to him that he was looking for vampires in the wrong direction. Shifting a part of his brain to assume the role of those he was hunting, he began to ease himself into a manufactured personality.

Think like a vampire, he told himself.

As soon as he began the experiment, it immediately changed the focus of his attention, shifting it away from the help to study the rest of the audience. He was not long in finding his answer.

Of course, he thought to himself, of course. The master is not the one who pours the drinks, wipes up the messes, carries trays. Overlords do not service slaves—kings and queens do not clean toilets. Menial jobs were for menial types. You know, drops in the bucket—human beings. Winks.

Looking the crowd over, the detective knew he had found his villains. Not all the club-goers were vampires, of course. Some of the assembly were obviously just more human trash, like Morcey and himself, allowed in to be milked of their cash, used on the occasion when it seemed obvious they could disappear without any repercussions, or merely to help maintain a cover of if not respectability, then at least something that could be tolerated by the rest of the city.

London studied the revelers on both sides of him, those above and those below. Before a handful of minutes had passed, the detective was sure he knew which were the winks and which were the undying. There was something to them, something extra—an air about them that seemed almost incandescent.

The more he studied, the more he became convinced that there was indeed something—perhaps the degree to which the colors in their skin reflected the light—that was setting up a definite aura about each of those in the club that he would guess were vampires. Reaching for his drink, the detective ran the rim of his glass across his lips, drawing enough moisture to keep himself from getting too parched.

After weeks of having eaten no solid food, he could taste the juice of the small lime slice floating in his seltzer—so strong it was almost enough to make him retch. Again curiosity scratched at him, asking once more how he was managing to keep on going, week after week without eating. The detective almost gave in to the thought but, he caught hold of himself, refusing to spend any time wondering about it at that moment.

Later, he told himself, when we have the time to waste.

Then, he turned to the bar, setting down his drink. That was when the large mirror behind the array of bottles finally caught his eye. In the massive mirror, he could see the entire room, not only all of the dance floor, but all of the tables. Likewise, he could see all of the people in the club. He froze at the sight of them, fear creeping into his system, chilling him. All of those he had thought to be vampires, the auras he thought he could see about them before were even more pronounced in the mirror.

The thing that truly disturbed him, however, was that as shown by the mirror, the aura surrounding his body, colored the same as the vampires, was absolutely the brightest.

CHAPTER
TWENTY-TWO

L ONDON STARED INTO THE mirror, his self-image shattered—torn apart—by what he was seeing. What could it mean, he wondered. How could he appear in any way like those things he sought—those things he was growing to hate? Was *this* what Karen Tezzler had seen—what Martin Tabor had seen—that had made them think he was a creature such as they were? And if that was true, then why had the Muzz or those who came after him not seen it?

The detective raised his drink to his lips, ignoring the almost overpowering taste of the sliver of lime, draining half the glass with the one pull. He set it down, shaking, trembling from the force of the unanswered questions tearing at him. The bartender who had just served him came over, curious.

"Are you all right, sir?"

"Yes, yes," muttered London. "I'm fine, thank you."

"Can I get you anything else, sir?"

"No, dammit—I said I was fine!" snapped the detective, pounding his fist against the bar. Instantly regretting his reaction, not even certain where it had come from, he apologized immediately. Sadly, he noted that the bartender was more confused by his apology than by his earlier behavior. As the man moved off to his other customers, London wondered if his anger was just another thing he had in common with those he hunted.

The End of the Pier was their place. If they were the regular customers there, and that reaction seemed normal to the bartender where an apology had seemed out of place . . . then was he . . . becoming a vampire? Was it something that happened simply through contact with them?

As panic began to seize the detective he signaled to Morcey, letting his partner know it was time to leave. The balding man understood the message, nodding quietly. Although the pair had worked out a number of signals between them, they were all quiet, subtle things, arranged to keep others from knowing the pair were working together. Holding on to the edge of the bar to steady himself, London downed the last of his drink and then turned to go, only to find his way blocked by a man dressed in black—boots, pants, T-shirt, even his watch and the bandanna wrapped around his forehead. Putting his hand on the detective's chest, he pushed London back toward the bar, telling him in a voice loud enough to be heard over the band;

"Now, now, now, now, now. Bad form, friend. Very bad form, indeed."

The detective quickly pushed aside all of his doubts and fears for the moment, forgetting them to concentrate on his newest problem. Wanting to leave the club as quietly as possible, London answered in an even voice;

"I'm not your friend and I don't care how bad my form is. I also don't care what you want. I'm leaving."

"Oh, an angry one. Comes and shows the world his tasty-tasty and then says he doesn't want to play. Well, I say, *bop-bop*. Drebble says, *bop-bop*!!"

Out of the corner of his eye, London caught Morcey beginning to move forward. The detective made a desperate motion with his hand, warning his friend back. Not knowing what he was up against, he decided there was no sense in both of them going down if London's identity had somehow been discovered.

If it had not, though, then he had no idea what the man was talking about and did not want to jeopardize his friend for no good reason. So, trying to get himself out of the club without further incident, the detective answered;

"Look, pal; I've been about as civil as I know how to be so far but, that's it. This is all the nice you get. I'm leaving, and you're staying here. Now . . . get out of my way."

Drebble slammed London back up against the bar. The detective grabbed the other man's wrist as he tried to pin him against the curved top lip of wood, twisting it enough to make his opponent think that was how he intended to try to escape. Then, when Drebble began to strain to hold him, the detective shot his other hand upward, palm open, ramming it viciously under the other man's chin.

Drebble staggered backward a few steps but then moved forward again suddenly, making to grab London. The detective sidestepped the maneuver, grabbing up his Blackthorn, bringing it down in a swinging motion on his opponent's back. Drebble let fly a spitting curse, swinging around with blinding speed, catching London on the side of the head with his balled fist.

The detective tumbled over himself, falling away from the bar. Instantly he came back to his feet, seeing Morcey closing on the pair. Others were moving forward as well. London pulled in on himself, pushing the pain in his head away. Morcey slowed up, keeping his position within the crowd. As the detective eyed his antagonist, he studied the crowd as well, wondering if what was happening was something unseen before or merely business as usual.

"Drebble," called one. "What're you doing?"

"Bop time," he called over his shoulder, not turning, not taking his eyes off London. "This one comes in here, showing off all the radiating yummies, hanging the bar like he's the king of the world . . ."

"Drebble's got a right," came another voice. "Everyone has got that right."

"He's an outsider!" screamed back Drebble. "And I'm fall-down hungry! He's got too much—too fucking much for one man! It's bop time. *Bop time!*"

And then, before anyone could say anything further, the man in black rushed the detective—low and hard. London spun out of his path, letting Drebble slam his fingers against the bar. As the man howled, London cut the air with his Blackthorn, smashing it against the man's skull. Not resting for a second, the detective pressed his advantage, striking with the cane twice more, savage blows that rattled his opponent to the bone.

Another hit landed and the man in black's head bounced off the wood with a sickening, popping sound—teeth shattering against the curve of the bar, bloody enameled pieces spilling across the floor. The blow was a good one—too good. Feeling his teeth go filled Drebble with a renewed energy. He came up off the floor as if unfettered by gravity, cursing;

"Damn you, little man. You'll give sup or feast, one of the other. Drebble cares not."

"Drebble's an idiot," answered London. Holding himself in, regulating his breath, showing no weakness. Fresher than before, he leaned back casually on the bar, telling his foe;

"Read me right—bucko . . . I'll give you one thing, and that's nothing but pain. You're outmatched here. Go find someone who'll put up with your petty-ante or I promise you, I'll leave you dead on the floor."

The crowd buzzed. People on all sides quickly formed a semicircle around the pair of combatants. Behind the bar, the bartender released a line that lowered a shutter down over the massive wall-length mirror. Well, thought London, at least I know this is nothing special.

Money began to fill hands, people from all sides calling out names and times, amounts and degrees of damage. Others accepted the cash, giving odds on every call.

"Drebble down in ten—five hundred says crippled."

"Five to one."

"Mr. X down in five—four thousand says dead."

"Seven to two."

"Drebble in three—two hundred the stranger gets blinded."

"Ten to one."

On it went, London poised, sucking down breath, steadying his heart rate, preparing for the onslaught—Drebble walking the edges of the circle, hands elevated, muscles tensing, blood still dripping from his broken mouth. The crowd stared at both of them, each member picking their favorite. As the detective studied the faces around him, the auras he had seen before in the great mirror suddenly flashed in the eyes of those surrounding him. He realized that people without a flicker were being shoved to the back by the others. He could see that whatever happened would be covered by the vampires. No one from the outside—no winks—would see what actually transpired.

Drebble continued to swagger at the edge of the semicircle, kissing the women he fancied, some of the men. All of them licked at the blood trickling down his chin. One woman greeted the vampire warmly, holding him in a long embrace. She slid her tongue into Drebble's mouth, playing with him until she broke the embrace suddenly. As the surrounding vampires watched, she opened her mouth and extended her tongue, revealing one of Drebble's shattered teeth on its curled tip. The vampires stared at the tooth poised on the end of the smiling woman's tongue for only a moment before doubling over with laughter. Drebble waved his arms with glee himself, encouraging all those making up the semicircle to join in.

And then, as the man in black drew closer to the bar, dancing a loutish jig for comedy effect, London understood his movements. He had seen the clown act before—one antagonist playing the lout, amusing the crowd, calculating his moment of attack, waiting for an off-guard opening when his opponent seemed either amused or bored.

Shifting his position, the detective leaned back toward the bar, balancing himself carefully, looking all the world as if he could care less what Drebble did next, as if he was fooled by the vampire's tactics. Then, to finish the illusion, gauging the striking time of the man in black, London lifted his hand to his mouth as if to stifle a yawn, closing his eyes. Drebble launched himself instantly. The detective brought his walking stick up one-handed, bouncing it off the man in black's chin. More blood flowed, propelled on a hot wall of screams and insults.

London danced away from the bar and back toward the living wall surrounding him, skirting its edges but making sure not to get too close to any of the spectators. He had no idea how the rules worked in such games at the End of the Pier but, he had seen such sports often enough not to trust a crowd where people were betting against him.

"Tricky," said Drebble, "aren't you? Well, I guess that figures. Carrying around that much soul juice . . . must have a few tricks in your bag."

"You could still get out of this alive," bluffed London, hoping against sense his foe would take the option.

"Oh," answered the man in black, smiling his bloody, broken smile, "That I will."

And then, the vampire launched himself without any warning, tackling the detective about the chest. The two went down in an awkward, thrashing heap, the crowd dancing back out of their way with only a split second to spare. As the pair rolled around, Drebble suddenly found his way to the top. Straddling London, he slapped the detective across the face, shattering his nose. Blood sluiced down from London's nostrils, filling his mouth, gagging him.

"Hey, hey," cried Drebble. "Now we're a pair, ehhh?"

Not waiting for an answer, the man in black punched the detective in the side of the head, then took his hair in both hands and lifted his head off the floor, only to then slam it down again. Exploding white mist filled London's eyes. His hearing became an indecipherable blur of crowd noises and the sound of his own throbbing temples. Chaos ran through his conscious mind, distracting his will at every turn.

Not able to control his consciousness any longer he abandoned it, swimming down through the jumbled static it had become to his subconscious. Throwing all control to his instincts, he released his will, allowing his body to defend itself. Feeling the blows raining against his head in a distracted, painless way, he braced his hands against the floor and then pushed off with his feet, bringing them up and over Drebble's head. Locking his knees under the chin of the man in black, he pulled with all the combined strength of gravity and his legs. Before he knew what was happening, Drebble was slammed against the floor—chest first—hard and brutal.

Both the fighters came to their feet at the same moment. The man in black reached toward the bar—a brandy bottle that had not been within reach earlier had somehow appeared near his end. In one motion Drebble seized the bottle and smashed it open, gaining a five-inch-long, razor-sharp advantage.

"So," said London, stalling for a chance to breathe. "I see the bartenders are allowed to bet here."

"Let's just say they know their place—like you should have, new boy scum."

"Awwww," answered the detective slowly, flexing his fingers, readying his leg for the sudden jerk needed. "I didn't realize the rules called for those with balls to just curl up and die for those who just wished they had some."

Drebble remained silent, flexing his fingers, waiting for his moment. Needing to unbalance him the slightest bit, London tossed off a comment to break the vampire's concentration.

"Still, it wouldn't be good form to just drop my pants and let you feast, so I guess I'll have to fall back on that bag of tricks you were looking for."

"Ohhhhhhh," said Drebble in a mocking tone. "And what were you thinking of dazzling us with, hummm?"

"Something simple."

And then, London snapped his leg up, pulling Veronica from her quick-drop sheath. As the man in black made to duck under what he thought was a kick, he moved directly into the detective's attack. Before anyone in the crowd could react, suddenly, Drebble was toppling for the ground, clutching at his neck.

"Auugghhhh, ohhh, ohh—hhhelppp mmmme," he called, his words slurred in a choking gurgle.

Blood splattered in all directions, pumping relentlessly through the half-foot-long slash running across his throat. Shouts of triumph went up throughout the club, those who bet on the long shot collecting their winnings from those who had gone with the known. As London stood, sore and tired, backing away from the spreading crimson pool, Morcey pushed his way forward through the now-thinning crowd. Concern overriding caution, he came up to his partner, offering him a handkerchief. The detective took it and wiped it across the sweat and blood coating his face, soaking it through instantly.

A hand from the crowd offered another. Morcey accepted it, offering its owner a quick "thanks." Then he gave it to London who filled it as quickly as the first. The same hand offered another. Another "thanks" was given but, before the balding man could hand the square to his partner, he was pushed away as a howling London fell back against the bar.

The detective's eyes opened shock wide. He screamed as the same electrical stabbing that had burned through him in Karen Tezzler's apartment attacked him again. The force rolled over him, sizzling throughout his body. His eyes grew even wider as he stared at his arm, seeing visible steam rising from it. And then, as before, the voices of the dead filled his still-reeling consciousness, setting him screaming with agony.

Falling to his knees, he attracted the attention of all who had been circled about him. Content to scream with glee when he was locked in combat to the death, they now adopted looks of scorn as the detective strove to fight back the overpowering presences living within the dark recesses of his head. To the last of them, they took their money and their drinks, gliding back to their tables. The body of the man in black had already been taken away, the floor wiped clean, all traces of blood and broken glass removed.

When London finally seemed approachable, Morcey helped him to his feet, asking;

"Sweet Bride of the Night—what was that?"

"Same thing as the woman's apartment," whispered the detective. "Worse this time. More powerful."

As they made their way the few feet back to the bar, Morcey looked about for the person who had handed him the handkerchiefs, wanting to return the unused one. Looking down the bar, he spotted the man, chewing the one the balding man had handed him back earlier. Now not chewing it so much as sucking on it. Smiling at the pair, a movement molded of pure hate, he pulled the now-pink cloth from his mouth, slowly—threateningly—calling;

"So good to see you again."

London looked up into Martin Tabor's face.

"Who'd you bet on, Marty?" he asked.

"I don't gamble," answered the small vampire. "It's a vice for the weak of will, the dead of spirit. Not that such things will concern you for much longer."

Dropping the ruined handkerchief on the bar, Tabor began to move forward. Looking into the little man's intense eyes, both London and Morcey knew he intended to kill them then and there. Stepping forward, the ex-maintenance man said;

"Don't worry, Mr. London, I can handle this."

Without hesitation, Morcey reached hastily into his inner jacket pocket.

Tabor froze for a moment, giving the balding man the time he needed.

"Laugh this off, you jinch."

And so saying, Morcey pulled out a crucifix and held it aloft, threatening all around them with the sacred totem. For a precious, hope-giving moment, none around them stirred. But then, after the initial surprise had worn off, various of the crowd broke into different levels and pitches of laughter. Even Tabor stopped, grinning with satisfaction. Morcey turned to London saying;

"You know, I don't think this thing's gonna work."

As the pair looked at each other, bereft of ideas as to what to do next, suddenly a smattering of applause broke out from somewhere in the crowd. As those assembled broke ranks, a lone figure came forward from between them, clapping in a slow but respectful fashion. He was tall, lean, and feline in nature, a dark-colored man with close-cropped hair and deep, near-black eyes.

Coming up to Morcey, he gently pulled the crucifix from out of the balding man's hands, saying;

"Well, well, well—I see we have a fan of the cinema among us."

"Good evening, Jorhsa," guessed London.

"And, a pleasant good evening to you, Mr. London," answered the king of the vampires.

CHAPTER
TWENTY-THREE

"**B**UT WE HAVE TO kill them!"

"Martin," said Jorhsa in a quiet voice, still somewhat amused by the crucifix he continued to absently turn over and over in his hands. "Could it be you have forgotten just how things work?"

"No," the smaller vampire answered in frightened haste. "No, sir, no. It, it's just that this is the *one!* This is the one who killed the Muzz, who killed all of, who . . . Karen . . ." He said her name like a child remembering its lost mother.

"He has to suffer, Lord Jorhsa. He must," pleaded the little man. "He has to."

"Nonsense," replied the king of the vampires. "This is a man of mighty accomplishments. I'm sure Karen sensed the power within him—wanted it for herself—paid the price. Just like Drebble. Of course, Drebble was a greedy fool. Someone would have killed him sooner or later, anyway. Karen . . ." The vampire's voice took on a wistful tone.

"She was indeed a loss." He said the words almost with sorrow, standing still for a handful of seconds, lost within whatever memories of Karen Tezzler the mention of her death had brought back to him. And then, just as quickly, Jorhsa's smile returned, his tone again filled with cheer.

"But, losses can be regained," he reminded the assembly. "No, Martin, we will not be foolishly killing Mr. London. That would be a waste. And being wasteful is not what has kept us alive and strong all these centuries. Is it?"

"No . . . no, sir."

"Good little Martin. Now, I want you to go prepare the meeting room. Tell those council members present that I think we might have some fine entertainment in store for them."

Jorhsa watched Tabor move off toward the back of the club, stopping at this or that table for only a moment before going on to the next. He watched for only a supervisory moment, like a parent watching a five year old given some simple task, then the king of the vampires turned suddenly, asking;

"What are you thinking, Mr. London?"

"I think I'd like you to tell me how it is you know my name."

"Well, I could very well ask the same, but then I'm not a private detective, am I? I suppose someone in your line of work likes to know all the facts." Handing Morcey back his crucifix, Jorhsa said;

"Here is your toy, youngster. Take good care of it."

Then, the king of the vampires put his arm around London's shoulders. The detective did not resist the movement, waiting to see exactly what was going to happen next. Jorhsa moved toward the back of the club, following the direction in which Tabor had exited, urging London along with him. Again, the detective did not resist, sensing that at the moment he had no better option than to play the present scene out to the end. Morcey, sheepishly replacing his crucifix within his jacket, followed along as Jorhsa explained;

"I'm sorry—you were wanting to know how I knew who you were. Really—no big secret. Our people recovered the Muzz's body. Once we got it back we had our witches—yes, we have witches, too—lay their hands to it. They got the scene for us—your name, your connection to Xui Zeng Lu, how you killed poor Muzz. Amazing thing that."

"I just shot him."

Then, all of a sudden, Jorhsa stopped moving forward, turning to look into London's eyes. His hand came away from the detective as he questioned;

"Just shot him?"

He continued to stare deeply, asking, "Is that really what you would call it? 'Just shot him?' Are you actually so powerful that that is all you would consider it?"

"It is all right if I don't know what you're talking about, isn't it?" As Jorhsa regarded London, his eyes narrowing slightly, the detective continued;

"As far as I'm concerned, a big, dumb mug walked into twelve slugs and died from the experience. First, he walked into six and went down. Then he started to heal and get up again, so I blasted him another six times. That time he stayed down. Trust me, the gun did all the work."

Jorhsa's eyes narrowed another fraction of an inch, the left side of his mouth curling into a smile. Still holding his same position, he looked at the detective squarely and then answered him in a voice surprisingly earnest.

"I sincerely hope you can drop enough of your guard, just enough to enable you to listen to the things I tell you and believe them. I'll confess that I've waited a long time to meet someone like you. You're a fascinating man, Mr. London. Over the ages, just the mere image of the Muzz moving toward his foes across the battlefield was more than enough to inspire terror in all but the heartiest of them. His side pierced by a spear, he would simply draw it out and attack again. Sights like that froze his enemies in their tracks."

That said, the king of the vampires began to walk forward once more. London and Morcey followed him, listening to him talk. As they withdrew from the main body of the club, entering a long stone hallway hung with deep purple curtains, they looked about them, marveling at what they saw on both sides. The draperies were hung around matched sets of swords and shields, rows of each, weapons spanning hundreds of decades. As they passed by the collection, Jorhsa told them;

"This was his hall—these arms were all his, over the years. The Muzz . . . how can I explain it to you? At times he has been feared by the entire known world. Mr. London, try and understand the depth of my respect for your accomplishment."

Reaching over to the wall, the king of the vampires pulled forth a short bronze sword, a weapon at least two thousand years old. He hefted it easily, testing its weight, then handed it to the detective, telling him;

"Hold this, Mr. London—feel it. You slew the man who carried it—a man who stood at the side of Alexander as they strode together across the face of the world, conquering the Greek city states, toppling the Persian Empire from Asia Minor and my home of Egypt across the known world to the ends of India. You've slain a man whose paintings hang in the Louvre—who sailed with Erikson to discover the New World. Please, feel free to be impressed with yourself. You have the right."

Jorhsa stopped again, his voice dropping to a whisper. "After all, you're the man who killed Hercules."

CHAPTER
TWENTY-FOUR

L ONDON'S HEAD PULLED BACK a few inches. The detective looked at Jorhsa askance. He knew that at that point the vampire had no reason to lie to him but, he found that his natural suspicions, the traits that had kept him alive over the years, were making him skeptical nonetheless. In truth, part of his brain was perfectly willing to accept what it was being told. But, as much as London trusted that little voice—the one inside his head that told him what was real and what was not—what he was hearing was still so much to believe.

It was one thing to accept the existence of vampires, even to accept ones thousands of years old—but the things Jorhsa was telling him were too much for him to incorporate all at one time. Sensing this, the king of the vampires commented;

"Well, it's nice to see that there are some things in this world that can take even you by surprise."

"If I admit that there's plenty right here that's taking me by surprise, can I ask a few questions?"

"Of course," answered Jorhsa. "Come with me. We'll go to a place better suited for conversation."

They moved farther down the Muzz's hall, continuing on by his collected sets of swords and shields. London and Morcey continued to let their eyes wander from side to side, taking in each of the pieces. Some were battered and well worn, others in nearly perfect condition. The swords were of some interest to the men but, it was the shields that drew the greatest attention.

All of them were large, full-torso covering wooden circles, faced with bronze and backed with leather. Each bore its own distinguishing marks. Some were painted with pictures of horses, great birds, or dragon heads. Others were trimmed in ribbons of crushed, netted iron, set off with colored stones or tiles, or merely displaying centuries-old holes where some decoration had once rested, now long lost. Two of them showed the remnants of ancient leather curtains hanging from the shields' bases, most likely to act as leg protectors.

Unlike Karen Tezzler's collection, made up of scores of different pieces—all types and sizes and shapes from around the world, spanning the known ages—the Muzz's hall held only one type of set. All were from one part of the world; all from one time. That was until the trio reached the end of the hallway.

There, set back in a recessed show chamber scooped out of the wall, sat a magnificent beaten metal helmet. In the back of his mind, another ancestor voice—like the one that had explained the hunting patterns in the overgrown lot—began to speak to London. It explained to him that the golden chestnut color of the crest was natural, due to the fact that it was made of horsehair, a material not easily dyed. It pointed out the elongated cheek pieces, designed to better protect the wearer's mouth and throat, as well as the cranial ridge that not only added overall strength but ventilation as well.

London did not need the new ancestor voice speaking to him then to point out the beauty of the decorative relief work. The detective noted the incredibly detailed scene of centaurs and soldiers in battle all on his own.

Jorhsa intruded on London's quiet studies to offer, "Beautiful, isn't it?"

"Yes," agreed the detective, then asking a question supplied by the same ancestor voice. "Corinthian?"

Surprise filled the king of the vampire's eyes. When he questioned how London knew, the detective answered;

"Well, besides the relative obviousness of its overall style, it does appear to be hammered out of a single sheet of bronze. You never got that kind of craftsmanship in an Illyrian. Wouldn't you agree?"

Jorhsa smiled.

"Oh, yes. *I* would. But, honestly, I had no idea that you would. If you don't mind me asking, exactly how old are you, Mr. London?"

"I'm thirty-three. How old are you?"

"I sat through a celebration of my five thousandth and forty-fifth year just a few months ago."

"And he don't look a day over three thousand, does he, Mr. London?"

"I'm glad you have a sense of humor, little man," intoned Jorhsa, dryly. "Come this way, gentlemen. We have a larger audience in need of amusement."

And, so saying, the king of the vampires walked the last few feet of the hallway and then stopped to open the large, curve-topped doors protecting the next chamber. As the three entered, they were greeted by a large open area, surrounded on three sides by a steel-reinforced wooden barrier nearly four feet in height. As they moved farther into the heavily curtained room, London and Morcey both studied those sitting around the dais. Roughly half of the faces, like Martin Tabor's, they recognized, having seen them in the club earlier. The others they either did not know or did not remember.

Holding open a cleverly concealed swinging door in the barrier wall, Jorhsa indicated a seat for London. As Morcey followed his partner, however, the king of the vampires held up his hand, letting the balding man know he was to wait. When the detective protested, Jorhsa told him;

"You have a place here, this one does not. If he is to survive, he must meet certain requirements."

London stared at Morcey, searching to see how his partner was taking what was happening. The ex-maintenance man noted the detective's look, telling him;

"Don't sweat it, boss. Let's see what these monkeys got up their sleeves."

Morcey unbuttoned his jacket, freeing his arms, not knowing what to expect but, wanting to be ready for whatever was coming. Biting down on his lower lip, he turned his head one way and then the other, stretching out his neck. When he started to unkink his shoulders, one of those seated at the dais called out to him.

"What are you preparing for, wink?"

"I don't know," answered Morcey, not breaking his stride. "Why don't you tell me?"

A round of laughter went up from those assembled. Jorhsa smiled at the balding man, telling him;

"I suppose that would be the only fair thing now, wouldn't it? Very well, I will tell you. You have been brought into the presence of the high council. This doesn't happen to your type very often—not this way, as an equal—allowed breath and heart and reason. Shall I tell you why you are being given this opportunity for survival?"

"Yeah," responded Morcey, now certain of what was coming. He kept flexing, stretching himself out, purposely ignoring the vampire's eyes. Continuing to loosen himself up as if for hand-to-hand combat, he said;

"Thrill me, Barnabas."

"There is a bond between you and your friend here. Quite honestly, we would appreciate his company. Being equally honest, despite your jester's way with a religious artifact, it is the general consensus that we don't really care for yours. But, because we know to kill you outright would distress your companion, you shall be given your chance to impress us. As it seems you have discerned on your own, it will be a fight to the death. You may do anything you can to win."

Then, turning back to the dais, Jorhsa snapped his fingers in the direction of Martin Tabor.

"I cannot allow you Mr. London, dear Martin, but I can give you his friend."

Tabor rose without hesitation, staring intently at the ex-maintenance man, licking his lips. The small vampire removed his jacket, placing it over his chair.

Snapping his suspenders sharply, he made his way to the concealed door. As he swung it open, stepping out into the center area, London pushed himself upward, one hand tight around the top of his Blackthorn as he stood, protesting;

"What's wrong with you people—are you all crazy? Do you really think I'm going to just let you kill my best friend and get away with it? What the hell's the setup here, anyway? You would appreciate my fucking company, would you—start giving me a reason to give it to you!"

Jorhsa put his hand into the air at the level of the detective's chest. He warned London in a growling voice;

"Your life has been in our hands since you entered this building. We're offering you a tremendous opportunity here. We have our reasons and they will be made known to you—but—this question of your loyalties must be decided. If Mr. Morcey is worthy of survival, he will best Martin. If you are worthy of us, you will allow him his chance. Elsewise, you will both perish—now!"

London looked into Morcey's face. His friend gave him a tiny nod, assuring him;

"Relax, boss. Take a seat. I'm supposed to get worked up here because the CPA of the Damned is comin' for me? The world's gonna be short one more bloodsucker in a few minutes."

"You think so, you human scum?" asked Tabor.

"Oh, fuckin' A, man," answered Morcey in an easy, bantering tone. "I've killed real monsters, punk. The day I start gettin' worried about a chump like you, I'd better retire. We got secretaries at The London Agency that can handle the likes of you." As Tabor entered the arena, Jorhsa called out in a cautioning voice;

"Martin, are you sure you are prepared? You know how tricky quicks can be."

"I can handle one stupid unarmed wink."

Jorhsa sighed, and then announced, "Then have at each other."

Tabor smiled, his fingers opening and closing—once, twice. His arm muscles tensed as he hunched himself into a favored attack position. Morcey stood across the room, his arms folded, his mood unimpressed. The vampire took a tentative step forward, toes touching the floor first, heel coming down softly. There was a grace and an easy fluidity to his movements London had not expected.

Morcey uncrossed his arms, stretching them out from his sides. Closing his eyes, he opened his mouth in a yawn, a movement that actually startled Tabor in its unexpectedness. Then, having hoped for just such a reaction, Morcey reached behind his back, pulled out his Auto-Mag, and fired at point-blank range, blasting a massive hole in Tabor's chest. The vampire spun around twice and then bounced off the dais.

Stepping forward, Morcey fired again, and then again. Meat and blood smeared the dais, both shells erupting through Tabor's back, digging deeply into the wood and the steel barrier behind him. The vampire started to move away from the wall. Morcey quickly closed on him. Then, when they were only a yard apart, the balding man raised his arm and placed the muzzle of his weapon directly between Tabor's eyes. Another thundering blast was felt throughout the room as the vampire's head exploded, flying bits of bone and brain splattering in every direction. As the seemingly lifeless body fell, not wanting to take any chances, the ex-maintenance man moved forward. Standing over his foe, he placed the Auto-Mag directly over the small of the vampire's back and fired another time, shattering the man's spine.

Then he fired again and again, making an unholy ruin of the body beneath his feet. By the time he emptied the weapons' clip, Martin Tabor had been shredded into nonexistence. Morcey blew away the smoke uncurling from the barrel of his automatic. Trying as best he could to disguise the pain wracking his arm from the powerful weapon's overwhelming recoil, he dropped its clip into his hand and then slid in another from his pocket.

Slapping it upward into place, he looked directly at Jorhsa, smiling as he asked;

"Next?"

CHAPTER
TWENTY-FIVE

O ONE HEARD MORCEY'S rejoinder, of course—not even Morcey, himself. All in the room were still holding their ears, deafened by the thundering blasts of the balding man's attack. The heavy curtains hanging throughout the chamber had absorbed much of the noise, but it had still been more than anyone, even London, had been prepared for. The detective, shaken but relieved, gave his partner an inquiring look. Morcey returned him a tiny nod, letting him know he was all right for the moment. London flashed him a quick thumbs-up, and then asked Jorhsa, screaming at the vampire simply to be heard;

"Good enough?"

"Yes," shouted the king of the vampires. "Yes, enough. Good enough."

Leaving Jorhsa's side, the detective stepped down from the dais and went to join his partner in the arena. Clasping Morcey on the shoulder, he told his friend;

"You took an awful chance there, Paul."

"Hey, boss, no offense but, that's our business, ain't it?" His face taking on a slightly hurt look, the ex-maintenance man said;

"I appreciate you being concerned and all but, if you don't think I can take care of myself, what'ya let me join your organization for?"

"Well, that's not—" Morcey interrupted, cutting London off with a wave of his hand. Slight anger showing in his expression, he said;

"Like the chicken said, 'I knew the job was dangerous when I took it.' If you think I'm just in your way—that you have to watch out for me all the time—you just say the word and I'll take off. Anytime—anytime. But, until you say the word, don't be surprised if you don't catch me goin' through the Sunday Times help wanted section."

The detective apologized to Morcey, trying in as few words as possible to let him know that it was not any doubts he had about his friend's abilities, but only his fear of causing anyone else's death that had forced him to act as he did. While the two conversed, waiting to see what would happen next, complete hearing slowly began to return to those within the room.

As it did, the assembly of vampires began to shout back and forth, questioning each other over their opinions of all that had happened so far. Some reminisced over their first time within similar halls, standing where Morcey had stood, facing their first test. As threads of their conversations reached

London, the detective bellowed;

"Jorhsa! I demand an explanation!"

All of the assembled turned, staring at London and Morcey. Tabor's blasted remains still oozing blood at their feet, the pair struck defiant poses, waiting for their answer. The king of the vampires did not leave them hanging.

"Yes, I suppose you should have one, although I would think that everything would be obvious to you by now."

"Pretend we're not five thousand years old like the rest of you. Spell it all out, all right?"

Jorhsa made to answer but, before he could, another of the assembly spoke first.

"Wait. This is preposterous! How can we dare to tell our secrets to these—these—*nothings?!*" The king of the vampires wheeled on the speaker, throwing back at him;

"And I submit to all assembled—how . . . can . . . we . . . not? Look at his aura, all of you. Study the power that ripples throughout our Mr. London here. Are there any of you who have shimmered with such strength? When was the last beacon like that shown anywhere beneath the morning sun or evening sky? Their fate must be dealt with at once. He will join us or die, and it will be decided—now."

London stepped forward then, demanding;

"What are you talking about? For Christ's sake will someone here explain what this is all about? What fate? What is there to decide? I mean, really, why in the name of God would I want to ally myself with vampires?"

"Because, sir," answered Jorhsa, evenly, calmly, without a hint of deceit in his voice, "you are a vampire, yourself."

The detective took the news better than he thought he would—better than Morcey did. He realized even as he heard the words that a part of his mind had been wondering if what the vampire had just told him were not true. Everything Jorhsa told him after that fit neatly into place, answering all of his questions, explaining everything that had happened to him over the past two days.

The king of the vampires asked him if he had begun to note auras around others, possibly around himself. As London and Morcey took seats, the detective admitted that he had. Jorhsa interpreted the phenomenon for him.

"Everyone has a personal energy field," he said. "It is a measure of the life force within one, their soul, really. The more vitality, health, good humors, et cetera, a person has, the more this is reflected within their aura. It is that 'glow' people talk about seeing around pregnant women. It is a quite natural thing—the life force of two beings radiating through one. Really, the only people who don't have auras are the dead."

Sitting back in his seat, stretching his arms out across its massive back, Jorhsa continued;

"Don't let me do all the talking, though. Let these others assembled speak. Listen to them. Make up your mind."

Another at the dais leaned forward, then. He was much older in appearance than the youthful Jorhsa, but he possessed the same keen eyes and sharpness of appearance. He interrupted, first looking toward Morcey, saying;

"My name's Zhenmi, and let me say that was nice shooting, lad. Idiot Tabor—I knew Jorhsa was trying to hint that you might be armed. 'CPA of the Damned,' that was a good one, too. I hope we let you live, you're all right. But," he shifted his attention to London, "getting back to you . . ."

"Yes . . .?"

"Jorhsa's a good, strong, intelligent leader. That's why no one ever challenges him for the position. First and the best. But we'll be here all night if someone doesn't cut down to the meat of things. I figure there's only one thing you really want to know right now—*how* does a person become a vampire?"

Zhenmi caught London's eyes. Seeing he was right, he continued;

"I'll tell you how. They knock someone over the head and kill them—that's how. Steal a life, it becomes your own. You kill someone—their life energy flows to you. You want to know how you got a super-charged energy field . . . I'll tell you. Somehow, in your short time, you've killed a hell of a lot of people. Don't knock it. Means you'll live forever. Means you'll look that young forever, too, not worn out like me—but that's what comes when you start feasting too late in life."

London thought of the crackling pain he suffered in the hospital, the shocks both in Tezzler's apartment and in the front room of the club, piecing together what the older-looking vampire was telling him. Trying to second-guess the questions in the detective's eyes, the vampire said;

"And that's not the only benefit, is it? You fought the Muzz—all the others. You saw it—didn't you? You saw them healing right before your eyes. That's why Drebble didn't care if you knocked all his teeth out. What did he care? Ten minutes after you were dead he'd have grown new ones. Course, didn't work out that way—did it?"

Zhenmi had not anticipated London, however. Still somewhat confused, the detective asked;

"But does that mean Paul has received Tabor's life energies?"

"No. Killing with a gun puts too much distance between you and the victim. Unless you kill a lot of people all at one time, you have to be right on top of them, bashing their brains out, tearing out their throat with your teeth, running a sword through their ribs. You've heard the stories of tribesmen eating the hearts of their enemies to gain their power, or that stuff about . . ."

Now it all made sense. That was why the Muzz's power had not flowed to him—he had shot the Muzz. But he had been forced into direct physical confrontation with Tezzler and Drebble, and now, two more voices were in his head with all the others, including the ones they had brought with them.

Now, he thought, I understand what's happened to me.

But, even though what he was being told explained his own case, it created new questions that did not seem to make sense. Looking at the seemingly older vampire, he asked;

"But people are killed every day. Scores of them every day. Does that mean that half the people walking around are vampires?"

"No, no; it's not that easy," replied Zhenmi. "Hell, there's less than a hundred of us banded together. I'm sure there are plenty of others out there, somewhere, but they usually disappear before we can find them, help them get their balance."

As London sat, waiting for more, suddenly the older vampire's lecture was interrupted by an exotic-looking woman with flowing black hair. She told the detective;

"Most people can't handle the strain of their murders. They hear that first voice in the back of their heads, and right then they start going insane. You have to be willing to take responsibility for what you've done. Those that won't, or can't, can't hold the power—it fades. You have to want it, be willing to keep it at all costs. Then, it will sustain you throughout anything, even the centuries. After a while, the only aging you will experience will be the fading of your ethnic traits—once you've killed all men, you become all men . . ."

As the female vampire continued to talk, London let his eyes flit in this direction and that, taking in all that was going on in the chamber, without letting it appear he had lost any interest in what the woman was saying. He noted that Paul had settled into a position of utter boredom, wearing an I-wish-the-boss-would-hurry-up frown. It was a good act, but the detective knew his partner was worried.

And why shouldn't he be, thought London, I'm a little scared to death myself.

Finally, however, the circle of vampires had all taken a turn speaking. The detective smiled ruefully, suddenly realizing what had happened. Each of the council members present had provided him with a bit or piece of their story, allowing Jorhsa to sit back and study London while the telling had continued. The detective stretched his arms, unknotting his back. Bringing them back down, he placed his palms, one atop the other, over the knob of his Blackthorn, pushing it out at an angle away from his chest. Addressing Jorhsa, he asked;

"Well, so what happens next?"

"That, my friend, is up to you."

"No, I mean, I'm already a vampire, right? I've murdered enough people to get soul energy stored up to keep me going for a thousand years, maybe ten thousand? I mean, what do I need you for? I pay my dues and get a membership card and club house rights? What's the point?"

Jorhsa grew grim—silent. The others backed away from London and Morcey. Near the edges of the room, Zhenmi made a signal to a male figure back in the shadows, half hidden by the room's massive curtains. The man disappeared through some exit the detective could not make out. The king of the vampires spoke in a slow, deliberate voice.

"The point is, as they say, that you cannot go home again. You know what you are, and you know who we are. You are intelligent enough, I'm sure you have already determined on your own that you could not harm us as a group. Telling the media that there were vampires in this world would, at the best—and that is *if* you could get anyone to believe you at all—merely cause us to become oddities, or celebrities of sorts."

"Even when the murder angle was thrown in?"

"This is a world that likes proof. You would have to somehow prove we were what you claimed, that we did the things you claimed. And that," answered Jorhsa with a sudden ominous tone, "is something you would never get the chance to do."

He knew he was provoking a situation that he most likely could not handle but, London simply could not bring himself to give the creatures before him even a lying agreement to hold over him. Before he could help himself, he asked;

"Why not?"

"Because," answered the king of the vampires, "those who are not with us are against us. You are going to live forever—do you understand—*forever*. Everyone you know who is not one of us is going to die. You will be alone forever without family, without friends, without any contact with your own kind. And if you are against us, you will indeed be alone. If you try and stand on your own, you will do what others have done, draw attention to yourself, and thus to us. We will not allow that. Before we would, we would kill you and everyone close to you."

London took a deep breath, forcing as natural a laugh as he could. "Well," he answered in a casual tone, "I guess there's only one thing I can do."

The detective went for his Auto-Mag, but it was too late. No one within the chamber had thought he was convinced. They had gone through the ritual of induction too many times over the centuries to not know who was interested and who was repulsed. Before either London or Morcey could move, a dozen lesser vampires, all husky, impossibly strong males, swarmed out of the curtains and overpowered them both, kneeling on their backs, pressing their faces into the wooden floorboards.

"We're not going to kill you now," whispered Jorhsa, still sitting behind the dais. "I know what it's like to carry that many voices around in your head. I also know what it's like to think that what I'm saying is monstrous. But even I don't know what it's like to feel them both at once. So, we're going to release the two of you—yes, both of you—because I know how important that solitary friend can be. You see, Mr. London, take it from one very old Egyptian, I know you'll be back."

Then, the king of the vampires snapped his fingers and the twelve strong-arms pulled the detective and his partner up from the floor roughly, dragging them out of the chamber. The vampires moved their captives quickly through a series of rooms and stairwells and hallways, banging them against doorjambs, walls, railings. Then, suddenly, their captors opened one last door leading to the outside. Both men were thrown through it, falling a half-dozen feet into the alleyway below.

When they finally stopped moving, London and Morcey were sore and dazed, in no real position to defend themselves from what was coming. A large garbage Dumpster was wheeled over next to them. The two were stood upright, both pelted with several savage blows to further incapacitate them. Then, after that, they were thrown inside, one atop the other, London's walking stick pitched in as well just before the container's twin lids were slammed down into place.

As the two men tried to catch their breaths, they heard the sounds of chains scraping over and under them. Morcey struggled to gain some kind of footing so he could push upward against the lid but was too dizzy to do so. London, however, had his own problems. He had gone so long without eating that now the rotting stench inside the Dumpster was to him a suffocating nightmare. He retched repeatedly, spewing what little fluid he had in his stomach down the front of him.

The detective pushed up from the floor, only to have his hands sink down into the pulping garbage beneath him. As he pulled them free again, everything they touched repulsed him—sickening him to the core of his being. He brought one hand up in front of him, covered with cold fat. The smell of the greasy, rendered flesh made him gag, tears rolling down his cheeks. All of the smells repulsed him, pushing him toward madness. Horrified by even the air around him, he wondered when he would begin screaming.

Then, suddenly, the pair began to realize they were moving. Or, more specifically, that the Dumpster was moving. Both attempted to make sense of what was happening in their own ways but, they were still too stunned from before. At best, Morcey realized when they started traveling down an incline but, he could not attach a reason . . . at first. He did after a few seconds, however.

"Sweet Bride of the Night! They pushed us down a hill. We gotta be headed for the West Side Highway traffic. Boss, boss, com'on, we—"

The ex-maintenance man was given no chance to finish. At that moment the first of the three vehicles that would hit the Dumpster plowed into it, sending it careening off into different lanes of traffic. Brakes squealed all around them. Despite the lateness of the hour, the always heavy traffic on the expressway crashed into both them and each other, over and over. The chains burst after the second hit—the third finally knocked them off their wheels, sending the badly bruised and broken pair spilling across the pavement. Along with all the others.

Eighteen cars, three vans, one bus, a panel truck, and a tow truck were all damaged to some extent. Nearly seventy-five people needed aid of one sort or the other, forty-eight of them having to be hospitalized.

When the ambulances began to arrive, their attendants did not even know where to begin.

CHAPTER
TWENTY-SIX

I T ALL TOOK HOURS—WAITING for the ambulances, emergency treatment, getting to the hospital, being admitted, then getting seen by someone once they were there. London, of course, had healed without any problems.

As he had seen it happen to the Muzz and to Karen Tezzler, his broken bones had knitted in minutes, his torn skin had patched itself over. By the time the police got to him and Morcey, they were hard-pressed to believe they had both been in the Dumpster. The detective had given them a story about a wild street gang forcing them inside and then pushing them down into traffic. Claiming to be too dazed to remember any details, he had used the confusion to send the police off to look for other witnesses.

Then he had moved off and corralled an ambulance team. Holding up two hundred dollars, he pointed to Morcey and then told them;

"There's an easy way to do things and a hard way. 'Easy—take this money and get that man to the nearest hospital. No questions asked. Hard, I knock the three of you senseless and take him there myself."

The team looked into London's eyes and then gave him no arguments. As the gurney crew loaded the barely breathing man into the back, the driver put up his hand as the detective tried to give him the promised money.

"Forget it," he said, sliding into the driver's cab. "He's one of the worst here. He'd have gone first anyway." London threw the money in the cab, saying;

"Take it. Burn it if you want—I don't care. Just turn your siren on and don't turn it off until you get there."

The driver noted that the look had not changed in the detective's eyes. Forgetting the money on the seat next to him, he pulled away even as London was still climbing into the back.

Half of the loose wad of cash blew out the passenger window on the race to the nearest emergency room. Nobody cared.

By the time they left the hall outside of intensive care, they were exhausted.

"It's not fair," said Lisa, half crying.

"Nothing ever is," answered the detective.

London had called Lisa, telling her everything that had occurred. Next he told her to phone Pa'sha and let him know what had happened but not to tell anyone else. Both Lisa and Pa'sha owed their lives to the balding man, as did the detective himself. They would sit the death watch. Or, at least, that had been London's plan. As they walked down the hall from Morcey's room, Lisa told him differently.

"I have to tell you something, Teddy."

"Sure, anything."

"I didn't call Pa'sha like you wanted," she told him. "I called Dr. Goward instead."

Her tone told the detective she had not made an oversight. He waited. She continued;

"I had to talk to you first, and then I wanted you to talk to the doctor." Confused, London steered his partner into an empty visitor's lounge. Shutting the door behind them, he told her;

"I assume you had a good reason for not calling who I asked but, you don't mind if I'm curious to find out the 'why' of it all, do you?" When the young woman shook her head, the detective continued;

"Well, that's good. First . . . why don't you tell me what it is you wanted to talk about?"

Lisa set her lips together firmly, bending her head, turning her eyes from London. As he sat down in one of the box-shaped chairs lined against the wall, his partner took one as well, but one several seats down from him. When the detective asked if she was all right, she quickly shifted her weight and position in the chair, unconsciously pointing her body toward the door. Fighting her nerves, she finally said;

"Teddy—I, I have . . . oh, I don't know—I mean . . ." And then, after several more seconds of indecision, she suddenly blurted out, "I have to leave you."

She turned completely away from the door then, away from him, staring into one of the room's far dark corners. As London started to speak, she said;

"No, don't talk. Please. Don't say anything. I feel like a heel, but I can't help it."

"Sweetheart," he said softly, fighting his weariness, trying his best to understand, "I don't want to argue with you. God knows I'm not looking for any kind of fight right now. I'm just not sure what you're telling me. Do you mean leave 'me,' or leave the agency . . . what?"

She turned then, a bitter look in her eyes. Their normal soft blue hardened into a harsh, icy steel. London moved back in his seat without thinking, taken aback by the look in the young woman's eyes. Without turning away, without blinking, she told him;

"You don't even know. You can't even figure it out for yourself—can you?"

Lisa took several short breaths, rubbing at the back of her neck in frustration. London sat quietly, waiting for her to speak. Finally, she said;

"I, I want to help you with your work. I want to be a part of what we've started. But . . . I can't right now. It hurts me too much—to see you, to watch you and know I can never be any closer to you than, than a . . ."

The detective came out of his seat then, taking Lisa in his arms. She started to cry at the contact, hating him for understanding, hating him for caring about her in every way but the one that mattered. She let him hold her for a moment, but then somehow summoned the strength to push him away.

"I've got to go," she said. "I can't stay here, not with you—not with Paul dying down the hall. I'm going to leave the city." As London started to speak, she asked him not to, saying;

"Just let me talk. I'm going to go to the airport, or the train station—somewhere—anywhere, and just get out of town for a while. When I can look at you and not want to die inside . . . then I'll be back."

The pair stared at each other, separated by only a half foot of air, neither able to speak, neither able to reach out. And then, before either could do anything, a voice sounded behind them;

"Lisa, Theodore . . . ? Is that you?" London turned—Lisa looked over his shoulder. As Dr. Goward moved into view, he said;

"I've had the worst time finding you."

Lisa cut the doctor off, stepping away from the detective as she said;

"Talk to him—help him understand what is going on. Everything we talked about on the phone. Tell him, please. Will you?"

"Of course, my dear, but what . . .?"

The young woman crossed the room to the door, not turning back until she had reached the hall. Framed in its light, she stopped for only a moment, saying;

"Teddy, I'll always love you. Always."

And then she darted away, practically running down the hall to escape the presence of the two men standing in the visitor's room. The doctor looked at the spot where she had been for only a second, then asked;

"Are you all right, my boy?"

"Oh, yeah, sure," answered London, bitterly. "Lisa's just walked out on me, the doctors give Paul about two days at best, and the vampires know who we are. Things are great."

Without reacting to any of the news the detective had given him, Goward said instead;

"Let's go get a cup of coffee, shall we?"

The detective snapped.

"Coffee? What? What are you talking about? Paul's out there dying! I've got to get moving—I've got a hell of a lot to get done before–"

"Theodore!" bellowed Goward. "You will keep quiet for a moment and listen to me. You've taken a great deal onto your own shoulders. Circumstance has led you to think of yourself as the world's protector. Maybe not an unjustified title considering some of what's happened to you, but I think it's time you remember that Destroyer or not, you are just one man. And as the poet said, 'No man is an island.' Trust me—if you keep pushing people away from you, they'll keep going away.

"Now, I want a pipe and a cup of coffee. Lisa wanted me to talk to you about what's been happening, and I think she was right that I should. What do you think?"

The detective looked into the doctor's eyes for a long moment, searching for something that would allow him to turn away the older man's offer. Finding nothing, he said;

"Coffee sounds fine, Doc. Just fine."

CHAPTER TWENTY-SEVEN

ONDON WALKED AWAY FROM the hospital, the weight of its shadow burdening his shoulders. He could not help but think of Morcey stretched out in his bed, bent and broken, mazes of tubes snaking across his chest, patched into his nostrils and veins and organs. The ex-maintenance man's eyes had stayed closed, his breathing never rising above a whispering shudder.

Goward at his side, the detective pushed forward, slamming his stick along the sidewalk violently, counting off his mistakes with every click as it struck against the cement. He told his companion what had happened to himself and Morcey at the End of the Pier, letting the incredulous scholar know that there were indeed vampires in the world—and that he was now one of them.

After several blocks the pair came across an all-night deli. The doctor went inside for something to drink while London waited out on the sidewalk. Goward returned after only a moment with a cardboard container of coffee, asking the detective;

"Are you sure you don't want anything?" When London nodded, the doctor pushed him, "How long has it been since you've eaten anything—drunk anything?"

"Why?"

"Humor me," answered the doctor. "How long?"

"Well," said London, digging through his memory, searching for the correct answer. "I'm not certain, but I could swear its been six, seven weeks."

"Theodore," said Goward, taking a sip of his coffee, "doesn't that strike you as just a bit odd? I mean, you do realize that if what you told me earlier is correct, then you are living on the energies of the dead?"

"Yeah," answered London in a hollow voice. "I know. That's what I've been trying to explain."

"The voices . . .?"

The detective stared into the Goward's eyes, searching for the part of the doctor asking the questions. He found a mixture of professional curiosity and human sympathy but neither pity nor horror. Feeling safe, he allowed the terrors he had been suppressing to suddenly flood outward into his eyes. The pain of it reached out to the older man, snaking through his heart, tearing at his sanity.

Zachary Goward had seen many things in his lifetime of investigating the bizarre and the supernatural. He had talked to those claiming to have been abducted by UFOs. He had spied out African juju blood ceremonies and the haunted mansions and graveyards of the British Isles. In his time he had seen walls running with blood, witnessed Kalian Thugees slay an entire monastery full of monks, interviewed Charles Manson, and even walked on the dreamplane. None of it, however, had prepared him for a full look into the tortured darkness of London's eyes.

He stared back at the detective—not speaking—offering what comfort he could with his look alone. After a long moment, though, London suddenly broke their gaze with a blink, asking at the same time;

"Doc. You've got to explain this all to me. I'm seeing visions, for Christ's sake. What am I doing—dreaming about the day my mother died? My father? My brothers? Who were all those people I saw in Tezzler's apartment—the older ones—and what were they doing walking in my brain after I slept with that vampire? And while we're on the subject—what the hell did I do that for anyway? Why would I do that? Why did I do any of the shit I've been doing?"

The detective turned away suddenly, throwing his arms into the air, raging in the early morning chill.

"Have I been out of my mind? I've read the papers—there's been no mention of a fifty-million-pound monster destroying New Jersey? Am I the only person who saw that . . . that thing?! Am I? Or was it just another hallucination. Did I kill nearly two million people because I'm a lunatic who see things and hears voices?" And then London suddenly grabbed the older man's sleeve, shouting;

"You've got to tell me what's going on, Doc. Tell me—will you? Can you?"

Goward, appearing unperturbed by the detective's outbursts, took a much longer pull from his coffee, and then said calmly;

"We can talk, Theodore. That's what I'm here for. I'm not sure I can answer all your questions, but we won't know until we start."

"Well then," answered London, suddenly finding he could not stop himself from shaking, "let's get started."

"People saw Q'talu. Don't doubt that, my boy. As you should guess, they were treated as 'hystericals.' When it turned out there were scores of people claiming to have seen a hellish monstrosity ravaging the countryside, then—of course—they were 'mass hystericals.' I've kept tabs on the situation, using my credentials as a cover. The government's clamped a lid on the case, keeping everything as quiet as they have the UFO situation. Their investigators have never left the area, nor let anyone else in. Property owners, including the oil and gas people, have not been allowed to go back onto the land they own. No . . ." said Goward, taking another pull on his coffee;

"If I were to worry about anything, son, that wouldn't be it."

As the detective's suspicious eyes pinned the professor, the man answered;

"No, there's nothing else in what you said that I think should be worrying you, either."

Goward finished off his coffee in one last long pull, dropped the container in a nearby trash receptacle, and then said;

"Let's walk."

The two continued down the dark night street, heedless of the unsavory condition of the neighborhood around them. Walking past the shuttered and locked storefronts, London maintained a steady *tak-tak* beat with his Blackthorn while the professor stuffed his pipe.

Even though neither of them had planned their walk consciously, it seemed to have taken on the shape of a large circle. If they continued the way they were headed they would eventually end back at the hospital. Goward, finally finished stuffing his pipe, noted the change in their direction without comment. Slipping his pouch back into his side jacket pocket, he fired the bowl, released a large cloud of deeply scented smoke. His exhalation drifting behind him, he said;

"You cannot allow these things to seize control of you, Theodore. That vampire woman—now, all the legends about vampires suggest that they can control the minds of their prey. From what you have discovered about these creatures, they feed on the energy of their victims. She saw this aura of yours, knew you would make a fine feast, and so took you home and had at you. I suggest that you were tired, confused, and fell into whatever web it was she was spinning. The reason you survived is simply because you had far more energy than she could take. Those older souls you saw on the dreamplane while in her apartment, those were the dead she carried around with her, as you carry those from the Conflagration. When you vanquished her, you gained all her energy of the moment—her soul—and all the souls she has stolen."

"Then . . . ," replied the detective haltingly, "that was what caused the pain. Not the energy . . ."

"I believe so," agreed Goward. "It wasn't the power that hurt, but the burden that comes with it. You mentioned this Drebble character, said he claimed to be hungry—starving—yet the pain was even worse than when you slew the woman. He had no energy for you to claim, just the burden. I think that could explain why none of them wanted to kill you, my boy. The weight of souls you've got strung up within you is just too much for anyone to bear. Perhaps even you."

The professor turned his attention to his pipe, giving London a moment to think about what he had just said. Allowing himself several long draws on his pipe, he cherished the warm smoke, rolling it around inside his cheeks before letting the last puff escape. Watching it curl away into the darkness, he said;

"As to the dreams of your parents, your brothers. I don't want to upset you, Theodore. You're a man to whom the entire world owes a debt it could not begin to repay even if it knew the bill existed. Now you're looking to rid the planet of another plague it doesn't believe exists—running the same risks again of having to work behind the backs of those that you are trying to save."

"What's all that got to do with my parents, Doc?"

Goward took a deep, tobacco-less breath, and then stopped dead in his tracks. His face hardening over, he looked straight forward, staring through the detective, then said;

"It is my belief that whatever the thing we call 'Fate' actually is . . . it took control of the circumstances surrounding your life and protected you from birth so you could be the Destroyer. I do not presume to understand how this entity, whatever it is, operates, nor am I saying that you were fated to defeat Q'talu—only that you were the man chosen to defend the human race at that moment. I think your parents and your brothers were sacrificed by Fate to keep you alive until the moment in question. Just like the vampires you've killed over the last two days, just like the hundreds of thousands two months ago."

London walked forward in numbed silence. As part of his mind rose in minor protest, the rest decided it had to know the truth and opened the doors locking away the myriad voices living within him. Instantly, the distinctive sounds of Drebble and Karen Tezzler flashed through his ears, dragging along with them the uncountable scores of victims they had each held. The cries came in thousands of languages, tens of thousands of dialects—peoples from around the world, from every age and culture—their voices ringing in his brain while their faces flashed before his eyes.

Pushing past them, he hit the next wave, the hundreds of thousands he had caused to die when he had repulsed the invading Q'talu. With what was becoming practiced ease, he flowed through their howling protests and condemnations, letting them sift by like sand through his fingers, hardly pained by any of them, until he saw the Spud. He paused for a moment at his friend's image, amazed that he had not thought to look for him before, ashamed that he had hidden from him for so long.

Hello, Spud, he thought at his friend.

"Hello, Ted," answered the face he could see within his brain. "Long time, no see."

London shuddered at the memory of the destruction that had packed so many within his head, including one of his oldest friends. The detective was the only one who was supposed to die, just him, not the Spud, not anyone else—

"No, Ted. You weren't the only one Fate had ideas about."

London concentrated on his friend's image. The memory nodded, telling him;

"It's what had to be. We both had to be there. I realized that, that's why I came back. That's the only reason I came back. You can't shake destiny. You can just fail to live up to it. What do you think? How'd I do, pal?"

The detective continued to walk forward, his cane moving up and down, tears welling in both eyes.

You did fine, Spud, he thought to the image of his friend. Just fine.

"You, too," the memory agreed, and then it disappeared, swirling away in the sea of others, replaced by his brothers, and his mother and father.

Mom! he thought. Carl? Walter? D-Dad?

"It's us," came the blended response of four voices. "We're here. We've always been here."

Turning to Goward for a moment, blinking through the tears he could not explain, the detective asked;

"All this energy, Doc, all these souls, couldn't I—I don't know—*transfer* some of it to Paul somehow? I've seen those monsters knit broken bones back together, heal over torn lungs and ruptured hearts . . . couldn't I—"

But before the professor could answer, those within him assured him of what he already suspected. As the vampires had told him, only the one that took the life could use it. If Paul Morcey was going to survive on stolen energies, he would have to do his own killing and steal them for himself. Even as the small glimmer of hope died within London, however, the collective voice of his family sounded again, telling him;

"We're proud of you."

And then they were gone.

The detective wiped his eyes on his jacket sleeve, the contact reminding him of how repulsive he smelled. Pulling in on himself, he stopped the flow of tears and then cut off his sense of smell, redirecting it inward. Starting himself and Goward to walking again, he told the professor what had happened within his head. When the older man asked him how he felt, he answered;

"Better. I just answered a lot of my own questions. Honestly, I think I'll be all right now."

As he and the professor continued on their route back to the hospital, they talked of that which had happened in the last few hours. As they did, the detective assured Goward that he now knew what he was going to do. Walking back up the front steps of the hospital, London told the doctor;

"For once, everyone else was right and I was wrong. I've been playing this game as if I'm just some regular Joe that all the regular rules applied to. Well, I guess I'm not."

"No," agreed Goward, "you're the Destroyer. Like Solomon before you. He spent his life battling demons and locking them away from the rest of the world—sealing them in crypts with his magic. It says so in the Bible."

The detective looked at the older man and, half-smiling, asked him;

"You think I should go for being the new Solomon?"

"I think," said another voice from above them, "that you could if you wanted to."

London and Goward looked upward, staring at Lisa half hidden by one of the pillars at the top of the stairs. Before either could comment, she said;

"I didn't get very far, did I?"

When both men haltingly agreed, she stared straight at the detective without blinking and told him;

"I'm looking at you, though, and I don't want to die inside. Honest."

A warm smile filling his face, London limped his way to the top of the stairs, taking the woman waiting for him in his arms. As he hugged her to him, he said;

"You know, for the shy, retiring type, you're getting to be a real pain in the ass."

Lisa dug her fingers into his side, making him cough and then squirm in surprise. Without stopping, she told him;

"Takes one to know one, buster."

Goward, quite sensibly, turned his back on the giggles and clowning at the top of the stairs. Fishing his pouch out of his jacket pocket, he tapped his pipe's bowl against the railing next to him and then began to fill it again. He had no intention of interrupting their tender moment.

Fate, he was sure, would take care of that for him soon enough.

CHAPTER
TWENTY-EIGHT

"WHAT BRINGS YOU HERE?"

"What brings me *where*, grandmother?" answered London.

"To dis place?"

"What place be that?" asked the detective, maintaining his part in the often-rehearsed ritual.

"You choke to name dis place?" asked his inquisitor, an elderly, stick-thin black woman. "You run from de thought to name dis place?"

"This place has no name, grandmother. One cannot name what is not there."

"Den enter what is not..."

"And be where there is nothing."

The old woman was called Mama Joan. She was the guardian of the doorway to Pa'sha Lowe's domain. And, no matter how many times one had been there—and the detective had been there hundreds of times—she always insisted on the proper codes being given. Any variation, and whatever the powers were that lay hidden from the sight of others but easily at her disposal, would immediately be used against anyone trying to enter.

As London walked down the hallway in front of her, the ancient woman cursed him from over her shoulder;

"You are a damned thing, London-man. I do not like you be in my house. You be here too many times, you get my son killed. You bad for him, London-man."

The detective turned in the middle of the unadorned hallway, staring at the old woman. Leaning on his cane with one hand, he pushed his white hair back with the other, smearing the sweat of the evening toward the back. As it ran down his neck, he asked;

"Why for you say such things, Mama Joan?"

"You be a bad thing now, London-man. You seen the dark side of the day. Now you no more part of life—you part of that now—part of the death things. I wish you stay away from my boy. He still need his light."

London stared for another moment, then turned away from the woman, telling her;

"That would have worked yesterday. Then I still thought I was responsible for everybody. Now I know everyone's responsible for their own actions. And that includes your son, Mama Joan. If he goes with me—that's his decision."

Reaching the end of the hall, the detective turned to the left and headed down a moldering well of stairs marked with various warning signs of danger. As always, he paid them no heed, knowing the entire building was actually reinforced to the point where it was assumed the structure could withstand at least four rounds of mortar fire without permitting an enemy entry. As he started down the steel-braced stairs, the old woman's voice called once more;

"You eat the worms, London-man. My son don't need no meals from your table."

Ignoring the woman's words, the detective walked forward through the set of black curtains at the bottom of the stairs and entered her son's workshop.

"Hey-bo," he called. "Bang bang, big brother."

Pa'sha, hunched over one of his workbenches, waved London forward, calling;

"Come in, dead man."

"Oh Jesus, don't you start on me, too."

"You almost bought it this time—the End of the Pier wasn't the simple little defuse you thought it was going to be, was it?"

"No, not really."

As the detective came forward, he saw a hint of someone else peeking out from behind Pa'sha's three hundred fifty plus pounds. The person, bent over tinkering with the same equipment as Pa'sha, turned out to be a woman, one left a disturbing, bone-china white from a lifetime of avoiding the sun. London estimated her height to be no more than five foot one, her weight one hundred twenty-six. Her reddish, softly curled hair was cut to just above shoulder length. The detective told her;

"Nice perm."

Not looking up from her work, she took the length of solder she had in her mouth from between her teeth and answered;

"It was a bitch of a mess a couple of weeks ago. I hated it. I almost did a Curley Joe but my roommate convinced me to leave it alone. Now that it's growing out I figure I can live with it."

As she manipulated a computer chip into its proper slot in the contraption she was working on, she asked Pa'sha;

"Who's the hairdresser?"

"This is my little brother, Theodore."

She looked up then, taking in London. She noted his white hair, his cane, the drawn skin of his face, the look in the back of his eyes most would not notice. She caught the outline of Betty as well, despite the careful cut of the detective's suit. Coupling that with the facts she had, her eyes went down, searching for a hint of Veronica. Catching what she thought was a bulge of the knife, she said;

"Yeah—you're the guy I was listening to tonight." As London's head turned, Pa'sha told him, "Of course I sent her. If I was to be your backup in this—if I was to go in next—I wanted to know what it was might cause you to not come out. Little brother, this is Cat. She is my most trusted surveillance person."

London and the redhead shook hands. She held up the heavily modified rig on which she and Pa'sha had been working. It turned out to be a highly sensitive parabolic microphone. She told him;

"I was able to follow most everything that happened. Your run-in with Drebble—your friend Jorhsa and his stories about Hercules and killing so he could live forever—your goofy pal and his crucifix—even the good old 'CPA of the damned'..."

She patted her machinery.

"Got it all here."

"Enjoy the show?"

The woman's eyes drew narrow at the tone of London's voice. She stared at the detective for a moment, looked at Pa'sha to see if he had any vetoes for the questions both men knew she had, then turned back to London and asked;

"Is this all for real?"

"What? You mean 'vampires'—alive—in these, oh so, enlightened times? Or did you just mean can someone actually get their hands on eternal life by murdering everyone in the area? Or maybe you just wanted to know if my 'goofy pal' was going to live out the night?"

Before either of the two could say anything further, Pa'sha slammed a meaty palm against his workbench, sending various parts and tools and bits of equipment bouncing.

"Enough!" He lowered his voice to add, "What kind of idiots are you two? Whatever our enemy is doing right now, I doubt it resembles this conversation."

Turning toward Cat, the large man growled;

"Yes, there are vampires, and yes, they kill to live forever. I knew that and much more long before this. And as for you, little brother," said Pa'sha, turning his head back in the direction of the detective;

"Cat did not know about the Paul-man's condition. Lisa called me as you told her to—she gave me all your instructions and she told me what had happened to you and Morcey both. I did not say anything about it to Cat. Blame me if you be needin' someone to bark at."

London closed his eyes for a second and then opened them again, a different person looking out from them into the room. His defenses down, he said;

"My apologies. It's pretty certain Paul isn't going to make it through the night. The thought that someone could not appreciate that made me a little nuts. If we can forget it and move on, I'd like to get this show on the road."

"Theodore," answered Pa'sha, staring at his friend with concern, "are you sure you should not rest first? You have been pushing yourself very hard for quite some time now. Surely this plan of yours would—"

The detective cut him off, answered;

"You're the one who said the enemy is probably hard at work now planning his next step. Yeah, sure, I'd like a shower and ten hours in the sack—but it ain't happening. If Jorhsa thought I would do what I'm going to do next, he would have ended it back in his little arena. The only thing that sick bunch of fucks isn't expecting is to die—especially this morning. That's why we're going to do it now. You got everything ready?"

"I do if I understood Lisa correctly."

Pa'sha rose from his seat, crossing to a far corner of the work shop. Both London and Cat followed him. As he walked, the weaponeer said;

"You and I and one other are going to enter the End of the Pier on a sweep-and-clear mission. We will kill all within and then I will bill you an enormous amount of money."

"Apparently you understood more than just Lisa correctly," answered the detective with a wry smile. "I take it you have some special new playthings for this?"

"You take it correctly, too, little brother."

Lifting a quart glass bottle filled with clear liquid from out of a neatly packed bag holding three more just like it, the weaponeer displayed it in his hand, not giving it over to London. The detective noted that the top of the stopper-plugged bottle was circled with several layers of dusty paper. Pa'sha explained;

"Self-igniting chemical bottles. I think very effective considering what we shall be doing. You put concentrated sulfuric acid and gasoline inside. Then, after you seal it, you boil equal amounts of sugar and potassium chlorate—not chloride, please—until they crystallize. Then you fill paper with the crystals and tie it round and round a bottle. Throw the bottle hard enough so that it breaks and—*voila tout!* Instant napalm. A wonderful toy—no?"

"What guerrilla nut case thought up that thing?"

"Oh, Theodore," protested Pa'sha. "I got the recipe from the U.S. Army's *Improvised Munitions Handbook. Technical Manual 31-210.* It is a very handy book."

"Yeah, I'll bet. What else we got?"

Reaching into an open box of haphazard ammunition, Pa'sha pulled forth a shell, showing it to London.

"Now, the majority of the area we will be sweeping through is underground, is it not?" London nodded. Pa'sha continued;

"That is what I thought. Which makes explosive rounds out of the question. Most likely these subbasements and the tunnels connecting them are very old—meaning very unstable. Our lovely Pancor Jackhammers will have to stay at home. Indeed, halls and tunnels—might as well be trench fighting—all long barrels will have to stay home. This, however, is all we should need."

The detective took the bullet from the weaponeer's out-stretched hand. As he looked it over, Pa'sha explained;

"Formerly a hollow-point round. I have filled each tip with both mercury and one BB. This I have then glued over. On impact, the liquid metal, pushed from side to side by the BB pellet, will mushroom most impressively, making a much bigger hole than an ordinary hollow point."

As London replaced the round in its original box, Pa'sha said;

"They will work very nicely in our Auto-Mags. Cat will be using a Heckler & Koch MP-5. Only 9mm, true, but each of its magazines contains thirty rounds. Much better coverage. It will give us many good opportunities to reload."

"You said 'Cat.' As in she's our third?"

"You don't have a problem with that, do you, gimpy?"

"I don't know," answered the detective in dead earnest. "On the one hand, you seem to have my big brother's recommendation. On the other, however, I've found people with mean mouths to usually have a dangerously over-inflated opinion of themselves and their abilities."

Cat colored around her ears, her starkly white skin betraying her anger. Before she could say anything, though, Pa'sha again interceded.

"We need a surveillance person on the way in who can turn into a fighter on the way out. Cat is the best I could get on short notice. And the notice would have to be exceptionally generous before we could do better."

"Just making sure, big brother." Turning to the redhead, London told her;

"You'll pardon my saying so, but we're going up against a minimum of three, four score ruthless monsters. It took twelve .38 dumdum hot loads to bring down just one of them. All I want is for you to understand, these are the most vicious, hard-to-kill sons of bitches you will ever see in your entire life—if you live out the morning."

"You trying to scare me?"

"Well, yes—actually, I am."

"Pa'sha offers a job—" answered the woman defiantly, "I take it. I take a job—I do it. That's all there is to it."

"I'm not trying to scare you into backing out, I'm trying to scare you now so when you see one of these maniacs break through a brick wall with its fists you won't panic and freeze up. It's an old line, but you really won't be any good to anyone dead."

The woman stared at London for a moment, trying to gauge his actual intent. Looking into his eyes, she saw the truth in his words, the thought of what he had told her actually shaking her somewhat. Realizing he had meant nothing more than what he said, she answered in a somewhat softer voice;

"You're a real sweet-talker, London. I think I'll be able to handle myself. But," and then, suddenly, Cat smiled—half from nerves, half for luck—and added;

"Thanks for giving a rat's ass."

Strapping on the new Auto-Mag Pa'sha was handing him, the detective told the woman;

"Least I could do for someone stupid enough to go on this assignment."

Cat slipped on a shoulder bag of the chemical bottles, saying, "One with the most wounds buys breakfast."

London slid extra clips for his Auto-Mag into his inner jacket pocket, muttering;

"Ohhhh, cute." The detective eyed Pa'sha with an evil glance, "This one's a real charmer."

The three dropped the banter then, however, concentrating on making sure they had everything they needed for the assault to come. Finally, certain they had gathered everything, the trio started up the staircase to the main floor of the weaponeer's bunker home.

"Maamaa," the large man called out. "I am leaving now."

Mama Joan appeared from one of the many doorways in the hall at the top of the stairs, answering her son.

"Yes, but will you be coming back?"

Pa'sha narrowed his eyes at the old woman, telling her, "What happens— happens. That is the way of life. I am telling you I will be back. If you want to worry and fret up some other possibility—who am I to stop you?"

The old woman said nothing further in response. She stood in the door- way in grim silence, watching as her son and his companions exited out the front door. Then, as always, she moved forward to secure his home and await his return.

Outside, the three started for the van Pa'sha had arranged to be waiting for them when suddenly London stiffened. Looking first this way, then that, he searched the early morning darkness for a presence he could feel but not pinpoint. As the weaponeer's hand curled around the butt of his Auto-Mag, the detective laid his own hand on his brother's arm, cautioning him;

"I'm not sure . . . I don't think it's danger—I can't say exactly what's going on—but someone is watching us."

London shut his eyes, blocking the overused sense, picking up a trace of warmth and an impression of a heartbeat coming from the left.

"Someone over there," he finished, pointing toward a spot of darkness pouring out from the building directly across the street.

As he pointed into the center of the coal-black shadow, a figure moved forward out of it, walking directly for the trio. Both Pa'sha and Cat could im- mediately tell that it was a man, but nothing more. London recognized the intruder—waited for him to join them. As the man stepped into the strong ring of light in front of the weaponeer's building, the detective stared into the impassive face before him. Since he had pointed toward the man's hidden place in the shadows, London had known him to be the older Oriental who had saved him from the trio of vampires at Mrs. Lu's. Search as he might, however, he was not able to read anything from the elder's eyes.

"So," the old man said, "you are finally ready to do battle against the Gaun Cee Qui."

With no other course open, London answered;

"Sure am. Want to join us?"

CHAPTER
TWENTY-NINE

"I WANT YOU TO KNOW that I hate you more than I hate any other living thing."

As their van made its way easily across town in the nonexistent traffic of the early morning, London answered the elder Chinese, saying;

"Well, to tell the truth, Sparky, at this point I could care less. You want to tell us your story and tell us what gives with you—great. You don't, then shut up and jump out at the next light. We've got work to do."

"Smug. I was smug. That was how I lost my place."

"What place is that?" asked Pa'sha from behind the driver's wheel. The old man sat on the edge of his seat, somehow rigid but relaxed at the same time. His eyes unblinking, not looking to the sides, but not looking straight ahead either, he answered the weaponeer in a slightly warmer tone.

"Thirty-four years ago, I was a businessman. I had both riches and power. My holdings were based in Hong Kong and Taiwan, but I had my hands in every pot—a fishing fleet in Australia, clothing factories in Burma, Korea, plantations in the Philippines, orchards, too. But like many men before me, I grew bored with what I had. I wanted something more. Something that mere wealth could not give me."

Cat turned in her seat to study the speaker. She noted the corded veins running down his arms, the taut binding of all his muscles, even those in his neck. She also got the distinct impression that even though he was not looking in her direction, he was aware of her observations. Whether he was aware of her or not, however, he continued to tell his story.

"One day I heard a tale that intrigued me. It told of a great time approaching, one that would give an ordinary man the chance to be like unto the gods. I wanted that chance. To start, I converted several of my holdings into cash and then used it to refurbish an island monastery brought low by the war. I gathered its monks and told them they could return and work their lands again. The only thing I asked in return was that they train me. They agreed."

"Train you for what?" asked Pa'sha.

"For everything," answered the old man.

His short, razor-cut hair was still a glossy black despite his age. It reflected every bit of light coming in from the streets. Standing straight out from his head, it bent under the weight of his hand as he ran his palm over it, then sprang back up again as he continued;

"I quietly converted many of my holdings to cash, distancing myself from my family and friends at the same time. When the moment was right, I staged my own death and then dropped out of public life. Going to the island, I left behind silk sheets and limousines to begin my training for the Moment. In my youth I had studied the martial arts. I grew quite proficient in several disciplines. It was my way—to be best at everything. Then, was different, though. Once I put myself into the monks' hands, I had to learn all styles of fighting—all manners of offense and defense."

Pa'sha stopped for a red light while the old man talked. It was true that there were no other cars in any direction, but the weaponeer knew that it was no time to be stopped for running a red light when carrying an arsenal the size of which they had in the van. The old man kept talking as if he had not noticed.

"It was almost a joke. I who had been a veritable king became the lowest of peasants—every day, tilling fields, carrying loads of water and sand and wood, pulling weeds . . . and practicing. I practiced with staff and chak and sword. Once one weapon was learned, then was learned the way to overcome it. And then another, and then another, and then another. And at the same time came the studies that went with each art. I can still hear their lessons . . . 'What good to be able to crush a brick if you do not know which one is your enemy. Will you crush all the bricks in the world?' Miserable monks."

Tension rolled through the van, coming off the elder in waves. Giving out a heavy sigh, he continued his bitter story.

"Over thirty years—working, training, and studying the ancient words— twenty hours every day. But I knew it was worth it. For when the Moment came, I would be the savior of the world—of the universe. All the pain and humiliation would be made paid. But after all of it—the monks said I was not worthy. That I was too proud. They said it was ordained . . . that Fate would pass me by."

The old man turned toward London, his flashing eyes tearing at the detective. His iron fingers folded into killing wedges, the blood draining from their heavily callused edges.

"I am the one who worked for it. Not you. I am the one who should have been the Destroyer."

And then, London put one hand to his face, squeezing his eyes as he laughed. The noise of it bounced through the van, the force of it threatening to choke the detective. He sputtered through his amusement;

"What an idiot. You *wanted* to be the Destroyer? Pal, you don't know how lucky you are."

Without thinking, unable to bear the sound of London laughing at him, the old man launched his fist at the detective suddenly, giving no warning. Before it could connect, however, London raised his Blackthorn, driving its iron-hard tip between the man's fingers, splitting his fist, deflecting its fury.

And then, his humor abruptly broken, the detective reached out and caught the old man's wrist. It was a gentle, but firm gesture, one which signaled no attack. Pulling his face close to the other man's, London told him;

"You want a taste of what it's like to be the Destroyer . . . you got it."

And, so saying, without thinking about what he was doing, the detective raised both his hands and cupped them to the old man's forehead. Instantly, images began to form in the other man's mind—winged monsters diving from on high, people torn apart by talons and fangs, infants screaming in terror, cyclonic mountains of fire, burning their way through buildings, incinerating all within, howling nightmare screams flooding every corner of his brain, the voices of a thousand dead, ranting and blubbering for release, visions of people dying by the thousands, tens of thousands, hundreds of thousands—each of them blindly screeching, gibbering, howling, accusing—

The old man knocked London's hands from his head. He opened his eyes cautiously, blinking them rapidly, praying aloud that when he stopped the only thing he would see would be the inside of the van. In the driver's seat, barely aware of what had transpired, Pa'sha hit the gas as the light finally changed to green. Cat sat clutching her shoulder bag of chemical bottles, frightened by what she had seen although she had really seen nothing she could explain as frightening. It had all come at her too fast—Pa'sha's call, listening to what transpired within the End of the Pier to London and Morcey, seeing much of it only by watching outlines on her heat scanners.

Destroyers, she thought. Vampires. People living forever through murder. People fighting monsters, training for decades to do it.

Suddenly she realized she was carrying bombs and guns, riding along on a mission of extermination. Without batting an eye she had signed on to go into a building and help kill every living thing in sight.

What was I thinking? What the hell are we doing here? This isn't happening . . .

Her thoughts were broken for the moment, however, as London stretched across the way to put his hand on her shoulder. Squeezing gently, he said;

"You all right?"

Not questioning how he knew to ask at that moment, she nodded dumbly, biting her lip, watching as he turned back toward the old man, asking him;

"What about you, pal? You want to cut out?"

The old man shook his head, waving his hand before his face for a moment, trying to speak again. Coughing out the first few words, he stammered dryly, his throat straining;

"No. No. I have spent too long . . . so blind. I've been . . . trying to, to manipulate Fate as if it were . . . a child's ball." Then, finding his voice, he said;

"I came here to this country to discover why I was 'robbed'"—the word burned bitterly in his mouth—"of the honor of being the Destroyer. I tracked you down, watched you, waited for my moment to humble you . . ."

A slight sob broke the older man's voice. Suddenly ashamed of himself—of his entire life—he cried;

"Can you forgive me?"

"Sure," answered London quietly. "After all, you haven't done anything to me. I'll forgive you, if that's what you want. But I don't think it's *my* forgiveness you're after." The man sat quietly for a long moment, and then said;

"Jhong."

Somehow knowing the old man was telling him his name, the detective responded;

"Ted."

And then, London took the man's hand in his own, shaking it firmly. Before Jhong could respond, however, Pa'sha asked;

"So, are we all the best of friends, now?"

"Like the rabbit said, 'It's a possibility.'"

"That is good news, little brother. Because . . . we have arrived."

"To market, to market," said Cat in a cold voice. "To buy a fat pig."

"Home again, home again," answered London. "Jiggity, Jig." Pa'sha pulled over to the curb and shut down the van's engine and lights a half a block from the End of the Pier.

CHAPTER THIRTY

THE QUARTET WAS JOINED in the van by two of Pa'sha's men. The pair had been on duty since London and Morcey had first entered the End of the Pier. The five men were silent as Cat played her equipment against the dark club front. She told them;

"It all looks pretty clean. I can only spot four bodies moving around upstairs. That's it. Where everyone else is, is anybody's guess."

Lisa had found a set of floor plans for the club in an article about the building's past. It mentioned tunnels below the club used during Prohibition. The author was certain they had been built by at least the time of the Civil War, but much of his evidence hinted that they were probably constructed as much as a century earlier. London knew that at least part of the tunnel structure was there—he and Morcey had been dragged through it. Cat's instruments could find nothing, however.

"Nothing unusual in that, of course," she said, folding up her heat-reading equipment. "This kind of gear is designed for penetrating modern construction. If there are hundred-year-plus-old chambers under this place, they're going to be made out of big stone blocks and nothing reads through that. If we're going in, we're going in blind."

"Won't be the first time," answered London.

As the four began to gather up their equipment, the senior of Pa'sha's men reported;

"We be watch some long time—see many go in, not so many come out. They be ninety, one hundred, maybe, don't be come back out. Still in there somewhere."

"I know that, Zarin," answered Pa'sha.

"Then let us guard you, Daddy-man," answered Zarin, his hand coming to rest on the weaponeer's shoulder. "You go in there with two old men and one tiny female? Take us then, too, Daddy-man. Don't be die this cold morning."

"Be good to us," said the other. "We go home without you, Mama Joan be wicked mad."

Pa'sha looked deeply into the faces of both men. He could see that each of them felt the same. He also knew, however, that although they were both excellent scouts, they were not the best of fighters. Looking to spare their pride, however, he told them truthfully;

"Long ago, a commander I had told me, 'Pa'sha, if a mission need more than four, then it be need a hundred more.' I gave you your jobs for this night—and I tell you both true—I don't ask cowards to sit in the dark, by themselves, and count the dead as they walk in and out. If we be not back in . . . what say, little brother? Two hours?" The detective nodded. Pa'sha continued;

"If we be not back in two hours, you call for Mama Joan, tell her let loose the Murder Dogs. To be avenged is not so good as to be alive, but it will have to do. Now, get back to your posts, and keep you watch for the dead. And don't worry about Mama, she no boil your bones for my doings."

The two men exited, heading back for their stations. Inside the van, Cat, Pa'sha, and London all began to check their gear. Only Jhong had nothing to take with him. Cat quipped;

"Traveling light, eh, Fu Manchu?" The elder pointed one finger upward, in the fashion of one man quoting another, and answered;

"'The individual must be self-reliant and, in a sense, self-sufficient, or else he goes down.'"

"Yeah, great," responded Cat, struggling with the shoulder strap to her chemical bottle bag. "Whose pearl o' wisdom is that—Confucius?"

"No," responded Jhong absently. "Luther Burbank."

As Cat continued to struggle with her straps, the elder stepped outside into the space between the back of the van and the car behind it. Placing his arms behind his back he stretched them to their limit, going up on his toes at the same time, flexing all the kinks from his system.

Cat stepped out beside him, still trying to get her various bits of equipment into place. Without coming down from his toes, Jhong suddenly reached forward toward her. His hand snaked back behind him again before the woman realized what he was doing. Then, suddenly, she found that the tangle her straps had become was unsnarled, everything hanging neatly at her sides.

She thought to say something in return, started to even, but then found she could not. Images were flooding her head—remembrances of the bizarre things she had seen and heard so far coupled with imaginings of what was waiting for her inside—all combining with her already taut nerves. Her fingers curled unbidden into fists—her eyes closed, head trembled, red curls bouncing back and forth from the strain of trying to ignore what she was getting into. And then, Jhong's voice came to her in a whisper;

"Do not hold it in. If you do not admit you are afraid now, you will do it later—most likely at a very inconvenient time."

Cat caught hold of herself, almost blurted out a lie, and then said back quietly;

"Okay. You win. I'm afraid. Aren't you?"

"No," answered the elder, now up on one foot, stretching the other above his head. "I am prepared for whatever Fate has to offer. I tried once to change Fate's mind. I found such practices are not extremely rewarding. From now on, I believe I shall take what comes as it comes."

"There are vampires in there," the woman reminded the elder. Pulling out of his last stretch, he came back down on two feet, and told her;

"There are vampires everywhere. These just have their own club."

"Not for long," came London's voice from behind them. "Shall we go among them?" Cat lifted her parabolic mike from its holster, aiming it for the front door.

"No better time," she answered.

As the four approached the entrance, the woman examined the locks and hinges, telling the others;

"I'm not picking up anyone in the immediate vicinity. So, leave the door to me. I can pop this thing in a second." As she began to work, the redhead observed;

"These guys sure aren't very security conscious. No wall dampers, no infrared, no foils—simple deadbolts on the doors. Their grasp of technology is about seventy years out of date."

"I guess," offered Pa'sha, "that it must be easy to put things off until tomorrow when you know that tomorrow is never going to come."

And then a soft click was heard as the door came open in Cat's hands. As she re-aimed her parabolic inside, London and Pa'sha pushed past her, their guns sweeping the area, looking for targets. The four moved in, closing the door behind them. They advanced on the main ball room area, gliding quietly across the black-and-white floors. Then, all stopped as Cat raised her hand. She shut her eyes, counting the voices coming to her through her headphones, then held up one fist, raising two fingers. All knew what she meant.

Jhong took the point, disappearing into the dim light of the club. As the others watched from their hiding place, suddenly the two vampires Cat had heard approaching came into view. They walked across the dance floor toward the bar, chatting quietly, unaware that anything was amiss. As they did, Jhong rose up out of the shadows behind them. Before they even knew they were under attack, the elder's left foot had slashed out, caving in the skull of one. Before the first one could hit the floor, Jhong had caught the other in a vicious hold, one that both immobilized and silenced.

As the others approached, Jhong used one foot to smash half of the other vampire's ribs and then brought his heel down—fast—hard—smashing it through his victim's breastbone. Blood pumped up out of the vampire's chest, far too much, far too fast to allow him to heal. The broken vampire died, only small, wheezing sounds marking his passing.

The vampire in Jhong's grasp stared forward as the detective approached him. As Cat and Pa'sha took up outer positions from where they could watch for other vampires that might be about, London asked;

"Okay, Mabel—spill it. Where are the others?"

"Fuck you," sputtered the strangling vampire. "Jorhsa should have killed you when he had the chance."

"Yeah," agreed the detective. "You're probably right."

London pulled Veronica from her leg sheath. Pulling the knife up to face level, the detective plunged it into the vampire's left eye, twirling it around, scraping the socket until suddenly the eye popped out and bounced down the vampire's shirtfront. Gurgling hisses escaped from his lips, intense sounds of raw pain reduced to whispers. London poked the vampire in the chin with Veronica, asking;

"So, Mabel, like I asked before—where are the others?"

The hissing screams continued, the detective's only answer. Ignoring them, he stuck the blade deep within the vampire's chest, repeatedly, turning it sideways before each extraction. As Jhong calmly held the man in place, the detective asked again;

"Where are they? You know that one of two things is going to happen. Either you're going to talk, or someone else is going to come along and we're going to make them talk. So fess up, Mabel. You're getting as tired of this as I am."

The detective dug Veronica about a half an inch under the skin of the vampire's shoulder and then started carving his way to the man's throat. As London dug the blade in around the aortic artery, the vampire finally relented.

"All right, all right," he pleaded. "Everyone's downstairs in the main meeting room. Back through the hall to the judgment room—you remember."

"Yes," the detective's mind flashed to earlier in the evening, "I remember. Now, tell me, what goes on in the main meeting room tonight?"

The vampire closed his eyes and relaxed in Jhong's grip, no longer fighting the elder master. Opening his eyes again, he told London;

"That's for us to know and for you to find out."

And then, with all his remaining strength, the vampire shoved himself forward onto Veronica, slicing his neck open before either the detective or Jhong could stop him. London withdrew his blade even as the elder let the dying vampire slide to the floor. As he stepped away from the ever-growing pool of blood puddling outward from the two bodies, Jhong asked;

"Do you think something important is happening in this main meeting room?"

"Well, I don't know, but I guess we're going to find out."

The elder merely smiled as he and the detective regrouped with the others. Moving into the back hallway, they quietly passed the rows of swords and shields, London noting that the Muzz's helmet had been removed from the recessed show space where it had previously been displayed. Not bothering to comment on the detail, the detective moved forward instead, opening the large curve-topped doors leading into the next chamber.

Entering, they passed the dais and steel-reinforced wooden barrier on their way through the heavy curtains to the door the detective and Morcey had been dragged through earlier. London retraced his way to where he and his partner had been forced outside, then took the alternate path, descending into a much older part of the building.

As Cat had predicted, the walls farther down were much thicker, formed out of massive blocks of cut stone. Then, interestingly enough, after they had descended another few stories, the large blocks gave way to walls made of much smaller, newer bricks. Cat whispered to the detective;

"Probably they added on this section later. The large block looks like a hundred, hundred-and-fifty-year-old construction. These walls . . ." the woman ran her hand along the moist bricks, getting their feel before continuing;

"This seems like the last thirty, forty years. Probably tunneled it out and added it right after World War II. A lot of construction like this got done on the quiet in the late fifties, early sixties. Probably claimed it was a bomb shelter."

"I wonder what they do in this place of theirs?" asked Pa'sha.

"Nothing we'll like," answered London. "I'm sure. Let's keep going and find out."

They made their way down roughly another two stories when finally they came to a space where the floor leveled off. Although there were more stairways leading off in other directions, the detective gave everyone a hand signal indicating he wished to check out the door before them. Cat unholstered her parabolic, checking the door for sound. After a minute, she reported;

"Something on the other side—but not right on the other side. There's noise, though, human noise at that—but I think we're safe opening it up."

Taking the woman at her word, London took the knob gingerly, turning it slowly, looking to avoid any unnecessary noise. Opening the door a crack brought the sound of chanting to the quartet's ears. As London opened the door enough to be able to take a peek, he could see that they were entering a balcony-like affair. What this balcony overlooked, however, they could only guess.

Leaving Pa'sha to watch their backs, the other three crawled forward to see who was chanting, and why. Cautiously peeking over the balcony railing, they saw their missing vampires. As least two stories below them, standing between circular rows of stone seating, the vampires chanted, surrounding a round altar at the center of the room. All of them wore long, draping robes—many of them helmets, turbans, and masks.

As London strained for a better look, he made out the figure of Jorhsa standing at what he presumed to be the altar head, presiding over what seemed to be a human form lying under a sheet. On the other side of the altar stood a woman draped in clinging silk, holding a sword. As she approached the front ranks of chanters, suddenly the detective realized that a number of people were being held in place. Those being held were not costumed, but they were bound and gagged, some of them shackled. Then, as London watched, the figure with the sword moved forward, running it through the first of the captives.

As the chanting grew, the detective saw the same electrical show beginning that had occurred when he had killed both Karen Tezzler and Drebble. The woman with the sword struck again, and again, slaying those offered before her one after another, striking down each victim in time to the chanting. Horrified, fascinated, London watched as the mere human's tiny souls flickered, leaving their bodies. He could see the frail auras, could track the movement of the energy fields as they left their now useless bodies.

After only three such murders, London was able to comprehend what he was seeing. Those being slain were sacrifices, simply cattle being used by the vampires to bring the body on the altar back to life.

The detective was sure because he had recognized the executioner—or, more exactly, he had recognized what she looked like wrapped only in silk. Although more than one voice within his head found the notion unbelievable, London himself had no doubt that the woman closing on her fourth victim was Karen Tezzler.

CHAPTER
THIRTY-ONE

TURNING TO THE OTHERS, London told them;
"We've got to break up that party—now."
"How the Hell do we get down there?" asked Cat.
"Mr. London, Mr. Lowe—search for a way down. Ms. Cat, please to cover me."

And, with that said, Jhong leaned forward, grabbed the edge of the railing, and then threw himself out and over it, falling rapidly into the midst of the vampires below. Landing directly in front of Karen Tezzler, he kicked with all his might, sending the woman staggering backward, blundering into the altar behind her. She hit it dead on across her breastbone, slamming against it hard.

Above, Cat came to the rail and laid down a pattern of covering fire. Not bothering to aim, she blasted the surrounding crowd randomly with her MP-5, only caring that she hit vampires. Jorhsa threw off his headdress, ordering;

"Karen, kill the sacrifices. The ritual must not be broken. Feric, Dorma, Sengel—kill the intruder here. Jack, Russel, Dobil—take a crew—get the one above."

The three heavyweights Jorhsa had ordered forward tried for Jhong, but instead of backing off from them as they expected, he charged instead, ducking through their ranks. Coming out on the other side of their protective ring, he hit Tezzler from behind again, both his feet landing harshly at the base of her spine. She went down once more—hard—one knee slamming the floor painfully at an awkward angle.

Jorhsa moved forward to attack Jhong himself, but suddenly one of Pa'sha's chemical bottles broke open on the back of a member of the assembly, covering him and three others near him with its flaming contents. Two more bottles broke open on other parts of the crowd, shattering its collective concentration, replacing much of its chanting with screams.

Cat fired again into the crowd, emptying her first magazine. She ejected it smoothly, her hand slipping quickly into her ammo bag, pulling another out and slamming it into place in seconds. Leaning over the rail, she shouted;

"Hot lead brunch, everybody. Grab your trays!"

Her finger tightened, sending another dozen rounds into the vampires below. She chose her targets carefully, trying to excite riot, looking to disrupt the ceremony. She also had to take care not to hit Jhong who had placed himself firmly in the middle of everything that was happening, darting through the flaming bodies inflicting damage at every turn.

Tezzler had recovered her feet and returned to her executions. She had slain five of the twenty captives in total before she had been interrupted. Now, as the others in the room attempted to stop the elder master from reaching her, the vampire went forward once more, sword in hand. She waited for the proper moment in the chanting, heard the proper words, and then slashed forward, killing the next in line.

Chemical smoke filled the air of the underground chamber along with the thickening smell of gasoline and burning flesh. Whatever ventilation provisions might have been made in the past, they were proving to be not enough. In the gallery above, her field of vision sorely reduced, Cat was forced to limit herself to only occasional quick shots. She dared throw no further bottles, not knowing exactly where anyone was.

Ignoring the blinding billows, Jhong made a high leap, trying to pass the wall of vampires between himself and Tezzler, but instead landed atop two of them. Raising one foot quickly, he tightened the toes of his other, digging them down into the soft fabric of its slipper. Then, using them to clutch the head beneath his foot, he pushed off with a twist, snapping the neck beneath him. He landed on Tezzler's back just as she killed her eighth victim.

Leaping up again the moment his feet touched the woman, he kicked both legs out to their zenith and then brought them in again fast, crashing them against the sides of the vampire's head. Pain shot through her as bones broke in the left side of her skull. She fell to the floor again, screaming in agony, fumbling for her sword, trying to call forth her healing powers and regain her feet at the same time.

Her fall forced the elder to leap wildly for a clear patch in the crowd, but his move was anticipated by the vampires Jorhsa had set to bringing him down. Throwing themselves into his way, they managed to grab hold of him when he landed—each pinning one of his hard-muscled arms. As they toppled backward, others of the group leapt upon the three of them, raining blows wherever they could, hitting their fellows as often as Jhong.

Jorhsa shouted above all the madness.

"Keep chanting—our prayers must flow. The rhythm must be correct. All must merge in harmony. Karen—*hurry!*"

Needing no encouragement, Tezzler continued down the row of her victims, dispatching the thirteenth in line with another single stroke. As she withdrew her blade, moving on toward the next sacrifice, Jorhsa further berated his other followers, cursing them to calm themselves—not an easy task. Gunfire blasted somewhere in the distance, turning heads, but not breaking the vampire's chanting. The echoing reverberated throughout the chamber, drowning out the undying choir's melody, but not its rhythm's intent.

Fire still raged, burning on the stone seats and walls where it made contact. A score of the vampires were still smoldering, the flames that had been crisping their skin having only been put out in the last few moments. Their king sighed in despair as he watched those trying to subdue Jhong. Despite their sure hold on the elder, they could not disable him. Strong as they were, his knowledge of both leverage and the body's pressure points gave him a distinct advantage until—

"Hold him, Dorma—Sengel! Now we have him!"

The one called Feric advanced on the struggling cluster warily, hunting knife in hand. As several of the vampires managed to finally secure firm holds on the elder's legs, Dorma and Sengel struggled to pull away from Jhong's body, stretching his arms while trying to clear an attack slot for their companion.

The elder, half of his mind working to maintain a winning balance against his foes, set the other half to wondering what had happened to his companions. He had begun to feel concern that not only had London and Pa'sha not made their way to the floor, but that Cat's covering fire had stopped as well. Pulling in a deep breath, he reminded himself;

"As you told the young woman . . . self-reliance."

All around their small area, the smoke began to clear ever so slightly. As Jhong struggled, the choir continued its chanting under Jorhsa's direction. They hit another signaling chord. Tezzler's sword flashed up, slicing into another sacrifice. Her hand twisted the metal inside the body of the woman before her. She looked into the sacrifice's eyes, thinking—a mere fifty or sixty . . . so young—and then twisted the blade, severing the dying woman's heart from its arteries. Her death rattle flashed, her blood poured—body fell.

And then, from his position, Jhong could see the body on the table stirring. Fingers twitching—shoulder, knee—moving. He craned his head in the other direction and saw that there were only three more victims between the woman with the sword and the end of the line. Sucking in a deep breath, he eyed the approaching Feric coldly while tensing himself. His muscles swelled in size as he concentrated, tightening themselves to a steel-like hardness. The vampires holding the elder struggled to maintain their grips, knowing their target was about to try to break free.

And then, suddenly, he relaxed totally, throwing them all off balance. Feric rushed in, trying a desperate knife thrust. It did not work. Jhong pulled Dorma forward, blocking Feric's attack with the vampire's body. As Dorma's grip loosened, the elder snapped his arm free and then struck rapidly, blinding Sengel with two slapping blows. Near the altar, Karen Tezzler struck down the eighteenth sacrifice.

Jhong reached forward with both hands, catching up the hair of the two vampires holding his legs. Twisting his fists, he ripped out great handfuls with each motion. It did not loosen the grips of those holding his legs, however. Powerful as he was, the elder had underestimated the strength of the vampires. As he jerked backward, other vampires rushed forward to restrain him once more. Feric circled, coming in for another attack. Another spate of gunfire erupted from the doors leading to the outer halls.

Wrenching her short blade free, the executioner snuffed the life of the nineteenth sacrifice. Feric closed. Jhong snapped his wrists, flinging the hair in his hands into the vampire's face. Bristling edges stabbed the vampire's eyes, stinging and painful, blinding him. Jhong shook two of his new captors free, only to receive a powerful kick in the face from one of the choir. He dodged another, pulling the four vampires holding him along the floor with him as he did. As the rest of the assembly around them tried to move out of the way and maintain their song, suddenly the zenith note was hit.

All activity around the altar stopped. Karen Tezzler advanced on the last sacrifice, an investment banker who had thought the End of the Pier might be just the place to meet a wilder kind of woman. Curses for his stupidity filled the banker's mind as the executioner's hand came up, driving her sword through his heart. His life hissed from him, his eyes screaming hate for a second, then blanking over. The choir stopped singing—Jorhsa turned away from the struggle, pulling the sheet down away from the face of the body before him.

Everyone except those holding down Jhong cheered as the Muzz sat up smiling.

CHAPTER
THIRTY-TWO

"WELL, MUZZ," SHOUTED JORHSA, straining to be heard over the echoes of the gunfire still dying in his ears, "welcome home."

Again the crowd cheered. The massive man waved one of his trunk-like arms to everyone around him, saying;

"Looks like you've been having a little fun without me."

"Only the preliminaries, old friend," answered the king of the vampires. "After all, how can you have a real party until the guest of honor shows up?"

The Muzz laughed, warming the crowd. Most had already healed from the wounds they had received from both the previous bullets and chemical flames. Spotting his ancient war helmet across the room next to a complete change of clothes, the vampire threw aside the sheet still covering his legs and pushed himself off the edge of the altar, landing solidly on two of the bodies Tezzler had sacrificed. Blood pumped out of the ruined lumps, sluicing up through his toes and across the red-splashed tiles of the chamber floor.

"Ahhh," he said warmly as the squishing warmth covered his feet, "just like the old days."

Of course, as those congregated had expected, the Muzz no longer appeared Chinese. Having died, his features had reverted back to their original nature—dark Mediterranean skin, deep brown eyes, large curved nose, bristling, black hair. Like all of his kind, the giant had the ability to take on the look of those around him. He had lived in Chinatown so long he had acquired the Oriental features with which he had died almost without realizing it. But now that he had both died and been returned, he would have to start over again. Striding through the wallow of corpses, he said;

"I feel like such a pig—look at the size of the meal I just had, and yet I'm still hungry."

At the same time those around him chuckled, twenty voices cried out within the vampire's brain, seeing their remains through his eyes, screeching in horror as he trod over their bent limbs. Blinking once, the giant silenced their annoying chatter with the practiced ease of three thousand years. As he stretched first his arms, then his legs, unkinking the lingering traces of rigor mortis slowing him down, he stepped up to Karen Tezzler, smiling at the sight of the blood streaking her arms and chest and face. Understanding the obvious, he embraced her, saying;

"Thank you, little pigeon."

"A pleasure, Lord Muzz. After all, it's not as if you wouldn't have done the same for me."

Looking down at her, noting the depleted strength of her aura, he realized immediately that she must have been recently brought back from the dark just as he was. He crushed the woman gently to himself, smearing his naked chest with the blood still dripping from her. Tezzler's arms entwined him, covering his with further red streaks, her fingers and palms leaving scarlet splotches on his back. Gently, the massive vampire kissed her, then said;

"I think it's time we showed the good people of this city something." As murmurs of agreement rose throughout the crowd, the Muzz asked;

"The Blessed do not die at the hands of winks! That is not the way it works. Am I right?" As a cheer went up throughout the room, the Muzz continued, shouting;

"I don't know about the rest of you, but I've got an appetite. Who wants to go to dinner?"

Then, before anyone could say anything else, Jorhsa interrupted, saying;

"Muzz. Although it wasn't quite planned—we do have a little snack for you."

The giant walked over to the struggling group of men and women still holding down Jhong. Taking the elder's measure, he told the others in the pile;

"Let him up."

As the knot broke up, Jhong came slowly to his feet, feigning disinterest, but carefully watching the giant out of the corner of his eye. Walking slowly in a tight circle, bending and stretching as he did so, he waited for the Muzz to speak again—knowing his type—knowing he would.

"Little man, I'm going to have fun taking you apart."

"Correction," Jhong informed him, "you will have fun . . . *trying*."

"He's right," called a voice from the back of the crowd. "And you're going to have to try real hard, too."

Then, before any of the heads in the crowd could turn to the sound, London, Pa'sha, and Cat all opened fire, blasting away at the assembly. Jhong seized the moment, grabbing the sword from Tezzler's hands. Leaping forward at blinding speed, he stuck it through the Muzz's side, piercing his intestines, stomach, and a kidney. He pulled the blade out with a ripping twist, danced back a step, and then thrust again—this time without success. Before the elder could penetrate the Muzz's side a second time, the vampire managed to catch the sword in his bare hand.

"Nice try," said the giant, wrenching the sword out of Jhong's grasp. The blade sliced the Muzz's fingers and palm severely. Not seeming to care, the vampire shifted the sword to his other hand, saying;

"Now—try it again."

Jhong shifted his eyes rapidly from left to right—twice—and then smiled, moving forward as if that were exactly what he intended.

At the same time, the rest of the assembly rushed the doorway, enraged at the effrontery of the winks plaguing them. London and the others lay down a withering barrage of fire, blasting the legs out from under the first two waves of their attackers. As the front ranks fell, those behind them were slowed, having to either stop or crawl over their fellows. The trio took full advantage of the fact, continuing to blast into the crowd indiscriminately.

They emptied clip after clip into the vampires, at first bringing them to a halt, then sending them stumbling backward as some in the crowd began to fear the worst. Where London and Pa'sha's rounds blew vicious chunks out of those they hit, Cat's rapid fire blasted enough smaller holes in her targets to compensate for her lack of stopping power.

A number of the vampires had ceased to move, having taken too many mortal hits. Others lay where they fell, tangled with the dead, too broken or too weak to do anything except begin their healing process. Seeing this, the detective knew that if they did not finish off the enemy wounded immediately they would soon again be among their attackers. Reaching up for the filter mask hanging around his neck, he slipped it on, ordering;

"Nuke 'em."

Pa'sha and Cat slipped their own masks back up at the command. As the vampires began to withdraw, the trio reached into their bags, each bringing forth fire bombs. Within seconds, scores of the vampires were burning, screaming in agony as the billowing chemical flames ate through their flesh. The detective and his companions followed those bombs with more, then moved forward through the burning crowd, blasting open the heads of any they found still moving.

On the other side of the fight, however, Jhong had found himself with his hands full trying to keep out of the reach of Tezzler, Jorhsa, and the Muzz. Unlike the majority of the others in the chamber who over the centuries had forgotten how to fight or never learned the way of it in the first place, the elder was facing a deadly threesome, each not only a skilled fighter, but capable of working within a team as well.

At first they had simply taken his measure, not trying to deliver any killing blows, not allowing any. Finally, however, even though only a few minutes had gone by, the king of the vampires could see that the battle within the chamber was going badly. Making a private decision, Jorhsa ordered;

"There may be more of these within the compound. Muzz—kill this one, then direct the battle against the others. Karen, you come with me."

The Muzz moved forward as ordered, not thinking to question the commands of a man he had obeyed for nearly thirty centuries. As he did, the king of the vampires directed the woman next to him, so recently dead, to follow him to the other side of the altar. Across the room, still directing the slaughter of the crowd, London spotted Jorhsa's retreat. Pulling down his mask, breathing in the acrid fumes rapidly filling the chamber, he shouted to be heard over the deafening silence created by their gunfire.

"Can you and Cat handle this?!"

When Pa'sha simply smiled and nodded in return, the detective gave him a look back that only the massive weaponeer would understand. Then, tossing his friend a short salute, London turned his back on the pair and limped away as quickly as he could around the far side of the now-retreating tide of vampires. Pulling his mask up again he headed for the altar, disappearing behind the crowd and into the smoke. Watching the detective's departure only to be sure of his position, the pair directed their fire to the center of the crowd, working to eliminate the coven once and for all.

In the meantime, on the other side of the slaughter, Jhong and the Muzz were still circling each other, continuing to take each other's measure. Both of them aware of the fact that they were each facing an extraordinary foe, they extended their dance, waiting for the right moment, watching for the opening that might lead them to victory.

The Muzz led with his sword, keeping the blade between himself and the elder at every moment. The viciously deep slices in his hand had already healed over, now nothing more than pink welts crossing his palm and fingers. Planting his bare feet solidly after each step, he continued to move forward, working at subtly backing Jhong to the wall.

The elder, on the other hand, had spent his time doing his own healing. He had been severely pummeled by those who had held him down. When he had been released, his entire upper body had been a mass of agony. Blood had already begun to darken under his skin. Thinking his way past the pain, however, he reached a place within himself from where he could push it aside. Conquering that, he then straightened his back and began to take the fight to the Muzz—beginning by backing off to study his opponent, a move that made sense considering that it was the same tactic the vampire had chosen. As their tense, revolving duel drew itself tighter, the Muzz called out;

"Like the fumes, little man? Doesn't bother me, you know. Breathe it in, do a little damage—doesn't matter. All gets healed by the time I take in the next breath. Rather convenient, eh? Course, it'll kill you. Right?"

"Faster than you could, I'm sure," replied Jhong through closed lips.

The elder had already shallowed his breathing to protect himself from the drifting smoke. He recognized his opponent's attempt to both worry him over the fumes and awe him with his powers, as well as trying to get him to talk so he would suck in more of the noxious atmosphere. The Muzz answered;

"Oh, no. Don't worry, little man. The smoke might cripple you up somewhat, but I'll be what kills you. I'm going to break you into tiny pieces and throttle you until you're dead. Then I'm going to suck the life out of you and keep you in my head for the rest of eternity. The only things you'll see forevermore will be the things I do. Maybe I'll just kill gookiewinks for a while.

Rape Chinese babies, kill Jap women . . ."

The Muzz got a faraway look in his eyes for a second, blinked it away, then shared the remembrance.

"I was raping a pregnant Chink bitch, oh, about a year ago. She couldn't handle me—too tight. So I told her, 'Hey, I'm too big for you, don't worry. I can fix that.' Know what I did, I cut open her gut and stuffed my old wanger in there. Fucked her and the kid at the same time. Blood was pouring out of her—both of them, really. Just splashed out over my legs. She lasted almost fifteen minutes. It was close as I get to a religious experience these days."

Looking for an angry response, the vampire asked, "What do you think of that, little man?"

"I did the same to a woman once—only with more skill."

"What makes you say that?"

"You lived."

The Muzz smiled and then laughed, admitting when he could again talk;

"Oh, yeah—okay. You're good—You're real good. Probably should have known. Guess we're going to have to really fight after all."

"That is something else you should have known."

And, saying that, Jhong took two long steps backward, then feigned forward. The vampire swung his blade in a smoothly controlled arc, seemingly cutting off the elder's attack. Jhong backed off in sloppy fashion, pantomiming near disaster. The Muzz watched his retreat carefully, trying to decide whether or not he was being set up. Jhong looked up into the vampire's hard face, meeting his eyes for a moment, then blinked. He tried to make it seem natural, as motivated by fear as possible.

The Muzz moved forward on long strides, cutting the distance between himself and the elder instantly. Jhong backpedaled in panic, heading for the wall. Then, two steps from the moist bricks, he turned and threw himself upward, his left foot making contact with the wall. Swinging his right foot higher even as he pushed off with his left, he rebounded from the wall, flipping upward through the air.

Before the vampire could react, the elder came down behind him. The Muzz swung around, stepping backward at the same time, putting his back to the wall for protection. Jhong went down on his back and then threw his knees up and over his head. Pushing off with his hands, he drove both his feet into the Muzz's genitals. The air rushed out of the giant, leaving him defenseless for only a second. It was enough.

Regaining his feet in half that time, Jhong aimed a devastating blow for the vampire's left kidney, driving his hand a half dozen inches into the Muzz's flesh. The giant's mouth opened wide in surprise and silent pain, spraying the air with spittle and a few droplets of phlegm. He attempted to bring his sword up, but the elder blocked the vampire's wrist with his own and then snapped the same hand forward, smashing it against the giant's face. The vampire's head slammed against the wall—his teeth shattered—one eye closing over.

Not finished, the elder dropped and knocked the vampire's feet from beneath him with a sweeping kick, grabbing the sword from out of his hand as he fell. Even as the Muzz was falling, Jhong stepped up to the giant and drove his heel into the vampire's genitals again, and again, and then again. This time, the Muzz found his voice, his screams coming long and loud. Standing over the vampire, the elder looked down at the creature's shattered, ruptured penis and told him;

"Very good. Now, the next time you rape a gookiewink who is too tight, perhaps you will not have so much trouble."

Even though blinded by his pain, the Muzz managed to respond, saying;

"Something tells me, I may not get too . . . get too many more next times."

With one swift motion, Jhong swung the sword in his hand in a sweeping cut, slicing open the vampire's neck. Blood spurted upward in gushing arcs, pumping violently. With only seconds left to the last of his eighty-some lifetimes, the Muzz formed his left hand into a fist. Struggling to bring it to his chest, he tapped it to his breast, then raised it in classical salute to the elder standing above him.

Understanding the gesture, bearing his enemy no malice, Jhong returned the salute and then watched as the light passed from the eyes of Hercules for the last time.

CHAPTER
THIRTY-THREE

TEDDY LONDON MADE HIS way carefully through the close corridor, tapping at the walls here and there with his Blackthorn, knowing that he might find trouble around any of its sharp corners. The detective had been amazed to discover a segment of the decorative tiles on the floor lying on its side, exposing a dark drop hole hidden behind the altar. He had stared at it for a long second, frozen for that moment, not believing the lengths to which Jorhsa had planned his citadel.

How much more of the place is like this? he wondered. How many more little tunnels—and maybe booby traps—does he have hidden around here?

London's brain immediately filled with voices, opinions being offered on what to watch out for from dozens of his ancestors. The detective moved carefully, feeling his way through the dimly lit halls, trying to both find a safe path and ingest all the incoming information. It had not been quite so difficult when Pa'sha and he had made their way down from the gallery earlier—not to see, anyway. They had run into the threesome Jorhsa had sent to stop them, though. And the others that followed.

The two friends had shot down the first of them, over and over, finally blowing them to enough pieces to stop them. Cat showed up behind the pair, missing the first wave but catching the second. The smoke had so filled the chamber above that she had suddenly found the high ground to be of no advantage. Her added firepower arrived at an appropriate moment, though, allowing the trio to sweep the area in time to give Jhong the cover he had requested.

For a while, the detective had been surprised at how quickly the vampires fell, but a number of voices spoke to him, filling his mind with pictures of cities from the past. It showed him the cultures that created them, all peoples whose times had passed—swept away whenever they forgot whatever group knowledge it was that had once made them strong.

The vampires had been like that. They had gotten so accustomed to the easy life, herding "winks," networking and partying, seeking out each new cold-blooded monster they could and initiating them into their little club that now they had forgotten how to fight, how to really be savages. The voices whispered to him that once monsters lose their savage lusts, replacing them with more "practical" ones, they have always fallen.

Might be, he thought to himself. But most of them didn't fall without a struggle. You won't mind if I keep my eyes open, will you?

The ancestral voices did not answer him. He was beginning to realize they never would. They only knew how to speak out on what they understood best. They did not really interact with him, but they would always be with him. For the moment, he was grateful enough for that.

As he made his way through the twisting corridor, he wondered if Pa'sha, Cat, and Jhong had survived. He had great faith in their abilities, but he also knew all too well as of fifty-seven days earlier the price such contests commanded.

Well, he thought, maybe I'll be lucky. Maybe I'll be the one that gets it this time.

And then he chased the thought away, realizing that he did not need to hear from any of the defeatists stored within him. Allowing the tracker who had talked to him in the abandoned lot to lead his body along in the pursuit of Jorhsa and Karen Tezzler, he sat back and took a look at why he was doing what he was doing. He could think of many reasons to justify halting his chase—among them the amount of pain and damage it might cause him. He was fairly sure none of his friends was ready to cut up twenty human beings just to give him another round of existence.

He also knew that there were more monsters loose in the world, and that stopping these two was not going to make very much difference. And then, one of the voices coming not from his racial memory but from his own brain told him;

"Yes it will. Jorhsa's an organizer, a protector. He teaches the others to blend in—to manipulate society and feed off it. And besides, you took a job—you took a retainer."

The voice in his head laughed at him for even considering the option of backing out.

"You *have* to do it. You got paid."

London passed through another set of doors, suddenly finding himself back in the club's dance room . . . where he had killed Drebble . . . where he had first looked into the giant mirror behind the bar. He noticed that his feet had stopped moving, paralyzed at the edge of the dance floor. Inside his head, a warning voice whispered throughout—

The two he was after were somewhere close at hand . . . it did not know if they were aware of his presence . . . it also did not know where they were, but it did know, however, that if it were going to set an ambush for someone, that this was certainly a good place to set one.

A very good place.

Then, suddenly, blinding lights came on in the ceiling, bathing the detective. Two arrows flew from opposite sides of the room, ripping through him—the shorter one tearing into the arm he had raised to shield his eyes, the longer one piercing through his chest and back. Only the warning he had received had kept the damage from being worse.

The detective stumbled back through the doorway, stunned, howling in pain, his cane lost. Falling in the darkness, he doubled up in agony, fighting the waves of shock he could feel rolling throughout his body, urging it to relax. *Jesus, not* now, he told himself, almost laughing. *Oh, brother, not now!*

Catching hold of the shorter arrow—a voice he had not before heard identifying it as a crossbow bolt—he started to pull it upward, ripping pain seizing him. The same new voice protested, telling him to break it off for now and worry about the head later. London countered, lifting his arm to eye level so the voice could see that since its time, people had started making crossbow bolts out of galvanized steel.

Then push it through, the voice told him. *The head is back-barbed. You'll just tear up your arm if you jerk it out. Push it through.*

Gritting his teeth against the pain, the detective closed his tearing eyes and began pushing the bolt through his arm as the sound of footsteps approaching reached him. Jorhsa's voice called out;

"Not a very good entrance for an avenging hero."

Ignoring the taunt, London worked the bolt through his forearm, biting his lip to keep from screaming. Blood bubbled up out of his throat. Sweat washed down his face, stinging his eyes. His teeth broke through his skin as he dragged the slick length from his arm.

"Oh, Theodore," came Jorhsa's voice again. "I can hear your wheezing a mile away. Don't bother with amenities. Go ahead and scream. I'm sure the pain is staggering. Please, don't mind us. I assure you—we understand."

Continuing to ignore the vampire—listening to his sounds, but not his words, merely to keep track of his position—the detective grabbed hold on the arrow piercing his body with both hands and then pushed. The shaft slid slowly, painfully, every inch of its passage a nightmare. London gave it another shove when suddenly one of his voices asked him;

You know where one of them is, but where is the other one?

The detective let go of the arrow, fumbling weakly for his Auto-Mag. The tracker strained London's ears, answering the other voice, telling the detective;

The woman is moving in.

London took a deep breath, fighting his growing fatigue, trying to assess his situation. He knew that his position was a good one; he was well hidden in the hallway shadows. Indeed, if he were not, Jorhsa and Tezzler would have already hit him again. The detective had known that was why the vampire king had been calling to him, even without the help of his ancestors.

They did remind him of Tezzler, however. He had forgotten her—had not thought that far past his pain, had not realized that Jorhsa's comments had been providing distraction as well, giving the woman a chance to shift her position.

Hell, he told himself, I never even noticed when they pulled her out of my head and got her walking again.

Knowing she was most likely in place by now, he lifted his weapon, trying to steady his hand. He could not. Taking a deep breath, then letting it go slowly, he struggled to calm himself. He did not wonder at how he could survive the arrow in his chest. He had seen far too many tissue reconstructions lately—survived too long without food and water—to start wondering about such things now. Then, without warning, the Auto-Mag fell from his hands, too heavy for him to hold.

"Damn," he whispered. He cursed his wounds, cursed the dizziness threatening to drift him off to sleep, cursed the blood still bubbling up out of his chest. As a wave of nausea washed over him, suddenly he remembered the look in Tezzler's eyes just before she had begun healing in her apartment. Realizing he could afford neither pride nor conventional morals any longer, he said to himself;

"Fuck it—why not?"

Taking another deep breath, he opened himself to the energy within him. For the first time in the two months he had carried it as a burden, he allowed the current to flood rather than trickle past the barriers he had erected against it. The energy surged through him, cleaning his blood, knitting the tear in his arm, cooling the sweat running down his back and face. It poured over and out of and through his chest. The feathered shaft still sticking out of his breast suddenly burst into flames, disintegrating into ash—less than ash.

Sucking at the strength pouring through him, not wanting to die any more than any other man, he felt his chest heal over, the wound in his back close up. As he tried to control the process, he felt his bad leg returning to its full power, watched a boyhood scar on his knuckle disappear, saw dry skin on his palm moisten and blend back into the rest—

"Enough."

He said the word aloud, taking command of the runaway power. Finally understanding what had happened to him two months previous, he gave all the trapped souls within him his blessing and then freed them. Those still remaining within the detective boiled out of him, flooding away into the club. They exited him by the hundreds of thousands—the unsubstantial globes of light he had seen on the dream plane in Karen Tezzler's apartment. As they had then, the billowing, shining spheres moved in a variety of patterns, curving around each other, passing through each other, the walls, London . . . everything.

Lost in the dazzling display, the detective felt along the ground, searching for his Auto-Mag. As he did, suddenly he heard voices from behind him.

"Little brother, what is happening?!"

London turned, yelling to Pa'sha, "It's all right. Come on."

Finding his weapon, he hefted it upward, then slid his back along the hallway wall, making his way out onto the dance floor. Behind him, Pa'sha, Cat, and Jhong followed at a distance—not understanding what they were seeing, cautious despite the detective's assurances. In the outer room, London heard a trace of Tezzler's voice, then saw her. She had abandoned her crossbow, abandoned even any pretense of stealth. Standing in the middle of the room, she was pulling the energy globes to herself through force of will.

"More." He heard her voice like a noise in the wind.

"More," she called again, her last word before she started screaming.

As London watched, suddenly the energy draw became too much for her. Tezzler tried to stop the influx into her body, but it was too late. The vampire had allowed the energy too much access to her system, one not built to contain so much power. In seconds her skin was flaming, crackling away from her disintegrating muscles, charring bones. Seconds after her last words, the few bits of her that had not been consumed dropped to the ground, splintering against the dance floor.

And then, the last of the souls sped away from the detective, leaving him whole, but merely human once more. Not careless enough to remain a target once the blinding cover of the escaping soul force had left him, London leapt and rolled, ducking down behind the closest table. He crashed it over on its side, only to hear Jorhsa's voice coming to him from the direction of the bar.

"Ah, another noble Destroyer. How repetitious."

Risking a look, the detective saw the king of the vampires sitting in the center of the room, his hands atop the table before him. The bow he had used on London was nowhere in sight. The detective stood, making his way toward Jorhsa cautiously, saying;

"I think I finally understand." The vampire king kept his gaze fixed on the detective, but said nothing. London continued, asking, "You were the first—weren't you?"

Jorhsa merely lifted his eyebrows, shifting his eyes from side to side in response. Knowing he was right, the detective said;

"Five thousand years old, I should have seen it earlier. Five thousand years ago . . . you were the first Destroyer. You were the first man to turn back the Q'talu."

"I'd take a bow if I felt like standing, but you'll forgive me. I'm just too tired."

Forgetting the others, London sat down at the same table with the vampire, feeling no threat coming from the man who could now snap him like a matchstick if he so desired. Bursting with the need to know what had happened before, the detective asked;

"How? How did you . . .?"

"You mean, how did I stop the Q'talu without miles of gasoline and chemical storage vats to blow up in his face? How did a man living in the desert during the Bronze Age turn back the most powerful monster in all of creation?"

As London waited for the coming answer, his scalp tingling with the overpowering eagerness consuming him, Jorhsa answered in a voice so weary it sounded drugged.

"Magic, some. Faith, some. Mine and other people's. Just like you, though, I'm the only one that reaped the benefits . . . I'm the one that was flooded with all the loose souls in the area when it was all over."

The vampire tried to meet London's eyes, but found he could not. Staring back at the table, he said;

"I met Solomon, too—after his battle with the Q'talu passed. I'd kept myself alive for twenty-five hundred years, killing and killing and killing, knowing it was all worthwhile, knowing it would be justified in the end. My astrologers had told me the Q'talu would be back. Once I came to understand the power within me . . . what it could do . . ."

Jorhsa shuddered, then suddenly picked his head up, stared straight into London, and admitted;

"I fed it. I told myself that I *had* to do it, that the world would need the Destroyer once more, alive and whole and hale, filled with knowledge and ready to combat its greatest enemy. What were a handful of lives against the returning threat?" His head turning away again, he said;

"And when the Q'talu did return, no one would rally to me. No one would believe in me. Without the faith of others, my magic was useless. Solomon saved humanity that time, filled with passion, his oh, so burning righteousness. I'd gone to Israel, what was it, maybe a hundred years before Q'talu was to return, because the astrologers had said that was where he would arrive. I watched him, Solomon, watched him save the world—a world that by that time only feared and hated me."

The others had come out into the dance hall behind the detective. As they stood around the table, Jhong heard the first Destroyer describe how he went to Israel, as the elder had come to New York. Like the others, he did not interrupt as the vampire continued;

"After that, then . . . I don't know. I stayed alive out of confusion for a while, then hate. Finally it just came down to habit. As the world began to spawn others like me, people who could hold on to and choke down another's soul without conscience enough within them to feel regret, I gathered them to me, sheltered them, trained them, held them together."

And then, the vampire looked up, asking, "Fair pathetic, wouldn't you say?"

This time it was London who turned his eyes away, not able to meet Jorhsa's gaze, not wanting to subject the eater of souls to the pity he felt for the monstrosity the onetime savior of humanity had become in the end.

EPILOGUE

L ONDON, JHONG, AND JORHSA made their way quietly into the room while Pa'sha and Cat kept those outside busy. The two moved carefully through the dim light of the ICU, knowing they would have only a few minutes at best. The detective pointed toward one of the beds in the room, saying;

"That one."

As they came up alongside the bed in question, London reached down to his leg sheath and slid Veronica out. Then, leaning over the bedrail, past the snaking tubes, he gently shook his partner's shoulder, whispering urgently;

"Paul. Paul. Wake up!"

After a moment, Jhong tapped London's shoulder, motioning him to move aside. The detective let the elder pass, then watched as he slid his hand behind Morcey's neck, feeling for just the right nerve. Massaging it correctly, Jhong was rewarded by the opening of the balding man's eyes.

"This will only break the coma for a matter of seconds," said the elder. "You must act quickly."

Shoving Veronica into Morcey's hand, London snapped, "The vampire, Paul—kill him!"

Acting without thought, the ex-maintenance man struggled his hand upward weakly, aiming the blade for Jorhsa's heart. The vampire leaned over as far as he could, putting himself in the way of the knife. Its point bumped against his skin, but the hand propelling it was too weak to even break the skin. Reacting quickly, though, Jorhsa thrust his body upward, snagging the sharp tip against his skin, drawing blood.

But suddenly, Morcey's hand began to fall away. Quickly, Jorhsa clasped his hands around Morcey's and shoved Veronica forward, forcing the knife deep into his chest. He winced at the pain for a moment, then gave London a determined look and twisted the blade into his heart, jerking it back and forth with a violent fury.

As the detective and Jhong watched, Jorhsa's hands fell away from Morcey's as he began to tremble. Feeling a massive churning building within himself, the king of the vampires smiled at the detective, nodding. Then, having finally had far more than enough of life, he tumbled to the floor and allowed himself to die.

London and the elder retreated to the hall. As light began to pour from the doorway behind them, the detective pulled his Auto-Mag and fired it into the ceiling of the intensive care area, paused, then fired again. The small crowd of nurses and aides confronting Pa'sha and Cat ran down the hall, disappearing toward the nearest exit.

A minute later, Paul Morcey, whole and hearty, healed of all wounds, scoured of all blemishes, burst from his room, shouting;

"Boss, boss! Boss, Sweet Bride of the Night, what the hell's goin' on?"

"We are all getting out of here," shouted Pa'sha as soul energy flooded the hall, leaking through the floor, floating through the ceiling. The weaponeer thrust a ball of clothing at Morcey, telling him, "That is the 'what' that is going on."

"But," asked the ex-maintenance man, pointing back toward his room. "What about them?"

"Jorhsa?" asked London, not understanding the question, tugging at the sleeve of his partner's dressing gown. "He's dead—I'll explain later. Come on. Let's go."

"No, not 'him.' Them."

The detective turned, looked, and then understood. From out of the intensive care unit, the half-dozen men and women that had been stretched out in the special area's other beds began to stumble through the door—confused but overjoyed. Cat pointed down the hall, shouting;

"Look!"

Up and down the hall, every door was opening, patients of all sizes and ages stumbling out into the shining light, some of them walking for the first time in years. Old men and women, no longer blind, no longer cancerous, no longer dying, not understanding the miracle happening around them, laughed and danced, some screaming with joy, all of their faces smiling, soaking with tears.

Throughout the hospital, on every floor, in every room, the escaping vitality did its work, healing, curing, energizing, giving life, robbing death of its meals to cleanse five thousand years of guilt and shame. By the time Morcey had pulled on the pants and T-shirt and shoes Pa'sha had given him, the five had no trouble slipping away in the commotion.

Outside the hospital, they made their way through the overjoyed patients clogging the stairways. At the street, the group made quick good-byes, knowing that even though there was little chance of anyone remembering them very clearly after everything else that had happened, it was still best to fade away from the area as quickly as possible.

Jhong gave everyone a brief nod and then turned, disappearing into the early morning without a backward glance. Pa'sha shook both Morcey's and London's hands vigorously and then unlocked his van, hurrying Cat inside. The detective and his partner stared back at all the confusion behind them for a moment and then turned away, walking off down the sidewalk.

As London explained to Morcey what had happened since the night before, the balding man exclaimed;

"Hey, boss—you ain't limpin'. And, and your hair, it ain't white no more."

"It's been a busy night."

Morcey accepted the answer, laughing at the way things had turned out simply because he could find no other response within him. The detective started to finish his story, but then suddenly stopped. The pair had come up along the deli where London and Goward had stopped the night before. Telling Morcey to wait for a moment, the detective ducked inside, returning a minute later with a small brown paper bag overflowing with things rapidly picked from the shelves.

Handing Morcey a sixteen-ounce Yoo-Hoo and a family pack box of Twinkies, he then pulled out a loaf of French twist, actually still warm from the early morning delivery truck. As his partner shook the wax-coated carton in his hand to churn up the chocolate drink inside, London pulled free the end of the loaf in his hand and stuffed it into his mouth. He bit down fiercely, biting away pieces, one after another, needing nothing more to wash them down than the hunger-driven saliva swelling in his mouth.

Finally, having cut the edge off the gnawing need that had been tearing at him for two months, he slowed down enough to start chewing. His mouth half full, he looked at Morcey and then swallowed, pulling in a deep breath through his nose as his face broke into a smile.

"Ahhhhh," he sighed, happier, more satisfied than he had ever been in his entire life;

"Fresh bread."

Starting on his second Twinkie, Morcey asked, "It don't get any better than this. Right, boss?"

The detective nodded, taking another bite out of his loaf at the same time. Happy to be alive, and understanding why.

Finally.

THE LAST BEST FRIEND

PROLOGUE

THE SMALL BUT ENTHUSIASTIC throng of men packed themselves in around the oblong box in the center of the room like refugees crowding an over-laden dinner table. Their eyes shone from a fairly standard variety of emotions. Some reflected disbelief shaded with greed, others' flashed a more refined image of desperate hope mingled with avarice. Fear and dread were present as always, along with the ever-turning crank of desire, the true motivator of the type of men now jammed body-on-body around the intricately locked mahogany box.

"Gentlemen, your most energetic enthusiasm warms my heart to its happiest depths."

The speaker was a tall, compactly built black man wearing an outlandish top hat and feathered vest, standing far to one side of the knotted crowd. He was younger than some present, older than most. As the majority of the assembled turned at the sound of his smooth, velvet-like voice, his handsome, moustached face smiled widely, allowing his inner self the satisfaction of a hidden moment of amusement at the crowd's expense. He had earned it, he felt. He deserved it. True, the joke might all be of his making, but it pleased him, so he continued to grin.

"You are eager, which is delightful to me, but, why not? Truth to tell, you all certainly deserve such emotion this night—yes? After all, you have waited now a very long time, eh?"

"Too long, Lowe," snapped one of the crowd. "We were promised a return on our investment six months ago. So far we haven't seen crap. That better end tonight."

"Oh, I promise you, good Mr. Conti, sir, all 'crap' comes to an end this evening. You have not been admirably patient, it is true. But, you have been patient enough to allow for the promised work to be completed."

"Well," asked another in the bunch, his fingers bridging, then intertwining, his anxiety easy to read and amusing to the grinning man known to those assembled as Baron Lowe, "what are we waiting for then?"

Yes, thought the smiling man; *what, indeed?*

With a clap of his hands, the group's host summoned two servitors. Both a shining, deep ebony black, they moved through the tight-packed crowd, letting it be seen that if they were not allowed to approach the oblong box with their sets of keys that its contents would never be revealed. The mostly white crowd allowed them passage, parting the way a line of sports cars will for a tanker rig on a crowded highway—with no generosity in their gesture, merely self-interest.

"'And I saw the dead, small and great, stand before God;'" quoted Lowe mostly to himself as the various locks were opened, "'and the books were opened and another book was opened, which was the book of life.'"

The two retainers inserted their keys with a rhythmic unison, unlocking the box's restraints smoothly as if the action were a thing learned through much practice. All around them, the throng began to press forward again, their fanatical anticipation shining in their eyes.

"'And the dead were judged out of those things which were written in the books,'" continued the evening's colorful host quietly, "'according to their works.'"

At that point the last of the varied locks was finally defeated. Without a word, the servitors lifted the heavy wooden lid from the oblong box, then moved it toward the back of the room, away from the greatest body of the crowd, back toward the man called Baron Lowe. The group took no heed of their actions. Having served their purpose, the pair had disappeared from their radar. With the lid removed, the throng's patience evaporated as they rushed the box, all competing for the first glimpse of its contents.

"'And the sea gave up the dead which were in it . . .'"

What the assembled saw was the well-dressed body of a man, tall, thin and emaciated. His eyes were closed, and his skin discolored, but he was readily recognized by those around him.

"'And,'" the evening's grinning host whispered as he signaled for his retainers to take their positions at the secured doors, a raised finger cautioning them to wait for just the right moment, "'death and hell delivered up the dead which were in them . . .'"

The man within the oblong box was so quickly identifiable because most of those assembled had been present three days earlier when he had been murdered right before their eyes, hung by their host with a thick length of hemp which broke his neck, emptied his bowels and stopped his heart. They had all seen it; had examined the remains for themselves—*knew* in no uncertain terms that the man had been absolutely dead at that time.

"'And they were judged every man according to their works.'"

As the assembly stared, their host took a backward step toward the door through which he had entered. He did not move with guile; there was no need. The crowd's eyes were all fastened intently on the dead man's body—on the dead man's *moving*, shifting body.

"He's done it!"

"He's alive!"

"This is it, all we were promised."

The dead man's head, striped with distorted purple welts, lurched to the left, and then, its eyes opened—wide and unblinking. The assembled screamed with delight, their mouths all grunting different sounds signifying relief and joy. At the same time, the assembly's host signaled his men to open the pair of opposing doors where they had stationed themselves.

The assembly went wild as the corpse grabbed at the sides of the box, pulling itself erect.

"Life!" screamed one of the crowd, "it's goddamned life everlasting!"

As the throng cheered, the reanimated corpse reached out for one of the waving hands flapping near its head. Catching hold of it, it's bloated face smiled as it drew the hand to its mouth and snapped off two of its fingers. At the same time, the two retainers stepped aside as the cleverly-fashioned secure doors opened. The design of their posts allowed the pair to easily side-step the parades of animated dead shambling into the arena. The corpses moved slowly, many with an awkward gait, but the room was not large, and in moments they had it filled.

Men screamed and dodged, many stumbling directly into the grasping arms of the oncoming horrors. Some struggled, but it did not matter. Their necks were ripped asunder, eyes gouged, chests and spines and skulls torn open before they could think. Blood splashed across the floor in torrents and slavering, rotting tongues lapped it up eagerly.

"'And death and hell,'" said the grinning man in the flamboyant hat as he disappeared through the room's back door, locking it as he did so, "'were cast into the lake of fire.'"

And with those words, the old man laughed—a deep and cleansing sound that echoed across the courtyard before him—the pitch of his noise responding to the wild screams piercing the night behind him.

"You wanted immortality, gentlemen," he announced as he walked away. "Well, now, those of you who survive . . . *enjoy*."

Outside the obscured building, the man called Baron Lowe and his men walked off into the pelting rain, the terrible cries bleeding out into the night from the solidly locked complex of no consequence to them whatsoever.

I

As his cab pulled away, the nervous young man in the ill-fitting suit picked up his bag. Never having left his home village before that morning, now he stood in New York City, his mind snapping over the million differences between his homeland and this strange new place which he had seen just on the trip from the airport to the Manhattan corner on which he stood.

No time to waste—

The thought flustered the young man. Quickly he turned around to face the yellow-and-black-painted-brick building behind him. Walking up to the front door, he knocked, then waited. When no one responded he knocked again, then suddenly cursed himself for his failed memory.

"Oh, misery," he spoke the words quietly.

If I can't even get this much of it right . . .

Worry permeated the young man's mind. He had a message to deliver to a man he was told he would find within the bowels of the building before him. He had been given a ritual to perform, and already he had bungled an important step. Now, if people were to be believed, his life was in danger.

"This is not a cigar shop I'm sending you to," his uncle had warned him with an almost frightening gravity. "The people within are truly dangerous. There are those who have tried to gain entrance there without correctly performing the ritual and they have never been seen again."

Grasping the doorknob before him the young man found that it turned readily, as he had been assured it would. Entering the foyer within, he closed the door behind himself, then paused before the interior door. As he waited, he spoke nervously to the far-too-close walls around him.

"I am most sorry for the knocking," he said to the air. "I knew not to do it, but I forgot myself. Please do not turn your back on me because of this mistake—I, I beg of you, do not ignore me, for my message is most insistent."

The young man pulled at his collar, his mind flashing with a rush of thoughts he could not contain.

"Do it right or dey will not respond." He remembered his uncle's words, heard them in his ear once more. "Not respond at best, that is. I trust you to do dis thing, but I warn you that you must be serious, and treat your mission seriously, and treat dey people you will find in dis place most seriously, or you may never be returned."

He had not thought much of what his uncle had told him then. Indeed, he remembered his sneering answer, "you are saying they would harm a simple messenger?" When his uncle's mood did not change as he had imagined it would, he had barked, "and these are the people you expect to help us?"

The young man shuddered, remembering also the stinging slap he had received. He had felt ashamed then. His uncle was a well-respected and venerable man, but one too elderly and frail to make the journey to New York. That he had chosen his nephew over other candidates showed great faith. Ashamed for a moment, still the youth had been proud of that fact.

Now, he was merely worried—worried and a bit frightened. As he continued to stand quietly in the foyer, looking over the various apartment names on the building's tenant roster, he did not push any of the buzzers. Nor did he knock again. He had been taught the routine. He remembered it. Now he would simply stand and wait until the old woman came.

Eventually, because he had done as he had, the locked inner door clicked internally and then opened cleanly, propelled by the stick-thin forearm of an elderly black woman.

"What bring you here?" she asked.

The woman's appearance upset the youth even more than the waiting had. Although in his mid-twenties, the firsts he was encountering that day were beginning to pile up faster than he could handle them. After all, he had never been further than twenty miles from home before. Never been on an airplane. Never worn a suit and tie. Never before been told that if he said one word out of place he would be killed without a second thought. And, until he looked into the old woman's eyes, he had not believed such a thing could be.

"What brings me wh-where, grandmother?" he answered the old woman, palms sweating, tongue drying.

"To dis place?"

"What . . .," the youth hesitated, a centuries long split-second passing before he started again, "w-what place be that?"

"You choke to name dis place?" asked the woman harshly, her eyes drilling under the young man's flesh. "You run from de thought to name dis place?"

"This place has no name, grandmother," calm, calm, he screamed within his mind. Say the words, "One can not name what is not there."

A pause with the weight of mountains settled on the young man's back, and then suddenly, the old woman smiled, saying;

"Den enter what is not . . ."

"And be where there is nothing."

The ritual completed, the youth found himself shaking. Tears formed in both his eyes. With control he would pride himself over later, he allowed neither of the droplets to roll down his cheeks, but kept then in place through force of will. Unconcerned, unimpressed, the woman asked;

"Why be ye here?"

"I ha-have a message."

"For me?" snapped the old woman. "For Boney Pete, for Santa Claus, for St. Michael? Can you speak?"

The last word ended with a tiny but moist mote flying from the woman's lips to splatter against the young man's face. His lips stiffening, shoulders straightening, he threw his words forward like a weapon.

"For Pa'sha Lowe," he practically screamed. Without reaction, the woman merely turned on her heel.

"My son is this way."

As he watched, the old woman walked down the unadorned hall behind her. The young man continued to stare for a long moment, then, making the sign of the cross, he forced his legs to move one after another and followed her down the dark hallway. As he moved along, the youth ignored the doors to either side, not knowing what lay behind them, suddenly keenly aware they were none of his concern. Reaching the end of the hall, he followed as the woman turned to the left and headed down a moldering well of stairs marked:

Danger . . . Stay Off . . . Danger

He ran his hand along the railless wall as they descended. The stairs seemed sturdy enough, as if the sign were a distraction of some sort, but he continued to steady himself anyway. Finally, after several more twists and turns, he was lead into a darkened chamber.

"Pa'sha, baby," called out the old woman. "There is a . . . someone to see you."

At the far end of the room, an enormous black man turned from a work-table covered with half-built handguns and other, more formidable weapons, a large smile filling his round face. He stood with an abrupt motion, revealing a six-and-a-half-foot height hung with three-hundred-and-thirtysome pounds of solid meat. His quiet voice seemed out of place coming from his massive frame.

"And who are you, little brother?"

"My name is Christophe Boyer. My uncle is Francois Boyer. He sent me here."

Pa'sha stared at the younger man, his brow creasing. His mother made to speak, but the weaponeer casually silenced her with a wave of his hand.

"Tell me, Christophe, what race are you?"

The younger man pulled at his tie, his nerves tightening as he answered matter-of-factly, "I am mulatto. What is it to you?"

"Just gathering information." When Christophe's face remained unchanged, Pa'sha told him, "That you were Haitian was announced as soon as you opened your mouth. Your accent is as clean and clear as the streams that feed the Trois Rivières. Now that you have told me you come from money—"

"What?"

"Oh please, little brother, our island has an old saying, 'the rich black is a mulatto; the poor mulatto is a black.' Whether your people are still prosperous is not important. Knowing what you think of your background gives me advantage, yes? Has Francois taught you nothing of the world?"

Pa'sha made a dismissing gesture, moving his head from side to side while waving his hand slightly. His mother smiled, turning to withdraw. A look in her son's eyes, however, caused her to stay.

"Now," the weaponeer continued, concentrating on his guest, "while I hold all the cards, and you have yet to draw from the deck, tell me why it is you are here."

"My uncle sent me to tell you that there is a great need for you in your old home."

"This tells me why you made a trip, but it tells me little else. Might there be some specifics to your tale, or did old Francois forget to give you any?"

Christophe bristled at what his young ears heard as ridicule. His thin fingers curling unconsciously into fists, his voice lowered as he said, "No one may speak of Francois Boyer in such a manner."

Pa'sha was amused at the younger man's naivete, but he managed to hold back his laughter. He could not mask his smile, however, as he answered, "Calm yourself, boy. I would no more insult my sweet godfather than I would cook and eat a ribboned rooster. Now, stop wasting time and tell me why you be here."

"It is your father," answered Christophe, his tone humble, eyes lowered, fingers once more hanging loosely at his sides.

"My Pa'pe?" said Pa'sha, eyes unblinking, brow creased. "What trouble could he bring to our island?"

"There is rumor thick as delta silt. The old seals have been broken, the old religion filled with flame." The younger man's voice began to grow louder, his words running faster. "Many have flocked to him for the secrets of life, only to disappear. Important men, rich men, white men … but, you know, you don't be making the rich, important white men vanish, even on Haiti, and not turn to find trouble sitting your doorstep next morning. De Baron Lowe be bringing plenty trouble down on everyone."

Pa'sha turned toward Mama Joan, staring into her eyes. His mother returned his gaze, defying God, Jesus and the Holy Spirit as well to dislodge any of the tears she had ever refused to shed over the husband she had not seen in so long. After an eternal second, Pa'sha turned back toward Christophe.

"I don't think it be mine Pa'pe that is causing trouble for anyone."

"I have no reason to anger you, and," the younger man's eyes bounced from the weapons piled on Pa'sha's table, to the size of his corded arms, then back to his eyes, "it would be a most damned fool's errand to do so, but I must tell you again, as my uncle has told me to, it is de Baron that has done these things. It is he who must be stopped."

"My father," answered Pa'sha, chips of anger flinting his voice, "can not be your problem. My father is dead!"

"No, sir," answered Christophe quietly. "Not anymore."

II

"So, my godpa'pe," said Pa'sha, speaking to a compactly built, older black man in a cleric's collar, "what for you need to bring me home with such a tale, eh?"

Across the gloomy, overly warm barroom, the priest sat back in his wheelchair and smiled weakly, his arms raising, outstretched. Pa'sha crossed through the place's few patrons to face Francois Boyer, bending as he did so, encircling the old man with his huge arms. The two hugged each other quietly, refusing words, each holding back wells of emotion. Two fans, one rusting, one new, fought the stifling heat within the room as best they could.

"I be sore pleased," whispered Boyer, his voice wavering. "To have you here again. Home again."

The men broke, Pa'sha pulling a close-by chair to himself. As he pushed his massive frame in between the arms of the old wooden piece, he held his breath as his weight settled against its squeaking joints.

"I don't ask why for you no return before dis," Boyer added. "Past is past, and time spent crying on it be just more dead minutes. I be old enough, and too glad to see you now to worry on when I couldn't."

"And why be you so glad?"

Pa'sha stared at his godfather with a dreading curiosity. The weaponeer knew something terrible was happening. Christophe's agitated mood both in New York and throughout the trip back to Haiti had given him that much.

Besides, thought the big man, *no one would call me back to this place without a damn fine reason.*

"Because there be a long darkness coming, snorted from de nostrils of a raging quartet of horses, terrible beasts that no man can ride, that no woman wants to see, that no child should ever know."

"That be one powerful reference you make," said Pa'sha. "I'm sure you know that."

"I've spoke de mass near fifty year, I know which book I'm quoting. I do so 'cause it's powerful frightened that I be. Dis place be conquered now, at least by night. De first horse, de white horse, it dances in de square every night, its rider swinging his bow, ruler of all he surveys. And de red horse be right behind him, his horrible voice braying for all to hear."

Pa'sha simply stared, understanding his godfather's metaphor all too well. Raising his hand, he signaled the bartender that he could use a cold beer. The scarecrow of a man brought a large mug to the table filled with a golden brew so rusty in color the weaponeer could tell he would need more than one of the lime slices in the bowl in the table's center. Fighting back the heat with a deep swallow, Pa'sha pointed to Boyer's drink, asking if he needed another. As the old man shook his head while taking a polite swallow, Pa'sha, pointing at the spent 40mm shell casing in Boyer's hand, said;

"Perhaps for the best. It must be a powerful drink to be served in so potent a glass."

"Just a left-over from when your president, de one your country said was unfit to rule, but who ruled on and on anyway, sent his army to us to teach us how best we should rule ourselves." Boyer brushed an amber droplet from his moustache, continuing, "it was quite an experience. Out of nowhere, suddenly a shadow passing across de land, and all Haiti wondered if dis time around America would burn us all to death, the way it does its own people when dey resist its will."

"And, was anyone burned to death?"

"Not nearly enough."

Pa'sha eyed his godfather for a moment, then laughed aloud when the old man smiled, no longer able to hold back his own amusement. Taking up the brass cylinder before him, Boyer lifted the gunmetal cup to his godson, banging it harshly against Pa'sha's beer mug.

"To life, Pa'sha," he said, "to just de one, and no more."

"One is all I need."

Both men tilted their arms and worked at draining their drinks as Christophe entered the bar. The younger man joined them at their table, signaling the bartender to bring him a beer as well. Pa'sha doubled the order.

"I will never understand why you like this place, uncle."

"I like de name," replied Boyer, amusement still twinkling in his voice.

"That Dark Inn," Christophe responded, his eyes darting from one shadowy corner to another. "Well, it certainly be a dark enough place."

"Is that all de name means to you?" When the young man answered in the positive, Boyer snorted, waving his nephew off with friendly disgust. As Christophe turned to Pa'sha, the weaponeer told him;

"The name, I would guess, it be a salute from the poem by Walter Scott, 'To that dark inn, the grave!'"

"What does Haiti need a white man for to name its taverns?"

Pa'sha sighed. He thought of answering Christophe for a moment, then sighed again and let it pass. Boyer chuckled.

"Wisdom has entered your life, I see."

"It usually comes to those of us who live long enough." The large man took a long pull from his newly arrived mug. With a pause, he smacked his lips, then finished the last of his second beer, biting the two pieces of lime that slid down to the rim. The weaponeer sucked their juice, pulling at the citrus fibers as they mingled with the last golden red drops. Settling the mug on the table, he asked;

"So, now tell me, why am I to believe that my dear Pa'pe has not only left his own dark inn, the one I helped lower him into, but that he is now the magnet drawing us all over the edge toward the inferno?"

Francois Boyer raised his weary head, staring unblinking at his godson. His eyes looked tired, tired from age, tired from staring out over a world gone just a bit madder with each passing day, tired of having to drink in more pain than the soul to which they were the mirror could bear.

"Because, my poor boy," he said, looking on, feeling older, hating the world more with each word, "dere be zombies walking de land."

"Zombies," Pa'sha spat the word like a curse, signalling for yet another beer. "Please, there be no connection between such dazed fools and my Pa'pe. Drugging the living is one thing . . . no one makes the dead to walk again."

"Someone does," answered Boyer with a shudder. As Pa'sha started his third beer, the old man whispered, "this be not dey same tribal nonsense we lived with when you left us. Dis be somethin' new. Somethin' evil."

"Uncle's words be most true," added Christophe. "I have seen dese things. The dead walk."

"Do not play with me, boy."

"He be not playin' you, Pa'sha. Some new and horrible darkness has come to play with us all. Christophe has seen with his eyes young, and I've seen it, too. And more. When de stories came in, of de dead walking once more, of blood spilled, of sacrifices made, of men disappearing, and all of it being laid at de feet of a whisperman named Baron Lowe, I made de journey to de poor patch where we laid your father down."

Pa'sha sat still, his head bent, one eye struggling to face the words spilling toward him.

"He was not dere. Only de piece of limestone we set to mark his place, and a deep hole, already flooding with weeds . . . that was all that waited for me."

"And you have seen him," snapped Pa'sha, his blood suddenly hot, muscles knotting. "You have watched him staggering on moulder legs, pointed to his peeling skin, dangling entrails? Were his eyes still in his head? Teeth in his mouth?"

"There are those who have seen . . ."

A large fist slammed against the table. Heads turned at the explosion, but only slightly. The day was hot, and those few patrons inside were accustomed to pain dancing cheek to cheek with belligerence.

"Take me too them. Find me these witnesses."

"People speak only in de third person about dese things. You know that, boy," snapped Boyer, his strength rushing from his body. "Who will swear to seeing de dead climbing from their graves? Who will attest to witnessing de march of the zombies? Voodoo? Here on Haiti? Don't you know dat be all the old past ways, long forgotten? We be so much more civilized now."

"And so civilized you are, you cower from threats you say do not exist." Pa'sha signaled the bartender, calling for a round of the 40mm rum drinks. "Well, I agree. I scoff right with you. My Pa'pe is not crawling across the land, dead eyes staring to nowhere, dead hands clutching at air . . ."

"Pa'sha, please–"

"No!" The weaponeer slammed his fist again, grabbing the first of the drinks being placed on the table by the barman. Tossing it off quickly, he reached for another of them. "If I am to do something—*anything*—then I must believe. And I do not."

The large man tossed back the second rum, barely feeling the burn as its blurring fingers wrapped themselves about his reason. His massive fist encircling the last drink, he growled; "You know the words . . . 'Except I shall see in his hands the prints of the nails, and put my finger into the print of the nails, and thrust my hand into his side, I *will not believe!*'"

As Pa'sha tossed back the third drink as well, he rose from the table. The quick ascent staggered the weaponeer for a moment, but he caught himself on the edge of the table, then turned and headed for the door. Boyer called after him.

"Where are you going, boy?"

"To the cemetery," he snapped. "To take a head count."

III

Pa'sha stumbled over a mossy rock in the darkness. His hand grabbed automatically for the wooden gate to the abandoned church cemetery, ripping the rusting screws of the upper hinge from the grey wood. As the fungused boards splintered under his weight, the weaponeer was thrown off balance, plummeting unceremoniously to his knees on the overgrown gravel path. His fall was broken by the dense foliage that covered the long forgotten patch. Indeed, so long had the place gone untended, choking vegetation hid most of the grave markers still standing.

"Oh, Pa'pe," he sighed, "My fault this is. A true thing I say now—yes?"

Staggering to his feet, Pa'sha moved on through the darkness which hid most of the graveyard's features. Although the moon was shining brightly, it hung at little less than a quarter in the sky, illuminating just enough to mark the weaponeer's way if he concentrated on what he was doing. His brain was somewhat freed from the effects of the trio of drinks he had downed so rapidly on top of his beers, but still the big man had trouble in pulling all the pieces he had together within his mind.

Too many things made no sense to him. That zombies roamed the Haitian night was nothing new. But in his time he had lived on the island long enough to know the truth about such matters. He knew, for instance, that voodoo was based on a belief in a Christian God mixed with lesser Haitian and African deities—the *loa*. He knew that the native religion was concerned with possession of the living, and that the *houngans* and *mambos*, the priests and priestesses of the faith, did not concern themselves with the Hollywood nonsense of the walking dead. Pretending to powers on that level was something left to the sorcerers—the *bocor*—and even most of them made no pretense about being able to actually raise the deceased from their final slumber.

"But someone," the large man muttered, "someone wants people to believe that my poor Pa'pe—twelve years rotting in the heavy dark—that he now be bocor himself, and powerful enough to rise up flesh without blemish or maggot, terrible enough to take the place of Jesus in the pulling of men from their charitable sleep, setting them to the pain of living once more."

"You make that sound like a bad thing."

Pa'sha froze. The thin voice, one almost recognizable to the big man, had come from somewhere in the darkness, somewhere too close to be considered comfortable.

"It is more than a bad thing," replied the weaponeer, wary, suddenly immensely focused on the fact modern travel restrictions had left him virtually unarmed. "It is a horrible thing. A screaming blasphemy."

"It is a truth," the voice whispered.

"Then it is a damned truth," answered Pa'sha, his eyes straining to spot anything loose and sturdy which he might pull to himself, "and you are a damned thing for spreading it across the land."

"You have come a long way to walk in dey darkness this night," the voice spoke again. Listening to the words carefully, Pa'sha heard a cruel slyness in their tone, a smug self-assurance which warned him to immediate caution. No longer looking for the speaker, the weaponeer busied himself with his search for any kind of defense. Spotting what appeared to be a recently erected cross, he did not bother to question who might have been buried in such a forgotten spot, but instantly grabbed at the affair, wrenching it from the ground. Little more than two sections of painted two-by-four, Pa'sha pulled the boards apart, holding one to the ready in each hand.

"We all walk in darkness, my friend," answered the weaponeer, continuing on to the far corner of the long abandoned cemetery, the place where last he had seen his father. "It is realizing that this never changes that makes all the difference."

Only some thirty yards from his father's resting place, Pa'sha picked up his pace, threading his way carefully between the mostly crude and crumbling monuments scattered haphazardly about the overgrown necropolis. Although he did not allow it to show, the weaponeer was beginning to experience a slight sense of dread. Many of the mounds he passed had been torn open, dug away, defiled by someone or something. It was a sight that would not have left him comfortable, even in daylight.

"You know what you will find at dey end of your quest, don't you, Pa'sha Lowe?"

"No man knows his destiny," responded Pa'sha with authority. If they did, what would be the reason in continuing on?"

"Like yourself," answered the still-hidden voice, chuckling at something private and faraway, "they simply must see things for themselves."

And then, as Pa'sha neared his father's plot, he stopped at its edge, his conscious mind finally accepting what he had been told—what his instincts and emotions had accepted long before. Seeing the gaping wound in the ground where his mother and he had so long ago planted various flowers and then watered them with tears, he shouted;

"End this game! Show yourself, and tell me why for you needed to drag my poor Pa'pe from the cool bosom of that sweet dark rest the Lord saw fit to give him?"

"Nobody dragged him nowhere, my poor, sad foolish one," the chuckling voice answered. "The trumpet call came, and didn't he do his duty and answer it. And I was sore pleased to see dey glee with which he took to doin' my holy work."

Off to one side, a figure moved from the shadows, approaching Pa'sha with a steady gait. "You say all men walk in darkness," it called to the weaponeer. "Well den, maybe I be no mere man."

With a clap of his hands, the dark form somehow encased himself in a sudden light, the fingers of which splashed across the cemetery. As Pa'sha stared, he saw a man dressed in splendid silks and feathers. The brilliance surrounding him made his features and many other details a mystery for the weaponeer, but still much was left which could be made out. One thing Pa'sha noted immediately was that around the glowing man's feet walked an odd assortment of chickens, some all black, some whose feathers were streaked with white and even yellow. On each of his shoulders sat a long-tailed bird, both with fierce claws and large beaks, both with crested heads and staring eyes. Various lizards and a number of large spiders peeked out of the man's many pockets while a vast cloud of insects spun madly above his head.

"Where is my father?" asked Pa'sha.

"So impertinent," laughed the glowing man. "But, since squeaky wheels are supposed to get dey grease, perhaps I should send some good and trusted guides to take you to him."

The glowing man made no gesture, spoke no words. The light shining from him changed in no way Pa'sha could discern. And yet, from all around the graveyard the rustling of grass was heard as two score pairs of feet began shuffling forward.

"This foolish lump who now offers us his face after showin' only his backside for so long thinks he has power here. Instruct him, my children."

Eighty legs moved forward, tightening a crude circle around the weaponeer. Hefting the longer of his two boards, Pa'sha immediately scanned the cemetery, looking for the quickest way back to the front gate. As the first of the surrounding forces approached him, the large man matter-of-factly swung one of his two-by-fours with a surprising speed, smashing the head of the closest figure, spraying himself with its blackened blood and shattered teeth.

Zombies, thought Pa'sha, his own blood freezing, mind numbing. *These things really be zombies!*

The first assailant slumped to the ground, its hands still clawing at the air even as its body crumpled against the soil, fingers still trying to drag it forward. At the same time two more of the stumbling figures reached for Pa'sha, but he stepped back from them, again swinging his larger board with violent accuracy, caving in first one's head, then the other's, both with the same blow.

The bodies folded in on themselves like the first, but there were still many more coming, and not all of them appeared as fragile as those first he had dispatched.

I've got to get out of here.

"And how will you do that, mere flesh, with so many of your brothers lookin' to keep you here where you belong?"

Pa'sha froze. The glowing man-thing had read his thoughts. Shuffling, rotting bodies continued to push through the wild grass and weeds, crushing their way toward him, but still, he could not move, could not think fast enough.

"What are you?" cried the weaponeer, his eyes riveted to the glowing man. The approaching zombies forgotten, he screamed at the figure;

"What *are* you?"

"I am dey truth and dey light, and dey revelation's herald. I am your destiny, dear Pa'sha, your ancestor. I am dey hand on dey future's door, and I'm turnin' dey knob right now, boy, and I'll be draggin' your damned soul down to the pit where it belongs—right next to your damned Pa'pe!"

"No!"

Pa'sha screamed the word as suddenly both his hands swung out in a blind fury. The shorter of his boards caved in the chest of one of his attackers, knocking the rotting thing backwards into a few more of those shuffling forward behind it. The longer board crushed its way through one head on Pa'sha's other side, and then another still, but it jammed there, the nails of it caught in the shattered skull and brain of the dead man grabbing for the weaponeer's throat. The now blind thing twisted violently as it remembered pain, the sudden turn wrenching Pa'sha's weapon free from his hand as the zombie stumbled off into its fellows.

"Kill him, my children," mouthed the glowing form, the words broadcast for Pa'sha's benefit, "Tomorrow night, at the devil's stroke, when we march from King Henri's Citadelle, he must be at our side. So, drag him to us, make him understand dey glory of dey judgment to come!"

"Yes," growled Pa'sha, slamming his remaining two-by-four against his palm, "come on to me, you stinking remains, you come and try to teach me something."

With a roar Pa'sha leaped forward into a mass of the approaching zombies, slamming away with his board, tearing skin, breaking bones, scattering those coming at him with the unexpected savagery of his attack. Blood splattered from his arms as broken nails raked along their lengths. Hair was torn from the big man's head, his left ear and cheek laid bare, his back cut open by grasping hands and snapping teeth.

The zombies fell one after another, however, their ribs shattered, legs broken, skulls ripped free. Pa'sha ignored how their headless bodies would thrash about, how arms shorn from torsos would continue to drag themselves along the ground—spidered fingers crawling blindly—searching for him, feeling, clutching. He ignored the sprays of fluid that would splatter against his chest and face as he smashed away at his enemies. And, he ignored the questions in his mind, the reasoned voices nearly paralyzed by those things they were witnessing which they could neither explain nor accept.

"I will not think on these things," he growled, more at the glowing man than to himself. Panting, he dug his feet in as he added, "I will not think on anything, do you hear me, except your destruction."

Pa'sha gasped down a great breath of air. The weaponeer was running out of strength, his endurance sorely taxed. Still, he noted, he had severely routed the glowing thing's forces. And then, as Pa'sha sucked several more deep breathes into his burning lungs, the ground began to shake as a hundred hands, some still wrapped in skin, some nothing more than bones and gristle, began clawing their way to the surface of the cemetery.

"I cannot be destroyed, boy," answered the grinning figure. "Can dey wind be destroyed? Dey mountains?"

"For the wind," gasped Pa'sha, "one builds a wall. And for the mountains . . ."

Pulling his pocket watch free, keeping his mind clear, the weaponeer turned its stem counter-clockwise, then jerked it loose altogether. Tossing it into the mass of human light before him, he shouted as he leaped away;

"For the mountains there are other means!"

IV

"And then what happened?"

"The watch did as she has waited to do, she exploded most nicely, sending force and flame in many directions, and chasing away whatever the thing be that came to me at my Pa'pe's grave."

"But what happened?" asked Christophe. The young man was bent over Pa'sha's back, cleaning the wounds the large man had taken. As he pulled bits of twig and leaves and broken fingernails from his skin before cleaning and bandaging the various cuts and scrapes and bitemarks the weaponeer carried, he said, "To the thing, the zombies, to you?"

"Nothing much more to tell, I'm not so saddened to say. Gladly would I tell of triumph and battle, but for me to use my sweet Vivian, this means I had nothing left to give. She has always been my hole card, as it were. Like many women, to turn her loose is to bring down upon the world much noise and great confusion. Vivian traveled with me so that if all were lost, I still might have an option for which my enemies might not be prepared."

Pa'sha jumped involuntarily as the ointment Christophe was applying burned him unexpectedly. Apologizing for his lack of control, he finished his story.

"Also like the best women, my Vivian had a fiery core that made her most special. In her case that core was phosphorous. It set a great many fires which resulted in a most beautiful bounty of smoke. All of it helped cover my escape from the cemetery most nicely. I started running before she exploded, and kept running afterward. When I stopped at the graveyard gate to see what all had transpired, I found the glowing bastard thing had disappeared in the explosion."

"You destroyed him, yes?"

"I sorely wish so, Christophe, lad, but I do not know. I could not chance to look. There were still zombies everywhere, of course, many on fire. Quite a few seemed lost, but many still were putting forth the effort to continue their affair with me. I was tired, wounded and very confused. And frightened as well. It was time to withdraw."

Pa'sha closed his eyes against another burning stab of cleansing pain. As Christophe pronounced his ministrations finally at an end, the weaponeer thanked him for his help, adding an apology.

"I must ask forgiveness of both you and uncle Francois. I was rude and stupid earlier, and neither passion nor disbelief are adequate defense for such ignorance."

"It was . . . I mean . . ." embarrassed, the younger man struggled for words. "It was understandable, anyone . . ."

"Thank you, Christophe," answered Pa'sha. "You are kinder than I deserve. Now, tell me, have the zombies ever yet come so far into the city as here?"

"No, sir. Not really . . . once some were . . . no, not that anyone knows of for certain."

"Good, let us trust things remain of that fashion." Rolling over onto his side, Pa'sha told the younger man, "My first day home has been not so much a success, eh?"

"You are still alive," offered Christophe. Pa'sha roared with laughter.

"Finally, our island has a philosopher equal to walk with the Greeks. Ah, boy, you lighten my soul more than it deserves. Can I ask of you two boons?" When the younger man agreed he could, Pa'sha said, "Safe we should be 'til morning, I think. But still, I would wish for you to keep vigil until the sun cleans away evening's shadow. Uncle Francois and I will have much to do come the morning, and we need what rest the world will allow us."

"You said 'two boons?'"

"Yes," answered Pa'sha, his eyes heavy with the need for sleep, "Some packages will arrive tomorrow for me. If you will sign for them and wake me when they come, I will see what I can do about ending all this misery before it crawls much further."

"Packages?" asked Christophe. "What are they? I mean, what is coming; what is in them?"

"Boom boom," answered the weaponeer.

"Boom boom?" repeated the younger man.

"Yes," replied Pa'sha in a dreamy voice. "The most beautiful boom boom."

And then, Pa'sha drifted off, and Christophe's remaining questions were answered with snores.

The seven large Federal Express boxes waited for Pa'sha in Francois Boyer's dining room, entirely blotting from sight his grand oaken dining table.

"Ah, the most dependable men of Fed Ex," said the weaponeer with satisfaction, rubbing his hands one against the other, "when it simply *has* to be there the next day."

"What is here, my godson?" asked Boyer. "And who sent it? And how did they know you were here?"

"I sent them, godfather," answered Pa'sha as he tore open one of the oversized, oblong boxes.

"But what is it you sent?"

"When the 10th Mountain Division came to Haiti as part of Operation Uphold Democracy, ah, what a delicious name—how I miss the delicate irony of the Clinton administration. But, pardon, I was speaking of the 10th Mountain, and how they came armed with a most effective rifle, the M16A2, a most wonderfully designed piece of equipment. Even when fully loaded, it weighs under twelve pounds, and yet maintains a maximum effective range of 400 meters, in the right hands, of course."

Pa'sha pulled one of the four M16s from the first box. Handing it over to his godfather for examination, he then started in on another of the boxes.

"But here is what makes it a true wonder." Pulling forth another handful of deadly metal, he held it out for inspection as well, announcing, "the M203 40mm Grenade Launcher. For only the addition of another three pounds, one can most effectively increase the destructive capabilities of the modern warrior."

"And why would you send such a thing here to yourself?" asked Boyer, turning the weapon in his hand over and over. "I thought you did not believe in zombies."

"Before I arrived, I truly did not," answered Pa'sha. "But I have always believed in you, and if the word from your house was that zombies were dancing in the street, well, who am I to not bring along a few musical instruments of my own to help make the party more lively?"

"And what do you believe now?"

"I believe things have changed greatly here in our island paradise since I attended seminary . . ."

"You?" Christophe's surprise poured out of him, a noise so amazed it bordered on the insulting. Pa'sha smiled.

"Yes," he answered quietly, his strong voice fading. "My Pa'pe, he was a wonderful man—the sun would not set until he was safe home. He was an usher for the church and a right hand to the priests, like your uncle Francois here, for all my years. I knew from when my eyes came only to his knees that I would be a priest one day. All for him." The large weaponeer looked toward a blank spot on the wall, seeing something else for a long, still moment. Finally, however, he began to unpack his boxes once more as his voice returned.

"But, then he was murdered. There was much of it to do with politics and the government. Port-au-Prince has always been the devil's pit it is today. I called on the authorities to avenge me, and they laughed. I called for the people to rise up, and they divided their response—some laughed, most slunk away, and at least one called the authorities so they could come and beat upon my poor coconut head until it sensibly stopped talking." Pa'sha continued to pile weapons on the table, throwing boxes to the floor, attaching the launchers to the rifles as he finished his story.

"At that point I prayed for justice, but none came. Since the authorities and the people would not help me, I left Haiti. Since God would not help me, I left the church."

"And now that you have returned to your home," asked Boyer.

"One thing at a time, Godpa'pe." Turning to Christophe, the weaponeer handed him a great wad of cash and ordered, "I need you to go to That Dark Inn and gather all of their brass serving cups. Do not spend every dollar doing so if it is not necessary."

When the younger man hesitated, Pa'sha explained.

"It is a reasonable price that is charged to send weapons through the mail. Ammunition, however, incurs a most magnificent charge. I was hoping to pick some things up locally since the M16 was used here by the Americans, and then by the UN peacekeepers afterwards. But, having seen our enemies last night, I am thinking perhaps a special touch shall be needed. See what you can do, eh?"

Christophe ran for the door. Stopping in the doorjamb, he turned, looking at Pa'sha. He held his pose for a moment, then suddenly broke into a large smile and continued on his way. After a few seconds, Pa'sha said;

"I think perhaps the boy is getting the idea."

Boyer smiled in response, then laughed. After a moment, Pa'sha laughed, too, then went back to work.

Pa'sha, Boyer and Christophe worked throughout the remainder of the morning and all the afternoon, preparing the special shells the weaponeer had decided to cobble together. As he explained it to his godfather, "These zombie creatures, they are a new thing to Haiti as you said. They are truly the dead raised from the grave. I do not know how, nor do I care. My only idea right now is to put them back where they belong. And with the beautiful children I have in mind to create, that should be a thing most easy."

The first thing Pa'sha set Christophe to work at was cleaning the 40mm brass shell casings gathered from the tavern. They needed new primer, which the weaponeer replaced with fulminate of mercury he simply took from bullets friends of his godfather had on hand. When still others Boyer trusted arrived, they were put to work packing the shells with gunpowder which would become their propellant. After that, the projectiles were filled with various loads.

Some were stuffed with white phosphorus, some with magnesium—both very flammable. Another set were filled with bundles of nails wrapped in paper tape. Still more were filled with dime-sized slugs. While the others worked on packing these, Pa'sha labored with a small welding set, piecing together sets of ball bearings by joining them with a coil of thin steel cable some three feet in length when stretched out. These he would load into one of the 40mm shells, chuckling as he did so. When questioned, he explained;

"I can not guarantee that these children of mine will perform as I envision. Offspring so rarely live up to their parents' dreams, but the idea is that when fired, the ball bearings will spread out, joined by the cable, which will hopefully cause some wonderful mayhem."

All gathered grinned, or at least nodded with satisfaction. As the afternoon wore on, all of the special rounds were sealed with wax and labeled as to what type of shell they were. Finally, as the small band who Boyer had gathered to face what was coming finished their preparations, Pa'sha held up one of the 40mm packages they had created.

"Now," he told them, "since these sweet rounds were made for a weapon that was never designed to fire them, we may find that some of them could be, oh, shall we say, problematic."

"He means difficult, troublesome," one man told a friend.

"Are these things children or wives?" asked a balding fellow good-naturedly. As all the men chuckled, Pa'sha continued.

"My friends, just remember that these are low-velocity shells; they do not have the penetrating power of a common pistol round. But, the size and weight of the loads will make up for that."

"And let me add something," said Boyer. As all heads turned, the old man said, "I can not go with you to Henri's castle tonight. Wheelchairs, they be not meant for climbin'. But I will be with you in spirit, and I will be prayin' for you, beggin' Jesus to stand your sides and help you in dis righteous act. God's gentle mercy be with all you, and all you ... you watch you selves, and end dis thing tonight.

"Tonight."

The men nodded, some clapped their hands. Everyone thought the idea of a last drink was a good one, and two bottles were passed until they were drained. Then finally, when not a single drop further could be brought forth, the seven gathered in the hot room who could stand did so and made for the door with their weapons on their shoulders, ammunition on their belts, and prayers on their lips.

V

High above the island's once-fertile northern plains stood the Citadelle, built by King Henri Christophe at the beginning of the 19th century to defend against invaders who never came. It was the largest fortress in the Western Hemisphere, Haiti's most revered national symbol, a brilliantly constructed monument to cruelty that had cost some 20,000 conscripts their lives and which now stood in ruins, mostly unvisited, practically forgotten.

"I was named for the king, you know," panted Christophe as the seven worked their way up the 3,000 foot mountain, Bonnet-a-l'Eveque, upon which the Citadelle sat like a crown.

"I was named for my grandfather," responded one of the older men in the crowd. As the slow procession continued, one of his friends said;

"But your grandfather's name was Umbura."

"My mother's father."

"Oh, that is different," responded the man. After a second, though, he added, "But his name was Michael, and your name is Louie."

"This is true," admitted the first speaker. "But he had always wanted to be called Louie."

The small troupe laughed, even Christophe, who knew their nonsense was aimed at him.

"Too bad the cannon are still not above, eh?"

"It depends," answered Pa'sha. "If the zombies are waiting there for us, perhaps giving them cannons would not be a good idea."

"Waiting for us there, cannons or not," added another man, "is still a good idea. For them, that is."

The others had to agree. The Citadelle was an impressive fortress, stretched across a mountain peak with sheer cliffs on three sides, its only point of access easily defended by any within.

"She had over 350 cannons at one time," Christophe said. "They say it took three months for each of them to be moved from the island floor to the mountain's top. Some of them are still up there, but they are worthless now."

"We will be worthless if we do not reach the top before darkness descends," snapped Pa'sha. The others, sensing his mood, fell silent, understanding the wisdom in his words.

The seven still had at least a half hour's climb ahead of them. Making merry had its merits, but they were drawing too close to the Citadelle to fall off their guard. On top of all that, Pa'sha was trying to pull together the facts he had into some kind of scenario which made sense.

Trying to make sense of the walking dead, a voice within his mind asked him. *And have you explained this thing yet?*

The weaponeer scowled at the question. Indeed, all the facts he had left him confused. His father, a most religious man, rises from the dead and promises rich men everlasting life in exchange for great sums of cash.

But why would a dead man need cash, he wondered. Things keep pointing toward the coming of the Apocalypse. But again, if one is bringing about the final judgment, what need is there for cash? To buy a new suit in which to meet Jesus?

And again, how could it be his father? Yes, the weaponeer did believe the dead could walk. Although he had never seen the bocor who could manage the feat when first he lived in Haiti, he had seen enough the night before to convince him that some powerful new evil had visited his home with abilities far beyond those of the local sorcerers.

But, the reports of this murderous Baron Lowe talked of a man. A normal, human man. Not a zombie—not a rotting corpse. The man he had been told of during the day was an articulate figure, clever and theatrical. The zombies he had seen the night before had been growling, numb things. Animated beasts, puppets, not planners and thieves.

There was much more that puzzled the big man. Why was the glowing man bringing forth the zombies? Why were they marching from the Citadelle? Why at midnight? The end of the world was the end of the world—when it finally happened it was to happen everywhere at once, across the face of the entire world—and it was to be directed by powers somewhat far beyond the glowing man and his flock of chickens.

There is something here I can not see, thought Pa'sha. *But, if I keep moving things, sooner or later that which is hidden shall be brought into the light, and I will see it then.*

Hefting his weapon, checking the breech, he thought to himself with finality, and then this will all be dealt with, one way or the other.

After some twenty more minutes, the seven were finally within the walls of the Citadelle. They had beaten the falling sun by a margin great enough to allow them to set a number of powerful lights in place. After that, Pa'sha placed a man at each of the lights, both to act as sentry against the zombies and guard for their illumination. He then went over the use of the flares each man had, reviewed how and when to use their various types of ammunition, and then just sat back to wait.

They did not need to wait long.

It was Louie who first heard the distinct chatter of barnyard fowl. Cocking his weapon, he turned his head this way and that, calling to the others, asking in a loud whisper if they heard what he could hear. All could hear the clucking and pecking sounds, though none could tell from which direction they came. Nerves began to wear; trigger fingers began to sweat. And then, an orange shimmer began to grow within the walls of the Citadelle.

As the men watched, a seed kernel of light burst free from the ground, vines of illumination growing quickly upwards, wrapping around each other in the form of a man until finally the glowing figure Pa'sha had met the night before stood in the center of the Citadelle's vast and over-grown courtyard.

"Ah, Pa'sha," it called, its voice mocking, "such a good boy. Always so dutiful."

No one spoke. The weaponeer held back on giving the signal to fire. After all, he thought, he had dropped a powerful bomb in the very center of the creature before him only twenty-four hours earlier, and the act had obviously had no lasting effect. Before he tried something so futile again, he wanted to know as much as he could about his foe.

"You talk most familiar for a thing I don't know but as a graveyard thief," the weaponeer called out. "What for you bothering people with all this nonsense, eh?"

"You call dey end of humanity 'nonsense,' boy?"

"The end of the world don't need no financing," answered Pa'sha. "Plenty people pouring enough money into that I'm thinking Heaven don't got need to spend no cash. You ain't no angel, thing. God's right hand won't be where you sit."

"I sit where I choose, and my legions will cover the Earth while I recline in admiration. You what I came for, boy. You ready for to get in line?"

"You saying you want mix it up, we be most excellently ready for that, zombie-man."

"You too clever by far, Pa'sha Lowe. Like your daddy-man. Two big pains in dey ass." The glowing man threw its arms out to its sides, fingers pointed toward the fortress's floor. The seven defenders shuddered as the ground responded instantly, trembling and cracking.

"But dat pain goin' ease itself, dis day. And I be the laughin' one." All about the Citadelle, torn and ragged hands began to push their way up out of the soil.

"Tonight the big night of sacrifice," shouted the glowing figure. "I went to some fine big trouble to ensure all the most tasty meat be here for the last offering. When you all be dead, I be a god, and my revenge be finally complete."

Everywhere around the seven, zombies began to rise from the ground. Struggling to understand what the glowing thing had just said, Pa'sha threw its words to the back of his mind as he shouted to his fellows.

"No more waiting, good brothers. Fire as you will."

The Citadelle erupted as seven rifles blazed as one. Wasting no time, the defenders blasted at the zombies as the things dug their way up out of the ground, taking off their heads, shattering their chests, before they could even gain their feet. Limbs were torn apart and sent flying, spines were disintegrated, skulls shattered.

Working his way down to the Citadelle courtyard, Pa'sha used his ammunition carefully, lining his shots to take out two or more of the zombies at a time, firing his rifle rounds in bursts of three only, doing his best to explode the heads of the rotting monsters so as to rob them of both their eyes and teeth.

"You are formidable, true," called out the glowing figure, "but you have bullets and bombs in numbers finite only, and the dead of Haiti number far beyond such as you can count in lead or explosives."

"Then I will break all their necks for them once more, and then yours, monster."

"You can not stop me, Pa'sha boy," answered the floating form over the violent noise ringing from every corner of the mountain top castle. "So far, you have done everything I need for you to do. Think you can stop now?"

"I have done *nothing* for you."

"Please, you have made everything possible."

"How?!" The weaponeer screamed the word, even as he fired another of his specially cast shells. Released, its ball bearings tore across the courtyard, the steel cord holding them together slicing near a half dozen zombies into sections before it shattered, one of the balls flying off and burying itself in a wall, the other dragging the cord with it, plowing through the body of one last zombie, its tail wrapping around the thing's head, whipping its decayed face.

"You have been most helpful to me," answered the glowing thing gleefully, "I need sacrifices, you brought them here to me. I needed you back in Haiti, you came with speed most enviable."

Pa'sha slid a purely explosive round into his launcher and fired. It struck the ground directly beneath the glowing figure, sending a cascade of shrapnel and fire upward, all of it passing through the floating form with no discernable effect.

All around the weaponeer, the others battled with the ever-approaching zombies. No matter how many they slaughtered, blew apart, decapitated or otherwise maimed, however, a dozen more crawled upward out of the ground or staggered in from the surrounding hills. One by one the men ran out of bullets. One by one they ran out of the special rounds they had helped make hours earlier.

"This is why I told you I would be here," laughed the glowing figure. "Only so much could you carry to dis height. Far from dey graveyard, you thought, forgetting dey thousands who died to build dis place. Now, you have no where to go; my poor dogs are all about, and you are quite finished."

And, at that moment, one of the seven screamed. Out of ammunition, he had taken to beating back the zombies clawing toward him with his M16. Eventually, though, no matter how many he piled at his feet, their animated limbs twitching beyond reason, the grasping hands caught hold of him.

The others ignored his screams as his chest was torn open, his organs pulled out of his body, eyes plucked, blood slurped, fingers munched upon—not because they had no compassion for him, but because they were all but minutes from the same fate.

"You wondered at dey need for money," the thing laughed again. "All magic takes offerings. Money *is* magic, boy, didn't you know that? It's not real. It don't exist except in men's minds. The things I pray to, dey give me power, but only enough to get for dem what dey wanted."

"And what do these things want?" Pa'sha bellowed the question, still firing, still directing his remaining forces.

"I'll tell you, boy."

As the glowing figure spoke, the zombies stopped their forward march. All about the remaining six defenders, the walking dead froze where they stood, heads rigid, hands unmoving, feet solidly in place. Their eyes staring, mouths half open, flies buzzing about them, worms slithering out of their flesh, dropping to the ground, the zombies waited at their master's command as the glowing thing revealed his final jest.

"What else, Pa'sha . . . they want you."

The weaponeer made to speak, then fell silent for lack of anything to say. Some of the still remaining others called to him, but he gave them all the signal to hold their fire. A scant ten yards across the courtyard from him, the thing continued on, explaining itself.

"Foolish boy, I gave to you few helpers so you would be easily scooped up. Enough to make you feel you commanded a force, not enough to stop my beasts."

You gave to me?

"Twelve years ago, your daddy-man was tricked into supporting my bid for de immortal. All along, he think he be helpin' one in need. Too late he figure dey truth. No escape for de old Lowe. But, his soul too pure. With him knowin' de truth, no deal for me, no power. God things take his soul and laugh at me, let me know mine is next, unless I can give them you."

No, thought Pa'sha, not this, Jesus. *Let this be anything but, but . . . this.*

"I make you think de government kill you daddy. You forget de church, turn your back on de only thing what can save you. I wait, wait for the stars to become right again . . ."

Not you . . .

"Wait for dey right time, de appointed moment, gather money to buy de proper offerings, rare gems, sacred things used since de beginning of time . . ."

Not you . . .

"Now, my altar is built, and de things dat want you soul so bad, holy boy," the glowing figure moved toward a large mound of rock centered along the back of the courtyard. At it, the two human servitors who had aided him all along, decorated a large flat section of stone, placing upon it several wooden chests. "Righteous boy, stinkin' little saint, consecrated fuckin' bastard . . . now," the thing paused to laugh one moment longer, then threw open the two chests, "dey wait no more."

Sickening black lights oozed forth from the twin boxes. Within, two sections of the same crystal, separated for tens of thousands of years called to each other, pulsating from the sudden nearness of each other, yearning.

"Thirty some years, I work for dis moment."

Two of the defenders aimed their weapons at the glowing figure and released their remaining bullets in continual streams. The lead passed through the form, tearing up the ground, shattering another zombie, killing one of the illuminated thing's servitors. The floating figure was not harmed in any way. Almost without thought, the thing sent its zombies forth to devour those who had fired. The others watched, helpless, faces twisted with grief. The glowing man laughed at their pain.

"De gods, dey mark your daddy-man, I give him to dem. Dey mark your soul, I help smother it. Turn you from the church, break your shield . . . you could have denied me, so true—if you had but hung on to de faith, all done for me. But no, too weak you were, blame God. After that, all is mine, just need bring you back at de right time . . ."

The black lights began to entwine, dazzling bits of brilliance trapped in the ebony tentacles of merging power. At the same time, the zombies began to move once more, all of them heading for Pa'sha.

"Now, it all be finished, *godson,* all but the throwin' of you to dose what you been promised to, and de collectin' of de power I done waited so long for to be mine!"

"*No!!*"

The sudden scream coming from deep within Christophe's throat, the young man threw himself from an upper wall, a lit flare in each hand. His aim all too true, he landed atop the altar, his body shattering as he hit the solid slab. Ignoring the pain of his newly broken bones, he stabbed with his flares, driving one into each of the gem boxes.

"Christophe, don't—"

Boyer's plea came too late. The chests rocked violently at the touch of the burning chemicals, exploding outward with a force which made all within the Citadelle turn away. The young man was incinerated instantly. At the same moment, the protective glow that had surrounded the floating man vanished, dropping him to the ground. Above Bonnet-a-l'Eveque, the sky darkened over, the stars fading behind a rushing billow of gray, ichorous clouds.

Boyer lay on the ground where he had fallen, crippled once more. He gibbered in a tongue none of the others in the Citadelle understood. It did him no good.

"Run, my brothers."

The remaining pair of defenders joined Pa'sha in making their way toward the gaping front doorway of the dying structure. Behind them Boyer shouted pleas, begging for their mercy.

"Pa'sha," he screamed, "Help me!"

A thick revulsion building in his throat, the weaponeer turned to view the scene in the courtyard behind him. From all corners of the Citadelle, zombies staggered forward, marching toward Boyer. In their center, the man who had pretended to be his own best friend, who had played the role of loving uncle and concerned godfather, screamed until his throat ripped, tasting his own blood as rotting teeth dug into his flesh at a thousand points at once.

"I'm so sorry, godpa'pe," Pa'sha spat the title in disgust, "but as you said, I be too weak to do much for you now."

The large man turned his back once more, heading for the exit. He could not fathom how such magics worked—how two simple stones could hold such power, and still be so easily negated. Neither could he understand the greed and hatred which had driven his father's best friend to betray him, to condemn him to torments Pa'sha could not imagine, to sacrifice his own nephew, and to hate the weaponeer to where he would do those things he had done.

Behind the retreating men, the screams grew to a mad shrill tenor the trio could not bear. In the sky above, massive thunder peals exploded, heralding scores of devastating lightning strikes, but still none of it could drown out the terrible cries which followed the men all the way to the bottom of the mountain.

The three staggered in the lashing rain, desperate to keep each other from falling over the trail's edge. As a score of lightning strikes came down at once, all pummelling the castle ruins, Louie said;

"You know, they say ol' Henri, his ghost still walk de Citadelle. Maybe now, maybe he gonna have some company, you think?"

"Yeah, maybe," his companion answered. "Dey can be best friends in Hell."

Pa'sha stared up through the driving rain for a long moment. He thought on what he would tell his poor mother, twelve years a widow, all for nothing. He thought for a moment on Christophe's sadly wasted life, as well. He remembered his years in the seminary, equally wasted, like his years since. All his life flashed through his mind in a split second, ending on the words spoken by his fellow survivors a moment before. With a sigh, he quoted a line he suddenly remembered from the distant past;

"'My name is death;'" the poet had written, "'the last best friend am I.'"

And then, he continued onward through the mud, ignoring the thunder, turning his back on the lightning, desiring only the cleansing feeling of the driving rain, praying for the sacred blessing of forgetfulness.

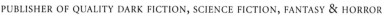

AVAILABLE SUMMER 2008

THE CTHULHU MYTHOS ENCYCLOPEDIA

BY DANIEL HARMS

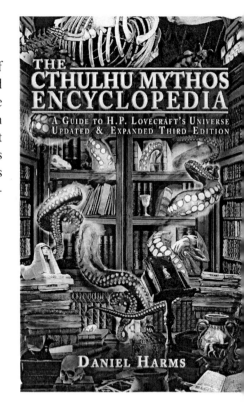

This is the third edition of Daniel Harms's popular and extensive encyclopedia of the Cthulhu Mythos. Updated with more fiction listings and recent material, this unique book spans the years of H.P. Lovecraft's influence in culture, entertainment, and fiction.

LIMITED, SIGNED
NUMBERED HARDCOVER: $45.00
ISBN: 1-934501-03-4
TRADE PAPERBACK: $17.95
ISBN: 1-934501-04-2

Printed in the United States
203949BV00003B/1-36/P